The Starship Sneak

ORIGIN STORY BOOK 1

Marc B. DeGeorge

D0838583

MUSEMARC
STUDIO

MuseMarc Studio, LLC.

Cover Design by: Lance Buckley

Author Photo by: MuseMarc Studio

ISBN: 978-1-956487-00-8 (digital), 978-1-956487-01-5 (paperback)

First Edition: **November 2021**

9 8 7 6 5 4 3 2 1

Acknowledgments

A story may be written by one person, but it takes many to turn it into a novel. To that end, I'd like to thank the following for their contribution to turning my typing into reality.

First, my dedicated and awesome reading group, Brennan Bishop, Ben Pick, Salone More, Tracey Canole, and my new friend John Blenkinsop. Thank you for your critical commentary, positive support, and friendship. My amazing editors, Savannah Gilbo, Brittany Dory, and Ariel Anderson. You have been a huge help in making this book a reality. Thank you. Also to my wife and family, for giving me the time to forge this first work...and all the ones that come after.

One

WHEN I WAS TWELVE, my father left us, taking my big dream with him. That same day, the Galactic Empire encountered its first alien species. It was a historic moment for humanity, but, just like my dream, it didn't last. The aliens attacked, and now, light-years from my home, a war rages. Not that I care. I might be happy if the Empire lost. It's their fault my father is gone.

We were going to be the protectors of the common people! With his legal talents and my...well, I'd learn a few skills by the time I joined him...we'd be the best in the business here on our humdrum minor planet of Angelcanis. Together, we would save the planet, starting with a few missing pets. We'd have respect, be famous, and most importantly, we'd be a family doing great things together.

Since the bastard left us—my mom and me—I've had a bit of a crisis coming up with some new plans. Unlike my buddies, I'm not amazingly talented at anything. They're smart, charismatic, adept, and every other positive word I can think of. Me? I can't even make a decent decision on my own. Thank the Goddesses I've got my buds.

Only for the next two months, though. Then they're off to take their two-year post–high school mandatory education somewhere away from our happy little town. Somewhere far away. Unless I can do something about it.

"Dude!" Grady Sugiyama, one of my said buds, grins at me with a mouth full of square, hyper-polished teeth as we stand just outside of his excessive family home. "It's only two years. We'll be back in no time."

"Yeah, but what am *I* going to do for two years?" I plead, likely for naught. "Couldn't you just do your compulsories around here? You're guaranteed a job the moment you get out anyway, dude."

"True, but come on, dude, it's Yeomanry! Coolest city on the planet? Why don't you go?"

"Because I didn't get anywhere near the grades you did?" I shoot back. "Because I don't have all the awesome extracurriculars that you've got? 'Come on' yourself, dude. I'm not getting into anything but a local school."

I'm taking the day to convince Grady and Afton, another one of my buds, to stick around with me and attend the community school here in our town. Not that I would ever expect anyone would want to do that. It's really dull around here. Duller than the flat brown paint used to color every standard domicile in town, including mine.

That's why I brought a lure with me—call it a bribe if you will. Yesterday I told Grady that my NaiNai gave me a family heirloom, and he, the historical aficionado that he is, went totally nuts. Then, when I told him it's really cool, but it's fragile, and I didn't want to bring it by, he wouldn't take no for an answer. Grady said he just wanted to scan it on his parent's high-resolution surveyor so he can "study" it when I'm not around, but I'm planning on doing him one better. That way I can hook him into staying around.

So here we are, waiting for Afton just outside Grady's parents' three-story domicile. It's way oversized for three people, but that's because his parents are big shots. Mine's only one and a half stories because my mother is a civil servant.

"So? Did you bring it?" Grady pries, his eyes sparkling.

Before I can answer, Afton trots up to us from across the street, a serene smile on her face. I toss her a nonchalant salute. Then Afton presses both her hands together, fingers upright, and bows slightly as she smiles.

"What the hell is that?" I ask, scratching at my cheek.

"Saying hello and wishing you peace in the ancient way...dumbass." Her response goes from sweet and pleasant to growling and ugly. That's about par for the course with Surela Afton Jee. I call her chaos on two legs. Long, athletic legs that put her half a cranium above me. She's a total sport-head, but she's got mental muscles, too. We could never let her hang otherwise. Then again, she probably wouldn't have hung out with us for the last seven years if she couldn't talk our geek-speak.

"Okaaaay...anyway...did you talk to Kayley today? I was hoping to get her help with something."

She smirks at my failed attempt to play down my inquiry. "What's the matter, Rancy pants? Do you need her to tie your shoelaces, or are you just worried about how much time she spends with Parrish?"

"No," I reply, "she can hang with Parrish if she wants."

"Are you just saying that because they used to date?" Afton swipes a finger in the air. "Oh, point me!"

"Dude! Give it up," Grady says. "You two have known each other since you were kids, right? And you see her every day. That's nineteen years times three hundred twenty-two times per year that you've had to tell her how you feel. Six thousand one hundred eighteen times! Kayley will always be your friend, and that's it. Accept it already. It's more constant than the speed of light!"

"Your math is fudgy, dude," I reply. "No way I'd be able to tell her anything until I learned to talk...and speed of light may be constant, but it's crazy bumpy. Just ask your dad."

"My dad already reminds me *every* day, thanks."

Grady—his awesome full name is Mutsumaji O'Grady Sugiyama—has a lot to live up to. His parents are ship designers, but not the modest kind that decide where the plumbing and lighting go. His mom's hull designs are so successful the entire Imperial Space Fleet uses them, and his dad came up with technology to make faster-than-light travel way smoother, faster, and safer. Which is great because accelerating up to that speed takes like forever. It doesn't work yet, though. Once Grady graduates, his dad is pulling him in to work on the project. If his dad can wait that long.

"Yeah, sorry, dude, I didn't mean to salt the wound."

"That's a totally nasty phrase," Afton says, wrinkling her nose. "Never say that again."

"So let's see it already!" Grady says, nearly climbing on top of me to look at my heirloom. I'm cool with his bully tactic because I don't want to drag out the painful conversation about the love of my life and how I'm totally not worthy of her. They'll just bust on me until I beg for mercy if I let them. Today, however, I'm not giving them that satisfaction.

Bribe time!

I swing my pack around and take out an old wooden box that my NaiNai gave me to hold the heirloom. She said she got it from her grandmother, who got it from her grandmother, and so on. It might actually be from one of the old colony ships. That could make it like a thousand years old. Maybe more. It hardly looks more than a hundred. Humans have only been on Angelcanis for about three hundred years, a drip in time compared to the five millennia that the Empire has been around. If I had to guess, this thing could have come from Albion, the Empire's homeworld. That would make it extra cool if it did.

So anyway, the box.

It's got some old writing on it. NaiNai says it was handwritten, but she can't read it. Neither can I. It's too complex to figure out, and it must have been a total pain in the ass to write it by hand. That's an ancient art that I've only ever seen one person practice. He's willing to teach you, but the amount of money you need to pay him for such a useless skill is not worth it.

I open the box for Grady, and he peers inside with wide eyes. The item inside is a strange-looking chunk of metal that gives it weight on one side with these plastic feather-shaped things on the other. NaiNai says it's part of an ancient game, but who'd want to play with something this old? It would break in two seconds. Maybe people back then didn't have any decent entertainment, so all they did was sit around and look at some weird object in a box. What a life.

"Dude! This is so totally ancient!" Grady says. As an aficionado, he's excited by anything old. Not old as in you should throw it away, but as in having a lot of history. As I said, we've only three hundred years of history here on Angelcanis, which barely fills up a semester of school. We have to steal other histories from around the spiral arm to have a proper historical education.

"What is it?" Afton asks, taking her own glance into the box.

"If I knew, I'd say so, Surela," I reply and get an elbow in my ribs for my sarcasm. Then another for using her first name. I've no idea why she doesn't like us using it, but it's a definite no-go zone. I'm still willing to step on the occasional land mine if it scores me points.

"Thank you, Rance," Afton smiles, all syrupy, but I know what's coming next won't be sweet at all. "Thanks for wasting ten minutes of my life I'll never get back. You're just as clueless as we are about this thing. Next time just grab something from the trash bin, and we'll play a game of twenty questions instead."

"Well, I think it's cool," Grady mumbles. This is it! This is my chance to hook him.

"Hey," I say with a sly grin, holding out the box to Grady, "tell you what. If you stay local for the next two years, I'll let you hold on to it for a little while."

Grady's jaw drops, and for a moment, I can tell he's envisioning some kind of antiquarian heaven before him. He's so still that I worry I broke my friend. But a few seconds later, he blinks and shakes his head.

"Dude, no way," Grady says, giving me an apologetic grin. "I prefer to live past the moment when I tell my parents that I've changed my mind."

"Yeah," Afton adds, "*murdered by parents* is not something you want to have on your death certificate."

"Aw, come on, dude!" I whine, and I'm not proud of it. "It's just the compulsories! It doesn't matter if you excel at them or not!"

"It matters to my parents," Grady replies, wrinkling his mouth up, "and so I've got no choice."

I sigh. I tried. No way he's going to stay, even if he wanted to. His parents would literally execute him if he deviated from their master plan for his life. I often envy Grady for his knowledge and sheer talent, but I'm not so sure I'd trade places with him.

"What about you?" I turn to Afton, trying my best to give her the most charming tone I can muster. I learned it from Kayley, who's the master of the sweet talk. She even won the school competition for best smile. If you ever see it, you'll want to say yes to whatever she asks of you.

"I am *not* staying here," Afton replies. She drops a hand on my shoulder. "Sorry, but it's as good as done. No way I'm living alone with my mom for the next two years so she can yell at me every day. Besides, the girl you should beg isn't me. Get it?"

She's right, of course. Afton is usually right. She's just behind Kayley in the "Rance Is Wrong" rankings. I'm on my hands and knees to these two because I don't think I'd ever convince my dream girl. She really will blast off to the stars someday, and I'd hang on to her safety strap and go for a ride if I thought I could even be a decimal point percentage of what she's capable of achieving.

Little Miss Student President really is too good for me. If we hadn't been friends since we were kids, I would doubt she'd give me the time of day, but I'd be wrong about that. Kayley is good to everyone, and that's just one of the million things I love about her.

"Yeah," I reply to Afton with a nod that leaves my head hanging. "I get it. I just don't know if she feels the same way."

"Don't be a droopy daisy," Afton says and smacks me on the side of the head, just gentle enough to show she cares and hard enough to get the message ingrained into my brain. "Talk to her already."

"But you're really running out of time, dude," Grady says. "In two months, she's out, I'm out, Parrish is doing his mandatories at boot camp, and Afton..."

"Officer Candidate School," Afton fills in when Grady looks at her. "Maybe. My brothers got in, so I think I've got a chance. If not, then anywhere but here."

It's an obvious reminder that I'll be the only one left in this dead-end town, and it's all because I couldn't keep my dad around. I know I shouldn't blame myself for it. It was his choice, after all. Still, if there was something I did or said, or didn't do or say, I really wish I could take it back.

The more I think about everyone leaving, the tighter my chest gets. I just wish that there was some way that I could make it possible for us to stay together. At least for a little while longer. Then I know I'll get up the courage to do the things I only dream about.

A siren wails across the street. It's the same air-raid siren they test every day at noon, only it's four o'clock right now. Everyone on the street pauses and glances around. We do, too.

"Why are they doing this now?" asks Afton.

"I don't know, but the authorities don't make noise unless there's a real problem," Grady replies, clenching and unclenching his fists.

"It's probably just someone playing a bad joke," I suggest, not believing my own words.

Down the street, a woman shrieks, and we spin towards the sound. Without warning, two strange craft streak by, buzzing us. The power of their draft nearly knocks us over. Grady grabs me to steady himself, and I him.

Whatever they are, they're huge, much larger than any ships that I know of. They're built of stuff so dark that it's like two black holes just flew by. I think they dropped something as they went by, too. Not sure what, but...

We see the flash of the blast before we feel its concussive effects. A light so bright that I shut my eyes and turn away. It's a good thing, too, because the detonation's pressure wave blows out from ground zero and whips everything in front of it like cream in a blender.

I find myself on the ground after it passes. I try to get up, but my head is spinning so much I can't tell which way is up. I feel like I just got tackled by one of Parrish's teammates. Only his teammate was an explosion so powerful it just leveled an entire building down the block.

"Oh man," Grady says, "Angelcanis just got moved up to the front line."

Two

THE CRY OF THE siren mixes with shouts and screams all around us, and just like that, my worries about the future are wiped away by what's happening *right now*. The ground rumbles, and the air vibrates with explosions—some of them too close for our liking. Panic is our shared mode. We search for shelter and choose the alley between Grady's house and the apartment building next door.

"How did they slip through our defenses?" Grady asks, his wide-eyed stare searching the sky for an answer. I'm wondering who "they" might be, though I could guess—aliens. Though why they're attacking our little planet is a mystery.

The satellite defense shield erected around the planet was supposed to be impregnable. If they slipped past it this easily, then these whoever-they-ares are hyper-advanced.

"I don't know," I answer and get back to a more practical topic. "But do you think this is the best place for us to be?"

"Not really," Afton answers. "We should find a shelter. No offense to your house, Grady, but that fancy construct isn't going to help us if a bomb drops on it."

"Where the hell is there a shelter?" I ask.

"No freaking idea, but staying here is a bad idea."

A bomb explodes on the opposite side of the building next to Grady's, sending us slamming into the wall. I'm blinded by a flash of light as the side of my head impacts the brick. I crumple, falling onto one of my friends. I don't know which one, but they twist underneath me and grab me by the shoulders.

"Rance! Up!" Afton shouts. "We've got to move! Grady's basement!"

"I thought we just said no to Grady's house?"

I hear the groan of defeated metal flexing way past its design spec. My arms and legs find a way to get me up, and I shoot out from the alleyway. The only direction I want is away. I'm not waiting around for a building to fall on me.

"Rance!" Grady calls from behind. I pause and turn back. He's there, on the ground, struggling to get up.

I fight my better senses and dart back. Afton's there, too. We both get a shoulder underneath and carry him to safety, just before the apartment building crashes down behind us, spewing dust and dirt in all directions. We dive onto the lawn across the way, protecting our faces from a nasty remodel. Debris covers us, turning us into cement zombies.

I can't hear much, but at least I'm moving. I roll to one side to check on Grady—he's okay, just in shock. Afton pushes herself up on the other side of him and shakes the discombobulation from her brain. She looks at me, and I at her. A simple nod and I know she's okay.

"Good call, Afton," I say, glancing back. Amazingly, the apartment building fell towards the street, leaving the Sugiyama homestead relatively intact. Only the wall facing the alley shows signs of serious damage. "But I think Grady's place as a shelter is definitely out."

"Oh, dude," Grady says, catching sight of his home. He coughs and dusts himself off as he sits up. "Good thing my parents weren't home, but boy, are they going to be pissed."

"Not something to worry about now," I say, offering him a hand. "We're out in the open. A single pebble flying at the right speed in our direction could be a problem."

A pair of those obsidian ships zoom overhead. We duck, expecting more bombs, but we roll a good save—no attack. I help Grady up again, wiping the concrete dust from his head. It's no use, really. A cloud of the stuff hangs over us, likely to invade our mop-tops once again.

"Ideas?" I ask, glancing at my shell-shocked companions.

As if to answer my question, Afton's Sergo buzzes. She pulls it from the cargo pocket of her pants and dusts it off, but it doesn't get any cleaner, so she just answers the call.

"Afton?" Parrish's voice comes on. He's worried, which hopefully means he's safe. I really hope that means Kayley is too. I motion to Afton to turn the volume up. Maybe they'll know something about my mom as well.

"Hey," Afton replies, her voice hoarse from the dust, "where are you?"

"We were five minutes from Grady's when the attack happened," he replies. "Now we're just holed up at Kayley's place...Are you okay?"

"We just dodged a bomb." Afton coughs. "Now we need to find safety. Grady's house took some damage, so that's out."

"Anyone hurt?"

Afton makes a quick examination of us, then replies to Parrish in the negative. I check myself again and find the side of my head scraped and tender. That's where I used it to stop the rest of my body from colliding with the wall. It doesn't hurt much now, but I expect tomorrow it's gonna sting—if we're still with the living at that point.

"Can you guys make it to my place? Do you think?" Kayley's songbird voice comes through the speaker, and I catch my breath. I want to go there. Call it trauma or just nerves, I don't care, but seeing her gorgeous face would make me feel a whole lot better.

"Good idea," I say.

"Sure," Afton replies. "If we can avoid blowing up along the way."

"Afton's right," Grady says. "That's a long way to be dodging bombs."

"Do whatever you have to do to get safe," Kayley, our de facto leader, commands. "If that's not here, then—"

A secondary explosion knocks us off our feet, and we meet the ground faster than we can react. Flames shoot towards the sky from a gas feed. The heat that radiates off it is so intense, I have to put my hand up to block it.

"Guys?" Kayley calls worriedly.

"I changed my mind," Afton shouts. "We're coming to you!"

Before Kayley can sign off, Afton is on her feet and yanking Grady up after her. I'm left to fend for myself, but it doesn't take me long to follow as they dash down the street. We dart through another alley and come out onto the main thoroughfare.

It's a crummy choice.

A lump hits my throat as I take in the carnage. Hysterical people are racing for cover around an immense crater in the street. Three buildings are ablaze and in danger of collapse, and there's no sign of emergency personnel anywhere. If that wasn't bad enough, I spot a pair of those ships speeding down the street, ready to create more destruction.

"Turn around!" Afton shouts and darts back down the alley at high speed. Now, I'm not out of shape, but Afton is an all-star runner. Compared to her, Grady and I are snails.

When the next bomb hits, we take a dive. Afton's already out of the alley and turning right. She's got no idea we've hit the deck. I try to call after her, but the building crumbling behind me puts that on the back burner.

I grab Grady underneath his shoulders and yank him up. My friend must be so zonked that he doesn't know what to do. I give him a push forward, and it finally connects. He sees me, and his legs get going.

"Where's Afton?" Grady cries. I just shake my head and point. We follow in her steps, but we can't go right when we get to the street. A building has fallen, blocking the entire road. We have to stop and check around for another way.

"This way!" I point towards an intersection, but before I can move, Grady grabs my arm. I turn to see his face, pale and tight.

"What if she's in there?" Grady says, high pitched, pointing to the former building.

"No way, not Afton!" I shout back above the din of sirens and roaring flames. "Don't worry, we'll meet up with her on the way!" I yank on his arm, but he refuses to budge.

"What if we don't?" Grady asks, his breathing getting faster.

"We will! We can't stay here, anyway!" A rumble under our feet punctuates my statement. It also wakes Grady up, and he drops me a nod. We're off again.

I know where Afton was going, but that shortcut is blocked. We've got to go all the way around, and that puts us in real danger as there's no cover this way. Plus, it will take longer, so Miss Gold Medal Marathon will be at Kayley's long before we are.

If she makes it safely, that is.

I'm just glad that Kayley is okay, but that thought leads me to another—my mom. As far as I know, she was home, and the house is far enough away from downtown that exploding things won't be anywhere near there. I put that in the "to freak out about later" file and double up my run.

A sound like the sky being torn open cuts across our heads. I throw my arms up to protect my skull but realize the futility of that and drop them. That could have been a missile, but there's no reason to stop and check. It would be long gone before I could spot it.

"Air defense!" Grady shouts in between ragged breaths. My own lungs are screaming for a break. We have to keep going, though. Missiles overhead are a sign of us still being in the wrong place.

We turn the corner after a long stretch of a block, and Grady finally gives up. He collapses onto the lawn of someone's house and goes flat on his back. I dodge his sudden rest stop, but my legs fail me, and I also go down. Only I can't control my fall, and I face-plant into the dirt.

"Dude," I gasp, scrambling to get up. "Dude, we can't rest. Not here."

"I know." Grady's chest is heaving hard, and I'm getting worried that he's going to have a literal heart attack. I wish he'd get out more, but then again, I should, too. "I just need a minute."

"Come on." I crawl over to him. "Maybe KayKay's got some of those spicy pickle things that you like. If we go now, you can be stuffing your face full of them in two minutes. We're almost there, right?"

"Almost." Grady shuts his eyes, and I get a sudden shot of nausea. I really hope he isn't about to have a meltdown. I grab his shoulder and shake him.

"Hey, you still with me?"

"Yes," Grady groans, "go away, Mom. It's not a school day."

"No time for jokes, dude. Let's go!"

A flash goes off in my peripheral, and I know it's another detonation. This one is far enough away that we won't feel anything but the pressure wave. That could be enough to get my buddy up and moving, so I'll wait for it.

It comes and goes like a strong breeze, and as hoped for, it gets Grady to sit up. He glances up at me with a grimace. Since he's well familiar with what I look like, he just scans around. He's fine until his eyes catch on something down the block.

Grady suddenly gets to his feet and backs away, eyes popping out of his head. He's sighted something that he doesn't like, and now I need to know what the excitement is all about.

Close to where the bomb must have gone off, there is a successive chain reaction of road plates—heavy steel road plates—casually lifting into the air to the height of ten-story domicile complexes. A hollow pop and a puff of sparks and smoke follow each.

"Dude," Grady says in a voice low enough that I know something bad is happening. "Gas main..."

I glance down the road and realize every plate that goes off gets a little closer to us.

"We've got to warn everyone in these houses!" I shout.

"No time, dude!"

Two blocks away, the fronts of two buildings blow off in a burst of flame and glass. Then the two across the street follow, showering the road with metal and concrete.

I run to the front door of the nearest house and bang on the door.

"Hey! Hey! You've got to get out now!" I yell, but Grady grabs me and pulls me away. I stumble to catch my footing and then follow along as he jets into the street.

If Grady pulling me away wasn't enough incentive, the next two buildings that light up definitely are. The clang of airborne road plates coming back down to impale themselves into the asphalt is the final exclamation point on an already intense message.

Another building goes up, and it's way too close. The heat from the air blast scalds my neck and throws me into a vehicle. Grady goes down a little easier, landing on someone's shrubbery.

I pick myself up, gagging for air. The impact shoved all of it out of my lungs, and now I'm so dizzy I can't see. I have to get Grady and keep moving before the blaze in the gas main blows out the building in front of us.

I stumble over to where I think Grady is, but all I find are prickly branches that stab into my hands. I can't speak, so shouting for him isn't happening.

Instead, he finds me. But it's not him. The hands that grab on to my forearms and haul me along are stronger, thinner...and softer.

"Found you!" Afton says and swings me forward to put me in front of her. As my eyes clear up, I see Grady waving us towards a metal shed. It's not much, but it's better than being out in the open. I get a surge of energy and take off towards him. If we can just wait out this chain reaction, we'll be okay.

Then the next explosion goes off.

Three

"ATTENTION, CITIZENS, THIS IS not a drill. This is not a drill. Please direct your attention to an emergency message from your Prime Minister on Angel-1. You may also sign on to Angel-4 for a simulcast. The broadcast will begin in ten minutes."

I awake to the most beautiful sight that I could ever hope to see. A pair of steel-blue eyes, wide set around a button nose on a heart-shaped face, create an intense contrast to the scarlet waterfall that hangs down around them. The eyes radiate such a sense of tranquility that I can only surmise I've died and gone to see the Three Goddesses. I'm certain that I'm staring at one of them right now.

"I've definitely gone to heaven," I whisper, and feel a dreamy smile bloom across my face.

"Hey, you're awake," Kayley Scarlett Garmonichnyy, my personal goddess, says in that dulcet soprano of hers. She turns to someone behind her and adds, "Guys, Rance is awake!"

So I'm not in heaven then. That's okay. This is better.

As I glance around, I see we're in the Garmonichnyy family den, an immaculate place. I would recognize its gold-embossed floral damask wallpaper anywhere. If not for the ivory hutch with its vid screen and the pair of matching sofas and lounge chair, I'd believe we were in a holy place. Kayley's parents don't even entertain in here, which means if they were home, they'd be yelling at us right about now. They're probably out with some high-ranking city official, which is a good thing since they won't see me begriming their perfect sofa.

"Just in time for the Prime Minister's speech," Parrish says as he leans over me. "Lucky you...How you feeling, guy?"

Parrish Waafajin Beltrami is lean and strong and not your typical sport-head. For one, he wears glasses like Grady does. Only he substitutes gel caps on his eyes when he's competing. Also, his chestnut-toned face is chiseled from a magical stone that makes girls faint when they lay eyes on his stunning features. Okay, I'm exaggerating, but even I, who have no real idea, say he's one hot dude. It's just another reason why my courage fails every time I think about asking Kayley on a date. This perfect example of male attractiveness is my competition. And Kayley, the perfection that she is, must have thousands of Parrishes after her. I don't think I could ever win.

"Okay?" I reply with a modest level of uncertainty, and I sit up. Of course, Parrish, the epitome of nobility, helps me get there. He is a great friend and a secret geek with one of the biggest collections of star charts this end of the spiral arm, which Grady and I covet...often. I can't ever hate this guy for being awesome.

"I called your mom," Kayley says. "She's fine. There was no attack by your place."

I smile my thanks to her, though I think the edges of my mouth have been curled upwards ever since I woke up and saw her gazing down on me.

"Oh good, you're not dead," Afton says, coming over to glance at me. She's holding a cold pack to the back of her head, and there are scrapes all over her arms and face. I'm not worried about her, though. If Afton hasn't lost her snark, then she's just fine.

Grady, amazingly, has not a scratch on him. His mound of hair is more messed up than usual, but that's not so uncommon. He's managed to hold on to his glasses, too.

"So what happened?" I croak.

"A boom," Afton replies, "a big boom. You got that much before your face fought with the side of a tree, didn't you?"

"Yeah, that last one was a doozy," Grady adds. "But it was strong enough to blow out whatever fire was underground."

"So how'd I get here?"

"Afton carried you," he answers, "lumberjack style. How's your stomach feeling, by the way?"

I shrug. I'm fine, other than my ego being wounded from learning that a girl carried me here, even if it was Afton, athlete extraordinaire. One of these days, I'm going to be the one that gets to do the saving. Then I'll be worthy of all the awesome people I hang with.

"Hey, the Prime Minister is about to come on," Parrish says, grabbing the remote and powering on the vid screen. "We should listen in. It's going to be important."

He tunes in to Angel-1, and without a second's pause the Prime Minister comes up to begin his speech. I pay attention because out of all the politicians I know, he's actually one who cares.

"My fellow citizens, I have some hard news to share with you today. Ever since our predecessors gained Imperial edict and settled on this lush planet, we have known only peace and prosperity. Angelcanis has been a gift to us, and we have tended to it as good shepherds should. Because of that, we have grown from a sustainable colony to one that now trades with the Empire at large. Our reputation throughout the Commonwealth is the highest of any of the prospective planets. We have the best soil for agriculture, and the Empire respects us for the high quality of our apprenticeship programs.

"That is why it truly saddens me to share with you this: we must turn from our peaceful ways and join with the Central Planets to fight those who have so savagely attacked us. My fellow citizens, make no mistake—we are now at war with an alien race! The discovery of intelligent life should be a reason for celebration, but as astonishing as this revelation is, we must put away our awe and replace it with alarm. As much as we would have hoped, this life form is not our friend. It is our terror."

"Why would they want to attack us?" Kayley asks as her fingers touch her lips.

"I will now turn this broadcast over to Defense Minister Crowley, who brings a message to us from the front."

The man who comes on is instantly dislikeable. He's got a menacing old look, with deep-sunk eyes and a pointy mustache underneath his hawkish nose. The whole thing is stuck on top of a wrinkled plank of a face. There's no doubt in my mind—this guy has to be a politician. I'll file him under "jerks who stole my dad."

"*Prospective citizens of the Empire, I know this will be difficult to hear, but there is something distressing that I must share with you. There is an obvious reason for this attack. We believe the alien menace seeks to seize our lawfully claimed territory and take it for their own malicious purposes. Now please watch the screen. The recent scenes of battle that you see are from Sector Seventeen. Yes, I have said that correctly—Sector Seventeen, less than a week's flight from your beautiful Angelcanis. That means if you want to protect the Empire's planet, you will have only a short time to prepare for a possible invasion. So, to that end, I am directing your Prime Minister to organize a defense! All residents of eligible age—please—we need you to defend your home and the property of the Empire. You may sign up at any government or military office. Again, make a serious consideration of it. Your decision may mean the difference between your survival or the horrible destruction of this planet that has given you so very much. Thank you, and may the Goddesses bless and protect us and our Emperor!*"

"Holy bones, he's asking us to sign up!" Parrish says, the sides of his mouth curving up when he speaks. Now, Parrish is no killer, but he was planning to join, anyway. He'd go sign up right now if there was somewhere open.

"Dude, you're totally going, aren't you?" Grady asks him, a small grin forming on his face. Parrish nods with the confidence of someone who has known what they would be doing since birth. I notice Kayley's slight reaction to his confirmation. It's not much more than a shift of her feet and a slight opening of her mouth, but since I've known her all her life, it's obvious to me that she doesn't want him to go. Peacetime service is one thing, but Parrish will be in real danger on the front lines.

"What about you, Rance?" Parrish turns to me, and I shrink back into my seat, my eyes avoiding his. I don't want to let him down, but I'm not sure I could do anything but die if I signed up.

Plus, I'd never do anything that minister commanded of us. He's an Imperial politician, so by my definition, he's someone to never allow inside your house. He'd let the entire population of our planet die before lifting a finger to defend us. The problem is, I know Parrish won't hear that from me, even if I tried to tell him. He's so hyped on this that slamming into a brick wall wouldn't stop him right now.

"He's not, but I might," Afton says plainly. Further explanation gets put on pause when she frowns and pulls out her Sergo to glance at the screen. It turns into a stare as she reads what must be a long message. Afton's eyes grow wider as she reads.

"Everything okay?" Kayley inquires. The question is innocent enough, but when Afton looks up from the screen, her eyes get watery.

"I...I've got to go," Afton says and runs out. The four of us watch her jet out, and we all share a furrowed look. Afton doesn't get emotional often, but none of us are too worried. She'll be back, or she'll call Kayley or Parrish if she needs us. And me, the bad friend that I am—I'm feeling lucky that her distraction has pulled the attention away from me.

For the five seconds that it does.

"Are you really not going?" Parrish asks, closing the distance between us. I know there's only one answer that will satisfy him, so I'd rather keep my mouth shut. He presses me with his eyes, and Grady joins him. So now I've got to reply.

"Come on, Parrish, you know I've got no skill to be a soldier," I reply, shaking my head. It's a poor excuse, and he knows it. But if I told him what I really feel—that anyone who signs up is likely expendable— he'd freak. I should convince him he's the one making a mistake, but I doubt I could.

"This is *different*!" he says, swinging a fist in emphasis. Before I can respond to his challenge, Kayley leans in front of me and cuts me off.

"And this is *serious*, Parry. You could die!" Kayley says. "Are you sure you've thought this through? I mean completely through?"

"Of course I have. The PM is making a call on a play, and I will not let our side down." He flashes a glare at me when he answers. I want to support my friend, but I don't want to be shipped off to some rock of a planet where I die when some big bug stabs me through the heart. That's exactly what would happen to me, too.

"Well, think it over again...please," Kayley says, her shoulders dropping.

"That still doesn't get him off the hook!" Parrish throws an accusatory finger at me. He can't beat Kayley in a verbal spar, so he picks me to beat on instead. Despite that, I still hold him up as the stellar constant of a good guy.

"Yeah, dude." Grady adds his voice to the verbal assault on my lack of conviction. "Guns may not be your thing, but you can do other stuff.

Isn't this the chance to do something real? You're always complaining to me about how you want to do big stuff. Get on board already, dude."

"That's not it, Grady," I say. "Kayley's got a point...You might not be coming back from this."

"That's what it means to sign up, dude," Grady shoots back, his eyes narrowing at me. "Are you that afraid?"

I shrug and hang my head. My buds aren't going to listen. The thought of war, of people getting killed, of my friends getting killed, doesn't sit well in my stomach. I'd sign up in an instant if I thought there was a way I could protect them and keep them from getting hurt, but I know there isn't, and that really beats me down.

"It's okay, Rance." Kayley does her signature smile that could convince the sun to shine in the middle of the night. "There are other ways to help besides fighting."

"Yeah, that's true." I appreciate the backup from her and can't help but smile back. No one could. "There's got to be a bunch of things we can do here at home. Maybe Mom has some contacts."

"Disappointing, dude," Grady says, dropping his gaze. I think he was really hoping for all of us to sign up together. Like Parrish and me, he's an only child. That's one reason we connected initially, but unlike Parrish and me, his parents are rarely home. That leaves a lot of lonely space in a three-story house for one person to fill up. Needless to say, he doesn't enjoy his alone time.

"Yeah, Rance," Parrish adds, "our planet needs us, and you're going to just stay here and do what? Play nurse with Kayley?"

"Okay, enough!" Parrish crosses the line, and Kayley calls him on it. I avert my eyes so that my buds don't see me rejoicing when she defends me. "Whether we like it or not, if we're invaded, we're all getting involved. You want to sign up? Fine, go ahead. I really don't think you should, but don't get on Rance because he's decided that the military's not for him!"

Commander Kayley can definitely silence the room. That's why she gets the final decision when we can't make up our minds. Usually, that only means choosing a place to eat or what cine to see, but she's made her point now, and none of us are going to contest that. No one wants to incur the wrath of Goddess Kayley.

"Sorry." Parrish hangs his head and reaches out to her.

Kayley takes his hand in both of hers and gives him a wistful smile. "We're going to be splitting up sooner than we thought, and none of us like it, but that's not in our control," she says. "All we can do is hope that it won't be long before we're back together again." She locks eyes with each one of us as she speaks. The gentle tone of her voice floats through the room and caresses my ears. I can see it affects Grady and Parrish, too. Their shoulders soften, and the tension slides off their faces. Kayley has that effect on everyone. Therefore, she's the queen.

Four

I TELL KAYLEY THAT I should go see my mom and offer Grady a place to stay for the night. His parents won't be home, and I don't want him to be alone. Not after all that's happened. He's going to have bad dreams tonight, I know it. I can't do much for him, but I can at least not let him be alone, if only for tonight. Tomorrow, he and Parrish will sign up, so Kayley and I have decided to wait in line with them. It's going to be the last time our little gang will be together. Maybe forever.

"Okay, I'm coming over early then," Kayley says. "I'll help your mom make sticky-rice porridge for everyone, and then you and I are going to have a talk, Rance, about what we're going to do until the war is over."

"Got it," I answer, but swallow hard after. I might have made the wrong choice. Military service could be easier than whatever Superachiever Kayley comes up with. Still, I get a jolt of excitement when I realize that she's going to be around, even after two months. It's strange to be thankful that war is keeping us together. I'm a bit ashamed, actually.

"Ooh, congee!" Grady rubs his hands together and beams at me with a hopeful look. "With ginger, chives, and goji berries, right?"

"Of course." I raise an eyebrow at him. "What did you think would be in it, dead animal?"

Grady's face nearly melts when I reply. He knows I'm joking, but just the thought alone is enough to make any Angelican cringe. No mentally stable human on this planet eats animal flesh. The idea itself is just too revolting to consider.

As Grady and I step out, we catch Afton crossing the street. She sees us at the same time and freezes in place. So we do the same and stare back at her until Afton takes the initiative and comes to us. She wipes a sleeve across her eyes and runs a hand through her ponytail along the way. And now I'm suspicious.

"Hey," Afton says, looking like she's trying to put a smile on her face. "You guys leaving?"

"Yeah," I reply, and watch her for a moment. Afton wrinkles her nose and looks away. I know something's up, but I continue as if everything is normal. "He's crashing at my place tonight, and then Kayley's coming over to help my mom make breakfast."

"Oh yeah?" Afton executes her mock interest poorly. I open my mouth, but before I can call out her act, Grady beats me to it.

"What happened?" Grady asks, his tone easier than his usual full-throttle style.

"My dad is missing," Afton says and chokes up. "His ship exploded in the middle of a battle. They don't know if he got out...or not."

"Whoa," Grady replies, which is what I would have said.

Afton's dad is everything to her. He's a ship's commander in the Imperial Space Fleet, and she looks up to him as if he were the sky itself. They moved here when she was twelve, which was when I met her. She'd lived on ten other planets before then.

We connected because I liked her total military-brat attitude and because she knew so much about ships. Her level of awesome drew Grady and me to her like magnets to metal. Since then, she's gotten closer to Kayley than to us, but she still hangs with the guys when she doesn't want to girly out.

I've only met Commander Jee once before, so I don't have a strong remembrance of him, but I feel like I know him because Afton always talks about him. I think her mom is really nice, too, but it's going to be really hard on both Afton and her mom if he's gone.

"Sorry to hear about that, Afton," I say, mostly because I have no idea what to say at a moment like this.

"Thanks." Afton reaches out and squeezes my shoulder. "Head not hurting anymore?"

Oh man, no sarcasm. Afton is in a really bad place.

"Yeah, I'm okay...Were you going to go back in?"

Afton takes a long glance at Kayley's house and inhales deeply. As she considers what to do, she lets the breath seep out.

"I'll walk you guys home first," Afton says. "I still need some air."

As we walk, Grady tells her about the plans for tomorrow. She nods along, half listening. I know her mind is on her dad, so I feel it's my duty as her friend to break her out of her gloom. I don't have many tools at my disposal, so I use what's handy and find something she'll want to talk about.

"How many bugs you gonna kill, Surela?" I ask and get a smack on the back of my head for trying to cheer her up. Her reaction is a step in the right direction, so I know my plan is working.

"Bugs?" Afton responds. "How do you know they're bugs?"

"Yeah, Rance," Grady says. "She's right. There haven't been any reports about what they look like."

I shrug. Once when I was young, I was sitting on the ground, eating a sweet rice ball that my mom gave me. I remember it was my favorite, the kind with a piece of fruit and a little honey in it. Suddenly this big-ass bug landed on it. I was so scared I threw the ball over our fence and into our neighbor's yard. I wouldn't do that now, of course. I'm not afraid of bugs anymore, but if there were going to be scary aliens intent on killing us, I'd think they'd be bugs.

In the thousands of years since the Empire was formed, we have never encountered an intelligent alien race before now. I would have expected them to be peaceful, but it's just as likely they'd be like the Empire—resource-greedy and endowed with an overinflated sense of their importance in the universe.

"Better if they're bugs," Afton says with a grin. "Makes them easier to squash. Try going up against some cute and fuzzy animal. We'd lose in fifteen minutes."

"I don't know," I counter. "A gigantic bug would be a total freak show. You'd only kill it if you weren't completely frozen in fear."

"Your opinion doesn't count, dude," Grady states in a flat voice, "since you're sitting this one out."

"I'm not sitting this one out," I shoot back. "I'm just going to do something different. Kayley and I are going to talk about it tomorrow."

"Ooh, you and Kayley?" Afton turns on me, walking backward. A mischievous, toothy grin flowers across her face, and she taunts me with a little skip and a hop.

"Yeah, what of it?" I frown, feeling the heat come to my face. I don't think I will get out of this one without at least a few beatings to my ego. But it's fairly beat as it is, so a few more hits won't matter much. And I'll take the abuse if it means her mood is improving.

"So then, where are you going to make your move?"

"What are you talking about?"

Afton rolls her eyes. "Rancy-boy, don't play coy." She gets in my face. "Didn't we just go through this earlier today? You've been pining your entire life over this. Or will you just wimp out and watch someone else get her?"

"Hey, I'm good, thanks. I don't need help from you."

That's a total lie, of course. I need all the help I can get if I'm going to step up to Kayley's class level. I won't ask her out before then. She's deserving of someone who can be as perfect as they can be, and I'm a bit far from excellence at the moment.

"Yeah, but," Afton says and spins to drop an arm around my shoulders, "Rance, come on now. You might be her oldest friend, but I'm her best, and she tells me everything. You've never really even tried, have you?"

"What?"

"Don't evade the question, snodgrass," Afton presses. "Face it. To date, you haven't made a single effort. I bet I could get Kayley to date me sooner than you could."

"No way! Kayley doesn't like—"

"Is there something wrong if she did?" Afton, monarch of the power play, glares at me.

"No, I'm just saying, she dated Parrish, so that means she's a bit more...traditional," I reply and have a moment of sudden dread. What if? No, it couldn't be. Kayley isn't interested in girls, not that I think, anyway. Does Afton know something I don't? Miss Jee has admitted to a bit more flexibility in her romantic interests, but that's hardly surprising. Her upbringing has given her the power to adapt. Afton will be whatever she wants to be. That drives her mother nuts, but it's never been a problem for us. She's our bud, and we accept her.

Even if she's choosing to be a total pain in my rear at the moment.

"You know what you need?" Afton grins at me, and I'm already suspicious. "Proper motivation, that's what."

"What are you talking about?"

"I saw you today...You're pretty good in a crisis, but you're a complete wasteoid any other time. You're always waiting for Kayley to tell you what to do."

"Thanks for the support, Surela."

"Careful, dude," Grady warns. "Second use in a matter of minutes... that's asking for trouble."

Afton's eyes narrow into a glare as she stares at me. Her hand goes to her chin, and her grin returns. This time it's a bit more sinister than her last one. I'm like an animal, hunted, the eyes of the predator on me, ready to strike.

"I'll give you nine weeks," she says. "That's how long basic training is. You've got that long to convince Kayley to go out on a date with you. After that...she's open. I won't stop her from going out with anyone. Heck, I might just see if she's interested in being my girlfriend."

"Kayley wouldn't date you...You're her friend!"

"Think about what you just said there, buddy."

"That's different!" I cry, my cheeks going from warm to steaming.

"Is it, though?"

I keep my mouth shut. As much as I want to disagree with her, she has a point. Kayley and I have been friends for so long that she may never see me as anything but that. I really wanted to make the moment I asked her out special, but with everything that's happened, I don't know if that moment will ever come.

It's scary to think about that moment, too. That's another thing holding me back. What would happen if Kayley said no? My world would end, that's what. I don't do rejection well at all—I blame my father leaving us for that. I wish I could at least have some clue how she might feel about me. Afton might know, but she'll never tell me.

"Well, she's not going to date *you!*" It's a poor comeback, but I seem to be on a roll with those lately. I really have to stop feeling sorry for myself and take a page from the playbook all my friends wrote. I wasn't always like this. There was a time before Kayley got in with the popular kids when I was just like them. Then everything fell around me like a crystal castle shattering. My dad split, and my friendship with Kayley went on hiatus. The only reason we reconnected is that she started dating Parrish. I really owe a lot to that guy.

"We'll just have to see." Afton chuckles. "But don't worry, you can still have visitation rights."

I'm not just some wannabe Kayley fan. She's done so much for me when I couldn't figure it out myself, which recently is always. And do I need to mention for the billionth time just how beautiful she is? To look at her is to look upon love itself. Okay, well, maybe that's over the top, but that's the way I feel when I see her. I'm flying through the stars when I'm with my KayKay. I've known her for so long, I can't picture my future without her in it.

I've got to take some action. I just don't know what action that is yet. That's because, just like Afton said, I'm a rock in the mud until someone's got a gun to my head. Plus, I don't know whether to believe our master of deceit or not. Afton has never shown that kind of interest in Kayley before, but I'll lose Kayley if I don't do something, and there's no consolation prize. I'd end up dating Grady out of convenience.

"So, buddy," Afton says, catching my eyes as I glance up. "What say you?"

"Okay." I sigh, hoping I won't regret this. "Nine weeks, and not a second sooner."

"You don't sound so confident, dude," Grady whispers in my ear.

I give him a shrug. What choice do I have?

Afton catches it and claps her hands together. "I can't wait to see what happens!" Afton says. "I'm cheering for you, Rancy-boy, but if you flake out on the perfect girl, you've got no one to blame but yourself!"

Five

WE'VE BEEN STANDING IN line for three hours already, and it's sweltering. I feel like I'm a melting ice pop, dripping its last drops onto the hotcrete of the pavement before it finally evaporates. Along the military base's fence, there are no trees to seek shade under. That's because it would be too easy to get over the fence by climbing up one. So we suffer for security's sake. Good thing Kayley isn't here yet. She's not good with the heat.

What makes it worse is that we were just informed they have too many applicants, and this is just one base out of hundreds on the planet! So they'll scan the line and dismiss anyone they consider not up to military rigor. I've never heard of the military turning down volunteers, but they must be so overwhelmed by the sheer number of wannabe bug-smashers that they can't handle them all at once. I bet they'll just wait until they can get the first recruits through training and then call people back when they're ready. My buds would be so disappointed, but I'm secretly wishing for it to happen. I'd get to spend more time with them.

Either way, it gives me more reason to not sign up.

"So, Rance, what are you and Kayley planning on doing together while we're away?" Grady's innocent question packs itself with all levels of entendre. He didn't mean it that way, but my buds wouldn't be my buds if they left a question like that hanging out there, untouched.

"Yeah, Rance, what *are* you and Kayley planning to do?" Afton echoes with a grin, and my blood pressure goes supernova. I'm not ready to discuss this in front of Parrish. I don't know how he'd react. He might still have feelings for her. It wouldn't be too cool of me to tell him on his way to a war that I want to date his ex.

"We haven't decided yet," I mumble. It's not enough to fend Afton off, but here comes Kayley, back from her shopping diversion and just in time to take some emotional heat off of me.

"Hey, I brought you all a going-away present!" Kayley says, then stops and presses her lips together, wondering why we're all staring at her. "Um...did I miss something?"

"Not at all," I say before anyone else has the chance to get a dig in. "We were just talking about our awesome plan to do our part here at the home base."

"Yes, I'm glad we talked and figured it out." Kayley beams at me, and I get all mushy inside. "I can't wait to do it with you, Rance."

Grady and Afton turn away with a snicker.

"Rance and I have something to tell all of you," Kayley declares, and we're all ears. "We're going to support all the single parents while their significant others are away. We're joining the local Families of Service chapter today! We'll help with chores, babysit, do errands, all that sort of thing. It's a good idea, right?"

"Wow, Rance," Afton says, folding her arms, "that's pretty mature of you. You think you can handle being someone's partner?" It's an outright challenge, but today I'm feeling up for it.

"Of course I can," I reply. "When you've been around someone their entire life, it makes it easy."

Kayley blinks at our exchange, and her eyes narrow after giving our guilty faces a thorough examination. So much for secrets.

"Okay, guys, unless you want me to give your presents to some random people online who don't have a great friend like me, you're going to tell me what's up."

"Nothing's up," Afton replies and shoots me a *keep your mouth shut* look. I agree with my eyes so that Kayley can't catch our brief communication. If she did, there'd be hell to pay. I'm in awe of my oldest friend. I've seen her strike someone down with just a "no." Just add that to the ever-growing list of reasons I'm crazy about her.

"Yeah, nothing going on," Grady repeats.

"Nothing going on, KayKay," I affirm, hoping she believes us. No one is safe until Kayley decides she does. Unfortunately, she's not sold yet. She folds her arms and turns to Parrish, who's been quiet today.

"Well, Parrish, it seems like you're the only one I can trust. Are they telling the truth?"

Parrish isn't paying attention. Instead, he's staring down the line towards the front. I take a glance—oh! Now I see what's been keeping him quiet. While the rest of us goof off, my bud is trying to be on his best behavior because of some tough-as-steel dude in military blue pounding his way towards us. Parrish is so determined to get signed up today that I think he's pretending not to know us.

The rest of my buds swivel their heads to see what Parrish is seeing, and they get a bit of a shock because the soldier—I can tell by the gold on his collar that he's an officer—is right behind them. The aide that he's got with him is only a nano-degree less mean. Hard swallows all around, team. Here's your make-it-or-break-it moment.

"Well, good afternoon, volunteers," the officer says, dropping his fists to his sides. "So glad to see this much energy applied to the war effort. All of you are of age?"

"Sir! We're all nineteen!" Parrish shouts and snaps to attention. The officer drops his eyes on Parrish and gives him a once-over.

"Excellent, but I'll need to see your IDs as proof of that. Even after five years of being here, you all still look like children to me." Parrish sinks a little, but I watch him try to stay strong as the officer's aide collects IDs.

"Not all of us are signing up, sir." Kayley does exactly what I was hoping she wouldn't do. "My friend and I will support the troops here at home." She jabs a thumb at me when she says it.

This draws immediate scrutiny of my physical person. With spears firing from his eyes and a hard frown, it's obvious that General So-and-so here is about to kick me off the line—with absolute pleasure.

"Want to stay home with your pretty girlfriend? Is that it, son?"

Oh shoot. He went with that one. Grady and Afton instantly find an interesting spot on the ground to stare at. They're trying to be on their best behavior, and a glance my way will definitely put them in the delinquent zone.

"We'll come back to you," the officer says and turns back to Parrish, looking him over once more and nodding. "What's your name, son?"

"Parrish Waafajin Beltrami, sir!"

"Well, Beltrami, you seem like the kind of recruit we're looking for. I'm Lieutenant Colonel Nelson. Ever fire a weapon before?"

"Sir, no, sir! But I'm confident that I can squash any bug that comes our way, sir!"

"What makes you think they're bugs, son?" The lieutenant colonel raises an eyebrow at his statement. "What if they were cute and fuzzy? You think you could still kill them?"

I hear Afton draw in a big gasp. We all do. It's pretty hard to miss. Colonel Nelson swivels around and catches her mouth open, her finger pointed right at him. I grin. She's done it now—no way Afton's getting in at this point.

"Something you'd like to add, miss?" he asks, moving over to look down on Afton.

"Sir, it's just that I said that yesterday, sir!" Afton shoots up straight, shoulders back.

Now, Afton is tall, but this officer has double-digit centimeters on her. He bends down a bit to get closer. While he's doing that, she throws a glance my way to see just how excited I am to watch her get dressed down by this military hothead. It'll be something that I'll be reminding her of when she joins Kayley and me to babysit military brats.

"What's that?"

"That they could be..." She cringes. "Cute and fuzzy, sir, and that we'd be in trouble if that was the case, sir!"

"Hmm, excellent deduction." He takes notice of the muscles in her arms and nods approvingly. "How much can you lift?"

"She hauled me nearly a kilometer the other day, sir," I answer, trying to help. He swings back to me and shakes his head.

"Son, you're not helping yourself...and the question was for the recruit. Not you."

"Sir?" Afton's entire face brightens.

"You heard me. I'm signing you up right now, provided your age documents are in order. You afraid of shooting a weapon?"

"Sir, no, sir!"

"Excellent, recruit. Glad to have you on board. Now what's your full name and your port of call?" He brings out a tablet from behind his back and gets ready to tap in her response.

"Sir, Surela Afton Jee! My port of call is right here, sir!"

"Jee, hunh?" He puts a hand to his chin. "You got any family in the service?"

Afton squirms, and I know the colonel just rubbed on a tender spot. She must have thought of her dad the moment he asked the question.

"Sir, my father and my two brothers are all serving currently."

"I think I know your father, Jee. He's the executive officer aboard the *Neenance*, is that correct? Sorry about what happened. Your father isn't someone we want to lose, so don't give it a second thought. We'll find him."

"Yes, sir," she says, with nowhere near the volume she had before.

Afton looks relieved when the colonel turns away from her and back to the rest of us.

"So who else is signing up today?"

"Sir!" Grady does a solid mimic of Parrish's attempt at soldiering, and the colonel nods approvingly.

"Name?"

"Sugiyama, sir!"

The colonel steps in front of Grady and looks him over. I'm betting he's thinking the same thing about him as he thought about me. If that's the case, then there goes his chance. I'm throwing a small prayer to the Goddesses for him.

"Any chance you've got some relation to the Sugiyama drive?" the colonel asks.

"Those are my parents, sir!"

"Well, don't we have a bunch of young celebrities here?" He taps his pad. "Engineering, of course. I bet your parents wouldn't have it any other way."

"Sir, no, sir!" Grady's voice cracks when he tries to double down on the gusto. If the colonel heard it, he's ignoring it for now.

"How about you, Beltrami? Your parents build the first condenser rifle or something?"

"Sir, no, sir." Parrish shakes his head. "My parents aren't famous, just proud that their son is heeding the call."

"See that you live up to that, okay?"

"Sir!"

After he's confirmed my buds, Colonel Nelson turns to me, and I become the focus of his scrutiny. My gaze drops to the ground to avoid seeing what I know must be some severe disapproval. I don't even know why I care, but he's different from what I expected a military officer to be. I'd hate to say it, but he might actually care about my friends. Otherwise, why would he say what he did?

"Now you...what's your name?" he asks, with a little more kindness than I expected.

"Rance He', sir."

"So, Mr. He', you going to support your friends, or are you choosing the easy way out?"

"My skills are best deployed here, sir," I reply with a twinge of regret. Why did he have to put it to me like that? Of course I want to support my friends. Who wouldn't? But no way will I ever trust anyone with gold emblems on their collar, no matter how nice I think they are. Besides, he reminds me of my father.

"Oh? What skills are those?" He folds his arms and stares me down. I crush my lips together, but I don't give him the satisfaction of seeing me wince. This guy knows how to push my buttons, and I really dislike him for it. This is exactly how it would be for me in the military. There's no way I could handle that.

"No answer for that, Mr. He'? Come on, son, I'm giving you a chance to defend yourself here."

"I don't need to defend myself against someone like you," I mutter, and a flash of anger crosses his face. He heard me. I know he did.

"What's that?" he growls, hands on hips and leaning into me. "You want to speak up, son?"

"Sir, you don't need me, sir," I reply, and his anger dissipates into something more like disappointment. As he stares at me, I start feeling the same way. I don't know whether it's my father's voice or my own, but something inside me says that I should have said yes instead of hiding behind my lack of confidence.

"One day, I just might, Rance. Remember that." He leaves me alone and turns back to my buds. "Why don't the three of you come up the line with me? Let's get the rest of the docs out of the way so we can get you on base ASAP. You can have a moment to say your goodbyes if you need."

"Thank you, sir!" they shout together.

"Very good. I'll see you up front. Keep it brief, kids."

He walks away, and once we think he's out of earshot, we all let loose with a collective sigh, each for our own individual reasons.

"Well, you heard the colonel," Kayley says, taking up her position as leader now that the other boss has left. She spreads her arms wide, and the first person she wraps them around is—of course—Parrish. I keep my head from exploding by reminding myself that it'll be just the two of us for the next nine weeks.

There are hugs and handshakes all around before Parrish and Grady head off. Kayley, Afton, and I watch them go, but I wonder why Afton is hanging back. Maybe she wants to say something in private to Kayley. It wouldn't be to me, that's for sure. We had our talk last night.

"Oh shoot! I forgot to give them their presents!" Kayley says and dashes after them. "Stay here until I get back!"

Afton and I stand together and watch her run off. We're like two gawky children that just got told to stand still for our school portrait. We don't want to smile, and we hate standing in one place.

"Rance." Afton puts a hand on my shoulder, the sides of her mouth fighting not to curl down.

"What's up?"

"Take care of her, okay?" Afton's tone is serious, and a chill nips the back of my neck. "She...needs people to support her. I know you know what I mean." But then her sober mood flips, and she smirks. "At least until I get back. Then your grace period ends, buddy boy."

"Okay. Don't worry." I nod and smile, unsure of what to say. But then something pops into my head, and my mouth widens to match her smirk. "I'll be taking perfect care of my *girlfriend*!"

That was a three-pointer, Surela! Rance for the win!

Afton recognizes my well-executed counterattack with a nod. Then a grin comes to her face, and she glances around before grabbing me by both my shoulders.

"Oh, and speaking of that...I want you to do me a favor..."

"Sure, anything."

"Give Kayley a message for me."

"Okay, what is it?" I growl.

With no warning, Afton slides her hands up to grab my face and plants her lips right on mine! It's a sneak attack for the ages! How could I ever expect it? My three points get completely erased. I don't even want to calculate how many points her killer blitz is worth!

Overall, the kiss isn't half-bad. Not that I have that kind of attraction to her. Naturally, it's normal for a guy to have those thoughts, but Afton has never made my skin tingle the way Kayley's touch does.

Well, until now.

Six

"YOU GOT ALL OF that message?" Afton keeps eye contact with me to confirm.

"Uh-huh." I'm feeling dizzy.

"Good, because I won't tell you it again, and just so we're clear, that wasn't meant for you."

"Okay, I wasn't...uh, really thinking that."

"Yeah, good." She pats me on the cheek. "See you soon, buddy. Take care of your mom."

Afton turns to go and then stops in her tracks.

"What?"

"Kayley...and Parrish...and Grady." Her eyes have this hundred-meter stare.

"Did you forget she went to give them their presents?" I try to get back into my cool persona, but I'm feeling weak at the knees.

"No...they're coming this way...running fast."

"Afton! Rance! Take cover! Attack!" I hear Parrish shout. No way, another attack? I scan the area for cover. There's not much around, but as I see the shops across the street, I get an idea.

"Basement!" I shout, pointing at the storefront across the street. Parrish sees it and gives me a nod. I grab Afton by the arm, and she grabs me back. We shoot across the street in a matter of seconds, waiting for the rest of our gang to get there. We're about to open up the basement doors that line the sidewalk, but a shout comes our way.

"No! Not that way! You go down there, and you'll be making your own grave! Come with me!" It's the colonel, beckoning us back across the street. Afton shoves me forward, and we dart back to the other side again. The colonel opens a side gate next to the base and hustles us through.

That's when the first bomb hits—right where Afton and I were standing. The concussion knocks us all down, and the glass of the shop windows sprays everywhere, catching a few unfortunates who didn't make it to cover in time.

The colonel recovers quickly, rushing over to us to pull us up. He's gone in the next microsecond, flying over to a low graphite-colored structure and ripping the door open.

"Come on! Get inside!" he shouts as he waves us in.

A pair of those black ships streak overhead, and then the military base next door is engulfed in flames. I'm stunned. I just stare as fingers of blue and orange reach towards the sky. The heat of the explosion is intense. My hands fly to my face, protecting it, but I feel my eyebrows have been singed off.

Someone grabs my arm and spins me around. It's Colonel Nelson, shouting something at me that I can't hear. I imagine it's something like, *"You dumbass, you're about to become a bunch of charred carbon!"*

My survival sense comes back to me, and I follow his direction, heading over to the shelter and diving inside. The colonel is right behind me and the door slams shut behind him. A big wheel is on the inside of the door, and he turns it with a grunt, sealing the shelter from the danger outside. But bombs are still falling. Some are really close and rattle the entire shelter, putting us all in a panic.

"Alright, listen up, cadets, volunteers, civilians," he says, looking at me on that last one. "We are well protected down here. They built this shelter to survive over a trillion joules of direct energy against it."

"How much energy is that, Colonel?" someone asks in the back. I try to catch the person who asked, but there's got to be a hundred people in this tight little space. Adults, children, soldiers, civilians, everyone who was just outside is well represented here. I hope there are other shelters like this, because there were many more people outside.

"You saw those bombs exploding outside?" the colonel asks.

"Yes, sir. We all did."

"They're not even close to that number." The colonel scans around the room, catching as many eyes as he can.

"Right, now," he continues, "we have supplies for all that can last a week or thereabouts, so the best course of action is to stay put and wait for the attack to be over."

"I'm worried about my mom," says a young boy near me. I agree with that. I hope my mom is okay, too. We're far from where I live, so if the attack is just here, then she's safe. I'm crossing my fingers, toes, legs, and arms, just to be sure. I'll call her once I get a connection again.

A big one strikes right near us and jolts the entire shelter like a child shaking a yuletide present trying to figure out what's inside. We're all thrown off-balance, and the ones who are standing—that would include the colonel and me—fall hard onto the graphcrete floor. A good thing it's more forgiving than the rock cement outside. I still bang up my elbow pretty good.

"You okay, son?" the colonel asks me, rubbing his own knee. I wish he would stop calling me that...I'm not his son, and the fact that he reminds me of my father only makes that thought more repulsive. I might give him a pass since he probably just saved my life, but I'm not going to forget he's just a military middle manager.

"Sure thing," I reply. I don't need to sound tough. It wasn't a nasty fall, but Kayley grabs my shirt and tugs me back towards the rest of the gang.

"Rance, you alright?" Kayley asks.

"We're all together, so why wouldn't I be?" That gets a shaky laugh from everyone and arms on shoulders all around. I'm feeling the sting of my elbow as Parrish rubs against it, but the shared chuckle and smiles help.

So we wait. I'm not sure how long because I didn't bother to check my Sergo. Who cares anyway? It must be a long time, though, because I catch my mind drifting. I'm having strange thoughts, like *How similar would Afton's kiss be to Kayley's? If we kissed, would I like it as much? More? Less?*

That last speculation makes me cringe. No way I'd believe that to be true, but more importantly, how did Afton expect me to pass that message on to Kayley, exactly? She was crafty in so many ways with that one, I can't even begin to count them. This is a no-win situation for me. I'm dead if I do, and I'm dead if I don't. And why am I thinking about this in the middle of an attack?

Also...does Afton know that was my first kiss?

I flash a glance over to Afton, who's got her arm around my destiny girl, with Kayley resting her head on Afton's shoulder. She catches me looking, but instead of gloating, she smiles at me. I can read all the worry and all the hope that Afton is feeling in that smile, and it confuses me to no end. Afton is supposed to be this impossible machine. Nothing breaks her, ever. Though if there was ever a day that did, this would be a strong contender.

"Dude," Grady whispers to me after a low rumble vibrates the floor beneath us. "This is some crazy stuff, right? You sure you still want to hang around here and get bombed into your next life?"

"You think it's gonna be safer out there, in the middle of a battleground?" I smack back at him. Even so, my body itches at the thought there might be people out there who are hurt bad. Innocent people—mothers, children, babies. It's too much to consider.

"For the front lines, no, but I'll be building ships, so I'm good," Grady replies.

"What happens if they bomb the factory you're working in?" I ask. I have to make sure Grady's got his head in the correct dimension of reality.

"Bombs don't work like that in orbit, Rance. They'd use missiles, and those don't even have to explode. Get your head out of your ass, dude," Grady says, a little too loud for the low noise level down here. A few adults throw us an uncomfortable glance.

"Hey, you two, stop it!" Kayley hisses. We both look at her like she's got a pair of horns sticking out of her head.

"We're just having a discussion, KayKay," I reply. I'm trying to keep things cool, even though Grady's aggressive comment has me shaken a little. Kayley doesn't take my comment in the way I intended, and her eyebrows dip as she leans forward and gets in my face. Not that I mind all that much, but it would be better if she was about to say something nice to me instead of giving me a beating with her tongue.

"You. Should. Stop. Talking. *Now*. There are..." Her eyes dart left and right as if to say *notice all the scared people around you?* "Children here. Got it?"

"Yeah, it's cool. We get it," I say. Grady nods in support. He knows, just like I know, there's no contradicting a command from Kayley. She doesn't need to be intimidating like Afton or even Parrish, but she's got her own means of shutting you up. Not that I see it much. Her smile is way more effective. This is more like her weapon of last resort.

She sits back, and Afton wraps her arms about Kayley's shoulders. She also drops a glare our way, but she's like a kitten compared to Kayley's full-grown tiger. It won't last, though. Neither of them will want to stay mad for very long. We all know there are a lot of bigger problems to deal with right now.

"Okay, everyone." The colonel stands up. "I've just heard from HQ over the base intercom. They think the attack is over, so I'm looking for a few volunteers to come do some reconnaissance with me. There might be people who need help out there, and we need to get to them as soon as possible."

Once again, I'm the target of his glance. If he thinks that I'm about to volunteer, he must be seriously nuts. I don't know why he wants to pick on me, but getting inside this shelter is the only command I'll follow from this guy.

Parrish's hand shoots up right away and receives a respectful nod. Afton, the competitor she is, can't wait to throw her hand up next. Her amount of enthusiasm is so exaggerated that even Kayley gives her the side-eye.

"Thank you, recruits. Anyone else?" The colonel looks around.

To my total shock, Grady raises his hand next. Never in the entire life cycle of a star would I ever have thought he would volunteer. He might not even realize what he's getting himself into. Now I'm thinking I might need to go as well to make sure he doesn't fall into a hole somewhere.

Then from out of nowhere, the Queen of the Team, my Kayley, grins at Afton and Parrish and raises her hand, too. Man, I'm looking bad now. I know everyone's about to turn on me with some level of expectation written all over their faces.

I'm too slow—it happens, and even the colonel gets his needles in on the act. I'm squirming as I consider my position. People need help, but what can *I* do? Blood doesn't bother me, but it's not like I could save someone if they were dying. I might even harm them more, and that's certainly not something I'd want to happen.

Then again...my buds are no medical experts, but they're going. I promised myself last night I'd be more assertive. If I don't go, that's a negative mark on my Kayley scorecard. It's more than that, of course, but the vision of Kayley shaking her head at me is what's forefront in my mind.

So up goes my hand. I smile a little to myself for doing it. Yes, there was a bit of peer pressure involved, but I made the choice myself.

"Well done, all of you." Lieutenant Colonel Nelson sounds like we just won some big battle for him. I think that's a bit like the reaction before the chain, if you ask me. Still, if it somehow gets my new-recruit buds promoted quicker, then I'm fine with it.

He grabs the wheel on the door, but then backs away and glances at Parrish. "If you would, recruit."

"Sir!" Parrish is feeling it, big-time. I bet he gets his second stripe before he graduates boot camp. He spins the wheel like he's playing roulette, and a second later the door comes unlocked.

"Careful, son, there may be debris on the door," the colonel warns. "Go slowly."

Parrish does as commanded, and the colonel's safety call is validated. A bit of dust slides in as he pushes the door open, covering Parrish in a mist of white powder.

"Okay, step back now," Colonel Nelson says and takes a step forward. "I'll go out first, then...What's your name again, son?"

"Beltrami, sir."

"What's your first name, Beltrami?"

"Parrish, sir."

"Okay, for today, I'm calling you Parrish. Okay with you, recruit?"

"All good, sir."

He is *so* getting promoted.

Seven

IT'S A DYSTOPIAN MESS outside. For about a kilometer in all directions, I can't recognize anything that resembles a building. The row of shops across the street have collapsed into such a pile of rubbish that it looks more like a recently opened junkyard than a place where you could have an awesome breakfast.

We search through the area where the hangar had stood, but we see no signs of anything, much less people. That's a good thing, of course. We don't want to find anyone. The state of this place is not conducive to survival. Anyone we found wouldn't have much of a chance.

"Did you find anyone?" Colonel Nelson calls to us as we head back. Kayley gives us a wave as she walks next to him. Seeing her so close to him makes me itch, but I'll put my paranoia away for now.

"No. The hangar was clear," Afton calls and waves back.

"We checked inside the one transport that was there. Nobody in it," I say, and the colonel nods.

"That's good," he replies. "That means they got the other ship out of there. Most likely the ground crew evacuated with that one."

"Did you find anyone?" I hope the answer to this is positive only if they're still living.

"Yes, they're okay, thank the Goddesses. All of base command went down into the shelter before the main thrust of the attack came. They've already been taken to main HQ for a debrief. I'll need to join them shortly, but first, I'll get everyone out of the shelter and on their way. Why don't the three of you join your friends and see if they need help? There's not a lot of light left, so you'll have to hurry."

"Thank you, Colonel," Kayley says with a big smile. I'm here listening and wondering what she needs to thank him for.

"No, Kayley, thank you. You've been a great help."

That, on top of the first thank-you, was not what I needed to hear. Why does she have to be nice to him? Doesn't she know he's only going to get our friends hurt?

"Oh." The colonel turns to Afton. "Make sure you keep yourself free for the next couple of days. By then, we'll have a new logistical plan for getting the recruits up to the base, and we'll be coming to collect you. Be ready."

"Yes, sir!" Afton snaps off a salute, though I can see the disappointment in her eyes. She was ready today, and she needed to go today. Sitting around is not something she's going to be enjoying much.

The three of us trot over to where Grady and Parrish are hiking up the rubble. Grady sees us, and he takes a break, wiping a shirtsleeve across his forehead.

"Anything?" I ask as we get close.

"No. You?" He's got this zoned-out stare, like he's been looking at the same pile of rubble for too long.

I shake my head. "Nothing, but that's good, right?"

"Not if they're buried so deep that we can't get to them with our hands," Parrish replies. He's about spent on his search, I think. There's some frustration in his voice, and my buddy is the kind of superhuman that doesn't get that way.

"That's what the rescue team is for," Kayley says. "Let's keep looking."

"Where haven't you looked yet?" Afton asks.

Parrish sighs, and he gets his bearings before turning to point down the row of stores, now turned to lumpy pancakes.

"We're there," Afton says and follows Kayley, who's already headed in that direction. That leaves me to follow behind.

Kayley's got a light, and she shines it in between the chunks of brick and concrete. I climb up to see if I can get a better vantage point, but wind up slipping and throwing up a haze of concrete powder into my face. It smells funny—like a combination of charred wood and liquid fuel.

I crawl up again and finally get to the peak, and I feel accomplished, like I just summited some great mountain. Not that I've ever seen one. Angelcanis doesn't have many mountains. I've only seen photos from other planets. If I ever get to a planet that's got them, I'm definitely going up.

"Rance, try listening for any sounds. Put your ear next to one of those holes." That's my KayKay. She's always got sharp ideas. Well, and Grady, too, though Kayley's are usually more practical.

The first hole that I listen to, I just hear the sound of air rushing in and out—no human sounds, for sure. So I try another. Same thing. I can see how this could quickly get tedious. No wonder Parrish and Grady are so zoned out.

"Anything?" Kayley asks.

"No, but I'll let you know." She better not ask me every minute. That would also get old, really fast.

Parrish and Grady give up on their pile and join us. I reach out to Parrish to give him a hand up. He could climb this without my help, but right now he's wiped out and he willingly accepts my charity. Grady waves me off and takes a moment to get his legs back in order.

"Where'd you check already?" Parrish asks.

"Kayley's got me listening, so if you want to do the same, try over there." I point across the pile from where I've been dropping my ear into holes. Parrish nods and climbs over.

After another hour of this, we're all beat. The sun is about to drop off the edge of the sky, and I'm waiting for someone to call it quits. Nobody does, though. If I had to guess, it's because we're all hoping for hope's sake. If there's someone who needs help, we want to be there for them.

"Hey, guys, it's getting dark." Grady's the first to hold up the white flag. "Maybe we can come back tomorrow."

"Just a bit more, then we'll go," I say, not believing that just came out of my mouth. Everyone agrees, though, and now I'm patting myself on the back because I just might be a good leader like Kayley, sticking to my morals and all.

I scramble, or rather, slide down into an area I think was the back of some clothing store. My ear goes to a hole, and I get still. Of course, nothing. Why would there be?

"Hello? Anybody down there?" I yell into the hole, just for fun, and because I'm so tired, I don't care about looking like an idiot.

But then it comes. A weak but audible "Help!"

"Guys! Guys! I just heard something!" Unless I'm hallucinating, that is.

Before I can even look up, the four of them are next to me, ready to dig to the other side of the planet.

"What did you hear, Rance?" Kayley asks.

"Someone said help. I'm sure of it."

"Which hole?" Parrish asks. I point. "Hello? Can you hear me? Are you okay?" he shouts down the hole, then turns his ear to it.

It's obvious. He hears it, too. Yes! I'm not hallucinating! That much is good. The other part about someone being alive is also a plus.

"Okay, we hear you! Hold on, we're going to try to get you out!" Parrish turns to me and points at a chunk of concrete. "Help me lift this."

The concrete is as heavy as the situation for whoever's down there. We don't really pick it up as much as we shove it out of the way. Now there's a big opening that we can see down—sort of. After a meter or so, it goes blacker than my no-windows bathroom when the light goes out. I pretend like I see someone down there, but I don't, really.

"Kayley, bring your light over here," Parrish says.

As soon as she aims it down the hole, someone's hand becomes visible. It's bloody and dirty but otherwise intact. It's also not that far down.

"Are you hurt?" Parrish calls down.

"Not bad, but I can't move my leg. It's caught!" the woman calls back up to us.

"Okay, we're gonna figure out how to get you out of there!"

We all look at Parrish for a plan, but he looks to Kayley, so the rest of us follow his gaze and turn to her.

"We're going to need some rope, and..." Kayley looks at the hole. "This hole needs to be wider."

"No problem," replies Parrish, and he starts to rip a bunch of rubble from around the edges.

"Careful!" Afton says. "You don't want any to fall down on her!"

Grady and I help to get the debris away from the hole as Parrish rolls it back. Very little falls in, so we're doing a good job. Kayley keeps the light on the woman's hand and talks to her so we know she's okay—as okay as someone with a leg stuck under an entire building can be.

"Rope?" Kayley asks. That's our one sticking point. Until Grady remembers something.

"I've got an idea...It's not rope, but it will work!" he says, his eyes lighting up. "Be right back!"

He comes back with a thick cable. Like something you see the power techs use. Like always, Grady is right—it will work. Now all we have to do is figure out who's going down there to release her from the rock.

"Rance, you go down and get her free," Kayley commands me.

"Me?" I can't think of a single reason I might be the best choice for the job. Parrish should do it, or maybe Afton would be better since she's lighter. Certainly not me.

"You're strong enough to move anything heavy and light enough so the rest of us can pull you back up." Kayley's pointed stare says she's not accepting any reply but a yes from me. I guess that means I'm going.

I wrap the wire around me, just under my arms, and tie it as tightly as I can. Then Parrish tries it and makes it secure enough to lower me down. Kayley is still talking to me with her eyes. Her look now says *I want you to come back safe*. Kayley hands me her light. And now that my Queen has expressed concern for me, I'm feeling lighter than the air itself. My buds should have no trouble lowering me down.

I sit on the edge as the others find the best way to ease me down. Then, when they're ready, I slide off and find myself suspended in the air. I raise a hand and give them the ready signal. My body suddenly free-falls for a frightening second before the cable goes taut and slows my descent.

When I get to the bottom, I try to locate the woman, swinging Kayley's light around until I see her.

"I'm here!" she cries. It sounds like she's in a lot of pain, which wasn't something we picked up on from up top. She's on the floor of what used to be the basement, and there's a massive shelf lying on top of her leg. The shock of the scene hits my face before I can hide it, but luckily she's not looking directly at me.

"Okay, miss, my name is Rance," I say, but it's more for me than for her. "I'm here to get you out."

"By yourself?" The lack of confidence in her voice is demoralizing, but I have to put on my brave act, anyway. She might not want me to help if she doesn't think I can.

"No, there's four of my friends up top. We just have to get your leg free, then they'll pull you up."

"My leg's stuck."

"Yeah, I'm gonna see if I can find something to lift up that shelf."

There's not much that looks useful down here—boxes of clothing, clothing hangers, a clothing rack...wait. That might work. I thank Grady for making sure I understood the principle of levers when we were young. It helped me pass a class, plus now, look at me—using it in real life to save someone!

"Okay, miss, I'm going to use that rack to lift the shelf off your leg. When I do, I need you to get yourself out of there, okay? Do you think you can do it?"

"Yes, I think so."

I wrestle with the rack for a minute. It's stubborn and doesn't want to come off of its mount. I grunt and fight with it before it pops out, but the pole is much heavier than I expected, so I wrestle with it again until I have it under my control. I find a nice chunk of concrete for my fulcrum, and now I'm ready.

"Here we go...three...two...one...go!" I press all of my weight on the pole to jack the chunky metal shelf upwards.

The woman moans but manages to push herself up on her elbows and begins to slide backward. Even with my lever trick, the shelf is painful to lift. I'm not trying to lift just it, but all the junk on top of it, too. It's amazing it moves at all.

"Rance? How's it going down there?" I hear Kayley call, but in my struggle to keep the shelf lifted, I get no more than a croak out of my throat. No clue if she heard me.

Some debris drops down. It's not big, but that's still a bad omen. If the rest of the rubble above is unstable, it could crash down on us. We need to get out now, but the woman doesn't look like she's clear of the shelf. She's trying, but we're running out of time. I could grab her and pull her free, but I risk caving in the whole area if I drop the shelf too quickly. It's getting heavy, though. If I'm going to move this along, I might need to take a risk.

Kayley would beat me if she knew what I was planning. Then Afton would, then maybe Parrish next, followed by Afton again. Of course, that's only if I survive. If not, they'd have to wait until they got to heaven to beat my ass. Those guys would be ancient by then, and there's no way they'd have the strength to even pull a hair from my head.

I count down in my head and release. The shelf comes down with a heavy thud with more force than I expected. I almost lose my footing as I grab the woman under her arms and slide her free. We get clear just as the whole section caves in, crushing the shelf and blowing dust all over the place. We both get covered, and I fall back, the woman falling on top of me.

"Rance!" Grady is the first to the hole up top. He peers down, but there's a haze above me, and I know it's impossible to see from where he is. "Dude, are you okay?"

I better check to make sure that's the case before I answer.

Eight

"RANCE, PLEASE! LET US know if you're okay!" That's my darling Kayley, and there's a bit too much desperation in her voice for me to just keep lying here. I need to answer, but I've got to stop choking on dust first.

"You okay, miss?" I ask the lady, who's still lying on top of me.

"Yes...yes...you did it," she says in between coughs.

Maybe I'm good at something after all.

She gets raised from the basement pit first. Then my buddies pull me up, looking fairly happy that I'm alive. They wait until I put my feet down on the stable ground, then all four of them attack me at once with pats and slaps. This feels more like a punishment than a reward. Until Kayley squeezes me tight and holds on for a long moment. Then my cheeks turn the same color as her hair.

"Guys, we need to call medical, get her to the hospital," Parrish says.

"Anyone still have a charge on their Sergo?" Afton asks, waving her device in the air.

"Nope," I reply. "Actually..." I dig into my pocket for the wallet-sized device, checking to make sure it didn't get crushed. They're not cheap to replace. "Oh, good, it's okay."

Kayley is already on it. She sends the emergency team directions while a medical technician talks her through a brief examination. As I watch her follow the instructions step by step, I think she could be a superb med-tech. She's gentle with the woman, but she moves through the once-over like a pro.

The woman's name is Anne. Her leg's not broken, the med-tech says, but she'll need to stay off it for a bit. Afton and Kayley help her sit up, for which she thanks them with a smile. She's grateful for all the care and attention, and of course, the saving, which I did.

"What's your name, young man?" Anne asks.

"That's Rance," Afton replies for me. "He's kind of a wimp, but his heart's in the right place."

"Surela!" I say.

"Just getting you back ahead of time because I knew you were going to do that."

I shake my head. She may have predicted the future this time, but she's no clairvoyant. "If that's the case, then I think I get unlimited chances today." I grin at her. "And maybe I'm thinking I'd like to use a few more."

"Try it, buddy. I dare you."

"Oh, you kids," Anne says, taking a moment away from her suffering to show some kindness back to us. "Always teasing each other like that. You two must be dating."

There goes everyone's self-control, except for Afton and me. We just stare at each other, speechless. Oh, the horror.

"Well, Rance, I don't think you are a wimp at all," Anne continues. "That was a very brave thing to risk yourself like that to come down and get me out. Thank you." She smiles. I smirk at Afton to make sure she knows I just scored like a hundred points.

"Good job down there, dude," Parrish says, laying a playful shoulder into my side. "You sure you don't want to put those skills to use where they could make a real difference?"

"Thanks, but I don't know what skills you might be referring to." It's a half lie. I know what I accomplished, but I'm not attributing my success to any level of skill that I have. It could have easily gone the other way, and Anne and I would have gotten buried under tons of reinforced concrete.

"Don't play dumb," Grady says. "I know you know what you did."

"You know," Anne says with a wince. Kayley drops down next to her and puts a hand on her shoulder. "You kids should sign up. That is if you haven't already. They could really use you."

"We have," Afton replies, glancing at me. "Well, some of us have, anyway."

"And the rest?"

"Rance and I were planning on joining Families of Service," Kayley replies, with a smile up at me. I manage a small curl of my lips. I keep telling myself I'm making the right choice, but every time I do, my chest gets achy. I'm happy to be spending time with Kayley, but when I think of my buds out in the middle of a war, it's the same feeling I get when I remember the image of my father walking out the door. If they go, I don't think I'll ever see them again.

"Hey," Parrish says, dropping a hand on my shoulder. I glance up at him to see the same kind of somber mood reflected in his eyes. "I didn't apologize for yelling at you last night. I just don't want us—"

"I know, dude." I pull my smile up again, but it falters. "The same thing's bothering me."

Today, we all had the reality of war give us a good smack in the face. It's pulled Parrish down from his ideological tower, and it's dumped him in the dirt with the rest of us. He's trying not to show it, but he's scared, and I'm scared for him.

"Hey, you know you could always work in the med corps," Parrish says, forcing a grin. "You've got a way with rescuing people, and you could be near to Grady if you get posted to a station."

As Parrish says it, I catch Kayley's mouth drop open, and for a second, she's got this lost expression written all over her face. It gets quickly covered up when she notices I'm looking at her. Kayley presses her lips together and gives me a supportive nod.

My heart gets ripped in two. If Kayley thinks I'm about to change my mind, she's gone off the deep end. But I can't say goodbye to Parrish, Grady, and Afton. Not when it feels like it could be the last time. I drop on the nearest pile of rubble and turn my head in any direction where there isn't one of my friends. Looking one of them in the eye is going to put them in a bad place.

"Rance?" Parrish asks, his voice small. I grimace because now I've gone and made him think it's his fault that I'm down like this.

"I'm cool," I respond. Again, it's another fabrication I put together from one part truth and several parts fiction. "I just wish this wasn't the way it has to be."

"That makes six of us," Afton says, dropping down across from me, sitting cross-legged. A second later, Parrish and Grady follow along and form up a circle, with Anne lying in its center.

"Why did the Empire have to pick a fight?" I ask no one in particular.

"What makes you think they did?" Anne responds, her tone verging on accusatory.

"They can't be trusted," I reply, keeping my eyes down.

Anne gasps. It's like she just heard me curse the Goddesses and my parents all at once.

"Rance! The Empire isn't at fault!" Anne says, then coughs. I feel bad for upsetting her, but if there is someone to blame for this mess, it's the Empire, and specifically the bureaucracy. The Emperor himself is too detached and too much of a nut to have caused any problems. "How could you say that? They've provided so much for us, and now it's our turn to help out."

"Maybe, but they've taken a lot, too, so I figure we're even."

Anne is lost for words. She glances around at my buds, hoping one of them will explain, but they wouldn't be my buds if they were so ready to betray my personal story to a complete stranger. I know she must think I'm some kind of delinquent, but I don't fault her for it. The Imperial government and all of its excess are fairly popular here. The people of Angelcanis are happy with them because they've been easy on us. Just wait until we join the rest of the Central Planets as a full member. I'll bet they'll change their minds then.

"Hey, did you guys see those ships?" Grady says, trying to change the subject.

"Who didn't?" Afton replies.

"Anyone count how many ships there were?" I ask, trying to run through the attack again. Everything is clearer in my mind than I remember experiencing at the moment.

"I only saw three," Parrish says. Kayley nods in agreement.

"I saw a half of one, then I ran," Afton says. "After that, I saw nothing but the shelter."

"I know!" Kayley says. "Everything was a blur, but something stuck out for me...It's kind of weird, but I remember feeling really calm in the shelter. I had no fear that bombs were going off right over our heads."

"Really?" I ask, catching Kayley's gaze. I remember her smiling, like she's smiling at me right now. Confident and strong, but soft and tender too. I can see all of that in her smile, and that's why I fall for her every time she does it.

"What about you?" Grady nudges me as he asks. "Notice anything strange?"

"Not really, unless you count how it was only the five of us who raised our hands when the colonel asked for volunteers." I don't know why I think that's strange, but it's true. Out of a hundred people in that shelter, many of them recruits like my buds, we were the only ones to agree to help.

I feel a germ of an idea grow in the back of my mind. I can tell that it'll be real and possible and could even be the answer that I am looking for, but before I can form it, Grady knocks me out of it when he slaps my back, laughing.

"Nice try, dude! We had to stare you down before you put your hand up," Grady says. "Consolation prize for you."

"But I put it up, right?"

"Eventually," Afton says. I'll take the credit if she's willing to give it to me.

"And I thank the Goddesses that you did," Anne says with a smile. "No one would have found me if it wasn't for the five of you."

The emergency team comes soon after and takes Anne to the hospital. She graciously thanks us over and over and even gives us a blessing before they take her away. My buds stand and wave while I fight with my brain to bring back that little insight I just had.

As it forms, I can see the five of us together. I don't know what we're doing, but we're enjoying it. We're getting accolades from everywhere because of what we accomplished, I think. We did something good, for sure. Maybe we helped someone. We...

A huge grin comes to my face when I realize that I've been looking at my father's and my dream the wrong way. I haven't been this positive about something in years. Now all I have to do is convince my buds to join me. It's going to take more than a family heirloom to convince them, that's for sure.

"So, Rance," Kayley says, walking up to me. "You think Grady can crash at your place again? I'm sure his parents won't be home, and you know how he gets..."

"Yeah, sure," I say, beaming at her like I just won a lifetime subscription to *Stars and Planets*.

"Great, he'll really appreciate that." Kayley turns to Grady to give him a thumbs-up, then she looks back at me, lifting an eyebrow when she catches the look on my face. "Actually, I think I'm going to come over for a little while, too, because I want to know what's got you so excited."

I grin at her and nod. My Kayley, nobody knows me better.

Nine

IT'S ONLY TAKEN A war—which caused the total destruction of a military base and our favorite breakfast spot—and the saving of one woman who would have surely died if we didn't...if *I* didn't save her, for me to be alone with Kayley again. If I have to go through all that every time, then my life will be very busy. I would do all that just to be with her. I'm just hoping I don't have to.

All my buds are killer to hang with, but there is just something about spending quality time with someone who's known you your whole life. The fact that I'm totally in love with her might also have something to do with that, but I'm not about to put too much emphasis on it.

"Mom doesn't mind two more people for dinner again, right?" Kayley asks as we wait for Grady to finish his shower. She doesn't need to ask. After all, she calls my mom "Mom." Shouldn't that be enough? And why would she mind? My mom loves to cook and feed people. If those people happen to be my buds, then it just makes it easier for her.

"Of course not," I say, but I don't really need to. Kayley knows. My mom is practically hers, too, though I don't like to consider that. KayKay would become my sister, which messes up all of my romantic thoughts about her.

Kayley drops herself down to sit next to me on the floor. We prefer this to furniture, and ever since we started sitting this way when we were young, we've decided to keep doing it. I don't need a couch to make me comfortable, anyway. I could be happy anywhere if she was there. For instance, if I was in a garbage dump with her, I'd be in heaven. Believe it or not, we were once.

"So, Rance." Kayley gives me this sly smile, but the smile mutates into an evil grin, and if I didn't know better, I would swear the lights just got dimmer. "Out with it."

"With what, KayKay?" I know exactly what she's talking about, but I take a naïve approach.

"You already know how not-stupid I am, Rance. Do you really need me to remind you?"

"Yeah, if you wouldn't mind..."

"Fine, but for that, you're going to tell me ev-ry-thing. Got it?"

I gulp and nod.

"Right after the med-techs arrived, I saw you in full think mode, and then you smiled to yourself." She pokes the side of my head with a delicate finger. "What was happening inside that brain of yours?"

"Oh, that." I shrug. "That was nothing."

"You're a horrible fibber, Rance. Now out with it before I go downstairs and tell your mom you think her rice is the worst thing you've ever eaten."

"Don't you dare! You know how much extra work she does just to make it fluffy like that!" I sigh. It's time to give up the charade. My hands go up in mock surrender. "Alright, I'll tell you."

"Great!" She leans forward and rests her chin on her hands with a smirk, just to tease me. "Off you go then."

"Well, you remember how I mentioned I thought it was strange it was only the five of us who volunteered?" I ask.

"Yep. Keep going."

"Well, got me thinking. Why just us? What's so different about us?"

"You really want me to list everything?" Kayley grins, making light of my philosophical question. Kayley likes to tease me when I get deep like this. It's okay. I know she's taking me seriously, despite her little dig.

"But then we actually pulled off a rescue. We actually saved someone. All of us. We all worked together and did something really good. Right?"

"Yeah, that was pretty cool." Kayley puts on a warm smile. "We never really did anything like that before, but I'm glad we did."

"Well, what if we did it again? Saved someone...and maybe did it again and kept doing it? I think it's possible. We could be great at it, too."

She's thinking, and by the look on her face, it's somewhere in between *Rance is a genius* and *What the heck is he talking about?* I wait anxiously for her verdict.

"That's a nice thought, Rance, but we don't know a thing about rescuing people. We got lucky today, and that is a wonderful thing, but..." She stops when she sees my whole body droop, but changes tactics with a cluck of her tongue. "Oh, come on now, were you seriously considering this?"

"I don't know...maybe. I remember my dad always said we would do together what he promised me. But then...you know." I sigh. "What we did today made me feel good...like I haven't felt in a long time."

"Hey." Kayley reaches out and touches my knee, giving it a squeeze. "Rance, I know I've got no business saying this, but you need to forget about your dad's promises. If you keep hoping for him to come back—"

"No, that's not it!" I blurt. Kayley cringes and withdraws her hand, rebuked. I regret my shout instantly and give her an apologetic smile. "Sorry."

Kayley returns the smile, though it's a sympathetic one. I know she just wants me to be happy, and she thinks my continued melancholy about my father is the one thing keeping me down. She's partly correct, of course, but the rest is all me, and I really need something to look forward to.

"We're already going to be doing something good, and important," Kayley says. "Supporting the people who are behind our volunteer militias is an honorable thing to do."

"So is saving people or...pets. Or whatever. We just have to do it, and the others will see that's just as important...and safer."

"I wish I could be so confident as to agree." Kayley shifts, leaning back and pulling her knees to her body. "Parrish, Afton, or even Grady won't be so easy for you to convince. Remember, you already tried to stop them from signing up, and that didn't go so well."

"But they haven't yet. Technically. We could still convince them," I say.

"We?" Kayley smiles and chuckles. "How did I become involved in your scheme?"

"Well," I begin, but falter. Other than hoping that Kayley would help me, I don't have a plan, and I haven't had a lot of time to think it through. All I had ever considered was how I could resurrect the dream my father and I had. It had included no one but the two of us until today. I can't put things together the way Kayley can. That's why I thought if I could convince Kayley first, she could get the others for me, but I'm seriously failing at that right now.

"Well," I start again, "everyone listens to you, KayKay. If you ask for something, everyone does it. They trust your judgment, and they'd follow you anywhere."

I catch a small smile hit Kayley's face, which she attempts to hide by tilting her head away to comb her hair behind her ear. She likes to think she's immune to compliments, but since I've known her my whole life, I can confidently say she'll take as many compliments as she can get. That's not so unusual, but everyone—myself included—has always told her how smart, pretty, and talented she is, just to gain her favor. It's propped her up a bit, but it's getting to the point where I'm worried about what will happen if one day she hears silence rather than that artificial praise.

"That doesn't mean I'd want to pull them away from their own dreams, Rance," Kayley counters. "I may not agree with them, but it's not right for me to ask them to change just because of that."

"Isn't that what you're asking me to do?"

"No! I just don't want to see you hurt, that's all," she replies, but when she's about to continue, she stops and stares down at her hands.

"I don't understand," I say, because I really don't. "So Afton and Grady and Parrish all get to risk their own lives for what they want, but I don't?"

"Rance, it's not like that." Kayley shakes her head but doesn't look at me. That's unusual. She's always on point with the eye contact, and I'm usually melting when her eyes lock with mine.

"Then why don't you—"

Kayley stops me before I can continue and looks at me now. Her eyes do connect with mine, but her face is hard. Instead of becoming a puddle, I just stare back, confused.

"Rance," Kayley says softly. "None of them have been through what you've been through. They also don't have the big dreams you do. I'm just worried that makes for a poor combination, and I'd like to protect you from making any bad decisions if I can."

"Why do I get such special attention?" I ask. At any other time, I'd be happy to get anything special from the girl that I love. But I don't know how to feel about her attempt to hold me back. I know it's well intentioned, but coming from her, my heart hurts ten times as much.

Kayley blushes and presses her lips together. Her other hand brushes her hair back, and I frown. That was not the response I was expecting. Kayley is resolute in her decisions and makes no apologies for them.

"Alright," she says after an awkward moment. "Since we have a few days before they have to report, why don't you and I spend some time to figure this out? Then, if it's something that makes real sense, I'll bring it to them...but only if it makes sense, okay?"

"Okay," I say, and give her a genuine smile. It's more than I had expected to get from her. The way our conversation was going, I really thought I would be back to zero again. I've got some hope now, towards what I don't really know, but I'm ecstatic that I've got Kayley on my side. I could soar into the stratosphere without any other booster.

"Oh, hey," Kayley says. "Afton said to remind you not to forget the message she asked you to give to me. What was it?"

Oh man. I can already feel my face getting warm.

Ten

THE NEXT MORNING WE all gather outside my house for one last hang-out—all of us. The others got their orders faster than we expected, and now they have to show up tomorrow for transport to another base, where they'll ship off-planet for their training. Kayley and I stand together while Parrish, Grady, and Afton face us a few paces away. I don't like how much space there is between us. It feels like we've already lost them.

"Hey, you know we're going to be together the whole day, right?" Parrish says. He must see the frown on my face, so he tries to buck us up. "Didn't you put together a whole plan for us today?"

When Parrish says *you*, he means Kayley. I didn't have anything to do with it, though I would have helped. She didn't ask, naturally. It was already done before she went home last night.

"Of course I did," Kayley replies. "If I had left it up to you slackers, we'd just be standing in the same place the whole day."

"Who are you calling a slacker?" Afton asks, giving KayKay the side-eye.

"Yeah, I second that!" Grady adds.

"You can't second that, Grady," I correct. "It's not a motion. It's an inquiry."

"I'm going to second it anyway," Grady replies, lifting an indifferent shoulder.

Cue the world-famous Kayley eye roll.

"Alright, so, where to first?" Parrish, always the squad commander. Parrish may call the audibles, but the decision-making power is definitely in Kayley's hands. Case in point: who made up today's itinerary? I don't think Parrish minds that much. None of us do.

"Breakfast!" Afton calls. "I'm starving!" Afton is always starving.

"Fine, we'll do breakfast...but quickly. We're going to the zoo this morning," Kayley replies, keeping a tight hold on the leadership reins.

"Zoo?" Grady doesn't look impressed. "You want to see animals, just look up! There are plenty of happy birds flying around...and if you're wondering why they're happy, it's because they're not locked up in a cage."

"Grady, we're not interested in flying scavengers," Afton says. "And I like the idea of the zoo. We haven't been there since..."

"Last month," Grady bats back. "We were definitely there last month."

"Bzzzt...wrong!" Afton gets in his face with a snarky grin.

"If you really want to know the actual date, Grady, it was just before last month," Kayley states.

"Close enough!" Grady says. "Why don't we hit a museum instead? Then we'll at least have some protection over our heads in case...well, you know."

Kayley's stare-down of Grady is a definitive answer. I don't mind either way. When those three are off-planet, I can still see furry animals and bad art anytime I want. On top of that, it'll be with the one person I really want to see furry animals and bad art with.

"Alright, let's go," Kayley orders.

As we're gearing up to get on the local landferry, the sirens blare out a warning. Great. That means another attack, for sure. We all share glances, and the puffed-up vibes we had deflate.

"Aww, not again," Parrish says, bowing his forehead onto his palm. The rest of us are more anxious than disappointed.

"Yeah, well, we still get to spend the day together...even if it's in someone's basement," I say, trying to keep it positive. That's not so easy, considering what we went through yesterday. "Though...we should get some gear together and prepare ourselves."

"Prepare for what?" Grady asks, tilting his head at me.

"Well, the last time we rescued someone, we didn't really have the right stuff to do it, so if we're going to do that again, better to be prepared, right?"

Out of the corner of my eye, I see Kayley clue in to what I'm up to. I know we said we would talk it through first, but she's not opening her mouth to object, so I'm going for it.

"Whoa, whoa, whoa, Rance." Parrish puts his hands up. "What makes you think we are going to go rescue people today?"

"Uh, the air-raid siren?" I say as we trot back to the house. My reply was fairly wise-ass, but it's also true. The zoo is out, and we'll get stuck in my basement for the next few hours, easily. Afton's going to be getting hangry, too. Maybe my mom's got some leftovers she can bring down there with us.

What strange things I think about sometimes. It must be the stress of the bombardment.

"Let's keep an ear out for people in trouble, though," Kayley says. Of course, no one argues with *her* about it. She flashes me a hidden smile, but Afton catches it as she darts a glance between the two of us. We betray nothing, and despite another attack, I'm feeling the surge of energy as KayKay backs me up.

We start heading back inside when an alien fighter flies overhead so low that we duck. It's not so low that it would cut our heads off, but it definitely feels like it would. The wind draft behind it is strong enough to have knocked us over if we were fully upright.

Two seconds later, a pair of our own air fighters chase after it. They're not nearly as fast, but they've got home-field advantage. I'm hoping that counts for something. Otherwise, this war is going to be over really quickly.

"Everyone okay?" Parrish asks, glancing around. We all nod or give him a thumbs up. He nods, takes a breath, and opens the front door to my house.

A sonic boom shakes the whole house as we step inside. Then a flash, and the next thing I know I'm face flat on the ground. Before I can register much else, the back of the house groans, followed by a heavy thud, with dust and debris flying towards us. We cover over each other, but we still get pelted with bits of fiber and rock.

I think a ship just crashed in my backyard!

"Mom!"

She'd be in the kitchen, for sure—that's where she is almost all the time. It's in the back of the house, right where the roof just collapsed. I jump to my feet and try to get there, but I'm not steady, and I crash my shoulder into the corner of the entertainment cabinet. I know that's going to hurt later, but right now I don't care. There's only one thing on my mind, and it's my—

"Mom! Are you here? Are you okay?"

The kitchen is a mess. One of the beams that supported the roof fell through the ceiling and brought most of it down. Debris is everywhere, and there's a growing flame on the cooking surface that is threatening to get a lot bigger if it's allowed to burn any longer.

"Mom! Can you hear me?"

A weak response comes from behind the fallen beam. "Rance, here..."

All the tension that my body was holding releases at once. But we're not out of the woods yet. "Mom! Are you hurt?"

"I'm not sure...but I'm stuck."

The rest of the rescue team arrives, and Parrish extinguishes the flame on the cooking surface with some sort of rag or cloth. I don't know what it is, really, nor do I care. As long as it's out.

"Okay, Mom, we're going to get you out." I wanted to help some people today, but I never thought that one of those people would be my own mom. We have to get her out of here before anything else falls. I take a moment to examine the destruction. That big beam is in the way. We'll need to move it, but I'm not sure if we can. I grab on to it and test just how heavy it is.

"No! Are you nuts?" Grady puts a hand on my arm and pulls me away. "If we move that, the whole ceiling could come down!"

"What if we went around the back?" Kayley suggests. That's a good idea and possibly the only way to get to her. I rush back out the front door, with Kayley and Afton right behind me.

"What the hell?" Afton says, stopping short. "Is that the colonel?"

I hadn't even noticed the squad of military vehicles pulling up in the street.

I get to the back, and I throw a glance at the crashed craft long enough to know that it's not one of ours. I feel a chill in my spine, but I keep going. The kitchen door is intact, but the wall surrounding it is bent, crushing the door. I'm not going to be able to open it.

I try anyway.

With a bit of a tug, the door opens, then falls off its hinges. I jump back to avoid getting hit by it, but then I'm through and looking for my mom.

There she is! Not trapped, but on the ground and shaken. I drop next to her, my hands reaching around her shoulders before I realize that it's not a good idea to move her.

"Mom!"

"Oh, Rance. I was just about to make breakfast, but..." She smiles up at me.

"Mom!" Kayley comes down next to me. "Are you in pain anywhere? Can you move?"

Leave it to KayKay to ask the important questions. I'm just glad to be talking to my mom. Glad that she's not hurt. Next to Kayley, there's only her.

"No...no, just...a little shaken up," Mom says, still smiling. She's got this thing about never complaining about anything. She could be dying, and I don't think she would moan once about it.

"Can you try to stand?" I ask.

"Maybe...let me try."

But before she does, a medic arrives. He catches my mom trying to get up and puts a restraining hand on her shoulder.

"Ma'am, let me check you out before you move. We don't want you to cause yourself any additional injuries." He glances at Kayley and me in a way that says he's got it from here, but I don't want to move. I can't move. This is my only remaining parent, after all.

"Buddy." The medic taps me on the arm. "Let me examine her and make sure she doesn't have any broken bones. I promise we'll take care of her. Awake and talking is a good sign, so there's a good chance there's nothing majorly wrong."

I feel Kayley's tug on my shoulder, and I take a breath before stepping back. We go outside, only to find my buds and a handful of military personnel gathering together. Colonel Nelson is there, which I find strange. I thought he was off at some meeting or something.

"Is she okay?" Afton asks. Everyone is concerned, of course. She's just the first to vocalize it.

"I think so."

"Everyone okay?" Colonel Nelson asks as he comes over. "Whose house was this?"

"Mine, sir," I reply. "Technically, my mother's house, but I live here, too."

He raises an eyebrow at my last comment, but doesn't pursue any line of questioning. "Alright, well, I'm going to need all of you to clear out of here, recruits included. This is now a restricted area."

"Sir, my mom is still in there."

"I'm aware, son. Just wait up front by the med transport, and you can go with her when they take her to the hospital."

Before I can say anything, a hissing sound comes from the crashed craft, and everyone spins to face it. A pair of soldiers lift their rifles into a ready position, and everyone backs up a few steps.

Smoke or steam rushes out of a portal on the side of the craft. My eyes lock on to it.

"Don't shoot! I mean you no harm!" A warbled, childlike voice comes out from within the smoke. It takes me a second or so to realize that it spoke in Empire Common. It takes me another second to realize how strange that is.

"Yes, we know," the colonel replies, taking a few hesitant steps towards the craft. "I am Colonel Nelson, from our military's intelligence division. As we discussed, I promise you will not be harmed."

As they discussed? What's going on here?

A limb begins to stretch out from behind the panel, and a foot appears. A fuzzy pink foot.

"Oh..." Afton says. "We are so screwed."

Eleven

"WHAT DO YOU MEAN by that, recruit?" The colonel turns on Afton. He steps up to her, his eyes serious. Afton, for once in her life, is intimidated. I could laugh, but it's not the best time to be counting points. Instead, I hide my grin behind my hand and hope she doesn't get it too bad from this military musclehead.

"Sir..." Afton stammers. "It's just that..." She stops. Her head isn't doing explanations at the moment. Like all of our brains, hers is trying to understand what the heck is behind that portal and if it is secretly plotting to massacre us.

But the creature that appears is not intimidating in the slightest. First of all, it's fuzzy. Secondly, just like its foot, it's all pink, save for a patch of black fuzz on the top of its head. The creature's eyes are big black disks encircled with just a tiny bit of white. It's got feet and hands just like we do, but there's also a pair of fleshy tentacles perched over its head, and a pair of triangle ears poking out of the top of its head swivel around like an old radar dish.

This thing is just too cute to be scary, and now I realize what Afton has been trying to say all this time. Nobody is going to want to shoot this thing. They might want to cuddle with it, though—and that's when they'll get us.

"Do not engage arsenal," the creature says, holding its arms and tentacles up. How does it know how to do that? That it's fuzzy, pink, or tentacled doesn't bother me, but is putting your hands and/or tentacles in the air the universal constant for surrender?

"We will not shoot," Colonel Nelson says and motions to his men to put their weapons down. "We mean you no harm."

"That is satisfactory," the creature says. "When is the requirement to make the introductories?"

"I have already introduced myself. Now it is your turn," the colonel says. I'm dying to ask it a thousand questions, as I know all of us are, but first off, what the hell is going on here? Isn't this the enemy? Why is the colonel talking nice to it?

"That is accurate," it says. "I am..." An incomprehensible bunch of sounds, whistles, and clicks come from its pointy-toothed mouth. "However, simplicity is recommended. The appellation is..."

We hold our breath and wait. Is it thinking of a nickname? Is it plotting how to murder us all simultaneously? All we can do is wait.

"Tim," it says.

"Tim?" the colonel asks, raising an eyebrow—and I agree. That's a bit too...common? To call a strange alien race by the same name that you might call your pub buddy is a bit weird, no? It could be a trick. Getting us to trust it, just before it eats us all.

"Listen," Colonel Nelson says, "if you are trying to choose an Empire Common name, let me give you one that would be more appropriate."

"That is acceptable," it replies.

"Well, first of all, would you consider yourself male or female?"

"That is accurate." Another brief answer that makes Colonel Nelson clench his jaw.

"Are you...omni...sexual?" the colonel asks.

"That is accurate," the creature replies, its huge disks blinking.

"Okay, well...I think you look male at the moment, so I'll call you... Teddy."

"Just like a dude to pick a male name," Afton mutters.

"What?" Colonel Nelson throws Afton a glare.

"Nothing, sir."

"The female does not respect your gender," the alien says. Afton's mouth drops open.

"I see." The colonel chuckles. He lays a glance on the shrinking Afton, then turns back to the alien. "So is Teddy acceptable to you?"

"That is accurate."

I personally can't believe this. We've connected with an alien race that is supposed to be our enemy, but they don't appear aggressive at all. This one is almost friendly, even though those claws and dagger teeth could slice us all up in an instant.

Oh yeah, and they're okay with being called by a name humans might find unremarkable.

"Teddy, I am very glad you have survived the crash." Colonel Nelson takes a step towards the pink creature. "I wasn't sure what to expect when you contacted us, but...here we are."

"We are here," Teddy repeats. "We are everywhere."

"I...suppose that's true," the colonel replies, seeming unsure. "Before we discuss more, I think we should find a better place to talk."

"My living room is open," I offer, for some unknown reason. But forget that. Our military is about to have a meeting with a representative of the enemy, and it seems like they meant it to be all very hush-hush. What is going on here?

"The room of existence is acceptable!" Teddy cries. I don't think anyone has ever spoken about two sofas and an entertainment center with such gusto before.

Colonel Nelson's face gets tight, but he agrees.

"Does anyone else find it freaky that his mouth doesn't move when he speaks?" Grady says in a low voice as we make our way around to the front. My mom is already there, getting loaded into the med transport. As I watch the medics get ready to put her in, I almost miss the creature's comment.

"Motion of the mandible is unrequired. Your language is untroublesome," Teddy says. He's a respectful distance away, so Grady jumps a bit when he answers.

"You heard that?" Grady says, turning to Teddy with an incredulous stare.

"That is accurate. Therefore, Teddy has responded."

That stuns Grady to silence, but I can tell his brain engine is still cranking away at full power. Out of any of us, he's the one that will want to know the most about our new guest.

My new guest, that is.

"Hey, Kayley...can you show everyone in?" I ask her. "I want to go check on Mom."

"Let Parrish or Afton do it. I'm coming with you." She clasps my hand and gives it a squeeze.

Mom is hanging out on the med-tech's stretcher while he's doing some sort of diagnostic thing to her legs. She gives us a smile as we get there. A big smile...like she's had one too many glasses of rosé.

"Hey, Mom, how are you feeling?"

"Just fine, Rance. In fact, I feel great. How's the house?"

"Um." I give Kayley a glance, and her level of uncertainty matches mine. "Should be okay, Mom. No worries."

"We gave her a booster to help her with her pain," the med-tech says, as if he's telling us about what he's having later for dinner.

Kayley and I sigh out an understanding.

"Will she need to go to the hospital?" I ask.

"Yes, we'll need to do a more thorough examination, just to make sure. You can stop by later."

Later?

With an alien creature sitting in my living room, having a chat with my buds and the military, I wonder just how much later that will be. I need to find out, so Kayley and I return to the house.

A guard stops us before we can get into the living room.

"Military personnel only," he says.

"But this is my house," I shoot back, "and I invited you. If you want to keep your stuff classified, do it somewhere else."

"Let them in, Private," Colonel Nelson says. As we step in, we see he's sitting on the nice sofa, next to one of his subordinates. Afton and Parrish are on the other, while Grady's just lurking in the corner and staring at Teddy, who, oddly, is on the floor.

"The proprietor of this domicile is available?" Teddy turns his head towards me, rotating it most of the way around like an owl.

"Uh, yeah." I'm so stunned, I can't think of anything more to say to a furry pink alien who's admiring the fuzzy carpet like it's one of his best friends.

"The domicile has torment?"

"Huh?"

"The house is not in pain, Teddy. It's not alive," Afton says.

"That is unusual."

"Not on this planet, it's not."

"Teddy." Colonel Nelson clears his throat and shifts in his seat. "I don't want to stop your exploration of our planet, but you contacted us with what you said was an important message from your leaders."

"This is accurate," Teddy replies, rotating his head back to place his enormous black eyes on the colonel.

"So then?" The colonel leans forward, looking like he's about to scold a two-year-old.

"The message is...excursion with Teddy is required."

"Now, Teddy, our peoples are at war. You understand that, don't you? Are you asking me to become your prisoner?"

Teddy doesn't so much blink as fold his eyes back into his head. I'm guessing that's the universal sign for *what?* Then he makes a sound like a coin being dropped into an old-fashioned vending machine. I remember the sound from an ancient cine I saw once.

"That is not accurate," Teddy says. "Extinguishment of conflict is required. Conveyance of communication is required for extinguishment."

Colonel Nelson's face is turning red. It's not a good look for him. "So you came all this way to get me to surrender my people? If that is it, Teddy—"

"*Surrender* is unrecognized. Pontificate the connotation." Teddy's tentacles intertwine themselves over his head.

"It means to give up," Parrish says, not in a friendly way.

"Escalation of tension is understandable. Teddy does not require giving up. Cessation of combat is appreciated. Explanation of communication is not possible. Conclave is required."

Okay, so they're not asking for our surrender. That's good, but I don't understand why they want a meeting. If it's with the military, then it could be an offer of a cease-fire, or a trap to get our generals in one place so they can assassinate them. Not that I think our military is ready to stop shooting.

"So let me get this straight," the colonel says. "You contacted us, and then came all the way here—thank you, by the way, for not dropping any bombs on us this time—to ask me to come with you so your leaders could give me a message that isn't about surrender? Can't you tell me what the message is about right now?"

"Nothing has dropped," Teddy replies. "Anguish over deceased is understandable." His tentacles unravel and then fold themselves into what I could only call his lap. He's sitting cross-legged. Sort of. His legs aren't long enough to cross. "Teddy has not received the communication. Conclave is of extreme importance. Carnage is unplanned."

"Well, Teddy, the sentiment is appreciated. I don't want to kill you, either, but you attacked us, and now you come here trying to take us somewhere to hear some message..." The colonel shakes his head, then folds his arms in front of him. "I'm sorry, but this is not something I think I can do."

"Conclave is extra special," Teddy tries.

I think I'm getting this now. The Teddys want to meet with the colonel, where they plan to offer terms on a cease-fire. That sounds all well and great, but these military types aren't interested in peace. If they were, they'd have no job. Heck, some of the Central Planets battle each other just to keep their skills up. I don't know how, but I have to get the colonel out of this discussion. Our Prime Minister would be a better person to speak for our planet. At least he wouldn't be thinking of fighting.

"No, I cannot accept that, Teddy." The colonel is about done. "If there is some way to stop this war, I want to discuss that, but I cannot go with you."

See? He's already finding ways to say no to a cease-fire. I don't care how nice Colonel Nelson has been to us. I can't trust the military. No way do I want to see our planet destroyed because they want to fight. This mess already resulted in my mom getting hurt. Who's next? My friends? Kayley?

My stomach twists the second I picture her wounded and crying in pain. I just can't allow that to happen. Not to anyone I care about. If I had the chance, I'd go retrieve the proposal and bring it back to the right people. I mean, I saved someone yesterday...I could deliver a message, couldn't I? Or is it completely nuts to be considering that?

"I'll go." The words come out of my mouth before I can even consider them. Everyone spins their heads towards me, their faces an exact visual of my own internal reaction.

"Rance, what did you just say?" Kayley's jaw drops so low, it must have hit the center of the planet.

"I said, I'll go."

Twelve

"YOU ARE ACCEPTABLE," TEDDY says, gun-turreting his head in my direction.

That's followed by a chorus of human voices shouting, "No!"

Now my ears are burning as they stare at me, and I think I just made a big mistake. I volunteered without knowing what I'm really getting myself into. The colonel is wiser than I give him credit for. This could mean that I'd be on my own, too, and that wasn't exactly how I thought it would be.

I could just say I was joking, but that doesn't really solve things. The colonel would still be in control, and now that I realize it, that's why I offered myself up. I don't want him to crash this peace ship right into a star.

"What about Mom, Rance?" Kayley asks. She has a point, but Mom'll be okay once she is out of the hospital. I'll visit her when I get back.

"Son, there's no way I can allow that," the colonel adds. "There are too many unknowns here."

"That's okay, I'm volunteering," I reply. "But not for the military. I'll be the planetary representative."

"No. I can't authorize that." The colonel shakes his head. He just doesn't like that I'm taking over.

"We have authorized it," Teddy corrects.

"You can't authorize him, Teddy. He's human," Afton says.

"That is not accurate. Authorization is complete." Teddy gets to his feet. "Rancid, departure is imminent. Transport is available."

"Uh," I put a finger up. "My name's not—"

The colonel and his soldier get up, reaching for their sidearms.

"I can't allow you to do that," the colonel says as he waves two more soldiers armed with automatic weapons into the room. "Failure to comply will be an act of war, and it will force us to take you into custody. It's your choice."

"Thank you," Teddy replies. "Determination has completed."

There is serious tension in the room. I have no idea if an alien race can show or even feel emotion, but all the humans in the room are definitely doing both, including me. One little false move could cause things to blow up—literally—and that would be bad for my house. It's busted as it is.

"Additional delegation is available?" Teddy asks, catching Grady as he steps delicately over to me. Grady's mouth opens, but only air comes out. I'm betting he wants to, so I answer for him. Besides, then at least I won't be alone if I crash and burn on this one.

"Oh yeah, he's totally going," I say.

"Rance!" Kayley shouts, and I realize that I've hit the Kayley penalty box. I'll have to make it up to her when I come back...if I come back. Still, I'm doing this for her.

"That's it." The colonel points at Teddy. "Arrest that...alien!"

Teddy buzzes like an old-fashioned alarm clock, which I guess means he's annoyed. An antenna-like thing pops out of his head, and there's a flash in the room. Now all I see is this big, glowing white blob in my vision.

"Teddy, what the heck was that?" I ask, blinking to get the huge white spot out from in front of my eyes.

"Popsicles," he replies.

"Rance, I can't see! Where are you?" Grady says, reaching out to me. I'm only about half a meter away—my living room isn't that big—and he slaps me in the face. "Oh, sorry, dude."

Ouch.

"Departure is imminent," Teddy states, but something's changed. The room is a lot quieter, and neither the colonel nor his men are saying anything. They're not even moving. As my vision clears, I see Afton's frozen like a statue. So is everyone else. They're...

"Popsicles..." Grady says, looking around.

"Teddy, what did you do?"

"Popsicles," Teddy replies again, as if that was a good enough explanation. I guess it is, since it's an accurate description of everyone besides Grady and me.

"Are they okay?" I ask, a lump forming in my throat.

"Existence is unaffected," Teddy replies.

Grady and I sigh with relief. It would be really difficult to explain to everyone's parents, not to mention I really don't want to see anyone dead. Not the colonel, not my friends, not the girl I—

I draw in a breath, trying to warm myself from the chill that just ran through my body. That's twice I've thought of Kayley as a corpse. It's not any better the second time.

"So...now what, Teddy?" I ask.

"Movement is recommended. Arrival for disembarkation is paramount."

Grady and I share a moment of complete disappointment, mixed in with a little bit of *what just happened?*

"You mean, you don't have any way to dematerialize us out of here and rematerialize us onto your ship?"

Teddy whirrs like my mom's brewing machine, then makes a bunch of pops and whistles. I don't know what that sound means, but I hope it's not bad. We tense, waiting for Teddy to make us into frozen treats like the others in the room.

"That is not accurate. Movement is required," Teddy says. I'll let Grady ponder that one for a bit. "Rancid, direction to the emergence."

"My name is Rance."

"That is accurate. Egress is imperative. Do not delay, Rancid," Teddy says. I let it go for now because Teddy is right. If we're going, we have to get out of here, now. We can't use the front door, as there are soldiers all over the front. The back door, which got crushed by the Teddy ship, is also not an option.

"Okay, let's hop out the window in the guest bedroom. That leads out the back to the yard."

"Good idea," Grady says. "Let's go." He takes one last glance at icy Afton, Kayley, and Parrish, then gets moving. I know why he did—I'm feeling the same way. It could be a long time before we see the three of them again. That wasn't what I had intended at all. I just have to keep reminding myself I'm doing this for them. It's something that I can actually do, and if no one has to fight, or die, anymore, then I'm going to try. It's what my father and I wanted to do.

Grady peeks out the window before he opens it and then hops through. He scans the backyard, then gives us the thumbs-up.

"Okay, Teddy, you're next." I realize Teddy might have some trouble getting up to the window's height since, well...he's not that tall. "You want a hand getting up there?"

"Unnecessary." Teddy's tentacles stretch until they reach the top of the molding around the window and latch on. In a movement that is too fast for me to catch, Teddy pulls himself up and flings himself straight through. I can hear Grady's gasp as he almost gets knocked over by a flying alien.

There's no way I'm going to let some fuzzy pink alien show me up, so I take a few steps back and make a running leap through the window. It's a respectful attempt, but I've got my hands up too high, and I scrape the knuckles of my right hand on the bottom of the window.

The burn on my hand distracts me from making a good landing, so instead of a nice tight tuck 'n' roll, I just belly flop onto the ground with a grunt. So much for scoring a point for humanity. Next time I'll just climb through.

"Well done," Teddy says.

"Dude, this isn't the time to show off!" Grady is serious and also right.

"Okay, we're out...Where's our ride?" I get up and dust myself off, then check the top of my hand. A little blood is coming out of the scrapes, but it's no big deal. I look at Teddy.

"Perigee has been achieved. Transport will occur in—" Teddy clicks and whistles the rest of his answer.

"Remind me to teach you about how humans tell time," I say.

"Confirmed."

"Is that it?" Grady asks. He's staring up at the sky above the house, one hand blocking the sun from his eyes. I follow his gaze and squint, but I don't see anything yet.

"That is accurate," Teddy replies.

And then I do. It's at almost the same angle as the sun, and since I don't have the best eyesight, the glare makes it hard to see. I've got it now, though...and I'm guessing it's a lot bigger than the craft Teddy came down in.

"Whoa...dude, that's huge." Grady takes the words right out of my mouth. I can always count on Grady for that.

"Hey, Teddy...isn't that ship going to get spotted?"

"That is accurate," Teddy replies. "Preparations for departure are required."

"We are totally ready, Teddy." I grin at my rhyme.

"Well done," Teddy says again.

Out of the corner of my eye, I see a pair of soldiers come around the back of the house to check out Teddy's crashed ship. They are in complete awe of it, so they don't see us. Grady also notices them and nudges me.

"Dude...company," he whispers.

"Yeah, I know," I whisper back. "Hey, Teddy...think you can popsicle those two?"

Teddy turns to stare at the two soldiers ogling his ride. He stays that way for longer than I'm comfortable with. I know they're going to turn and see us any second now.

"Yo...let's go this way." Grady turns to go around the opposite side of the house but then stops short. "Oh shoot...maybe not." He slowly spins around and tiptoes back to us.

"What?"

"More soldiers."

"Teddy? Can you popsicle them?"

"Unnecessary," Teddy replies.

"Really? The moment they get their fill of your smashed ship, they're going to—"

"Hey! What are you doing over there?" one soldier says, pointing at us. He starts walking over with his companion, who unslings his rifle, clicking something on the side that I can only assume is what you push to get the thing ready to shoot.

"Told you," Grady says.

"That is not accurate," Teddy corrects.

"Hey, we're speaking to you!" the soldier with his rifle shouts, but his companion grabs his arm and stops him.

"Don't get too close...It's one of them!" He unslings his own gun and clicks it.

Behind me, I hear the voices of the soldiers that Grady saw before. Once they turn the corner, they'll smash into us, and then it's going to get dangerous.

"Oh man," Grady says. "So much for our field trip."

"Gratin...that is not accurate," Teddy says again, and for a minute, both Grady and I forget about the soldiers with deadly weapons at the ready. We just look down at our fuzzy companion and wonder what he's getting at.

When the sky goes dark, our puzzlement is cleared up. I don't even need to look up to know why the sun just disappeared. Instead, I get the enjoyment of watching the two soldiers rotate their heads up and then quickly start backing away. I hear a sudden curse from the other pair of soldiers on the side of the house. I'll bet they're beating a fast retreat, too.

"Our ride is here," I say.

"This is now accurate," Teddy confirms.

The ship must be at least a hundred times the length of my house, though I can't see either end. I can't really judge the other dimensions, but it seems like the ship covers most of the homes in the general area. It's deep black but so shiny that we can see our reflections in it. I can even see over my house to the front yard, where the contingent of military personnel are all craning their necks back to take in the entire ship.

"Okay...I'll say it. It's impressive, Teddy." And I mean that.

"How do we get in?" Grady asks.

Just above our heads, a black disk drops from the ship. It comes down so fast we have to jump out of the way, and when it lands, there's this heavy thud and the ground shakes beneath our feet.

"Embark," Teddy says, and he steps on.

I glance at Grady, and he shrugs and steps on. I'm glad one of our heads is clear about what we're about to do. Of course, I want to do this, but I just wish that my friends, Kayley especially, were more open to it. Not that I had much time to convince them. I barely had time to convince myself. If I manage to get a message back here, then that's a big score towards my dream. Provided no one hates me when I get back.

"I really haven't thought this through well at all, have I?" I ask Grady.

"Not the time, dude!" Grady hisses, and he pulls me on.

"Wait! What are you doing?" one soldier shouts, his eyes opening wide.

Before I can reply, the disk launches itself straight up, forcing me down as gravity tries to keep us on the planet. The air resistance doesn't help, either. I glance up just in time to see us get swallowed up by a black hole in the ship.

Thirteen

IT TAKES A MOMENT for our eyes to adjust to the dim light. I notice we're not alone. There's a horde of fuzzy creatures surrounding us, staring back at us with their saucer-shaped eyes. They're all the colors of the visible spectrum: blue, black, gray, orange, yellow, a few red, and maybe even some colors we can't see. It's creepy how they stare back at us, their mouths open to show us their several rows of razor-sharp teeth.

Once again, Grady takes the cake by saying what I'm thinking.

"Dude..." he whispers. "What did we get ourselves into?"

We really tossed common sense out the window. Grady and I were so excited about the prospect of seeing an alien ship that we lost all sense of self-preservation. Here we are, the first humans on an alien ship, and we don't know the first thing about them. I mean, what if they wanted us to come on board so we could be their next meal? Those pointy teeth make me think they don't follow the Angelican diet.

"So, Teddy...uh...can you introduce us to your friends?" I ask casually, trying to keep calm.

"It is done," Teddy replies. "Awareness has been accomplished."

"Oh yeah? Great...but we don't know their names." A little broken laugh comes out of me.

"Knowledge is uncomplicated," says Teddy. He points his tentacles at the others. "This is Teddy."

"They can't all have the same name as you...and we just, like, gave you that name before we even got here." Grady gets this strange look on his face, like he's just broken his transaxle and can't seem to move forward anymore.

"Nevertheless, they are Teddy as well."

"Did you just say *nevertheless*?" I ask.

"That is accurate."

"Also, what is that smell?" Grady asks, and then I get a whiff, too. Like rotten eggs mixed with a little too much bad perfume. I can't decide if I like it or hate it.

"Yeah, Teddy...what is that?"

Teddy's big black eyes just stare at us. We stare back. All of the Teddys stare back at us, and no one says anything for a good two minutes. I bet if I didn't open my mouth again, they wouldn't say anything at all. Maybe this is where they decide if they want to grill or sauté us?

"So, uh, Teddy," I start, hoping distraction gets us off the menu for the day. "Maybe we should...meet your boss? Don't they have an important message for us?"

"Promenade," Teddy says and turns around, heading towards a corridor that seems a little low for us...well, for humans, that is. Grady and I aren't all that tall, but we both need to stay sharp, or else something hanging from the ceiling is going to slam us right in the face. The just-after-dusk level of light in here is not helping, either. I guess that this is already bright for their big googly eyes. We'll just have to be careful.

The walls and the floor are this smooth dark gray, with the occasional luminous light that flashes through a spectrum of colors. Also, there are no doorknobs, entry panels, or card slots. I do see some diamond-shaped holes massed together in patterns, but I have no idea what they do, if anything.

As we follow Teddy, I make a casual glance behind us, and the entire contingent of Teddys is quietly strolling behind us. I tap Grady on the shoulder and motion for him to look back.

"We must be a big deal," Grady muses.

"Yeah, well, how many alien species do you know, dude?"

"True, that."

"They might be following us because they're hungry."

Grady goes wide-eyed like he hadn't considered that. "I don't think I taste very good, Rance."

"Yeah, well, let's hope they think so, too." I glance back.

We arrive in front of a semi-clear wall. Inside is a room with a googolplex of square panels aligned in pairs, each set with a single Teddy behind it. I'm trying to figure it out, and if I had to guess, I'd say each one of their eyes is using a different panel at the same time. I spot one or two of them moving their eyes in separate directions at the same time. I've seen Parrish do that trick on occasion, and it is totally freaky. Add aliens into that, and it's out-of-this-galaxy nuts.

Teddy, our pink original, sticks his right tentacle into one of the diamond holes, and the wall dissolves in front of us. I might try, but there's no way to describe it without including the word *awesome*.

"What do you think, Rance? It's the ship's bridge?" Grady asks, whispering in my ear. Grady may have forgotten, but I haven't: there's no point in whispering because the Teddy sense of hearing is insanely good.

"That is accurate," Teddy says, answering Grady's question as I guessed he might.

"So we're going to meet your ship's captain then?" I ask.

"Also accurate," Teddy responds, "subsequently."

"So then, why go to the ship's bridge if we won't meet them yet?"

Teddy only responds in a few clicks and whistles that mean nothing to Grady or me, although now I'm determined to learn Teddyese, or whatever the name of their language is. Just to try it out, I make a few clicks and whistles of my own.

"Nonsense," Teddy says.

We follow Teddy around the side of the bridge until we get to another semi-clear wall. This time, he takes his short arm and sticks a claw into a diamond hole in its face. Once again, the wall disappears, and we follow Teddy inside. Teddy points to a low part of the wall that sticks out just enough for Grady and me to sit on. So we do, and now that we're turned around in the tiny room, we can look out on the bridge and feel less claustrophobic. The ceiling there is easily four times as tall as it is in this little room. It's a good thing we're now sitting.

The other Teddys have dispersed somewhat, although a few still look in on us in the room like we're some kind of aquarium exhibit. Grady smiles and waves at them. We can't do anything else.

The creepy thing is, a few of them smile and wave back. But what smiling means for them is to open their enormous jaws and bare their carnivorous teeth. Afton was only partially right about the cute and fuzzies. One point for me. I'll have to remember to tell her the next time I see her.

I wonder when or even if we'll ever get to see them again. They have to be worried about us...at least, I hope they are. Kayley is definitely going to let me have it, and she's going to let Afton, her enforcer, do all the damage. That is really going to hurt. I better make this count.

Original Teddy hops up on a stool-like box and waves his tentacles. We're watching him, so we don't see the floor open up beneath our feet. Not at first, anyway.

"Whoa! Rance! The floor is missing!" Grady grabs on to me as if he expects to fall into it and doesn't want to die alone.

"Mind the gap," Teddy says, as something rises from the blackness under our feet. We both dip our eyes down, afraid to move anything else lest we slip.

A rectangular panel about the same size as the hole in the floor floats up out of the depths and suspends itself just above our knees. Teddy does his tentacle-conductor thing again, and the hole scrapes closed like a giant rubbing two boulders together.

So now Teddy puts the tips of his tentacles down on what I'm going to call a table, and a ball of light appears above the center of it. A Teddy face appears inside of the ball and stares out at us with its unblinking eyes. Original Teddy clicks and whistles at the Teddy in the light ball, and then the Teddy in the light clicks and whistles back at our Teddy. This goes on for a short bit, and while it's happening, I'm listening for some pattern in the sounds or any sort of syntax in the Teddyspeak.

"Dude, what are you doing?" Grady asks quietly. I think he's got it by now that the Teddys can hear everything, but his curiosity has won out over his manners.

"Listening to see if I can figure out their language," I reply.

"You have no idea how to do that." Grady gives me this look like I just gave away all of the secret treasures my NaiNai has been handing down to me.

"It helps pass the time."

"How about talking to me?"

"Okay, what do you want to talk about?"

"Forget it." Grady sighs and turns to watch Original Teddy do his thing.

The light ball goes out, and the floor opens up again, but this time we're ready for it. The big dark monolith of a table sinks back into the deep. Grady and I glance over at Original Teddy, expecting that he will explain, but he just hops off of his stool and dissolves the wall.

"Promenade," Original Teddy says and heads out of the room.

"What was that all about, Teddy? Was that the captain?" Grady asks as we follow. We pick up two Teddys on our stroll out of the bridge: one white and one blue.

"That is not accurate," Teddy says, but nothing more. He heads towards a wall panel next to the little room, and we all go through. I'm trying to keep track, but I think this is a different way from before.

"Where are we going, Teddy?" I ask.

"Inspection," Teddy replies.

"What are we checking up on?" Grady beats me to the question once again.

"Rancid and Gratin," Teddy says and points one of his tentacles at the two of us.

"So, like, do you want to ask us some questions?" A little edge of concern gets into Grady's voice, and I'm uneasy, too. It's like we're about to start our first day on the job only to find out we're nowhere near qualified for the position we've just been hired for.

Then again, they might just be checking the tenderness of our flesh to make sure we're going to be good eating.

Just to make us even more anxious, Teddy doesn't answer Grady's question. So I turn to the white Teddy that's on my right and try to catch its attention by waving my hand in front of its eyes. It looks up at me, in what I think is a curious glance.

"Hey, can you speak Empire Common, too?" I ask it.

"That is not accurate," Original Teddy replies. "Only Teddy can speak your language."

"Okay, so then can you ask him a question?"

"Her," Teddy corrects.

I glance at White Teddy again, but there is no discernable difference, other than her color, that is. I try to imagine some girly things about White Teddy: long eyelashes, nail polish, or even a dress...but it's just too weird.

"Teddy is waiting," Original Teddy says.

"Um, what do you think of us?"

"You are unremarkable," Teddy says.

"Is that your assessment, or is that hers?" Grady asks.

"This is Teddy's assessment."

Grady gives me the side-eye, and I return it. If Grady can't figure this out, then I'm completely hopeless. It's frustrating trying to get any actual information out of the Teddys. I don't know if they're doing it on purpose or if Teddy's ability to speak Common just isn't all that good. Either way, this will be a very short diplomatic meeting if we can't understand each other.

"Destination is imminent," Original Teddy says, stopping in the middle of a long corridor and rotating himself left. One of his tentacles finds a diamond-shaped hole in the wall and plugs it. As expected, an opaque part of the wall dissolves, and I see a bright white light come forth. Maybe it's not that bright, but now that my eyes are used to dim Teddy-light, this seems harsh. Original Teddy thinks so, too, I guess, since he backs off and turns away from it. Blue and White Teddy also stop.

"Oh? Back already? My, that was fast, Teddy," a female voice from inside the room says in Empire Common in a strange, clipped accent. Grady and I share another one of our glances.

This just got interesting. No, I take that back—this just got totally mysterious.

"Now let's see...What did you bring me?" A hand—a female, human hand—grabs on to the edge of the wall, and a head—make that a beautiful female, human head—pops out from the room and glances around. Her hair is long, straight, and blond, and if I have to guess, she's a few years older than Grady and me.

"Ooh! Unexpected!" The woman's sapphire-blue eyes sparkle when they land on us. "Hello, gentlemen, welcome! Doctor Elizabeth Chapman, at your service."

When Grady and I just stare back at her, she frowns.

"Not much of a delegation, are you?"

"Huh?" I say.

"You're here as representatives of the Empire, are you not?" She straightens and steps out into the corridor, her hand still holding on to the edge of the wall.

"Well, just of our own planet," I reply with a smile. Good. Here's someone that's going to help us get this rolling and this war ended. Dad, your son is really doing it!

"Oh? And which planet is that?"

"Angelcanis."

"Hmm...never heard of it."

Or not.

"Where are you from, Doctor?" Grady chimes in. The doctor smiles at him.

"Honestly, I've no idea."

Fourteen

IT'S UNDERSTOOD GRADY AND I should be sharing a glance, so we don't. That's fine since I'm fighting the most male aspects of my instinct that want to say nice things to this woman. I can't believe that anyone but Kayley would get me warm under the collar. It's wrong and only makes me think about how I don't deserve her. I'm hoping that this charming doctor turns out to be crazy or a serial killer or something. That would make it easier on me.

"So are you ready, gentlemen?" the doc asks.

"Ready for what?" Grady says.

That draws a frown from the good doctor. "Surely you knew that you'd be getting a medical checkup, yes?" Doc Elizabeth asks, glancing between the two of us with a smile that would give Kayley a run for her money. "We need to be sure it's safe for you to be on board. As you may have noticed, this isn't a human ship."

"Of course," he says. "You're going to make sure we can handle the FTL...the past-light speeds that this ship is capable of achieving." His eyes dart around the corridor. "Which I bet is quite a few times faster than light. Maybe even faster than our ships. Maybe a lot faster."

Doc Elizabeth waggles her eyebrows. Point scored, my friend.

"So it'll be the Voight-Atlas physical and mental stress test, is that right?" Grady's on a roll.

"I'm impressed. Few know the name." The doctor's face brightens, and her smile reveals her beautiful, straight pearly white teeth. Of couse.

"Uh, I know a little about applying bandages." I just spit out my words, hoping to catch everyone by surprise. If I did, nobody mentions it. The doc tries to be polite and nods. My failure to impress is obvious. In some ways, I'm glad.

"Well, let's not keep you young gentlemen out in the hallway. Do come in, please." She beckons us in and then nods to the Teddys. "Thank you, Teddy. You may retrieve them in two hours."

The Teddys bow back to her, then turn around and head back the way we came. Grady and I, and presumedly Doc Elizabeth, watch them go. I'm a bit worried to see them leave, even though we're being left in the hands of a fellow human being. At least, we think she is.

Also...how does she know to call them Teddy? This place is getting more bizarre by the minute.

"Hop to, now, boys, we've got much to get through before they get back...and let me tell you, Teddys are extremely punctual."

We turn back to her as she pivots and saunters back into her space. That's when I first notice she's only wearing a light shirt, shorts, and no shoes. It makes me feel like I just strolled into her living room with my trainers on. Everyone knows that's poor form. Shoes come off at the entrance.

As we enter, I understand why it's so bright in here. It's the largest and tallest space we've been in since the bridge, and all the walls are white in severe contrast to the heavy gray of the rest of the ship.

The panel reappears behind us after we're inside, and I pause in the small space in front of it. Grady takes a few more steps inside, but then stops and looks back at me. I think he gets the idea about the shoe thing since he always has to take off his when he gets home. His parents have special slippers just for wearing in their house, and because I'm there so often, they gave me my own. I think they just got tired of me walking around in my socks.

"Uh, Doctor?" I say.

"Elizabeth, or just Liza. We don't need to be on such formal terms." She turns around and puts her hands together, beaming at me. I look down, avoiding her gaze, but that's the wrong decision, because now

I'm staring at her legs. Her very shapely legs. I think I'm feeling warm, and I wonder if Kayley can have Afton kill me twice over for being unfaithful.

"So yes? You had something to ask? Er..." She's searching to remember my name, but we never told her, so she's just being polite.

"Rance." I nod over to my friend. "And this is Grady."

"Thank you. Nice to meet you both! So, Rance, you wanted to ask me a question?"

"Well, I was just wondering why you weren't wearing any shoes."

"Oh, well, because they're not really necessary on the Teddys' ship, and I much prefer feeling the ground with my bare feet. You're welcome to do the same, if you like."

I stare up at the ceiling. Her gorgeous smile is getting to me, I can feel it, and if I have to compare and contrast Kayley's versus Doc Elizabeth's, I'm going to go crazy. If I thought he'd do it, I'd ask Grady to slap me across the face.

"You also are kinda...lightly dressed?" Grady asks. He doesn't sound embarrassed to ask it at all, which is unusual for him. Questions of a personal nature are not his forte.

"Yes, well, perhaps you haven't noticed, but the Teddys acclimate to a cooler temperature, so they think humans need the environment to be much warmer than it actually should be. Inside my compartment here, it's nearly thirty degrees Celsius. I'm normally warm, so it can get to be a bit much for me, sometimes."

Okay, so that must be why I feel warm, and for no other reason. I'm not cheating on KayKay, after all—yes, that's what I'm going with. When we get back, I'm going to prostrate myself before her and beg forgiveness.

"How do you know they're called Teddy?" Grady asks, slipping off his shoes. He's done it so many times, he doesn't even need to bend down anymore. Just a little pressure on the back of his shoe, and he slides right out of it. Mine have straps, so I can't do that.

"That's what they're called, aren't they?"

"Not until a few hours ago," Grady comments suspiciously. There's not much to this mystery, but I'll let him investigate if he really wants.

"Right then." Elizabeth claps her hands together. "This ship travels a bit differently than human star cruisers, so we need to get you all checked out and make sure you can handle the travel well enough."

"And if we can't?"

"Then"—our gorgeous doctor grins at us in a way that makes me uncomfortable—"we've got a solution for that, too."

"Okay. So what do we need to do to get checked out?" I ask, trying to get this over with. We've got actual business to attend to, and as pleasant as the doc is to look at, Grady and I came here to stop a war.

"Right, well, first things first," Doc Elizabeth says. "Let me find my tools."

She digs into a drawer and pulls out several sharp objects, a pair of clamps with some seriously aggressive teeth on them, and an elastic funnel-type thing with a hose attached to the end. If I didn't know any better, I would assume she was getting ready to torture us, not examine us.

"Okay, here we go!" Doc Elizabeth's voice is kinda singsongy, and now I'm wondering how much she's going to enjoy torturing—I mean, testing us. "Who would like to go first?"

"Grady would!" I say, and my friend glares at me with the intensity of an atomic blast. All I can do is smile apologetically and maybe say a prayer or two, hoping he doesn't die.

"Very good, Mr. Grady, shirt off and hop up on the table here, please. Rance, you can have a seat there for the moment if you like."

The doc points to what I would consider the pilot's seat in a fighter plane. It has some strange appendages attached to it, so that's where the similarity ends. I drop myself down on the edge and slide in.

It's more comfortable than it looks, though I wonder what it's for. In fact, I wonder what all of this is for—a human doctor on a ship full of Teddys? They must have their own medical staff. And where did she get all of this stuff, anyway? I ask out of curiosity.

"Please don't interrupt, Rance. I'd prefer not to damage your friend." She picks up a metal cylinder with a point at one end and presses the button on the side. The device whirs like a high-speed drill. When Grady's eyes fall on it, they grow to be Teddy-sized. He swallows hard and wets his lips. I can see the tension building in his muscles. Boy, am I glad I volunteered him first.

"What's that for?" Grady's voice shakes as he asks the question.

"Don't worry, Mr. Grady. This won't hurt a bit. I'm going to test the stability of your brain cells."

"How?"

"Well, something like this," the doc responds and engages the switch again. The device spins up to a terrifying whine, and I just can't watch anymore.

A yelp comes from Grady, and I stare at one of the pretty plants sitting in a big pot on the floor. It's tall enough that its top leaves are bent over at the ceiling. Yes—this is much better than watching my poor friend undergo whatever sinister test Doc Elizabeth has dreamed up. I mean, because she's pretty, and because I'm an idiot, I assumed that she's human. This is exactly how killer plants lure in their prey, and now I think she might very well be a serial killer.

Not to mention, the good doctor gets this big grin whenever she handles pointy objects.

I gather my courage by telling myself it's okay—the Teddys would have chopped us into small pieces already if that's what they wanted to do.

I hear Doc Elizabeth directing Grady to move this way and that and telling him what she's about to do next. It all sounds reasonable enough, but the tortured sounds that my friend makes when she does these tests keep knocking me back to square one.

She sounds like she's really enjoying this. Grady is definitely not.

"Excellent, Mr. Grady, you may get dressed."

I cringe. I take a breath to keep myself cool, but now I can feel her eyes on me, and l glance her way.

"Ready?" Her expectant gaze is burning a hole through me. "Don't look so worried. You've nothing to be concerned about, really."

"Yeah, dude, nothing at all." Grady's voice sounds broken, despite his attempt to calm me.

"I don't believe you, dude," I murmur and make my way over to the examination table, thinking I'd rather be riding on the outside of the hull than doing this.

I hop up on the exam table, and she helps me lie down. Her hands are warm, and that helps. They're also soft and gentle, and that doesn't. I'm expecting that she's going to turn into a bugbear and swallow me whole.

I really have to cut down on all the cine I watch.

To keep from going nuts, I think about my mom and hope she's doing okay. I'm not too concerned, as I know she's in excellent hands. Even though those med-techs were military, they probably took her to a civilian facility. The doctors there are decent, so again, all positives.

"Turn to your side, please, Rance," Elizabeth says. I comply, and she presses something cold against my back while holding on to my shoulder. "Good, now breathe slowly."

I wonder what Kayley is doing right now. Knowing her, she's probably mobilizing the entire planet to look for us. Kayley's an amazing leader, when she doesn't let her self-conscienceness get the best of her. Unlike me, she's had a great upbringing: two awesome parents, a good home, and people that always support her, no matter what. That might be her only problem, actually—too many people telling her she's awesome.

"Great, now sit up, please," Doc Elizabeth directs. "This might feel uncomfortable for a moment."

Afton and Parrish are probably on the way to training now, with that colonel. I hope that—WHOA, that feels weird! I get a huge chill down my spine. It's not painful, but it is extremely distracting.

I can't focus my thoughts again until the exam is over, and the doc tells me to get dressed. I happily take care of that in a microsecond.

The best part is I wasn't murdered, and I think I'm convinced that the doc is a real-life human being.

"So how'd we do?" Grady asks.

"Both of you passed with top marks, but Rance..."

Uh-oh.

"What did I do?"

"We really need to discuss your eating habits."

"I only eat my mom's cooking...mostly."

"That and a ton of junk." Elizabeth puts her hands on her hips. "Really, you need to make better choices. However," she says and holds up a finger with a smirk, "on this ship, we have that solved."

"Yeah, what do the Teddys eat?" Grady asks.

"Oh, you'll see," she says with a grin. And now I'm worried.

Fifteen

AFTER WE'RE DONE WITH the examination, Original Teddy shows up —right on time, as Doc Elizabeth said—and escorts us down the corridor towards the center of the ship. I think we're good on not becoming the next course at Teddy dinner, but I'm still wondering when we're going to meet the captain. It would be good to get this mission moving. Our world is waiting.

So I ask.

"Nutritional, before conclave," Original Teddy replies as we head farther into the ship. I think we're headed towards the rear, but we've been winding through so many corridors that I'm lost. Doctor Elizabeth strolls behind us with a sly grin on her face.

Also unexpected: she's holding hands with our other friends Blue and White Teddy. I have no idea what that is about, but the Teddys seem content to do it.

The corridor ends in a sizeable space, with no portal closing it off. I see a few of the diamond holes in the wall, so I guess there's a way to close something if needed. The room has several tables, each topped with a rectangular tray with short, clear walls on its edges. Several short cylinders surround each of the tables, and just like the rest of the ship, except for a few small buttons and holes along the walls, everything is dreary. Despite that, it's bright enough in here for us humans to see well.

Original Teddy motions us to one table and sits down at the head of it. Grady and I follow suit, taking the spots on the side next to him, with Doc Elizabeth sitting next to me, and the other Teddys hopping over to the other side. These seats are kinda low, so I have to cross my legs in front of me or I risk kneeing myself in the face.

"So this is dinner? Where are all the other Teddys?" I ask.

"They don't have set mealtimes, so they just eat when they're hungry," Doc Elizabeth replies. "Same with sleep and work. We're here late in their day, so most of them have eaten already. Most only eat once a day." She smirks. "Too bad...it's quite the experience to have the entire room full while the Teddys are recharging. They do enjoy their eating!"

"So...what do—" Grady begins, but the doc puts a finger to her lips. It stops him from talking, but I don't know if that's what she meant. I've never seen anyone make that gesture before.

A chime rings, and the bottom of the tray disappears, just like the table did in the meeting room. Since we've seen that before, Grady and I aren't freaking out. It's cool tech, and watching it for the second time makes me wonder how they make it work.

That is, until the bottom comes up again.

It's a little garden. There are colorful plants of all shapes and sizes: mini pine trees, orange cabbage kinda things, and even black celery. I'm guessing that some are edible for humans, and I'm sure the doc would stop us from munching down on something that isn't safe to eat.

Then I catch some movement in the mini forest, and I lean in to take a closer look. What I see is like a cross between a caterpillar and a ball of fuzz. It's about the size of my fist, and the fuzz seems to mirror the colors around it. It's not moving too quickly, so I wonder why it's in there.

Doc Elizabeth pulls me back by my shoulder, and I turn to look at her. She smiles and shakes her head at me. "It's not polite to put your head in someone's food," she says. "Also, it's a bit dangerous."

"Food?" Then it dawns on me exactly what she means, but before I can ask more, I catch a sudden movement out of the corner of my eye. It's so fast that I don't get what happened until I glance across the table to see Blue Teddy's maw, full of those dagger-sharp teeth, chomping away at a fuzzy form.

A microsecond later, a flurry of tentacle strikes snatches fuzzy forms out of their mini garden sanctuary. One even lets out a shriek, and now my stomach is shutting down any interest in trying something new to eat.

"Oh," Grady moans. "I don't think I'm going to eat this whole trip."

"Gentlemen, let's not insult our hosts on their ship...Have some!" Elizabeth chides as she breaks a stalk of the celery off and bites down on it.

"Yeah, I, uh, we..." I get distracted by the fuzzy slaughter. I can't look. The only place I find that's not horrific to direct my gaze is straight down. "We don't eat animals."

"Silly." Doc Elizabeth chuckles. "Those are not for us, and I doubt you'd be able to catch one, even if you wanted to. Here, try this. It's a bit like licorice."

She hands me a stalk of the black celery, and I stare at it to make sure it's not moving.

"What's licorice?" Grady asks Elizabeth, with a level of interest that I wasn't expecting from my friend. He must be starving to even be considering eating right now.

Instead of answering, she hands him a stalk of the black plant as well. I've decided that I'll let him try it first before putting it anywhere near my mouth. Grady isn't in any hurry, though. He sniffs it, examines it closely, then sniffs it again. I don't think he's fully convinced, but he takes a bite.

I am completely focused on Grady, anticipating his response. I can see his brain shift into overdrive as he contemplates the taste. His eyes open wide, and he lets out this melodic hum that I can only guess means he likes it.

"See? Isn't it delicious?" Elizabeth says. "Very good for you, too. Full of amino, omega, and citric acids—that's the bitterness you're tasting —plus some protein and some other vitamins. It's as close to a perfect food as you can get."

"Fresh is best," Original Teddy says and snatches a piece of orange cabbage.

Okay, so now I have to try it. I just jam it in between my molars and crunch down. A spurt of flavors hits my tongue: savory, sweet, spicy, and, of course, the aforementioned bitter. Doc Elizabeth is right—it's near perfect.

"So, what else can we eat?" Grady asks with renewed enthusiasm. I'm feeling it, too, even though a moment ago I was in a complete panic. Living things that move or scream are not part of my diet...ever.

"Any of the plants are fine to eat. Though, if you want my opinion, what you just tried and the little pine tree here have the best flavors. I'd avoid the orange cabbage if I were you."

As we're finishing up, a brown Teddy comes in, followed by another white one. The brown Teddy is fairly tall. Taller than any Teddy we've met so far and almost as tall as Grady and I.

"Conclave is available," Original Teddy says, and the bottom of the tray drops out again, replaced by a flat panel that rises to the top of the tray.

"So this is the captain?" I ask.

"That is accurate," the brown Teddy replies, and this Teddy comes to stand next to Original Teddy. Both of them make this strange motion with their tentacles, where they wrap them together in a spiral then unwrap them just as quickly. I'm guessing here, but that could be a salute or some other form of greeting.

"Wow," Grady exclaims, "you speak Common."

A rather obvious observation by my genius bud. But hey, this is new for both of us, so I'll give him a pass.

"Wait a second, Teddy." I frown, remembering Original Teddy's answer when I asked that question earlier. "You told me only you could speak it."

"That is accurate," Original Teddy says. "For Teddys present at that location."

"Conclave has begun," the captain says and raises a clawed hand to get us to watch the big illuminated globe hanging over the table. I have to blink because even though this spherical vid is cool, it hurts my brain to look at.

As the vid starts, there are two ships. The first one I recognize as an Imperial star cruiser, and the other, I'm guessing, is a Teddy ship because it's big and dark like the ship we're on now. After a few moments, the star cruiser opens up on the other ship, firing missiles and beam weapons in an all-out assault.

My mouth drops open, and so does Grady's as the Teddy ship flashes, then bursts into a trillion fragments, headed for every direction of the universe. The star cruiser turns and rushes away, avoiding the debris like some heroic scene from a big-time cine. Only I'm not feeling much elation over the murder I just watched.

"Tell me that wasn't real," I say. My eyes are so wide right now they must look as big as a pair of Teddy orbs.

"That is not accurate," says Captain Teddy. "This recording was transmitted by Teddy ship number four thousand seven hundred thirty-two."

"So...when is this from? Is it recent?" I'm wondering why they wanted to show this to us. I mean, it sucks, right? A bunch of Teddys just got blown up, but I don't really know how to feel about that. They're the enemy, but my personal experience with them hasn't been so bad. They've been nothing but accommodating to us so far, and Doc Elizabeth seems fine for having spent time with them.

"This is the first encounter," Captain Teddy replies.

"The...first encounter, ever?" Grady guesses, and that idea leaves my stomach feeling a bit queasy. Wait...did we shoot first? Are we the ones who actually started this?

"That is accurate," Captain Teddy says, waving a tentacle at the vid globe.

Oh man. Just seeing this is hurting my head.

"Rance..." Grady turns to me. I can tell he's on the verge of a total meltdown. Unlike me, Grady has always had a strong belief in the Empire. It's done his parents a lot of good, and they've gained a lot of notoriety from their work that he's going to reap the benefits of. Me? All they've ever done is take my father from me.

"Rance." When Grady repeats my name, it's usually not a good sign. "This can't be true. No way. We would never."

"I don't know, Grady, but it sure looks real." I glance around at our hosts for an answer.

"It is certified authentic," the captain insists.

"How can this be the whole story? All we're seeing is one side," Grady argues. I wince a little because his voice is growing louder, and when it does, it starts getting harsh. "We can't know the truth unless we have all the evidence, all of the facts!"

Well, I can say this about Grady. He makes a compelling argument. I'm leaning towards agreeing with him. And this doesn't excuse or forgive the attacks on our planet. The Teddys definitely have some explaining to do.

"Yeah, Grady's right," I add, but I'm trying to keep my voice down. Our furry hosts have only been kind to us so far. It would be good to keep it that way, considering we just saw how they eat. "We should see all the evidence."

"A typical answer for representatives of the Empire," Doctor Elizabeth comments. I get her wanting to be considerate of her hosts, but it wouldn't hurt for her to back her own race up, too.

"No supplementary recording exists," Captain Teddy says. Did I hear regret in his voice, or am I just assigning human traits to an alien race?

"Well, can you tell me why you attacked our planet then?" Grady asks.

"That is not accurate. We did not attack."

"Dude!" Grady is starting to squeak. "You blew up my favorite breakfast stop!"

Well, I'm stuck—what should we believe? I definitely remember being frightened out of my mind over bombs and explosions, as Grady does. I don't even need to try very hard to do it, either. If I close my eyes, I can hear the sounds and feel the rumble that shook the ground when the bombs exploded. It's terrifying, and I'm never going to forget it.

"Teddy," I begin, "you denied dropping bombs on us before, too, but you have to know people are dead because of the weapons you released. So, what's up? You want us to believe that our Empire attacked first, but you guys aren't innocent of killing, either. How do you explain that?"

"Loss of continuance is unfortunate," Original Teddy says. "Intention is not accurate. Neutralization of combat is necessary. Subsequentially, the conclave will be possible."

"Oh man, that's just great." Grady puts his head in his hands. "Sorry we bombed you? That's your line?"

"Teddy does not excel at combat," the captain says. "War is... unfamiliar."

"Gentlemen, I think a little bit of trust is called for here," Doctor Elizabeth says. "There is no sense in pointing fingers, and they did reach out to you first. Has there been an Empire contingent sent to discuss a cease-fire? Hmm?"

The doc has a point, and it's hard for me to not listen to pretty women, especially when they're making sense. They've conditioned me for this from an early age.

"Grady, what's the harm in hearing them out? Isn't that why we came here?" I ask.

"I thought we came here because you wanted to check out an alien spaceship," Grady mutters, rubbing his eyes with his palms. Grady's upset because, just like me, he really wants peace. After all, this is the very first alien race we've ever encountered. Are we just going to blow them up? Not a good way to start. I'm sensing an opportunity here.

"Damn straight," I say. "I want to do that, but I was also thinking about our planet and our friends. I mean, aren't we here to stop a war?"

"Well," Doc Elizabeth chuckles, "aren't we after a Nobel Prize?"

"What prize?" Grady pops his head up and glances at her.

Doc Elizabeth waves a hand at us. "Never mind, as you were..." she says. "Continue to save the galaxy."

"What is she talking about?" Grady asks.

"Forget it, Grady...and stop doing that with your forehead. You're going to get wrinkles early."

"That is not accurate," Original Teddy says.

"Exactly, Teddy," Doc Elizabeth seconds.

"So how about it, Grady? Let's reserve judgment for a moment? In the name of peace?" I'm hoping he'll say yes, mostly because I have no idea what to do if he says no.

With a long, drawn-out sigh, Grady considers, then nods. "Okay, dude. We'll listen."

Sixteen

"UM, CAPTAIN?" GRADY CLEARS his throat, and I'm wondering what he's about to ask. "Not to change the subject, but how is it possible that you refer to yourself and your people as Teddy when we just decided that name, uh...not that long ago?"

Not change the subject? He just did exactly that, and I'm still stuck on the last subject.

"Let me answer that if you please," Doctor Elizabeth says, and everyone turns to her. "The Teddys, as you call them—"

"They call themselves that, too!" Grady insists.

"Yes, well." Doc Elizabeth smiles politely. "They do so for your benefit. There is no exact name for the race you call Teddy—"

"We didn't call the race that, only him." Grady points at Original Teddy as he speaks.

"Yes, I understand." I think Doc Elizabeth is losing a bit of patience with my friend, who is very insistent on the accuracy of facts. "But hear me out, if you wouldn't mind."

"Yeah, sure." Grady's face is pinker than it normally is. I think it suits him.

"Right, as I was saying, they don't have a concept of individual ownership because they share everything. Thoughts included. Now"— she holds up a hand before Grady can open his mouth—"it wasn't always like this, but because of their firm sense of sharing, they created a technology that lets them share thoughts when they want to. Don't ask me how it works because, well...I've no idea."

This is a really interesting concept. Share...everything? That just brings up way too many more questions than I think we have time for right now. I do have a feeling that we're going to be on this ship for a long time, so I'm sure we'll have the chance to ask.

Grady is also thinking deeply about this. I know he is because his mouth is closed and he isn't interrupting anyone. We're a communal society on Angelcanis, but there is definitely my stuff and your stuff and their stuff. Like the way that Parrish likes to steal my rice sticks. That's not communal property. Those are mine, and no one should be taking them without my permission.

"Okay, I get it." I actually do, which is why I'm saying it. "So like, when we decided to call Original Teddy—"

"I'm sorry, what did you just say?" Doc Elizabeth furrows her eyebrows.

"Original Teddy?" I say again.

"Ah, yes." Doc Elizabeth nods. "I understand. An excellent idea, Rance. Go on."

"So yeah, Original Teddy." I point to him, and he seems pleased, though I have no idea what pleased, or any other emotion, looks like on a Teddy. "When we decided on his name—"

"Colonel Nelson decided on it," Grady corrects, and I give him a beady eye for interrupting me.

"When *Colonel Nelson* decided on it..." I throw Grady another glare for bringing up the man's name. "Original Teddy just uploaded the name to all Teddys, and so now they call themselves that name for our sake."

"That is not accurate...entirely," the captain says. "We have also decided on Teddy."

"Anyway...can we get back to the last subject, please?" I ask, trying to keep things on track.

"We have returned," Captain Teddy says.

"Why do you think that ship fired on your ship then?"

"Misunderstanding has been established," Original Teddy says.

"What kind of misunderstanding?"

"The kind where you want to take something that doesn't belong to you," Doc Elizabeth says. "Human history is rife with this kind of nonsense."

"So our Empire is trying to take your territory?" Grady asks. We've got the same screen open, for sure. I'll let him run with the questions.

"That is not accurate," Captain Teddy replies.

"They don't have any territory," Doc Elizabeth explains.

"You mean they're nomads?" Grady is trying to connect the dots. I'm not even sure where the dots are.

"That is not accurate." Captain Teddy sounds like he's stuck on repeat.

"The concept of individual ownership is very...for lack of a better descriptor...alien to them." The doctor is making a valiant effort to help us understand, but our basic understanding of the Teddyverse is still about a hundred million light-years from where it needs to be.

"So..." Grady says, and I'm rooting him on to figure this out for both of us. "The Empire...they're not interested in cohabitation, in... coexistence in the same sector. That's what you mean?"

"That is accurate." Both Captain Teddy and Original Teddy speak at the same time. I notice something about their use of Common that I hadn't notice before: they're sort of singing when they talk to us. One Teddy talking at once isn't too noticeable, but now that there's more than one, I can hear some kind of harmony or something like that. It's kinda beautiful.

"The Empire is only interested in one thing," Doctor Elizabeth says, and her voice gets dark when she says it. It breaks my enjoyment of Teddy-song, and I pull my attention back to her.

"Whoa, whoa, whoa, wait," Grady says and throws up his hands. "No way that the Empire is just going to shoot first and take what they want. We haven't gotten this far by just blowing things up and then stealing everything. I bet a single ship acting on its own started this. Now, if the Empire was trying to cover that fact up, that would make more sense."

"Yeah, true," I say and nod. Grady might be onto something. Screw-ups and cover-ups sound a lot like the Empire's standard modes of operation.

"An emergency has occurred," Captain Teddy says out of nowhere. "Action must also occur." He bends down and gets on all four of his limbs, with his tentacles forward. Then without warning, he sprints off down the hallway, the other Teddys galloping behind him. Original Teddy hangs back, sitting here with us as if nothing has changed.

"Do you need to go, Teddy?" I ask.

"Teddy is not required for emergencies," he replies.

"What's going on?"

"The Empire sends greetings." Teddy's tentacles wrap around the edges of the table and tighten their grip. "Take care."

"Teddy, do you mean—" I don't get to finish my sentence as the ship vibrates and lurches to one side, knocking us off our little stools and onto the floor with a triple thud. As light flashes across my eyes, I hear all three of us humans grunt. The ship bucks again, and we're thrown up and temporarily suspended in air, only to crash back down again. I land on my side and knock my head against the floor.

"That's not a greeting, Teddy! They're attacking us!" Grady half shouts and half groans.

"That is accurate. Take care. Retire to domicile is recommended." Teddy hops off his stool and ambles out, his tentacles reaching out to brace him against the ceiling.

"Wait, Teddy! We don't know the way back!" I shout, then realize we haven't even been shown anyplace to stay.

"I know the way." Doc Elizabeth winces and rubs the side of her head. "Are either of you hurt?"

"Define hurt, and I'll let you know," Grady says. He looks about as dizzy as I feel, and I'm not sure I can even stand, but I'm determined to try.

"You're likely unharmed if you're answering me with that tone of voice." The doc glances at me and frowns. "Rance, your head is bleeding. Can you stand up?"

"I think so," I say, but I'm not anywhere near confident about it. I push myself up, and I'm able to stand, but I'll keep my palm on the side of my head that feels wet and hope it's not too bad.

"Come here, Rance, let me see." The doc takes my head in her hands and peers at whatever wound is there. She's being real calm about it, which is impressive, while I'm waiting for the ship to jolt and knock us all down to the floor again.

Out of the corner of my eye, I see Grady come over, squinting like he just woke up. It's hard to see him fully, as the doc still has my head in a grip of death. I'm beginning to wonder if the cut is worse than I thought it was.

"Okay, you're fine, but let's get back to my quarters, and I'll seal it up." She glances at both of us. "Keep your hands on the ceiling just like you saw the Teddys do, and we should be okay if the gravity goes out."

"Can that happen?" Grady asks.

"Yep," Doc Elizabeth replies.

"Has it happened before?" he asks, his voice rising just a little.

"Yes, so let's get a move on." Doc Elizabeth jogs towards the door and raises her hands, pushing them against the ceiling. Grady and I follow behind, mimicking her moves. We all look like we're snowshoeing it down a tunnel full of black snow.

We make it back to her quarters with only a few jolts here and there, but I think that might just be the ship maneuvering and not actual hits from weapons. It's strange to consider humans are shooting at us. I wonder what weapons we have on board this ship. If those bombs were any sort of clue, they've got to be really advanced. All of this shaking and bumping of the ship doesn't make me confident about that, though. We're really getting pounded. It would be pathetic if we got killed by our own race, that's for sure.

"I wish I knew what the heck was going on," I say as the doc seals up my cut. I don't know what she's using, but it smells nice, and a little personal attention from Doctor Elizabeth isn't a bad thing. Gosh, what would Kayley say if she heard me say that?

"We can solve that." She turns to Grady and nods towards a panel on the wall. "Hey there, Mr. Grady, can you stick your finger in that top diamond? We can get a feed from the bridge."

Grady walks over to it and examines it with a healthy amount of suspicion, just what I would expect from an engineer. He then tentatively inserts his pointer finger into it and looks happily surprised when the only thing that happens is that a screen opens up on the side wall.

"Good, now the lower right one, and press it until you see the bridge come up. We're not going to understand anything, by the way."

"Obviously," Grady mutters, then jabs his pinky into the diamond void and watches the screen like he's flipping through vid channels at home.

"Is it really that easy to work the controls of the ship?" I ask the doc.

"No, but the Teddys modified the controls in here so that I could use them." She chuckles. "My spindly little fingers could probably get to the standard controls, but it's not safe."

After a lot of pressing, Grady gets the bridge channel. It all seems quiet and peaceful, not like I've seen in the cine where sparks are shooting all over the place and the captain is shouting out commands to bloody and beaten ship's officers who refuse to abandon their posts. I'm a tiny bit disappointed.

"Looks like we've turned around and are accelerating away from a star cruiser," Grady says.

"We're running away? Does that mean we're losing?"

The captain said they weren't that good at fighting, but how to explain the bombs dropped on Angelcanis? Luck? I'm not sure I can believe that. What I can believe is that Grady has already figured out how to read their tactical display.

"Not sure, but..." He points his finger at some small dots trailing our ship. They seem to be getting closer...quickly. "What are these? Missiles?"

"Do missiles normally move like that?" Doc Elizabeth asks as she finishes cleaning me up and turns to watch along with us.

"No, not missiles," Grady corrects. "Fighters."

Seventeen

THIS IS BAD, AND that's an understatement. The Teddys are trying to escape attack, and just like with fighting, they're no good at it. I drop myself down on Doc Elizabeth's exam chair and stare up at the screen as I grip the armrests.

"Those fighters...they're faster than a star cruiser, aren't they?" I ask Grady.

"Obviously, dude," Grady replies. "And they pack a nasty punch."

"How many of them are there?" Doc Elizabeth asks, her voice losing all of its prior cheeriness.

"Ten...a full squadron."

"Remind me to ask you later how you know about military ships, Mr. Grady."

We bring our focus back to those little dots chasing us. They're getting closer, and I'm squinting at the screen to see if I can figure out just how close they are. There's Teddy-writing next to each of the dots, so I'm guessing that's some kind of tactical information, but since I can't read Teddyese, I've got no idea what it says. I might not want to know, either.

The ship vibrates again but happily doesn't throw us on the ground. I'm guessing at least three of them are in range with their weapons, and it won't be long before all of them are pounding on our hull. I really hope it takes a lot to knock a hole in this Teddy ship. But if what we've encountered so far is a hint, I'm guessing it won't take much.

"I can't believe they're firing on us!" Grady shouts, waving his hands around.

Doc Elizabeth glances away from the screen with a troubled look on her face. Another hit rocks the ship, this one more violent than the last, and my companions have to grab something so they don't go flying. The doctor's copious collection of sharp objects in here only multiplies the danger.

"Believe it, Mr. Grady," she says, then snorts. "Pssh, if humans knew about the Teddys, they'd not be so aggressive."

When she says the word *humans*, my brain stirs. Then I get it—we may be on the ship that belongs to and is chock-full of aliens, but we're not Teddys. We're human! They don't realize they're shooting at their own people.

"Grady, do you think we can comm the star cruiser?" I ask, dropping my feet back to the floor.

"Why would we..." Grady looks at me blankly at first, but it doesn't take long for his supermind to figure it out. He snaps his fingers and points at me. "Yes! The Teddys were able to contact the military before. We should be able to call that ship!"

"Let's get to the bridge!" I cry and charge towards the portal. Grady spins and follows after.

"Boys!" Doc Elizabeth shouts. I check my step and reach my hands out to the wall to stop myself from crashing. Grady can't stop, and his skinny body slams into mine. We both turn around and stare wide-eyed at her.

"Why don't we comm the bridge first before you just try to bash in there, unannounced?" A voice of reason, for sure, but when the ship shakes again, any level-headed thinking I had evaporates.

"Why don't you call them while we're headed up that way?" I suggest.

"Do you even know which way to go?" The doc's got her hands on her hips, and I have to commend the consistent level of logical thought coming from her. Too bad we don't have time for it.

"We'll figure it out." I grin at her, and she responds by rolling her eyes. Grady opens the portal, and we jet out, hopefully in the right direction.

"If you get lost, I'm not coming to find you!" Doc Elizabeth calls after us.

If I had to bet on us getting to the bridge in any amount of reasonable time, I would have lost. After a few wrong turns, a rocking ship knocking us down twice, and a handful of very surprised Teddys, we make it. Is it lucky we made it at all? Absolutely. The Goddesses must be smiling down on us.

"Captain!" I yell, and all Teddy eyes converge on us. It's creepy. "We have an idea!"

"Unnecessary to converse at intensity," the captain replies, and I remember they have sensitive ears.

"If we can talk to the human ship, maybe we can convince them to stop attacking us!" I'm still talking loud, but I've brought my voice down several decibels. "We're diplomatic representatives, right? There's got to be a law against attacking a diplomatic ship."

"Perhaps that is accurate." Captain Teddy considers it while another rumble rocks the ship. It's not so intense here, so we're still on our feet.

The captain rotates to look at the multitude of screens, then brings his attention back to us.

"It is agreed," he says and turns one tentacle to point at the small room we were in earlier. "Await the interface."

Grady and I dash off into the cramped space and drop ourselves on the bench in the wall before the outer wall seals us in.

"Mind the gap," Grady says with a smirk, remembering what Original Teddy said earlier. Sure enough, the floor drops out, and the table rises up from below. Once the table is in place, the globe appears on the table, but it's blank.

"Are we supposed to do anything?" I wonder out loud.

As if to answer my question, the globe lights up, and a man wearing the deep blue of the military corps comes on.

"This is Captain Hillary of the Imperial Star Cruiser *Nebulon*. Who is making this call?" The captain is peering into the camera as if he's looking into a dark hole.

"Yes! We got through!" Grady cheers. Of course, Captain Hillary hears it, and his face goes red.

"Who the hell are you, and where are you calling me from?"

"Um, sir, I'm Rance He', and this is Mutsumaji Sugiyama." It takes me a second to remember Grady's actual name—I don't think I've ever called him by it. "We're calling you from the Teddy ship your fighters are currently attacking, sir. You're putting us and everyone on this ship —"

"Including a human doctor!" Grady adds. It's helpful, but minus points for interrupting me.

"Where are you from, Rance He'?" Captain Hillary examines me closely while his arms are moving around like a harvester at high speed over whatever terminal or desk he's sitting at. I've got to give the man credit; he took the call off the bridge, so we can't see anything other than him. That's why he's the captain, I suppose.

"Angelcanis, sir," I say with a level of pride that I think everyone should have for their home planet.

"Angelcanis? The colony that got attacked?"

"Yes, sir, that's us."

"So you're asking me to stop my pursuit, Rance He'?" He pauses his mad keyboard dash and leans closer to his screen. "Why would I do that? How do I know you're actually where you claim to be? You may appear human, but how do I even know you're who or what you say you are? I would appreciate some proper answers before I even consider it."

I'm thinking that this will not be as easy as I thought it might be. It also occurs to me that this could be the very ship that first fired on the Teddys, so no matter what I say, he'll keep attacking.

"Sir, did this ship fire on you?" I ask, trying that for my first verbal volley.

"What kind of question is that? We're pursuing an enemy ship, and we're at war. We have every right to defend ourselves." He blocks my attack with little more than a shrug. I'll have to try something different.

"Sir, we're on this ship because they have asked us to be representatives of our planet to discuss a cease-fire with the Ted—with the aliens."

"You?" Nope, he won't go for that, either. "You two boys barely look old enough to be recruited, much less representatives of an entire planet."

I'll have to put some firepower into my next counter. Otherwise, this conversation will go nowhere, and we'll be back where we started. I'm not looking to get blown to bits before we get anywhere.

I could use what we learned from the recording to throw the captain off his game. Even if I don't believe it myself, it doesn't mean I can't weaponize it. That might be a decent tactic, but there's got to be more. Man, if only Parrish were here...I'm no good at strategy.

Before I can try it, Grady speaks up. "Sir! My parents are Tadao and Elenora O'Grady Sugiyama! You know who they are, right?"

"I wouldn't be captain if I didn't, son. Do you have any way to prove that claim?"

Okay, nice thrust, Grady. How are you going to follow it up?

"Captain, all you need to do is contact them and put me on. They can verify who I am," Grady says, and there goes all of my hope in his making convincing arguments.

"I'm sure they can verify any image, but that still doesn't prove to me who you are." I can tell that Captain Hillary is about ready to hang up on us. In fact, he's reaching for a switch. "Unless you have something else to add, I'm going to be ending this conversation."

"But you'll be killing human beings, sir! Please, wait!" Grady begs.

"You haven't proven that's the case," Captain Hillary fires back, thrusting a finger at us. He's a definite candidate for unwarranted aggression against Teddys, and that just drops us back into the jeopardy we were in before we started this call.

This ship is sinking fast, and Grady and I are struggling to come up with a way to keep it afloat. We've only got one more chance before we become stardust. If only we could get a time-out to think. Freeze time so we can talk it through without so much pressure to get it right.

Wait, freeze? Yes, freeze! Popsicles! That's it!

"Sir, if you could contact Lieutenant Colonel Nelson on Angelcanis and give him a message, I'm sure we can sort this out. I'm sure he will verify who and what we are. He may even be eager to get us back," I say.

"But hopefully not because he wants to squash us into flatbread," Grady adds under his breath.

"Please, sir, this will only take you a moment, and if he doesn't tell you what you want to hear, then you're welcome to pulverize this ship into little tiny bits of space debris."

My anticipation rises as Captain Hillary lowers his arm and considers my offer. But my panic rises again as I see him reach for something. As he stares me down, he presses a button on his desk. I cringe and hope that wasn't the "fire all missiles" button.

"Ensign, get me in touch with a Lieutenant Colonel Nelson on planet Angelcanis." His eyes jump back to the screen. "I don't suppose you know where on Angelcanis I can find him, do you?"

Grady launches off a string of names and numbers so quickly, it surprises both of us. The captain relays that to his officer, and the call goes out.

"Okay, Rance He', what's your message for the colonel?"

Eighteen

THE MESSAGE GOES OUT, and while we wait for a response, I'm having serious second thoughts about what I chose to say. Both Captain Hillary and Grady gave me the most curious stares after telling them what I wanted to say. Maybe "Sorry for turning you into a popsicle and stealing your position as representative of the planet" was a bit too much, but with my life on the line, I was a little desperate.

"So, what are they like?" Captain Hillary asks, his tough outer shell cracking a sliver to show his more curious human self.

"Well, cute and fuzzy is as good a way to explain them as any. They're strange, too, but at least some of them speak Empire Common. It's been helpful."

"I wonder where they learned it," he muses, then continues to pry for information. "How many of them are on board that ship?"

"No idea, sir," Grady replies. "We've only been to three locations so far. One of those was the canteen." I give him back the point he lost before suggesting something that didn't work. Though compared to me he's still ahead, as I made three proposals that were all losers before getting one that hit pay. I haven't counted it as a win yet, since we're still waiting.

Or we were.

"Well, seems like we've gotten a response from your Lieutenant Colonel Nelson." Captain Hillary chuckles. "It appears your message rubbed the colonel a bit raw, son. You might be better off getting blown up."

"So...does that mean you believe us?" Grady asks in a tone of voice so meek I wonder if he's turned into a mouse.

"To be honest, son, it doesn't really matter at this point. He's ordering me to stand down and remove my ship from the fight. As his rank and jurisdiction over you override my authority, it's no longer my decision as to what happens to you. You're his problem now." The captain jabs a few buttons on his desk, then looks back at us. "I do have to say, I am impressed at your quick wits. Hopefully we'll never have to meet in battle again."

All the stress drains from my body, and I imagine that I've just jumped into one of Angelcanis' volcanically heated pools. They're only about half a day from my house and one of the best ways to relax. We all went after we graduated, and it's one of my best memories.

"So that's it?" Grady asks the captain.

"For me, yes," the captain replies. "Though for you...I would highly recommend that you contact the colonel as soon as possible. He will be expecting you."

"Yeah, we'll do that. Thank you, Captain." I smile and nod.

"Don't thank me. I won't hesitate to destroy that ship if it makes any aggressive moves. Whether you're on it or not." Captain Hillary leans forward once again. "I'm not sure what you're doing there, but I'm glad it's no longer my problem. Hillary out."

The Teddyglobe goes dark, and Grady and I slump into each other with a gigantic sigh. Crisis averted.

"Communications with domicile," Captain Teddy says. Now I realize that the cute and fuzzies were listening to our entire conversation. Maybe this captain is fairly sharp, too. "It has been prepared."

"Whoa, whoa," Grady says, holding his hands up. "We better talk about this first and come up with a solid explanation for what happened. Otherwise, we could be in some real hot lava."

"Unlikely. Volcanic activity is not present," Original Teddy corrects, and now I understand that some idioms probably don't translate well. Actually, I'd be surprised if any do.

"Okay, Grady...what do we say?" I ask the smartest human in the room.

"Dude, why are you asking me?" he complains.

"Honesty is recommended," Captain Teddy says. It's a good point. If we try to fib this up too much and get caught, it'll be a slaughter fest for Grady and me, the targets of termination. I'm thinking Kayley here, not any military personnel. We just had—and survived—the biggest military scare that I ever hope to have, but Kayley will do much, much worse if we don't give her a legit reason.

"We could just say the Teddys kidnapped us," Grady suggests.

"This is not accurate," Original Teddy says. That's correct—it's not accurate at all.

"Dude, not happening," I say. "They already know we were trying to leave on our own. Plus, that'll put the Teddys in danger, and that's not what we're trying to do here."

"What *are* we trying to do?" he shoots back.

"Find out the truth, of course!" But I'm just guessing. This brief excursion of ours has been worse than trying to choose a compulsory school to go to. We saved ourselves from becoming space debris, but that was just luck. I need Kayley here to help us figure this out. Maybe even the colonel. If he's not threatening to kill us, that is.

"Okay." Grady sighs and slumps his shoulders. "Let's get the call over with. We just dodged an exponential number of missiles. I was hoping to dodge one more today."

"Don't worry, we will," I say, trying to convince myself as I say it.

As we're connecting to Angelcanis, Doc Elizabeth comes in beaming. She strolls over to us and gives us both a literal pat on the back.

"Nicely done saving our hides, fuzzy and not," she says with a smile, then turns to the screen as the colonel comes on.

"This is Lieutenant Colonel Gabriel Nelson of the—" The colonel breaks off as he recognizes us. I can almost see the steam coming off of his face. His glare pierces through light-years' worth of space to stab us all right between the eyes.

"Rance! Sugiyama! Where the hell are you two? Explain yourselves!" The colonel is certainly less happy to see us than I'd hoped. Oh well. We're still not space dust...yet.

"On board the Teddys' ship, Colonel." Grady salutes him before he answers, but it doesn't get the response he was hoping for.

"You don't get to salute me, son! You're not a soldier, and as far as I'm concerned, your recruitment is on permanent hold until you make me understand what the hell happened!"

"Popsicles," Original Teddy says.

"What?" The colonel peers around the globe until he locates Original Teddy. "What do you mean by that?"

"I think what Teddy is referring to is their ability to short-circuit the nervous system with an electric charge." The doc folds her arms and gives the colonel a smirk. The stiff military man isn't in the mood for jokes. I wouldn't be either if I got zapped like that.

"Who are you?" Colonel Nelson peers at her with a healthy level of suspicion.

"Doctor Elizabeth Chapman. A pleasure to meet you."

"How did you get—" The colonel shakes his head. "Never mind. Rance and Sugiyama, start talking!"

"Well, the Teddy ship picked us up," I say, as if that was an obvious explanation.

"Teddy's ship picked you up?" The colonel glares at Original Teddy. "You've taken two of our citizens without my permission! I demand that you return them at once."

"That is not accurate," Original Teddy replies. "Teddy has not appropriated."

"Sir," Grady jumps in before there's a major misunderstanding. "We went with Original Teddy of our own free will. In fact, a few of *your* soldiers were about to shoot us!"

That puts a halt to the colonel's inquisition. His eyebrows jam themselves together, and I'll bet he's going to say that his men would never shoot at citizens. He is taking a moment to think about it, though, and while he does, his temper also cools a few degrees.

"What did the two of you do to make them take aim at you?" he asks. "Did you threaten them in some way?"

"Not at all, sir!" Grady insists. "Maybe they were just scared."

"Dismay is instinctive," Captain Teddy adds.

"Who's that?" Colonel Nelson is trying to find the voice's location, and I realize he probably can't see as well as we can in this dim light since his space is fairly bright.

"That's the captain, sir," Grady explains.

"The ship's captain? Let me speak to him!"

Captain Teddy steps closer to the globe, and the light emanating from the screen brightens up his brown fuzz.

"Captain," the colonel says, "return my citizens at once, or we will take them back by force. You've already experienced the firepower of one of our star cruisers. Now, since we're trying to create a cease-fire, I'd prefer not to, but we will if necessary."

"Colonel, that's totally unnecessary," I say. "Grady and I are fine. We chose to go with Original Teddy, and we're acting as the representatives of Angelcanis, so we're totally safe here. The only danger we ran into was that *Nebulon* ship firing on us."

"You don't become the official representatives of the entire planet just because you got on the ship first, son," the colonel replies, "or did you forget you went without my authorization?"

"What?" Doc Elizabeth turns on us. "You're not actually the Empire's representatives?"

"All the more reason to get them safely back on planet," the colonel replies.

"Oh, pssh." The doc waves a hand at the globe and the colonel. "They're in no danger here."

No sooner does she refute the colonel than she spins back on us, crowding Grady and me against the wall, arms crossed again. Her normal chummy mood has worn away to expose a fiercer disposition, and I have to say it's fairly intimidating.

Also, a bit sexy.

"Did you boys lie to me? Hmm?" Doc Elizabeth's tone contains every sharp object in her med kit. I swallow hard, remembering them with horrific detail.

"That is not accurate." Yes! Teddy is sticking up for us! "Rancid and Gratin have been authorized."

Well, I'll take the sticking up for us part. We'll work on the names later.

"Replacement is unnecessary," adds Captain Teddy.

"I'm not leaving you on that ship." The colonel is adamant. "That's just not a responsible thing for me to do. You are coming back."

"I think you are misjudging the situation, Colonel," Doc Elizabeth says over her shoulder. "I've been on this ship for quite some time, and

I'm familiar with it, as I am with the Teddys. They are in no danger."

"I'm sure you are, Doctor, but they aren't your responsibility."

"And how are they yours? I don't see any military uniforms on them," the doctor counters.

As we watch the two of them trade punches, I realize there's a good chance that we will go home, and that's not how it's supposed to be. I mean, I don't know *exactly* how it's supposed to be, but I know that going home is not what I want. This has been nuts, but it's also been amazing.

This is absolutely where we're supposed to be, and no military man is going to tell me differently. The doc is right—he's got no authority over me. I appreciate the concern, if that's what this is, but I'm here for my friends and my planet.

The only problem is we need the colonel's okay to do this. There's got to be some way to convince him we're the right dudes for the job. He's listening to us at least, which is more than what was happening before. If I could find something of value—besides us—that he'd accept in exchange...

"Colonel," I interrupt. "The Teddys showed us a vid that might change the outcome of this war. You wanted to talk about peace? Well, this vid might be the key to making that happen."

"Dude!" Grady elbows me. "What are you doing?"

"What vid?" asks the colonel, taking the bait in exactly the way I wanted him to.

"Dude," Grady whispers. "We don't even know if that vid is real."

"Maybe," I reply. "But it might be the only thing that keeps us from going home."

"The recording is accurate," both Teddys state. Once again, Grady forgot about their exceptional hearing.

"What vid, Rance?" the colonel asks again.

"Sir." I try the honorific to see if it scores points. "It's best if you come to see it for yourself...you know, when you come to pick us up."

Everyone gets quiet while Colonel Nelson considers my suggestion. I have no idea which way he'll go, but since I was able to convince that captain not to blow us into the next universe, I think I might be good at getting one over on the military.

It's better than that, though. If this vid is real, it could break the whole "you shot first" argument wide open. Whoever is running that ship would be in big trouble, and that thought alone makes me grin. I like the idea of seeing a ship's captain in cuffs.

"Alright, if it means a potential way to end this war, then I'll come. But"—he points at the two of us, still plastered to the wall. "Once I'm done, you're coming back with me."

Grady and I both let out our collectively held breath.

"Oh, and Rance?" The colonel leans back in his chair.

"Sir?"

"Contact your girlfriend. She's worried about you."

I wonder if KayKay knows he calls her that. I'm okay with it, personally.

Nineteen

AS WE MAKE FOR rendezvous with the colonel, we've got a little time to burn. Doc Elizabeth offers to take us somewhere we can reduce our stress. With little else to do but wait, we agree.

The place the doc picks is spot-on—the ship's oxygen-producing garden. If you can call it a garden. It's so overrun with plants that I'm not even sure any of the Teddys have done any cultivation or landscaping up here. A gigantic transparent dome that covers the whole thing rises out of the ship and exposes itself to whatever solar light is around. The glare is a little much, but it's not too different from being in the sun back home.

"I bet this is so much better than the recycled burps that are on an Imperial star cruiser," Grady says with his head tilted back as far as it can go. I do the same. The star's photonic rays are nice and warm on my face. I hope the Teddys have blocked out any radiation that might be damaging.

"Yes, it's wonderful," says Doc Elizabeth, then narrows her eyes at us. "You didn't smell any burps on this ship, did you?"

"Do Teddys burp?" I ask, glancing around at the thick jungle. There are many plants I don't recognize—some with leaves larger than the three of us combined. They rise to the top of the dome like botanical skyscrapers. Others are tiny; they line the floor and make a nice carpet to walk on.

"Yes, and it's horrible...like rotten eggs and perfume, mixed together." She wrinkles her nose, and Grady gets his instant recognition face on— eyes wide and mouth open like he's about to sing a song.

"Yeah, we've smelled that," he says, his face wrinkling.

"So, Rance, when are you planning to call your girlfriend?" Doc Elizabeth gives me a grin like a devil, and when she sees her question has hit its mark, she gets as gushy as a middle school girl getting the latest gossip.

"Kayley's not my girlfriend, actually. At least not yet," I reply, as reluctant as I am to correct her. Kayley deserves me being honest about our current status. It does ache for me not to fib a little, though. Especially after Grady and I pulled our disappearing trick. I hate to consider my actions may have made my chances with Kayley lower than low. They were small to begin with, but this could have won me the "Never Dating Rance" prize.

"Yes, but she's worried about you. And what about your parents? Yours too, Mr. Grady." The doc is staring at Grady's back as he strolls away from us, lost in the stars above.

"I'll call," I say. "I need to talk to her about our problems." I pick another direction and gaze up, looking for any recognizable constellations, but it's impossible. Enjoying the twinkling blanket of light that's draped over the dome is enough for now.

"Problems?" Doc Elizabeth follows me. "Like what?"

"Like not going home?"

"That's not something you have much say in, Rance. The colonel was adamant. Both of you will return with him once he sees the vid. Honestly, I think he's right. If he believes the recording, then there's potential for a scandal to be uncovered here, and that's *not* your problem to solve."

"Even if he believes it, he's got no actual way to prove it's real. His superiors will just say the Teddys faked it. I bet they've already covered it up. One ship and one captain? Both are so buried by now that we'll never get to uncover the truth."

That's just my personal dislike of the Empire talking, but even after our short time with the Teddys, I trust them more than I would any Imperial representative. Not one of those baby kissers is worth even a blade of grass in my backyard. Even the ones that got flattened by

Original Teddy's ship. I'm way biased, of course. Those gormless jerks stole my dad. They bribed or blackmailed him with something, forcing him to choose work over his family. He just said goodbye one day and never spoke to us again.

"Again, not your problem," Doc Elizabeth says. "Still, I think you should feel proud. You made the first contact with the Teddys and got them talking to the military, and that might just end this war. You should go home with your heads held high and spend time with your friends and family."

Not happening.

I don't feel like explaining to her why I know allowing the military to solve this is a bad idea. It creates too many other questions for her to ask, and the answers that I'll need to provide bring up way too many painful thoughts for me.

Besides, if I let someone else do it for me, what have I really achieved? Grady and I haven't accomplished all that much yet. If I'm going to be worthy of Kayley, I've got a lot more to do. If I don't step up and get to the bottom of this mess, then what am I, really?

How I do my part for my planet is still up for debate. Maybe I could convince the colonel again? No, nobody's that lucky. Certainly not me, and even if I could convince him, there's Kayley to persuade, and then my mom. The reason would have to be astronomically perfect, and I know there's no such thing as cosmic perfection.

If Kayley were here, she might convince him to let us stay, but then I'd have to convince KayKay to come with the colonel, and it might be too late for that. He's likely on his way right now.

"I don't really think Rance wants to go," Grady says. I look down from the sky view to see Grady smirking at me.

"Neither do you, dude," I shoot back with a grin of my own. "This ship is a tech marvel that I bet you're just dying to get your digits into."

"No doubt," Grady replies as he approaches. "But what can we do?"

"You boys are serious about this?" Doc Elizabeth's eyes dart between us. I think our recklessness is rubbing off on her.

"Doc, there's an infinite number of reasons why we've got to stay," I say, hoping she'll accept that. "I'll tell you, but can we just put it aside for now?"

"Fine, but I'll hold you to that," she replies. "And please, it's Elizabeth. I've a feeling we're about to become co-conspirators."

"Grady," I say. "What if we could find something that would convince Kayley to talk to the colonel for us?"

"We'd need to figure it out pretty quick, and you know she's not going to accept some half-loaded concept. It's got to be a full-on killer reason."

"What would something like that be?"

"What's really important to her?" Doc Elizabeth asks. "Besides you, of course."

"Kayley likes helping people," Grady suggests. It's good...but not enough. We've got to get specific.

"It's more like she likes to be the parent in the room," I say, thinking of many, many times she acted like our mom when we were together. We've all got moms, but she's our gang's mom. Kayley's always looking out for us. I have no idea how this is going to help us, though. Doc Elizabeth and Grady agree.

"Well, wait," I say, thinking out loud. "All we really need to do is have her come here, right? Then if she sees the vid, maybe Kayley can get the colonel to let us stay."

"She's not going to just watch the vid and then spit some words at him, dude," Grady counters. "You're missing like ten thousand steps in between all of that. But you're right about one thing: getting Kayley on board is first. If we can do that, then everyone will come."

"You're still making quite a jump there, gentlemen," Doc Elizabeth says and shakes her head. "You do realize you're talking about a young woman convincing a colonel to take a risk he's already stated that he's not willing to take? No, I say you're still headed home."

"Thanks for the support," I say, but I know she's right. We're back to the start again. I might be happier if I poked my eyes out. Why can't I do what I want without the damn military getting in my way?

I rest myself against a tree and chew on my lower lip. If Kayley were here already, she'd have this all tied up in minutes. I don't really know how she does it, but it's just part of the mystique that makes up the almighty KayKay. I could have a year and I wouldn't be able to solve this conundrum.

Grady and I must stay on this ship, at least until we're tired of it. Not that I think we'll ever get bored here. What is there to go back to, anyway? Sure, Grady could go home and continue from where he left off. But me? Other than my mom, there won't be anything to return to. My buds will still leave, and eventually Kayley will, too.

"I still think Kayley is the key, dude," I say. "She's always supported my ideas before, and she's got the skills to come up with something we're not thinking about. We've got to get her here."

"Yeah, true." Grady nods.

"You're certainly putting an enormous responsibility on her shoulders." Doc Elizabeth's eyes narrow. "Even if she was your girlfriend, that'd be quite a lot to expect. Are you so determined to stay here that you'd put all that on her?"

"You don't understand how capable she is, and she wouldn't even question me about it if I asked."

"She sounds like a remarkable young woman then." Doc Elizabeth folds her arms and paces around me.

"She totally is." Grady speaks up to support me. "Rance isn't exaggerating about Kayley. He's pretty useless without her."

Wait...did he just give Kayley a compliment by putting me down? Minus ten points for him then.

"Don't you want to see your friends and your parents again?" Elizabeth turns on Grady.

"My parents can definitely wait." He chuckles, but then glances back up through the dome.

"And our friends will come," I add, "but we have to get Kayley first."

"Okay, boys," Elizabeth says with a load of *I really don't believe you*. We both turn to her, each of us defiant in our own right. "So you've got one small piece of your puzzle. Congratulations, but you still haven't figured out how to get yourselves out of going home, and that's the bigger piece."

"One thing at a time...*Elizabeth*," I say, forcing out her name.

"Ooh, well done." The doc claps her hands together and smiles. "Now let's go call your girlfriend."

Twenty

"RANCE? CAN YOU HEAR me?" Kayley waves at me from the other side of the screen, probably more to make sure she's got my attention than to say hello. I wave back, anyway. It's as dark as a cine theater in the cubby attached to the bridge, so I'm sure it's hard for her to see us.

The Empire has had subspace tunneling tech for communications for a while now, but this is my first time using it to call home. If I wasn't acutely aware that I'm nowhere near Kayley's house, this would be like chatting with her on my Sergo.

"Yeah, KayKay, I can hear you. Are you okay?" I ask, with a bit of a casual attitude. Doc Elizabeth shakes her head. I'll bet she was expecting me to get all lovey-dovey with Kayley. Not in this current reality—even Grady would think that was strange.

"Of course I am! But what about you guys? We were really worried! And why is it so dark where you are?" Kayley is still trying to get a good view of us through the globe.

"Teddys like it dark," Grady explains. "Big eyes let in a lot of light and all that."

"Then come closer, I want to see you." Kayley leans in, her own eyes getting big...and is she crying? If she is, I'm really a bad dude for getting excited over Kayley's tears.

We do what she asks. As if there was any question. To disobey Kayley is to request Afton to stand on you with her heavy boots until you beg for her to let you up. She may be slim, but she's not light.

Kayley inspects us like we're a fine art painting, and I'm fighting to hold my grin back from seeing her. She's I don't know how many quadrillions of kilometers away, but it's like she's right here in the same room.

"You're going red there, Rancy," Doc Elizabeth says, and I curse her under my breath. I'm not sure why most women seem to enjoy knocking me down when I'm up on life, but I'll just hope they mean well by it.

"Who's that?" Kayley asks, trying to look around me. "Is someone there with you?"

"Oh yeah, Kayley, this is Doctor Elizabeth Chapman," I reply, and the doc steps into the light of the screen. Kayley's eyes get Teddy-big, and her jaw drops open, and I immediately second-guess introducing Elizabeth to the girl whose affections I'm trying to win.

"Pleased to meet you, Kayley," Doc Elizabeth says in her most charming clipped Common. "I've been looking after your boys...um, after Rance and Mr. Grady while they've been here."

"You have?" Kayley asks, with more accusation than curiosity in her tone.

The doc turns to me, nodding approval and ending with a grin. "I can see why you like her," the doc whispers as discreetly as she's able.

Afton's head pops into the image from the side, her eyes searching for something that isn't Grady or me. Once she locks on to Elizabeth, it becomes obvious what she was after. Afton's eyes narrow, like she just located her mortal enemy.

I never expected it would be so tense between the ladies. Then again, I'm so excited to see Kayley that I could be imagining the whole thing. Still, Afton keeps her competition face on.

"Hello." Doc Elizabeth nods to Afton. "A pleasure to meet you. I'm Elizabeth."

"Sure you are," Afton says and gets an elbow in her ribs from Kayley. "I mean, nice to meet you, too."

"Hey!" Parrish leans in from the other side, as much of his massive body as he can fit into the frame. "Parrish here." He sweeps his gaze over Grady and me, as if he's looking for something wrong. When he doesn't find it, he just gives us a big grin. "You guys alright?"

"All good, Parrish," I say. "Sorry about the popsicle thing."

"Popsicle?"

"Never mind, we'll tell you later. First...is the colonel on his way to us? It's important."

"I don't think so," Kayley replies. "Afton and Parrish are supposed to go with him...something about proving themselves under pressure."

"KayKay." I put myself up close to the globe. "You have to go with them! We need you to talk to the colonel for us! We can't let him take us back."

"What?" Kayley frowns. "Why would you not want to come back?"

Oh, I didn't consider that.

Okay, not that big of a problem. I just need to explain the situation to her better. If she understood why we want to be here, she'd agree. Just like before, when I had my idea of how to get my big dream going, Kayley listened and she understood. Sure, she didn't agree with everything, but just like always, she supported me. I can do the same thing as I did last time, and that will almost guarantee she'll understand. Kayley is a superb listener and equally intelligent. She'll get it in no time.

"Kayley, there's something big going on," I say. "Grady and I saw this vid; it proves that the Empire started the war! They shot first!" I have to take a breath before I go on. It's a bit dramatic, but effective. "We have to convince the colonel that the recording is real!"

"Okay," Kayley says, "but how does that convince anyone, including me, that you have to remain on the Teddy ship?"

Kayley is also seriously skilled at clearing away the nonsense and getting down to the core of anything. It's really difficult to argue with her when she won't stop making sense like that. No worries, I can do that, too.

"Someone has to remain with the Teddys as the representative for humanity," I reply.

"That was an extreme fail, Rance. Try again," Afton says, triumphantly calling out my bluff.

"Stop speaking, Surela, before you make yourself look stupid," I fire back. "Oh, wait...too late!"

Haha. Point me.

"We can't trust the military to be the representative here," Grady chimes in. "We think they're trying to hide that one of their ships shot at the Teddys first."

As powerful as the Empire is, it's really only just a handful of ad hoc alliances between the twenty Central Planets and the Emperor on Albion. It continues to function because it's in the best interests of everyone to keep it going. That doesn't mean every planet likes all the others. It'd only take a few of them to decide they don't want to play by the rules any longer to break everything apart. And it'd only take one controversial action—like a ship from one planet starting a fight with an alien race—to cause a complete meltdown of the system. Other than that, it runs smoothly.

"Well, I'm with you on that. The citizens of the Empire should know the truth...whatever it is." Kayley brushes her hair behind her right ear. "But you don't belong out there in the middle of it. I want you to come home...both of you.

"And Rance, what about your house?" she adds. "You've got to get back to make sure it's fixed before your mom gets home from the hospital."

"Actually," Parrish chimes in—Yes! Thank you, dude, ten points for the backup—"the government is doing the repairs. I was by there the other day, and I saw all the construction equipment. It'll be good as new in no time. Maybe even better."

It's three against one or a possible three against two if Afton's on Kayley's side. Parrish probably wants us back home as much as Kayley or Afton, but since he's always looking out for what's best for his team, he's less strict.

"KayKay." I stand, hoping she'll take me more seriously like this. "This is where Grady and I should be. Honestly, I've never felt more sure about anything. We need to be here, or I know something will go wrong with this entire plan. That's why I really need you here."

Well, there is one thing that I've been even more sure about, but I'll only be sharing that when I'm ready to confess to her.

"Okay, I understand." Great, Kayley's considering it. Seriously considering it. I know she takes what I say as truthful, and it is. I meant everything I said. I want her here with me, too.

But something's not right. Kayley is taking an overly long time to think about this. When I share my ideas, usually she responds in no time. What's the difference this time? I know that I've been fuzzy-headed ever since I got here, but I can chalk that up to being in a new environment. Did I not explain things correctly? She said she understood, so an answer should be easy for her. Right?

"No," Kayley says, and my heart falls out of my chest and through a crack in the floor. "No, Rance. That ship isn't safe. No matter how the Teddys have been treating you, they're still our enemy, and we're at war with them. An Empire ship could attack you, and there's no way I'm letting you get killed out there. You'll come home. I'll go with everyone to meet your ship, but you're coming back with us. That's final."

"What?" I whisper, mostly to myself. I heard her. Every inconceivable word.

As Kayley and the others say their "see you soons," the vid goes dark. Dark like the mammoth hole in my chest my hope just flew out of. Never in an eon would I have expected Kayley to decide against me. Not about this. Where did I go wrong?

"An extremely sensible young woman," Doc Elizabeth comments and smiles at me. "I think you are right about her. I can see she's quite capable."

I just stare up at her. I guess I won't be staying after all.

Twenty-One

AS WE COUNT DOWN the last few minutes before the Teddy ship meets with the shuttle carrying the colonel and Miss Extremely Capable, I pace across the hangar floor so quickly, even Afton would be hard-pressed to keep up. I'm still racking my brain for some way to get Kayley to convince the colonel to allow us to stay, but I'm doubtful that any sudden revelations will appear. She won't change her mind. In fact, her faithfulness to her beliefs is one of the thousand things I love about her.

All sorts of ideas cross my mind, from the vaguely possible to the outright ridiculous. I even consider confessing my feelings to Kayley, in the most impossible chance that she confesses back to me and we run away together. It is a nice dream that lasts about five seconds.

"Rendezvous approaching," Original Teddy says as he arrives with White Teddy. "Preparations are concluded?"

"Well, sort of," I reply, sounding like a little kid who was just told to go clean their room.

"Inflection is not positive, Rancid," Original Teddy comments.

No kidding. I can't think of anyone who would be anywhere near upbeat when their world just got eaten by the sun. And that killer star is the one thing I adore above anything else in life.

"Dude." Grady drops a hand on my shoulder and stops my pacing. "As long as we're on this ship, we can still do something."

"Yeah, it's that something that's got me burning holes in the floor."

The clank of the shuttle docking rings through the chamber and cuts short any more thoughts about time. What's got my curiosity now is how the Teddys managed to make ships from two very different species able to dock together. They are a totally resourceful bunch, and again, that's a thought for another time. I push it aside for the thought that's really occupying my mind—I'm about to see Kayley. Parrish and Afton, too, but no offense to them. They don't exactly make me feel the same way.

There's a hiss of air, and water vapor forms and clouds up the round hatch. I'm shaking in anticipation of who will be the first to come through it. I know Kayley won't be the first, but I don't think I've got it in me to wait very long.

A herd of Teddys gather around us as the first human...no, make that the first two humans step through. They're just soldiers. Probably the colonel's security. I'm not sure what they think a pair of assault weapons will do versus an entire ship of Teddys, but then again, I remember what Original Teddy said about them not being good at fighting. They are good at eating, though.

The two guards are unnerved by the encircling Teddys. I watch as they lift their weapons out of the Teddys' reach, apparently not noticing they also have a pair of tentacles that could easily snatch them out of their hands should it come to that.

The colonel is next to come through, and he scans the space until he latches on to Grady and me. He comes straight for us, giving Doc Elizabeth a nod as he walks over.

"You boys look tired. Are you well?" the colonel asks. That's a surprise—I expected more of a chewing out.

"Yes, sir," Grady replies. From the corner of my eye, I see Grady's hand twitch. He wanted to salute, but he stopped himself, likely remembering what the colonel said to him the last time he tried it. I guess I'm not the only one freaking out.

I glance past the colonel's tall form, expecting more people to come through the hatch. But none do. Total dismay cramps my lower back and creeps up my spine. Despite my dream girl crushing my dream, I'm shaking in anticipation of seeing her.

"Uh, Colonel...Kayley came with you, right?"

"They're waiting in the shuttle until I let them know it's clear," the colonel replies, and I hear the inflexibility in his voice. It's not what I want, but at least she's here. I can wait for her to come out...at least one minute longer.

I still don't know what I'm going to say when I see her. Sure, I've got the "hello" part down, but after that, what? She's got to know I'm upset about her decision. Is she going to just pretend that was the end of it? I can't.

"What are you worried about?" Doc Elizabeth asks the colonel. "Perhaps I can help assuage any of your concerns."

"My concerns are tactical, Doctor, not medical."

"Pssh, Colonel, no Teddy on this ship is going to hurt you or your men. I've been here for quite some time, and I have never felt in any way threatened."

"And how long is 'quite some time,' Doctor?" The colonel turns to face her straight on. The doc presses her lips together and stares back.

Grady and I already know that she has no recollection of how long it's been. The most we've been able to get out of her is that her earliest memory is waking up on the ship, in her room, with all the medical equipment still in boxes. She has no recollection of where's she's from, or even how she became a doctor.

I throw another glance at the airlock, and all my worries flood back over me. I'm only a few steps away from going home, and if the colonel so decided he could send me there right now. Sure, I'd get to see Kayley, but any opportunity to expose this attack would disappear. If I can at least hang on until the colonel sees the vid, that would be something.

"Colonel." I step towards him. "Please. We're all safe here."

He turns away from the doc and rubs his chin. I shrink under his gaze, becoming shorter by the second. He's got a full head and a half on me, so feeling small before his towering frame is already too easy.

"And what do you base that on, son?"

"The Teddys...they're not a violent species, sir. I think the vid will prove that." I slide my hands behind my back so he can't see how tightly crunched together they are. It wouldn't take much for him to punch a hole in my rice-paper bluff.

"Violence is not possible during conclave," Captain Teddy says, plodding in with Original Teddy and a contingent of all blue Teddys.

"Ah, Captain." Colonel Nelson turns away from me to greet him. "A pleasure to meet you in person. I'm eager to see this recording that you say you have. Where can I view it?"

"Conclave is available pending arrival of all passengers."

The colonel frowns—outmaneuvered by a Teddy. He'll have to put up a show of resistance just to hold on to his men's respect. Once that's done, I bet...no. I *pray* that he'll let everyone else on board. I was already boiling over before the shuttle docked. Now I'm about to go supernova.

But if I thought I was supercritical before, the moment my friends come out my body flashes hot and cold and my hands shake. Parrish is first. He greets us with a grin, which quickly fades when all the blue Teddys surround him. He's totally lost in an ocean of Teddys and has no idea how to handle it.

"Dude, it's cool." Grady laughs at Parrish's predicament and goes to rescue him from the Teddy sea.

I'm so caught up in the scene, I don't even catch it when Kayley bursts from the airlock. She crashes into me and wraps her arms around me in an instant. I'm so overtaken by the moment, I nearly forget to hug her back. She squeezes me hard, and I become a puddle in her arms. She's so warm and smells so amazing. Any intention I had to drop to my knees and beg for her to let me stay dissipates into the air.

Besides, I think I have a better way.

"Don't you ever do that to me again, okay?" Kayley whispers into my ear. She pushes me back to look me over at arm's length. A gentle chew on her lower lip and a knitting of her eyebrows says she doesn't approve of my condition. "Have you guys been eating?"

"Absolutely. They've got these tasty little trees and black celery that we can eat. Elizabeth even says they're extremely nutritious."

"Elizabeth?" Kayley tilts her head down like a mother cat protecting her young.

"The doc." I wave a hand over to our blond-headed medical professional, who's chatting happily with Afton. That's a surprise. Both of them keep glancing our way.

"I see." Kayley nods, then makes to turn back towards the shuttle. "Well, come on, let's get you some proper food...You look exhausted, too. I bet you and Grady were too busy exploring to sleep, right?"

"Yes, but—" I plant my feet down hard, jerking Kayley to a halt. She looks back, mouth open and forehead creased. "I'm going to wait for the colonel."

"What? Why?"

"He's got to see the vid, and I want to be there if he's got questions." He'll have questions for sure, but none that I'll be able to answer. I've already had this discussion with her, and it doesn't end well for me, so I've got to hold on any way I can. Once the colonel sees the vid, I'll have something to press him with.

"I'm sure he'll be fine." Kayley gives another tug, but I stay put. "Rance..."

"Just until after he sees the vid, KayKay, then we'll go. Besides..." I smile at her, trying to change the subject. "I really want you to see this ship. It's amazing!"

I look into her eyes, unafraid, because that isn't a lie. Kayley is just as fascinated about tech as any of us, and who could resist examining an alien spacecraft for the first time?

"Okay." Kayley smiles back. "But then I want you to get some sleep."

Twenty-Two

"SO THIS IS KAYLEY," Doc Elizabeth says as we travel towards the center of the ship. This, I realize, is in the opposite direction from the bridge and a bit farther back than we've been. Grady and I decided that watching the Teddys eat would not be a good way to begin our conclave, so we take a moving walkway to get to where we're going. It's not the fastest means, but at least we don't have to move our feet the whole way. It's a big ship, after all.

"Kayley was president of our graduating class," I say with pride. "She's interested in working in the medical field, though honestly, I bet she could do well in any career."

Kayley's delight in my talking her up is obvious. I'm cool with that —if I can make her happy, then I'm happy to make her happy, especially if seeing her happy makes me happy, too. She beams at me in her special way, and all the fuzz on the back of my neck stands straight up.

"Medical, eh?" Doc Elizabeth puts an arm around Kayley's shoulders. "Well, won't we be good friends?"

Kayley gives Elizabeth a hesitant smile.

The room we end up in reminds me of a circular cine theater, but there are no comfortable armchairs to relax in, only the standard Teddy stools—all in the ship's ubiquitous dark gray. We do our best to sit down on the squat seats while Captain Teddy and his ensemble of one white, two black, and another pink Teddy all stand to the side of the round table in the center.

Original Teddy takes a seat behind us by hopping up and launching himself off the row above with his tentacles. It's the most agile Teddy move that I've seen, and now I'm reassessing what level of physical nimbleness they can pull off.

"Conclave will now begin," Captain Teddy states. He scans all the humans with that passive Teddy-face that I've seen before. I still don't know what it means.

"Uh, Captain, perhaps it would be better to tell us what we're about to see before we see it," the colonel says. "That way we can know what to look for."

"It is self-explanatory," the captain replies. "Perception is the only requirement."

With that, everything gets dark, and the largest globe I've seen so far descends from the ceiling and ends up hovering just above the table. The screen turns on, and not long after, the Teddy ship's vid plays.

"That's the *Mursilis*," the colonel says. I hear some amount of wonder in his voice. "They're the only ship with crimson around their intake vents."

I lean forward and glance to my left, down the curved row towards where Colonel Nelson is sitting. I'm hoping to catch his reaction, but even with my eyes adjusted to the light levels on the ship, I still can't see him well. Kayley, who's sitting next to me, fixates on the globe. Her face is all confusion and disbelief. I wouldn't like to see her that way in any other situation, but right now, I could not have hoped for better.

It no longer matters to me if the vid is real or fake. I *have* to believe it, because not believing in it is a guaranteed ticket home. It's easy to believe that a war-crazy captain on our side shot first, anyway. The colonel knows, just like everyone in the Empire knows, we've got some trigger-happy officers. There was an incident not that long ago where two planets fought just because one side needed to test their new weapon.

Some in the Empire have this need to prove the superiority of their ways to everyone. I guess it makes it easier to claim planets and solar systems that way, when you believe it was yours for the taking all along. Then when you encounter a friendly alien race like the Teddys, you don't have to negotiate. You just shoot your missiles. And all this for what? More natural resources? Are the Central Planets really running out that quickly? This is exactly what used to get my father angry...but then he gave up and joined them. Now it's on me to do something, but I can't do it on my own.

I need the colonel.

As the lighting returns to dawn levels, everyone stirs. I see the colonel and his men stand straight up, clearly disturbed by what they've just seen. Perfect—it will be easier to make them agree we need the recording from that ship.

"Captain, I appreciate you showing this to us," the colonel says. "If this vid is real, it will have deep implications for this conflict. Which is why I must ask you—how sure are you it's real? Is it possible that someone manipulated this recording?"

"This is inconceivable," Captain Teddy replies. "Teddy can only be accurate."

"This...this was what you were talking about?" Kayley hisses at me as her eyebrows close the distance between them.

"Yeah. Everyone in the Empire needs to see this! One view and everyone will demand an end to the fighting! We need to—"

"We don't need to do anything but go home, Rance. That's what *we* need to do."

If I respond to her it's only going to result in me losing the argument again. I turn away and try to get the colonel's attention. He's conferring with his two aides, so a simple glance won't cut it. I give Grady a motion with my head and get up.

"Where are you going?" Kayley asks. I give her a "hold on" with my finger and walk over to the colonel. One of his aides notices me and watches as I step up to them.

"What is it, son?"

"Well, sir." I try the honorific again. "Grady and I have been discussing this, and we've realized that we're going to need to get the *Mursilis'* recording for any of this to have an impact. That's where the actual evidence is. Just like you didn't believe it, others won't believe the Teddy ship's vid, either."

The colonel nods. "That is what we were just discussing. What do you suggest we do about it?"

"We have to go get it, sir!"

"We?"

"Well, I suspect you're going to need all the help you can get." I tilt my head up and look him in the eye. "Didn't you say you might need me one day? I'm volunteering for this mission, sir."

"Rance." He gives me that grin that all parents give when they're thinking, *Look how awfully cute and naïve my child is.* "What I wanted you to understand then was how we need every eligible body to defend Angelcanis."

"But how is this different, sir? Aren't we trying to stop a war? Isn't that defending Angelcanis, too?"

Before he can reply, a hand latches on to my wrist and pulls me away. I jump, my head spinning towards my jailer.

"Sorry about that, sir," Afton says, dragging me back. "He's just really tired. I'll make sure he won't bother you again."

"It's not a problem, recruit," the colonel responds. "He happens to be right."

Kayley's enforcer drops me—gently—back onto the Teddy stool next to Warden Kayley. I wrinkle my nose at Afton, and she sneers back. So much for an intelligent discussion about this.

"Listen, Rance." Kayley leans into me and begins her talk. This is where she gives me all the logical reasons we shouldn't do something, and I have to listen. "This *is* completely amazing, and if it weren't for the situation, I'd be right there with you, but we're at *war* with the same race whose ship we're on. This isn't the place for us. We're not soldiers, and as much as the others are planning to be, Grady, Afton, and Parrish aren't yet, either."

I just nod and look down. Yes, of course she makes sense, and if it weren't for the situation, I'd let her leash me and take me back to the shuttle, where I'd go into hibernation until we were home. But I want to defend the people of my planet, just like Grady or Parrish or Afton. It's been my dream for almost as long as Parrish has wanted to join the military. The only difference is I don't want to take orders.

I've got to stay and help. It's where I belong. I can't just go home and be a babysitter when I know the truth is getting buried as we speak. I may not be a soldier, but I have to do something.

Staying here's my only option.

"Okay, let's go." The colonel's voice breaks me out of my dream and back into cold, hard reality. "Humans in this room, we've seen what we needed to see. We're headed back."

The colonel's gaze is directed at me when he speaks. I'm receiving his message loud and clear, but that doesn't mean I'll acknowledge it. I consider asking Original Teddy to do another popsicle attack, but that will only make Colonel Nelson furious. Then all potential for joining him disappears the moment he wakes up.

"Ransome Quigley He', did you hear what I just said?" the colonel says, putting his hands on his hips. "And yes, son, I am talking directly to you. You did well bringing us here to see this, and now let me return the favor by getting you back home safe. It's extremely dangerous having you all here, and I won't continue putting you at risk any longer. Understand?"

I glance at Kayley, who's looking back at me with the most glorious pools of blue that exist anywhere. I'm sure of this because I would never look into anyone else's eyes the way I look into hers.

"Let's go home, Rance," Kayley says with a hopeful smile. I don't want this to come between us, but it already has. She's the one who dropped the roadblock across the path to my dream. I get why, but I can't just lie down on this one. It's just too important to me.

"Colonel," I begin, but falter. Why? This is my chance, isn't it? All I have to do is say it and then pray to the Three Goddesses that the colonel says yes. It's a lot to ask for, but I think I deserve some positive things to happen to me after all I've been through.

"What is it, Rance?" the colonel asks.

"Colonel...sir," I say again, and now I think he's clueing into my scheme because he approaches, his hand moving down to the holster hanging off his belt.

"Out with it already," the colonel says.

"Sir, I'm not leaving."

Twenty-Three

"SON, I APPRECIATE YOUR desire to help," the colonel says. "So I'll humor you this one last time, but after that, if you decide to be difficult, my men will drag you back to the shuttle, understood? Now tell me what you think you can accomplish by staying here."

I open my mouth, but before I can speak, the ship jerks and the room blacks out. I hear Kayley gasp. She reaches out, searching for me, locking a hand on my arm when she finds me.

"What's going on?" the colonel says. "What's happened?"

We hear Captain Teddy's gruff voice say, "Malfunction is present," followed by a major disturbance of the air as if a large transport just flew by us. "Remain unmoving. Teddy will also remain."

"Upright is not recommended." That was Original Teddy from behind. "Have a seat. Safety is paramount."

"A malfunction? What kind?" The colonel mumbles something else, then he orders his men to sit.

"Mmm, ah, yes..." Doc Elizabeth chuckles. "We must be out of petrol."

"My guess is that this ship doesn't run on fossil fuels, Doctor," the colonel says, but I'm not sure if he's serious or not. The colonel is an intelligent man. I doubt he'd believe something still runs on liquified and fermented animal bones.

"I didn't mean my comment to be literal, Colonel," the doctor shoots back. "A total annihilation engine powers this ship. Sometimes some of the antimatter escapes and, well, causes problems."

"Annihilation engine?" The idea makes Grady all big-eyed. "Could the attack have damaged the shield holding the antimatter in place?"

"That is accurate, Gratin," Original Teddy says.

"What did he just call him?" I hear Afton whisper.

"That's really bad, guys," Grady says, and while I get the basic gist of the propulsion system, I don't understand the part where it gets bad. Hopefully someone will explain to us non-engineers.

"You mean," Parrish says, and I'm glad he's doing the "I don't get it" part for the rest of us. "If there's enough antimatter in containment, and the containment suddenly ruptures...there would be an instant reaction, and depending on how big, we could be history in a nanosecond."

Whoa, I wasn't expecting Parrish to be the one to make the explanation, but I shouldn't have doubted my bud to be as on point with the engineering speak as he is with calling a play in a game.

"Colonel, maybe we can help them...somehow," Parrish suggests.

"Not a bad idea," Colonel Nelson replies as he swings his light around the room, "but unless you are familiar with an alien propulsion system, I suggest we remain where we are."

A sudden jolt from the ship throws us all Parrish-height into the air. My arms flail about, trying to stabilize and prepare myself for the inevitable. I feel someone's fingers hit mine—it's Kayley. I reach out for her, and just for a moment, our hands connect, right before we—

Fall.

Kayley, Doc Elizabeth, and I let out a cry as we accelerate towards the floor. Or, I should say, the floor with a row of stools on top of it. I'm lucky. I have my hands free, which makes a difference because I don't want to get the edge of a stool in my eye.

At the last second, I make the self-sacrifice and throw my arms out, hoping to protect Kayley and Elizabeth from impact. I turn my head just enough so I don't crush my nose on something, but I still catch the edge of a stool with my forehead. That's not nearly as bad as what happens to my knee. It smashes on top of a stool seat. I also take another stool in the chest that knocks all the air out of me.

Thank the Goddesses Kayley and Elizabeth are light, though one of them is definitely a few kilos heavier than the other. I'll never tell which one. That wouldn't be gentlemanly of me. I'm also not worried about it because trying to breathe again is at the top of my priority list.

"Kayley, help me turn Rance over. He's not breathing!" Doc Elizabeth says, grabbing my sides to flip me on my back. All the while I'm gasping and struggling to get my lungs working again.

The doc switches on a light. The first thing I notice is how her face didn't escape injury, but she's still caring for me first. Kayley is also leaning over me, with serious concern in her eyes. She's not scared, just worried. I'll give her a smile to show I'm alright.

But first, air.

It comes back in stages, and I wheeze my way through a few breaths before a cough or two messes up the process. Doc Elizabeth sits me up and pats me a few times on my back until I get my rhythm back again.

"You still with us, Mr. He'?" Doc Elizabeth asks. "Or do I have to prod you with needles again?"

I cough again, but not because breathing is still a problem. From the corner of my eye, I see Kayley throw an arched eyebrow at the doctor. I imagine the devilish grin that Doc Elizabeth is giving her right now.

"Yes, by the color of your cheeks, it appears you're alive and well." Doc Elizabeth reaches up and dabs the gash above my eye with her thumb. "Now let's stop that bleeding."

As she patches me up, the others gather around her little light, staring down at me like I'm some lost pet. They're not uninjured themselves. Parrish is battered, but he's used to the rough-and-tumble of every sports match, and Grady looks like he just finished up an all-night design session. We've been better, for sure, but we're still standing. My friends are, at least. I haven't tried getting up on my smashed knee yet.

"We all here?" Parrish asks. Most of us give some form of guttural confirmation.

"Teddy is available," Original Teddy replies.

"What about the colonel and his men?" Grady asks.

"Oh my goodness, you're right!" Doc Elizabeth jumps up and finds them in short order. "They're here! The colonel is unconscious. I need some help, please!"

As Parrish and Original Teddy go to assist Elizabeth with the colonel, I slide myself over to rest my back on a stool, wincing all the way. That knee is going to be no fun when I want to get up.

We're in the dark again, but we gather in close so we can make each other out. Grady and Afton are sitting across from me, and Kayley tries standing. I hear her whimper as she puts weight on her feet and decides that sitting is better. She must have twisted her leg when we landed.

"Kayley, are you okay?" I ask.

She hums a reply that's somewhere between "yes" and "I'm not sure."

"If you need help, maybe I can give you a hand."

"Stop trying to act so tough, Rance," Afton says. "You got knocked hard. It's okay to show it."

"Offering advice now, Surela?" I smirk back at her.

"Yeah, I knew it." Afton throws a finger at me, though I feel it more than I see it. "He's fine. Same idiot as always."

"This idiot stopped me from getting hurt," Kayley says, and I try to hide my pleasure at knowing Afton just got humbled. I only wish I could have seen it happen in glorious bright light.

"Okay." Grady sighs. "So, despite the power loss, the ship seems like it's stable, and we've still got atmosphere and gravity, so I think we're doing well, all things considered."

"The colonel will want to get on the way the moment the power comes on," Kayley says. "He told me we'll have a limited time window to get back before they shut the approach to Angelcanis completely. After the Teddys attacked, they stationed an entire fleet around the planet. He also told me you were lucky to get a call through to him. If the captain of the *Nebulon* didn't patch you through his ship, the fleet would have disrupted your transmission."

"The colonel seems to talk to you a lot," I complain. Kayley just glances at me curiously.

"The colonel could try to contact his bosses," Afton suggests.

"He needs to be conscious to do that," I reply, peering over to where the doc is taking care of him. "And I need him to do something first."

"You were just complaining about him, and now you need a favor?" Kayley asks, her tone suggesting that I might have lost a few more points with her.

"Yes. He's got to get the recording from the *Mursilis*," I reply. "With that, we can expose their actions that started the war. The Empire won't continue the war after that. Then the colonel and the Teddys can talk cease-fire. With the war over, we won't have to worry about getting home."

"And the *Mursilis* is just going to let him get on board from what they consider an enemy ship and borrow the recording that implicates them?" Kayley bends down to examine my cut. "You must have really hit your head, Rance."

"Of course not. He'd have to sneak on and download a copy of the file," I reply with as much sense and reason as I can. I am dizzy, though.

"Yeah, he's brain-damaged, alright," Afton says.

"Rance is right. This war doesn't end unless we get that recording." Grady backs me up again. I'll throw him a few points for being a great friend.

"I don't want to see any more lives lost, on either side," Kayley says. "But it's not up to us to end the war."

"Then whose responsibility is it?" I counter. "The Teddys already made the first move by reaching out to the colonel. Someone on our side also needs to do the right thing, but we're the only ones who know the truth. If the colonel can do it, we should help him. If he can't or won't, then it'll be our responsibility."

As dizzy as I am, I'm feeling proud of my little speech. I think my dad would be, too. I feel a sharp pang of regret when I consider my father, but with or without him, I need to do this. If only to prove that choosing to fight for the people is the right course of action.

Grady's all the way with me, and Afton is considering it. I think she's looking for any excuse to not go home because staying out here means a chance to look for her dad. Doing so under the discipline of the military would be difficult. I'd like to help her, too, if I can.

Three pairs of eyes turn towards Kayley, our chief. Nobody contests that, and certainly no one else wants the job. But I've got to put on my boss shoes and get her to commit to this plan, or else a lot more people, and Teddys, will die.

"Okay, Rance." Kayley folds her arms. "Let's just say for a moment, we all agree to take some part in this idea of yours. First off, none of us have any training as soldiers, thieves, or whatever other requirements we might need to get on board an Imperial star cruiser. How do you suggest we do this?"

"Well, for a start, we've got Grady." Grady pumps his fist when I say his name. "He knows those ships just as well, if not better, than anyone on it. We've got the colonel for military strength, and as far as anything else, the rest of us can put it together. Let's not forget the Teddys. We don't really know what they're capable of, tech-wise. Not that they haven't already, but they may just surprise us."

Kayley's eyes pop wide, and even Afton is impressed. I bet they weren't expecting me to come up with anything, much less an entire strategy. I still don't want to be the leader, though.

"Uh..." Kayley is thinking of some way to contradict me, and I'm satisfied I got this far. True to her nature, though, it's not long before she comes up with something. "The colonel would never agree to this, Rance," she says. "As he's already stated, more than a few times, he is taking us home. No exceptions."

"Yeah, true," Grady says. "But what if we miss the deadline? That seems likely if we can't get the engine back online soon. We need power to disengage the shuttle from the dock. I'm not one for jumping from one problem to another without solving the first one. How do you propose we solve a problem we don't know how to solve?"

I grin. Grady's totally on team Rance, and not only that, he's come up with a solid comeback. I flash him a victory sign and get a foot in my shoulder from Afton for my show of support. I can tell she held back on that one. For a girl who spends a lot of time running, it could have been a lot worse.

Once again, we stump Kayley and she's not liking it. Her lower lip comes out, and she drops a side-glare my way. I'm not enjoying making the girl of my dreams angry, but I have to get this done. I really hope I'll have the chance to explain it to her so she understands.

"How do *you* propose we do that, Mr. Grady?" The colonel is up, and he's walking over to us. There's a wrap on his head that's got a little red stain on it, and he's not walking straight, but at least he's walking. He takes one look at me and nods. I think I even see a small bit of approval in his eyes.

"The only way we can, sir," Grady replies. "We do it together."

"Okay," the colonel says. "Let's talk."

Twenty-Four

YES! WE'VE GOT THE colonel opening up for discussion, and that could mean we can convince him to put our plan into action. Despite the soreness of my head and my knee, I feel a surge of energy pulse through me as I get one step closer to achieving a dream I've had since I was young. This could really be my moment!

But of course, it's not.

A sudden rumble rocks the ship and sends us tumbling across the floor. I twist and spin until I hit the table at the front of the room, whacking my sore spots hard enough that the universe flashes before my eyes. Grady and Kayley slam the table somewhere around me, with Afton not far behind.

"What now?" Afton grumbles, pushing herself up off the floor.

"Another engine shield could have ruptured," Grady says, his voice shaky. "I think anything dangerous would have vented out into space."

"That is accurate," Original Teddy says. "Recommendation for—"

"I get it," the colonel says, turning on a portable light. "Which only increases our need to leave. Everyone, get yourselves together. Immediately."

"Disembarkation is not possible."

"Listen." The colonel helps up one of his team members. "I know what we just decided, but that was before I understood how much danger we're in. We need to be off this ship now. Point us the way, Teddy."

"Excursion is not problematic. Vehicle is at issue."

"Did our shuttle get damaged?" Colonel Nelson frowns and tilts his head at our pink buddy.

"That is not accurate," Original Teddy replies. "Status of vehicle is unknown because vehicle does not exist."

"What?" It's not just the colonel asking. It's all the humans in the room.

"Intensity is unnecessary," Original Teddy says, lowering his tentacles to his ears.

"Sorry, Teddy," I say, remembering his sensitive hearing. "Your statement just surprised us."

"So, what happened to the shuttle?" asks Parrish.

"Interface was not accurate."

"You mean our jury-rigged docking port—the one that *you* designed —failed, and that jolt just knocked the shuttle loose from your ship?" I'm impressed at the colonel's deductive powers. "So we just get it when we get powered up again."

"Retrieval of vehicle unlikely," Original Teddy says.

I keep my rejoicing internal when I hear that. We're stuck here! That might be bad for the colonel and his men, but I'm not at all disappointed. This also means we have some time to figure out the best way to help the colonel retrieve the star cruiser's recording.

"And why would that be, Teddy?" the colonel asks in a very untrusting voice.

"Unknown," Original Teddy replies.

The colonel sighs. He's having the same communication issues as we did when we first came on board. I'm sympathetic.

"Colonel, if I may," Doc Elizabeth says. "What I think Teddy means is that since the ship has no power, they're unable to search for it, but they estimate it will be next to impossible to find it once the power returns."

"Why? It couldn't have floated that far away." I see the colonel's eyes get wide, and with his light underneath his face like that, he becomes the epitome of creepy. "Unless we were moving when the engine went out."

"That is accurate," Original Teddy says. "Velocity is currently..." He switches into Teddytalk. I think it's because he doesn't know the proper translation into Empire Common. I'm going to guess that whatever he said, it's plenty fast.

"With their engine, this ship is probably capable of ten times light-speed." Grady gets up and paints digits in the air with his finger. "If we were going anywhere near that, then the shuttle is long gone by now."

"Doesn't matter how fast we were going. If we can't see it on sensors, we sure as hell aren't going to find it by looking out the window," Colonel Nelson says.

All of a sudden, there's a sharp crack and a tremendous rush of air around us. The ship rolls to one side, and the colonel and his men fly past us and crash into the next row of stools as we all slide off our own. The colonel's light flashes once in our direction, then goes spinning away off some stools.

We're careening out of control, and it's dead dark again.

As we slide towards the next row, Doc Elizabeth grabs on to me, and since I was angled in Kayley's direction, I reach out to her, and she latches on to me. We all roll together until we impact the stools across the aisle, crunching into them. The ship angles again, tilting up, and we slide towards the center of the room. I begin to feel light, and a second later we all rise from the floor.

"Artificial gravity's gone!" Grady yells over the rush of the escaping air. I appreciate my friend trying to explain, but as we all float in the darkness, I think that's a given.

Grady must be somewhere off to my right, but it's hard to tell. At least the doc, Kayley, and I are all still clutching each other. Plus—small bonus—Kayley's prior death grip on my arm has turned into her arms around my waist. My mom always said to take pleasure in the little things. Especially when we're all about to suffocate. We've got to seal that air leak.

I wiggle my right arm free from Kayley's wrestler-hold so I can try to feel if we're anywhere close to hitting the ceiling. If I can grab one of those tentacle-holds, maybe we can get something across that hole, crack, or whatever it is. No breathable air in the room is a bigger problem than no gravity.

"Elizabeth!" I yell over a blast furnace's worth of noise. "Do you have your light?"

"Yes, I'll try to grab it." The doc wraps her arm about mine and lets go of my shoulder with the other. "What do you need it for?"

"Looking for the ceiling...whoa!" I feel something wrap around my outstretched arm and then realize it's Teddy's tentacle. I know he's close because that unmistakable Teddy perfume is beginning to grow in my nose.

Doc Elizabeth's light comes on, and Original Teddy is just above us with his feet planted on the ceiling. He's holding on to my arm with one tentacle while he secures himself with the other. It's a fairly convenient way to travel, especially in a zero-g environment.

"Teddy! We need to seal up that hole!" I yell. The only confirmation I get that he's heard me is that he breaks into a trot and spins. We rotate around him like a ship in close orbit. Just when I think he's going to continue spinning forever, he lets go.

This is, of course, completely unexpected, so the three of us are yelling and screaming at the top of our lungs as we hurtle towards the break in the bulkhead. Doc Elizabeth manages to aim her small medical exam light in the direction we're headed. I can make out the hole, and it's a major gap in the bulkhead. You wouldn't want to get your head near it unless you wanted someone to punt it out into space like some galactic game of kickball.

While we're doing our own impression of the ship—moving at velocity with no control or power—I realize we need to orient our feet towards the wall so we can stop ourselves with a safe part of our bodies.

"Help me turn us around! I want to put our feet on the wall rather than our heads!" I say, barely hearing my own voice. I hope they did.

It's a strange sort of wiggle that works to get us oriented in the right direction, but once we do, something occurs to me.

"What are we using to close that hole, Rance?" Kayley asks, and she just took the question right off my tongue.

"Uh..." I glance around but see nothing that might work. Even the stools are too far away to grab, and they're likely secured to the floor. Otherwise, they'd be floating around like cylindrical asteroids, threatening to knock us out.

Doc Elizabeth cries out. I turn to see what happened, and as I move, something thin and dark almost takes my eye out. It flips past and hits the bulkhead, bouncing off to head back in our direction a bit more slowly.

"Kayley, grab it! We can use that!" I yell, though I'm sure she's considering it already. What I'm wondering is where the hell it came from. With no way to turn independently from our trio of flying humans, I can't look behind us to find out.

As we impact the wall, Kayley reaches down and snatches it out of the air. I wrap my arm around her back so she doesn't lose contact and go flying off. It's a strange time to think about it, but here I am, pondering if this is the longest embrace we've ever shared.

The air rushing out of the hole shows no sign of stopping, and the noise is louder than Grady's last prototype rocket he built and launched in the field by our school. It was big enough to get out of the atmosphere, and it succeeded. I remember all of this as I pray to the Goddesses that this little patch will work. If the hole gets any larger, we could all be taking our last few breaths.

"Give it to me! My hands are free!" My voice is getting hoarse. I'm not used to this much shouting.

Kayley hands it to me and wraps both her arms around me again, freeing up my other arm. I've got the panel, or whatever it is, in both my hands, and I bend forward to put it in place. I'm hoping it'll just stick in place with the amount of vacuum on the other side.

"Rance! Don't get your hands any closer!" Kayley shouts in my ear. "You'll crush them if they're under that thing. Just push it towards the hole!"

She's right. I almost lost my fingers! I can just let it go with a little push and that should get it in place, hopefully solving our emergency. I don't even need to do that much. If I can get it in the airstream, it should just get sucked up.

It's a complete shock when the force of the air pressure rips it from my hands and sucks it towards the hole. The clang that the panel makes as it smashes against the bulkhead leaves my ears ringing long after quiet returns to the room.

"We did it!" Doc Elizabeth exclaims, and I hear Afton, Parrish, and Grady give a cheer. We all let out a collective sigh, and the two ladies on my sides give me a squeeze, grasp hands with each other, and share a smile and a moment of what I would call solid teamwork.

"Okay," Afton says with a sigh, "anything else going to go wrong today?"

Twenty-Five

"WELL." THE COLONEL RUBS the bump on the back of his head and finds the nearest stool to drop himself on. "I hate to admit it, but I think you're right, Mr. Grady. Our IFF transponder was on the shuttle, so we can call home, but no one will ever believe it's us, especially with the blockade around Angelcanis."

A short time after our latest excitement in the dark, the ship returned to normal function...mostly. We got atmosphere and lights back fairly fast, but the a-grav system took longer. I can thank Original Teddy for warning us before it kicked in. Otherwise, I would have collected another set of cuts and bruises to moan about.

"But, Colonel," Kayley interjects, "surely there's a way around that? Something you know? Isn't there someone you can trust to take your call?"

"Well, there are people I could call, but it's currently impossible to get through to them because of the heightened level of security around the planet. The Imperial military won't let a squeak pass by." The colonel sighs. "No, I'm sorry, boys and girls, but I can't get you home right now, and I need to continue my primary mission, which is to make contact and end this war. We've achieved the first objective, so ending this war is my goal from here on out."

"Colonel," I say, "we've pretty much determined that we need the recording from the SIR *Mursilis*. Especially if we want anyone in authority to believe us. Even if the Teddys don't want to fight, the captain of the *Mursilis* sure does. I bet he's not the only one."

"Rance, you're spot-on with that assessment," the colonel replies, "but there are also plenty who want an immediate end to the war. Thank the Goddesses that we may now have a way to do that."

Kayley slumps onto the stool next to Afton, who puts an arm around her. She bows her head—whether she's tired or defeated, I'm not sure, but I hope she gets her spirits back soon. We're going to need her. Kayley's always been one to bounce back quickly, so I'm not too worried.

Original Teddy ambles over to us and sits down next to me, his fuzzy head turning to examine the humans surrounding him, ending with me. I give him a curl of the side of my mouth, and he puffs up his cheek in reply.

"What do you think, Teddy?" I ask. "Any chance of you getting us back home with some kind of fancy tech that you haven't told us about yet? Maybe you've got a shuttle you'd be willing to loan us?"

He pops and clicks like an ancient analog clock setting its own time. I'm thinking that means no, but I'm waiting for him to respond. Based on my experience, he might not, but I wait a minute, just in case.

"Possibility is unlikely. Teddy achievement is monumental," he replies. "Ship also not completed. Maintenance is required."

What I think he's trying to say is the ship needs more work. This could mean they could do something if the ship was working, or it could just mean we'd better find some fast-drying adhesive and keep this thing from coming apart.

"Alright, listen up," the colonel commands, and we all snap our attention his way. "We need to lay some ground rules about this mission. Firstly, none of you are to put yourself in any more of a risky position than you are in right now. That means my team and I are the only ones to board the *Mursilis*. We can come up with a legitimate reason for being there—you can't. If you're caught on that ship, they could shoot you on sight."

"Does that mean we're really going to do this?" I'm mostly asking because I want to hear him say it.

"It means that I'm going to need your help, yes, but only while you're stuck here. The moment I can get you home, you're going. Other than that, I think you're probably as safe as anyone could be in the middle of a war."

"Thank you, Colonel," Kayley says. "Thank you for protecting us."

"My pleasure, Kayley," the colonel says, and he smiles at her. Seeing them share a moment makes my jaw tighten and my hands crunch into fists. Not sure why that is; the colonel isn't interested in her that way...is he? Or worse yet, is Kayley interested in him? I can't think about that, or I'm going to give myself a heart attack, and Afton will laugh all the way to my cremation.

"I'm going to need you to look out for your squad, too," Colonel Nelson says as he stands and starts to pace around. "Which brings me to rule number two—chain of command. We must have discipline in this matter, which means when I give an order, it must be followed. Kayley is squad leader, and that means she's in charge of you. She will make sure that everything I want you kids to do gets done. Are we clear on that?"

"Sir, yes, sir!" Afton and Parrish reply with gusto. The colonel drops his eyes down at me, awaiting my response.

"I got it," I say with a nod.

"Good. Now, last one, number three: though I know some of you wanted to sign up, you are not yet soldiers. Don't let your enthusiasm get in the way of good judgment. That means if there's a safer way to do something, you choose it *every time*. Not sometimes, not most of the time, but always. Is that understood?"

He gets his hearty acknowledgment once again from everyone, and even I give a half-hearted "Aye, sir." I can appreciate that he's looking out for us, even respect him for it. I'm *almost* willing to admit this one stiff-necked officer is actually a good guy. Especially if he gets that recording.

"Outstanding. Now let's get down to organizing our plan of attack." He sits back down, and Doc Elizabeth joins us as well. I can't see his two men, so I'm guessing they're still laid out.

"Let's start with what we know."

"Well, we know which ship allegedly did the firing," Grady says.

"Good. The *Mursilis*, that's Captain Hattusa's ship," Colonel Nelson says. "He's a gun-and-go kind of commander and would certainly shoot first at something that didn't look right to him. Though I have a feeling that he's not solely responsible for that decision. We'll get to that. What else?"

"We know the Teddys didn't start it," I try.

"Well, we *think* the Teddys didn't start it, Rance, or maybe we can say we want to believe that."

"We did not," Original Teddy says.

"We believe you, Teddy." Kayley tries to sound supportive of our fuzzy friend. He clucks in reply. I think that might be a thank-you.

"Colonel, the Teddys reached out to you to stop the fighting," Parrish says. "Isn't that enough?"

"I wish it was," Colonel Nelson replies. "Other than my local command, there's no other attempt to end this. None that I know of, anyway."

"No one on the other end of the spiral cares about a war against a bunch of furballs," Afton says. I think she's a bit cynical about the Empire's attempts to find her dad. I can't blame her. Making his daughter join the military as the only means of finding him is not sitting well with me, either.

Kayley wraps an arm around Afton. I can tell she also heard the despair in Afton's tone. Both of us have always been the sensitive ones in the gang. Grady too, sometimes, but he's never been one to act on his feelings. That's because his parents discouraged it.

"Your comment is valid, Miss Jee, but not something we need to consider," the colonel says. "Why don't we change over to what we don't know?"

"We don't know the location of the *Mursilis*," I suggest.

"Excellent, Rance. Intelligence about the ship and its location *and* the location of the data inside of the ship are all key to the mission. We need to know everything we can about that ship: armaments, crew strength and makeup, insertion and excursion points, and security capabilities. If I can get into the command net, we can find that information."

"Can you hack into it and create an IFF ident for us then, too?" Grady asks.

"Son, those systems and networks are not even remotely connected," the colonel replies. He sounds a bit disappointed in Grady, as if he expected him to know that. My friend is a genius with ships and their design, but he actually slacked off during networking class. That's another thing his parents got on him about.

"Teddy can gain admittance," Original Teddy says, and we all turn to him, expecting more. I'm not sure why we would expect more, since I already know that if there were more to say, Teddy would have said it.

"Then can *you* hack into it and create an IFF ident for us?" Grady asks with a chuckle.

"Nonsense," Original Teddy replies.

"Worth a try." Grady shrugs.

"Okay, what else? Either know or don't know." The colonel gets us back on track again.

"What are we going to do with the data once we get it?" Kayley asks.

"Tell *everyone*," Parrish says, with a lot of emphasis on the second word. "Absolutely everyone."

"True, but not exactly everyone." The colonel raises his finger to make a literal point. "Not at first, anyway. We'll need to get this to the people we can trust and any media outlet that isn't completely loyal to the Empire. I'm sure plenty of officers in the higher echelon would want to protect Captain Hattusa and his crew. Once the recording is out, we'll know exactly who's on our side and who isn't."

"There's something we don't know." I point out.

"Duly noted, Mr. He'." He glances around. "So if we put all of this together, we get our mission objectives: locate the *Mursilis*, find out its strengths and weaknesses, rendezvous with her, get on board, get the recording, and return—safely—then get the information to someone who can get it out to the populace. Are we missing anything?"

"Yes, sir," Afton says. "We haven't talked about the other side."

"Other side of what, Jee?"

"I think she means the Teddys," Kayley translates, though I bet the colonel would have gotten there on his own. He gives a nod of understanding.

"Well." The colonel looks down at Teddy, sitting next to me, happily making braids out of his tentacles. "I think we have some time to discuss that."

Twenty-Six

ABOUT AN HOUR LATER, we find ourselves back in the canteen, and Grady and I are dreading the slaughter fest that is going to occur with a nearly full room full of multicolor Teddys. Because of the ship maintenance—that's still going on, by the way—a lot of the Teddys didn't eat at their normal time, and I guess a little anxiety can make anyone hungry. That said, I can't believe how quiet it is in this packed room.

It goes exactly as expected, with those of us unfamiliar with Teddy eating habits losing their appetites and turning shades lighter than their natural skin tone. One of the colonel's men even loses what was left of his last meal, and he's escorted back to Doc Elizabeth's med room to calm his stomach.

So, after that uncomfortable experience, we open the dialogue with Original Teddy and his captain.

"So, Teddy," the colonel says, crunching on a bit of black celery, "we've seen your recording, and we're planning to retrieve the recording from our Empire's ship. Provided it shows us what we all expect to see, and provided we can get it out to the public at large, what will the Teddy, er, collective do once that happens?"

"Teddy will talk with everyone," comes the captain's ambiguous answer.

"That would be everyone in your...government?" the colonel asks.

"That is not accurate. Teddy does not administer."

"You don't have a government?" Kayley asks, her hands playing with a bit of the cabbage. I think she's hungry, but her eyes keep darting anxiously past the captain to see tentacles flying around, and she's thinking twice about putting any of it in her mouth.

"That is accurate. Administration is unnecessary," the captain states.

"Cool," says Grady.

"So then," the colonel says, "you will tell...everyone?"

Doc Elizabeth interrupts. "Colonel, the Teddys have a mechanism by which it is possible for all Teddys to learn about something that one Teddy experiences. It's a technology they have developed to govern themselves with no governing body. If there is discord with one or more of them, it becomes a problem that all of them will solve."

"I see. Thank you for the explanation, Doctor," the colonel says, and the doc smirks and points her finger at him.

I wish the Empire ran like that. Instead, we've got a Parliament that never seems to get anything done and a monarch with questionable priorities.

"So, Captain," Colonel Nelson continues, "you are aware that our shuttle is lost, and as we have already discussed, getting back to our planet is unlikely until we can get those ships to leave orbit. We're pushing forward with locating the Imperial ship that attacked your ship, allegedly starting this conflict. To do that, I am asking for your assistance. Would you help us find the SIR *Mursilis* and get on board?"

Captain Teddy does not respond, and the colonel frowns. I think he was expecting a prompt answer, but he's forgetting that we're dealing with an alien race, and they don't always act in ways that humans understand. I'm positive they'll help, though. As Doc Elizabeth mentioned, they want an end to this conflict. Just like most humans, it goes against their nature to have continued strife.

"Captain?" the colonel tries again. "What do you think?"

Still nothing.

The colonel is getting flustered, and I don't know how much longer he can handle the Teddy silent treatment. It wouldn't be good if he gets angry. We need to figure this one out, like now.

I turn to Original Teddy for some help, though I have to wait for him to stop chewing. In fact, I need to turn away completely until he's done.

Ugh.

"Teddy, this ship can locate the human ship on the recording, right?" I ask.

"That is accurate. Teddy is aware of its location," Original Teddy replies, as if he hadn't even heard any of what the colonel said before.

"Wait...you already know where it is?" The colonel is exasperated, and I pat myself on the back for being smarter than a guy twice my age who should be an expert at discussing military matters. "How do you know that?"

"Teddy is aware," Captain Teddy confirms, which doesn't answer the question.

"The Teddy ship that recorded the video may have tracked the *Mursilis*, sir," Grady offers. The colonel purses his lips and nods. That sounds to me like a reasonable answer, even if it's not exactly the truth.

"Where is she? Can you take us to the location of the *Mursilis*?" the colonel pushes.

"Unlikely," comes the captain's reply. It's disappointing but kind of expected. If the *Mursilis* is in Imperial space, then it's going to be a big ask to sneak this ship across the front lines and get hitched up so we can hop on. Of course, that's another problem entirely.

"Teddy, how did you get this ship down onto our planet without us noticing?" Grady asks, like he's cooking up an idea.

"Teddy ship can pretend," Captain Teddy explains.

"Pretend what?" the colonel asks.

"Make pretend," Original Teddy says.

The other Teddys in the room shuffle out, finished with devouring small, innocent creatures. They're heading back to their stations to fix whatever is left to fix. At least that's what I'm thinking. I wonder if they have recreation time or if they ever sleep. It's not the time to do a study, but I file it away as something to talk to Doc Elizabeth about later.

"This is completely frustrating." The colonel sighs. I can empathize. Understanding Teddy Common is not that easy and takes a bit of imagination.

"Maybe what Teddy means is that they can pretend *towards* an Imperial ship," Grady suggests.

"What do you mean, Sugiyama?" The colonel drops all polite behavior and swivels on his seat to aim towards Grady. "Are you suggesting that they can spoof our IFF systems?"

"No, not exactly, sir. I don't think they can pretend to be an Imperial ship...I think they can pretend to be anything *other than* a ship." Now we've all swiveled on him, anticipating further explanation.

"Okay, interesting," the colonel comments. "Do you mean they can pretend to be...atmospheric vapor if they want to?"

"Something like that, sir," Grady replies.

The colonel grabs his chin with his hand and rubs. We're all musing like that, considering how we can use this new possibility. Atmospheric vapor is not something that happens in space. That's why the name includes the word "atmospheric." There's none of that in the vacuum of space—exactly why they call it a vacuum!

"We could spoof them into thinking we were meteoroids, or space dust, or solar wind for that matter," Grady suggests.

"Maybe we could pretend to be some kind of anomaly," Parrish says. "That could draw them to us to investigate."

"Excellent suggestions, both of you." The colonel grins. "This could be exactly what we need to get close enough."

Of course, now that the colonel has decided to stop communicating with the Teddys, he's neglecting one major point: just because they said their ship can do what we require doesn't mean they *will* do that for us. The captain said before that it was unlikely that we can sneak up on the *Mursilis*. Now, I can't speak for what goes on in a Teddy's brain—or brains if they have more than one—but without confirmation of their assistance, we might as well be designing a new garden for my mom. At least we'd be guaranteed help there.

Now that I've gone and put the worry about my mom back into the forefront of my thoughts, I'll need to find a way to push it back down again. I'm sure she's okay, so let me think...What else can I apply my brainpower to?

"Teddy." Kayley gets their attention. "Could this ship pretend to be ionized hydrogen gas or something like that?"

"Camouflage is possible," replies Captain Teddy.

"If you did that, could an Imperial ship still detect us as a ship?" Kayley continues, and I get excited to see if she's onto something.

"Unlikely," comes the second confirmation from the captain. All the humans, including Grady, turn their attention away from him and towards Kayley.

"So could you help us sneak up on the *Mursilis* so we can get on board?" As Kayley finishes her question, I hear a collective inhale and hold from everyone, including myself.

"Unlikely," the captain replies, and our exhale becomes a mutual sigh. I'm thinking that the Teddys aren't turning down our request for support, however. They're just expressing their doubt about the plan, and it's getting jumbled in translation. I decide to test out my theory.

"Captain Teddy," I say, trying to choose my words carefully and keep in mind what Doc Elizabeth said earlier about the way they share their problems. "We all want to stop this war, right?"

"That is accurate, Rancid," the captain replies, and for the sake of the team, I'll ignore the name-calling for now. "Cessation of conflict is paramount."

"So, in order to do that, we need to get the recording from the ship that shot the Teddy ship, right?"

"That is also accurate," the captain replies again.

"What are you onto, son?" the colonel inquires, but gets shushed by Kayley and Afton. He grumbles something, but I don't hear it because I'm trying to keep my focus on Teddy syntax.

"Okay, then, we need our ship to pretend it's space gas so we can sneak up on the *Mursilis* and get the colonel and his men on board. Isn't that accurate?"

"You are accurate, Rancid."

We're almost there, but I still need to tread carefully. If I take a wrong turn, we might be back at square one.

"So..." I take a deep breath. "Let's go to where the *Mursilis* is and pretend to be something other than a ship, okay?"

The captain doesn't answer, and my heart drops out of my chest and falls down to my feet. Man, I was so close! I thought I had done everything right and gotten my point across in a way that the Teddys would understand. I guess I have a long way to go to figure them out.

The captain clicks twice, and I throw a slow glance over to him, waiting for him to turn us down.

"Delays must occur," the captain says, and I raise a curious eyebrow at his statement. "Renovation is paramount, then rendezvous is possible."

"I think he just said we can go once they fix the ship," Grady says.

"That is accurate, Gratin," confirms Original Teddy, and everyone cheers. Original Teddy joins in by creating a sound that sounds like me gargling my cold medicine.

"Captain," the colonel says amongst the rejoicing, "can your ship still connect to the Imperial network while repairs are happening? I need to get the data about the *Mursilis*."

"Potential is possible," replies Captain Teddy. "Risk of discovery is increased."

"I understand, Captain," Colonel Nelson says with a bit of a grin forming. "But you need not worry. No one will ever find out that I was there."

Twenty-Seven

"WE'RE ALMOST READY, TEDDY," the colonel says, his jaw tight as he drops himself onto a short stool in front of the terminal that the Teddys set up. It's just a few of us here in this back-closet space, mainly because no one else can fit. Why the Teddys chose it, I have no idea. I'm also confounded that they've provided an actual physical keyboard and touchpad for the colonel to use. Original Teddy says they made it, but...when did they have time to do that? It's only been like two hours since we came up with the idea.

"Do you think we can get access, Colonel?" Kayley asks, her arms folded. We're sharing a W-shaped corner to lean on in what is the darkest part of the room. It's all dark, really, and except for the colonel we're the only humans in here. So besides Original Teddy and his squat little Blue Buddy, there's not much else to look at. Teddys don't decorate much.

"Well, without knowing alien tech, it's hard to say, though it worked once before. That's how they contacted me," the colonel replies. That's not at all surprising for me to hear. Not after I just saw the keyboard, the touchpad, and before the hypo launcher they built to Grady's exact specs. On Angelcanis, we can rapid prototype stuff, too, but not at this level of sophistication.

That's where the rest of the gang is now, learning how to use the thing. The colonel's men saw it in action. It shoots a tranquilizer needle about as far as Parrish can throw a ball, which is far, and they liked it instantly. They mentioned something about not wanting to kill anyone, which sounds good. I just hope they're not trying to sedate themselves right now.

"System is ready," Original Teddy confirms after a few clicks and whistles from his Blue Buddy.

"Okay, let's go," says the colonel. He even cracks his knuckles before hitting the keyboard in a flurry of keystrokes. If Kayley hadn't rolled her eyes, I definitely would have.

As the colonel types away, we begin to see responses, which gets my interest. Could it really be this easy to use Teddy tech to break into our own Empire's highly secure military system?

Nope.

"Nuts," the colonel says and snaps his fingers before diving back in again. Kayley leans back against the wall. She's not concerned, so neither am I. It's just one denial of access, so no reason to panic.

But after the third and fourth time, Kayley's face gets sour, and Colonel Nelson slaps both his legs and lets out a sigh.

"Colonel, don't we have to start worrying about getting detected?" I ask, trying to sound as casual as possible.

"No, it takes several million attempts before an alert is created. That's because a hack is usually done by massive computer systems hitting that many attempts a second. A handful shouldn't cause any major alarms. It's when we get in that we've got to be the most cautious."

"How do you even know how to do this? Aren't you just a, uh, standard lieutenant colonel?" I follow up because these seem like some major intelligence techniques the colonel is knocking out. Plus, I'm wondering how he's had so much practice at it that he's that quick.

"They teach you this as a cadet, son," the colonel replies with a matter-of-fact tone.

Wait, cadets can hack into one of the most secure systems in the entire Empire? I find that hard to believe. I think there's more to Colonel Nelson than he wants us to know. If that's the case, I'm glad he's on our side. Let's just hope he's as good as he's not saying he is.

I'm still in amazement that I'm here, working with a military guy that I wouldn't have even said hello to a week ago. While I'm not ready to give all members of the military, or the government, a pass, Colonel Nelson is now on my cool list, along with Afton's dad.

I really hope Commander Jee is alive. For his sake as well as Afton's. Knowing what I know now, I wonder what really happened. I can't believe that the Teddys blew up his ship. It could have been friendly fire. Or worse—someone could have blown up the ship to cover up for Captain Hattusa's aggressive action.

"Yes!" Colonel Nelson claps his hands, breaking the tension, and we focus on him again. "We're in."

"Well done," Original Teddy says. I think he likes using that phrase. Hopefully, he thinks it means what it actually means.

Kayley and I get closer to peer over the colonel's shoulder. A regular info prompt now shows on the screen, ready to accept whatever requests for information he is looking for. I wish Grady were here to see this in action. Other than the minor hiccup getting in, you'd never know we were on an alien ship talking to our own network. Except for that smell, of course.

"Okay, Rance, get ready to copy this code down."

My breathing gets tight. There's absolutely nothing in here that I can do that with. There's probably nothing on this ship that I can use. Well, maybe with a few lessons, there might be something.

"Uh, Colonel, I don't have a stylus, tablet, or really anything I can do that with."

"Oh no? Here." He pulls a stylus out of his shirt pocket and hands it to me. I accept it, but this is only half of the problem—this thing can't write on the air. I need a tablet.

"It can write on the wall," Kayley explains, noting my distress. She leans in. "And it's luminescent."

"Ah." I can't think of anything more to say than that. Kayley's *really* close. Our noses are almost touching, and while she's never had a problem with removing the personal space between us, I can't say the same for myself. The heat is already hitting my cheeks, and that's saying a lot in the cave-chill temperature the Teddys keep in the ship.

"What?" Kayley asks with a frown, and then her own self-consciousness makes her pull back. She's still looking at me with the expectation of an answer, so I swallow and try to come up with one.

"Ready, Rance? Take this down." The colonel comes to the rescue, and he just jumped up a few positions on my cool list. I may start awarding him points soon. "78D437I_I059NE2," the colonel says, and I struggle to keep up. "Got that?"

"Yeah, I got it." Just barely, that is.

"Okay, coming quick, two more sequences. Make sure you get these. We don't have a lot of time."

"Ready," I say, expecting another code similar to the one he just gave me. That one wasn't too bad, and I got it down with relative ease, so I'm in chill mode.

"42P6OR32S17DFW3_L54GT038XV994ML   and PP453JU7N1NL29A_BD98FX01SM20WQ7 Got that?"

What the heck? What happened to the easy code from before? Even in this cool climate, I think I'm sweating.

"Got it?" the colonel asks again, this time with an itch of impatience.

"Wait! I'm trying to remember the second code! I mean the first of the second, or—"

"We don't have time for you to fumble around, Rance!" the colonel shouts. I see Kayley wince at the sound of his voice in this tiny space. "I need all those numbers back to me now, or in fifteen seconds, we're going to get spotted!"

"78D437II059NE242P6OR32S17DFW3L54GT038XV994MLPP453JU7 N1NL29ABD98FX01SM20WQ7," Original Teddy says, like a water sprinkler in rapid-fire mode.

The colonel turns on our little pink and fuzzy friend, wide-eyed. "You memorized that just from the one time I said it?"

"That is accurate," Original Teddy replies. "Teddy has uploaded the sequence."

"I think what he means is that he used their brain-networking to record the codes, Colonel," Kayley explains.

"Okay, whatever, great. Teddy, give me the first seven!"

We watch in awe as Original Teddy repeats back character after character as the colonel requests them. He makes no mistakes—at least I think he doesn't—and never even pauses to think about if the number or letter he just gave was correct. I would have had to double-check several times, and even then, I might have gotten confused.

"Thank you, Teddy. Well done," the colonel says, and Original Teddy vibrates in what I can only guess is self-satisfaction.

"What were all those codes for, Colonel?" Kayley asks.

"Just a second, I'm not finished."

Once again, we wait in silent anticipation as the colonel taps through another series of commands and responses. After a few rounds of this, a huge chunk of data streams down the terminal screen, and now I'm wishing the Teddys had brought a bigger screen to this closet. I also see a map of our target, but only for a microsecond.

"Was that the *Mursilis*?" I ask.

"Shush, let me concentrate," the colonel commands. "We're already past our deadline."

"What's that mean?" Kayley sneaks around the corner just enough to rub shoulders with me. She must be cold. I've got no problem with it.

"Meaning we're in serious danger of being found out any moment," I whisper.

It takes about another two minutes before the colonel gets Original Teddy to memorize some more numbers, then makes a hasty exit from the system. He even gets the Teddys to turn off the terminal before he spins around with a prolonged breath.

"We got her," the colonel says, "I needed those codes to spoof the system into thinking we were another cruiser, looking for data on the *Mursilis*...Thank the Goddesses it worked."

"So that means we're safe? We didn't get caught?" I flash an upbeat grin at Kayley, who returns it.

"Looks that way." Colonel Nelson stands up. "Excellent job, everyone. Let's get underway and get that evidence!"

Twenty-Eight

AS WE HAPPILY STEP our way out of our stuffy closet, an alarm echoes throughout the ship. We pause and glance at each other. A thousand bad thoughts go through my brain. I can only wonder what disaster is about to befall us.

"Teddy, what's going on, more engine trouble?" I ask.

"That is not accurate. Scan is occurring," Original Teddy replies.

"What kind of scan? Are we checking the ship for more damage?"

"That is not accurate."

"Well, what's going on then?" the colonel asks, out of patience.

"Spider is scanning," Teddy replies. It's the kind of answer I'd expect from Teddy, but it still doesn't tell us much. All I can imagine is that one of us tracked an insect on board, and now they're trying to get rid of it.

"Who is Spider?" The colonel is determined to sort this out. "An enemy? A friend? Should we be concerned?"

"Spider belongs to human federation," Teddy replies, giving us a little more to go on. The colonel then beats us to the conclusion. As his eyes go wide, I can tell he's broken through the Teddyspeak and gotten the answer he wants.

"Spider probes!" he says and curses up a storm. "They tracked us after all."

"Who did, Colonel?" Kayley asks. I'm sure the answer will come to her before he can respond.

"They must have traced our hack to this sector. If they've already spotted us, we're in trouble." The colonel turns to Original Teddy. "Did they?"

"That is not accurate. Spider is scanning adjacently," Original Teddy replies. "Identity is likely."

"Then I need to see the captain," the colonel replies. "I think I have a way to avoid detection."

Original Teddy clicks and whizzes, then takes off down the corridor. Blue Buddy follows right after, and now it's just three humans standing around, staring stupidly at each other. The colonel decides not to wait for an invitation and jets after them, dodging the low-hanging stuff on the ceiling as he goes.

Before I can have another thought, Kayley grabs my hand and drags me after her. I struggle to keep up as I'm looking out for my head and feet. This is faster than I've ever known Kayley to run. If Afton was racing us, my KayKay would be challenging her for first place.

"Hey, hey! Slow down!" I cry, hoping she will dump some velocity before we careen into a wall. I'm still tender from my little wounds, and I'm not looking to add to the collection.

"We can't!" Kayley shoots back. "We'll lose the colonel!"

Luckily, we make it to the bridge before we smash into anything hard. I'd expect that's where the captain would be at a time like this. The colonel is already there, breathing hard for someone on active duty. He's not out of shape, but I guess when you're that far from your boot camp days, it shows.

He's already discussing his ideas with Captain Teddy when we trot up to him. Their conversation is not without its pitfalls, but I think the colonel is getting through.

"So if you can transmit a wide-band SHF or EHF with a full-amplitude static frequency oscillation, you should be able to overwhelm their sensors," the colonel says.

Captain Teddy considers that for a moment, then clicks twice. He turns to a Teddy at a set of terminals next to him and zips and whistles. He looks back at the colonel and drops his tentacles to his sides. I'm guessing that's not a good thing, but I'm still hopeful.

"Oscillation is not periodically frequent. Recommend increasing," Captain Teddy says.

I have no idea what that means, but it doesn't matter. If the colonel understands, then that's enough.

"Look," Kayley whispers into my ear and turns me towards one of the big screens. She points to a pair of dots with Teddy scrawl next to them. I've seen this screen before, so I know it's the Teddy ship's long-range scan. It's showing our position in relation to the probes. I also see two other things: the probes are getting closer, and...we're not moving.

"Do you think they fixed the engine?" I ask Kayley. She won't know any more than I will, but I still hope for a confident answer from her to calm my nerves.

"No idea," Kayley says, and that's the best answer she can give. So much for my nerves.

"Captain, I don't recommend you oscillate the amplitude like that," the colonel says. I can only imagine how difficult it must be to explain scientific concepts to an alien race. On top of that, we're in a dire situation and words need to be kept short, so that's not helping, either.

"Half percentage is recommended," the captain counters. What that actually means is anyone's guess. They might be discussing a phase adjustment, but I'm no engineer. Grady might know...if he were here. I don't think we've got time to go ask him.

"I don't know about that, Captain," the colonel replies, "but we need to do something now, or we're going to get spotted."

"Understood."

The captain turns back to the Teddy next to him and clicks and whistles, to which the Teddy taps a sequence of buttons and whirs a response. Captain Teddy glances up at the screen we've been watching and waits for something. Following him, we do the same.

"What's he looking for?" Kayley asks the colonel.

"Not sure, exactly, but I'd guess he wants to see what the probes do based on the frequency settings he just put into their transmitter. If it works, then we're safe."

We turn back to the screen to watch the probes as they drift ever closer. There's not much else we can tell from the screen than that, and that's what's causing an ache in my brain. This is different from the *Nebulon* attacking us. The probes won't shoot at us if they come within range...at least I think not. I'm not about to ask the colonel if spider probes have weapons. I'm afraid of what the answer will be.

Then again, there's what happens after the probes discover us.

"Broadcast is not effective," Captain Teddy says.

The colonel drops his head and grimaces. But, to his credit, he's not ready to give up yet. He rubs his jaw and gives another glance at the screen. "What weapons do you have on this ship?" the colonel asks. "We could try to destroy them before they get in range. It's not the best option, but it's better than not doing anything."

"Eradication is not possible," Captain Teddy replies, and I'm worried that means what I think it means.

"Not possible?" The colonel's gaze shoots upwards. He's deciphering the meaning, and as I watch his frown deepen, I think he's come to the same conclusion I have. "So you really have no weapons on this ship?"

"That is not accurate."

Okay, well, that's better than I thought, but I have a feeling it still doesn't help us. The ship could have weapons, but they might not be effective against the probes, or they could just have small weapons, like a rifle or a pistol. Any explanation, provided quickly, would be helpful.

I glance up at the screen and see a blue circle around the probes— likely their scanning range. At the rate they're moving, they'll find us in just a handful of minutes. I don't know how I can help, but I'm not standing here and keeping silent any longer.

"Captain," I say, "did you mean that there are weapons mounted on the ship, or there are only handheld weapons available?"

"It doesn't really matter." The colonel's lament cuts off any response from Captain Teddy. "As the captain said, whatever they have won't solve our problem."

"Then what will?" Kayley asks, glancing between the colonel and the screen. "Can we run?"

"The moment we power on engines, they'll know we're here," the colonel replies. "The probes don't have a passive scan limitation for engine thrust."

Another alarm goes off, and while it's still not as annoying as a human one, this one has more urgency. We three humans all glance at the captain for an answer, but it's Original Teddy who replies.

"Guests are available," he explains while the captain warbles with a few of his bridge staff. I still can't decipher Teddy emotions, but their energy just jumped by a level of magnitude. Tentacles are waving and pointing in various directions, and their voices pitched up an octave. Whatever is occurring must be serious.

Rather than explain further, Original Teddy points to the screen. There's another dot that's appeared there. I take his meaning and pair it with the new target, and my stomach feels sick.

"That's a ship," the colonel says. "I can't tell whose it is or what their intentions might be, but if that's an Imperial star cruiser, their scan could reach us. Which means—"

"A big problem," Kayley finishes. If I were less concerned about getting killed, it might upset me that my girlfriend-to-be is finishing another man's sentence.

"Teddy, is that one of your ships?" I ask.

"That is not accurate," Original Teddy replies. Not what I was hoping to hear. In less than a minute, either the probes or that ship will know about us.

"Teddy, what about the pretend thing? Can we just hide from the ship's scans with that?"

"Pretend not available," Captain Teddy replies.

"Why not?" the colonel asks, his face getting red. "We just planned an entire mission around the assumption that we could camouflage!"

"Colonel," Kayley says, her voice soft, "perhaps we can figure that out later?"

The colonel glances at her and lets out a sigh. He knows she's right, but he's freaked, just like all of us. He shakes his head and stares at the floor. For a moment, I think he's ready to give up. Then he turns on me, and I take a step back.

"Rance, what do you think we should do?" he asks.

"Me?"

"Yes, I'm asking your opinion."

"We really need to get out of here," I say. "If we can't hide or fight, all we can do is run, scan be damned. We'd just better do it fast."

"Agreed, Rance," the colonel replies, and he turns to the captain. "If we can't fight a probe, then we've no hope against an Imperial star cruiser. Are the engines operational?"

"Percentage is likely," Captain Teddy replies. "Control not guaranteed."

"Not guaranteed?" I echo, letting that sink in. It sounds like we've got the power to the engines, but they might not work as expected. That's a problem. If we can't stop, we could run into something big, like a star. There's no coming back from a collision like that. But we can't very well sit around here and wait to be detected.

"Captain, it's your ship, so the final call is yours, but we seem to have no other options."

"Agreed," Captain Teddy says. "Prepare for secure. Speed is imminent."

"Rancid recommended to expedite," Original Teddy says and heads towards the exit. He glances back once, and I guess that means we should follow.

This time, I grab Kayley's hand.

Twenty-Nine

"WHAT DID THEY MEAN by secure?" I ask as we race down the hallway after Original Teddy and Blue Buddy.

"We're about to go very fast. Faster than even I've gone before," the colonel explains, right behind us. "Things get peculiar at multiples of the speed of light, or so I've been told. Based on my FTL training, we'll need to prepare ourselves for some unusual phenomena. In fact, we should find somewhere to lie down and secure ourselves."

"What? Why?" Kayley demands. "Is acceleration the problem?"

"That is not accurate," Original Teddy answers.

"Allegedly, you might see something that's not real and hurt yourself trying to run away from it." Colonel Nelson isn't joking. That flat face he's giving us right now says it all. "I don't know how or if the Teddys handle it, but we can't take a chance."

"There is no complication for Teddy. It is pleasant," Original Teddy says, always on point with the answers.

"Got it, Colonel," Kayley says. "Maybe we should go back to the doctor's space and get strapped in there."

"Possibility not available," Original Teddy says. "Acceleration is imminent."

"Whoa, wait! Where do we go then?" I stare at him, the lump in my throat growing.

Kayley and I share a hysterical glance, but happily, it doesn't last. The light goes on in Kayley's head, and she squeezes my hand and smiles. I don't know what she's onto, but I'm hoping, as usual, that she's going to save us all.

"Teddy, do you have berths—sleeping quarters—for us? Can we get to them in time?"

Original Teddy turns to his Blue Buddy, and they click and chirp at each other for a few seconds. I'm still trying to commit their sounds and patterns to memory, but they're just random nonsense to my adrenaline-boosted brain.

"Teddy says possible. We shall entourage." Both Teddys move out at a speed none of us three humans were expecting or can match. We push forward as fast as possible, but we're already low on rocket fuel after our last running competition. Original Teddy and Blue Buddy stop and turn to wait for us.

The moment the two of them lay their massive globe-eyes on us, they spin and burst down the corridor, legs and tentacles rocketing them forward. We try to mimic their movements as best as we can, but we suck at it, and we return to running. We're not that far behind when they stop along a section of the corridor that has repeating diamond holes every few meters.

Blue Buddy pops his tentacle into the hole, and the wall dissolves to open into darkness. I lean in and try to glimpse what's there, but it's not possible to see more than an arm's length inside.

"Colonel is recommended," Original Teddy says. The colonel dives in without another second lost, but he must have forgotten something because he pops back out, looking at Kayley and me.

"Wait!" the colonel says before the wall seals up completely. "The two of you, keep your eyes closed, and under no circumstances should you leave your berth. Got it? Be safe!"

As he disappears, the ship accelerates. It's not bad at first, but as the seconds tick by we've got to grab a handle on the ceiling or risk flying down the corridor. Neither of us want to splatter like red paint all over the Teddys' nice wall. I thought we were going fast when we ran from the *Nebulon*, but this is completely different.

Blue Buddy dissolves the wall across the hallway and beckons us in.

"Rancid, K-K-Kayley, immigrate immediately," Original Teddy squeaks. "Peril is now possible."

"Wait, I thought you said acceleration wasn't a problem! And what about you?" I shout as Kayley shoves me through the portal. I'm stunned at the change in tone from Teddy, and perspiration drips down my forehead. I'm not worried about us. We've got our space now, but for the Teddys still out in the hallway, and on the rest of the ship...

"Teddy will not be compromised, do not discomposure."

The portal closes behind us, and the space brightens enough for us to see. Kayley scans around for a bed but instead finds a flat pad on the ground surrounded by a short wall. It reminds me of something you might put your baby in so they don't crawl away.

Kayley pulls me in and down into the Teddy crib. She orients herself so that the force of the acceleration pushes down on her feet as if she's standing, and I follow along. It's a good plan, and if I wasn't still preoccupying myself with the distress in Original Teddy's voice, I'd have thought of it myself.

"Rance, what are you doing?" Kayley's voice is full of stress. "Get back in here!"

"I *am* here, KayKay, right next to you. What are you talking about?" Then I glimpse Kayley walking into the berth from outside. I blink, but she's still there, looking down at me. Another blink, and then she's gone.

"Wait, Kayley, why are you out?" I say, now completely confused.

"What are you talking about, Rance? I'm inside! Right here!"

It hits both of us simultaneously—the phenomenon that the colonel was talking about. We're experiencing it, and it's getting worse. The walls become transparent, and now we can see through the ship's entire structure, straight out to space. I shut my eyes, take a deep breath, and hold it. It could be my last.

"Oh Goddesses, Rance, close your eyes!" Kayley cries, but I don't need anyone to tell me to do something I'm already doing. I feel her reach for my hand, and I grab it. She's here, next to me, and she's real. I can feel the smoothness and warmth of her hand in mine, and we press closer, our shoulders touching. It's our confirmation to each other that we haven't become translucent space ghosts or dissolved away into the solar wind.

Just my luck that the only way I can lie next to the girl I love and hold her hand is for some extreme situation to force it to happen. I suppose I shouldn't complain. We're here, by ourselves, together. I'm deathly afraid of opening my eyes, but my quick squeeze of her hand gets returned.

If this is heaven, I'm scared to know what it looks like.

"Rance," Kayley says softly as the ship shudders, and the pressure on our feet increases by another exponent.

"What's up?"

"Tell me why you like me."

What? How does she know? Did Afton tell her? I feel my heart blow itself out of my chest. Of all the times to confess my feelings to her, why does it have to be now?

Hold on. I have no idea if she's just trying to take her mind off this insanity, or if she really knows how I feel about her. I choose to play dumb, hoping that's the best plan.

"What do you mean?" I ask tentatively.

"What's my redeeming quality?" she asks, a furrow of uncertainty running through her words.

That last breath that I was holding now comes seeping out of whatever lung pocket it was hiding in, and I feel the blood drain from my chest before it gets pushed down to my feet by the acceleration. So that's what's she's after—just some comfort, not an inquisition into my feelings.

Remind me to offer a thousand merits to the Goddesses when I get back home.

"KayKay, you have like a million amazing qualities." I'm amazed that she still does this. Kayley is the most beautiful, most intelligent, most mature...most perfect girl I have ever known, but she still doubts herself. I chalk it up to the fact that all her life, people have been telling her how amazing she is, and she's grown so used to hearing it she gets all insecure when someone doesn't. It's stupid, and it makes me mad. I wish I was better at helping her see she doesn't need praise to know she is as kick-ass as she is.

"Name one," Kayley says, and she's just pushed the challenge to the hundredth level. I think I'd rather open my eyes and expose my brain to whatever madness is out there.

"I...I don't know if I can name just one. You...you're amazing, Kayley. Right now, with all that's going on around us, I don't think I would want to be with anyone else."

"Please, Rance...just tell me one..."

My heart stops pushing out of my chest and falls out of my back. How can I not respond to her plea? The girl I love is asking for my help. I need to answer.

"Well, for one thing, we wouldn't be here if it wasn't for you, KayKay," I say.

"You're the one that jumped on this ship like an idiot."

"No...not here on this ship. I mean, here, in this room, safe. That was your idea, and it's not the first time. Remember that time when we tried to cross that frozen lake? How Grady nearly drowned because he thought his calculation of how much ice it took to support his weight was accurate?"

"Yeah, I remember that," she responds, and I can hear in her voice that the memory is making her smile. "Grady was so off."

"Then you should also remember how you got the rest of us organized and figured out how to save him from that icy mess. That was all you, Kayley. He would have died if you hadn't taken the lead. You're our leader, KayKay, and always will be."

She doesn't respond right away, and I'm hoping I didn't say something stupid in there somewhere to ruin my praise story. I start thinking back through my words, trying to guess which one messed it up for me.

Then Kayley does the unexpected. She leans over towards me, and somehow her lips find my cheek. Her kiss is so soft and gentle that my eyes shoot open reflexively, but I'm not seeing anything. I want to burn the moment her lips touched my face into my memory for all eternity.

It takes her curling up next to me and resting her head on my shoulder to realize that my eyes are still open. I don't understand what my visual sense is registering, though. I can't even begin to describe it. The Teddys were right, though—it is beautiful.

"Goddesses," I whisper.

"What is it?" Kayley asks, sounding sleepy.

"I don't know...but it's amazing. Take a look, KayKay."

"What? Are your eyes open?" She rolls onto her back, still tucked in beside me. I glance over at her to see if she's looked yet, but she's still got her lids shut tight.

"Kayley," I say in my softest voice. "Trust me. Open your eyes."

She does.

"What...what am I seeing?"

"I have no idea, but it's amazing, right?"

"Yes. It is."

It's still nothing compared to my Kayley, though.

Thirty

"ALRIGHT, LISTEN UP, TEAM," the colonel says as he paces back and forth in the canteen. "First up, good job getting yourselves secured and keeping safe during acceleration and a, uh...extremely fast decel, and thank you for stepping up and helping to get us back on track. Everyone feeling okay?"

"They're all fine, Colonel," Doc Elizabeth replies, then strolls over to Grady and pokes him in the cheek. "Except maybe this one. He opened his eyes in the middle of our multi FTL boost."

Grady's mouth is hanging open, and I swear I'm going to see drool dripping down the side of it any second now. I can only wonder if what he saw was the same as what Kayley and I experienced. We're fine, but he's acting like there's a big dent in his thinker. I hope that's not what happened. We need his smarts to figure this mission out.

"Kayley and I opened our eyes," I say. "But we're fine...How come? I mean, I'm not complaining."

"Clearly, it affects everyone differently. But don't worry, he'll be alright," the colonel states. "That kid has more intelligence than any of us. Even if he lost some, we'd never notice."

"That's true," Doc Elizabeth replies, and she pats Grady's cheek as she smiles down on him. Grady turns his head up at her and gives her an airy grin.

"Right, so, let's reorganize and get back to it. We're running out of time. Based on the original fleet timetable that I had before we arrived, the *Mursilis* will soon join up with the main fleet." The colonel scans our ragtag group. "Someone list out our accomplishments and to-dos."

"We've located the *Mursilis*," Parrish says. "Though we don't know how far we are from her, as of now."

"We've built—well, actually the Teddys built for us a very effective tranquilizer weapon, and even synthesized the drug that goes in it. We've enough to fill two guns," Doc Elizabeth says.

"We know how we're going to get close enough to the ship to transfer you over," Kayley says to top it off.

"Good, anything else we've accomplished?"

"Not dying," Afton adds.

"Fair enough, Jee," the colonel replies. "This is a mission that I want everyone to come back from. Safety will be important. Okay, what are we missing? What do we still need to do?"

"Figure out our location and approach to the *Mursilis*, study the ship's internal configuration, define the shortest route from insertion to the target, and prep all of our equipment." Kayley knocks it out of the park.

"Outstanding!" The colonel swings a fist through the air. "Are you sure you don't want to join up? I bet you'd make one hell of an officer."

"Not really my thing, Colonel, but thanks," Kayley replies. Afton gives her a mock pout and drops her head on KayKay's shoulder.

"Alright." Colonel Nelson scans across the team as he considers something. "Afton, Kayley, you're with me on *Mursilis* review. Grady and Parrish...well, mostly Parrish...you're on assist for equipment prep with my team."

"What about me, Colonel?" I ask, feeling left out.

"You and Doc go talk to the Teddys and negotiate our arrival to the *Mursilis*. Apparently, the engine is working again."

"Me?"

"Yes, you. You're the one who took the initiative to get us on board this ship, so the Teddys trust you. Doc Elizabeth has spent the most time with them, so she knows them best and can advise you. You're capable of this, Rance, so go make it happen."

Yes! This is like some military cine where the hero gives a motivational speech and inspires the troops to victory. Heck, it makes me want to jump up and snap a spirited salute to him, with a "Sir, yes sir!" as I charge into the fray.

Except it's not a safe thing for tall humans to charge around on a ship made for creatures less than chest height. So Doc Elizabeth and I make our way to the bridge in normal sauntering mode, and we manage not to hurt ourselves.

We find Captain Teddy in the middle of the bridge, clicking and chattering to all the Teddys sitting behind screens. Once he's done giving commands or saying whatever he is saying, he glances up at us with a solid stare.

"Uh, hi, Captain," I say. "Can we talk about getting to the *Mursilis*?"

"Unlikely," the Captain replies, and he turns away to chatter and click at a few other Teddys.

I'm lost for words. I give Doc Elizabeth an uncertain glance, but she only smiles back. I guess I should try again.

"Yeah, so, Captain, we need to get to that ship with the recording on it," I say. "We were hoping to talk to you about that."

"Patience, Rancid," the captain replies in his serious, flat tone, and wow, I think I just got rebuked by a Teddy.

I'm at a total loss as to how to approach him a third time. I get that he's busy, but we've also got stuff to do. The colonel is counting on me to pull through on this, and I'm not going to make myself look like a dunce for not making it happen. That would become one of those things that Afton doesn't comment about, which is worse than being picked on by her.

"Let me try something, Rance." Doc Elizabeth puts a comforting hand on my shoulder and steps past me to get closer to the captain.

"Hi, Captain, how is the ship?" she asks.

"Engine is ineffective." The captain turns to a screen and reads off it. "Maintenance is critical."

"That bad, huh?"

"Wait a second," I jump in. "We just crossed a solar system or two to escape an Imperial ship. How can the engine not be working?"

"...cannot maintain at velocity." I missed the first part of what he said. Either that, or he wasn't speaking Common at first. I get what he was trying to say, though—we've burned out the engine with the ludicrous speed we were trying to maintain. Just because the ship can reach eight hundred percent light-speed doesn't mean it likes to be there. Who knows what other forces are at work when you're racing around at that speed?

"So we can't move at all? How long will it take to fix?" I try to keep the urgency and anxiety out of my voice. Not that I'm at all sure Teddys understand that kind of inflection.

"Unknown," the captain says.

"So we're dead in the water?" Doc Elizabeth asks.

"That is inaccurate. There is no fluid complication. Life status is also maintained."

"I think she means, can the ship move?" I'm translating Common to an alien that doesn't really understand the language, anyway.

"Forward velocity is possible."

"Oh, great! How long until we get to the *Mursilis?*"

"Ten millennia," Captain Teddy replies, and I'm not sure I've heard him correctly.

"You mean ten hours?"

"That is not accurate. Ship is not capable of more than..." He adds in some Teddy measurement here. Of course, that doesn't help much. I'll have to take a guess.

"So let me get this straight, Captain. You're saying we can move forward, but...not that fast?"

"That is accurate."

Uh-oh. If the ship can't move fast enough to get us there before the end of our lifetimes, then we are really going to miss our chance.

"Sparkle is effective," Captain Teddy says, as if he's sensing my distress and is offering something to help ease my worry.

"Sparkle?"

"I heard them mention this once before," Doc Elizabeth explains as she turns to me. "It appears they have another way to move the ship, though it's not through propulsion."

There we go. Doc Elizabeth proves her lengthy experience here is valuable. Now, if I can only guess what a sparkle drive is. If it's not propulsion in the strict sense, then it has to be some way of displacing or folding space, or something like that. Grady told me about the theory of it once.

"Like a...what did Grady call it?" I'm racking my brain, trying to remember. Then it smacks me in the face. "I got it! A blink drive."

"A what?"

"It's a way of disappearing and reappearing in space somewhere else by traveling through other dimensions." I'm trying to remember how Grady described it to me. "Essentially, you do a shortcut around three-dimensional space, so you don't actually have to move. You just suddenly show up where you want to be."

"Well, that is useful."

"More than that!" I reply. "We won't have to worry about being spotted on our approach to the *Mursilis*. We'll just pop in right next to them, drop the colonel off, then pop out again. At least, that's how I think the technology works."

Wait a minute...If this sparkle drive thing was available, why didn't we use it to escape the probes? This I've got to know. I ask the captain.

"Knowledge was not available for distribution," the captain responds.

"You were keeping it a secret? At a time like that?" I'm not sure if I want to believe that the Teddys are keeping stuff from us. "Why tell us now?"

"Problem is solved," is the captain's response. Certainly, it's an answer, but I glance at the doc, hoping she might elaborate.

"Well," Doc Elizabeth says and shrugs. "It's like the captain said. Remember, Teddys don't like to have conflict within their group. So, whereas they didn't want or need to tell you before, it now solves a problem for the entire group. That's what I'd guess, anyway."

"But you knew," I say and frown at her. "You just said so before. Why didn't you bring it up?"

"Listen." The doctor throws up her hands. "I'm a doctor, not an engineer. I said I remembered hearing about it. That's a lot different than being familiar enough with it to suggest it during an emergency."

"Okay, I get it. We should share this with the others." I start to turn but pause, realizing something. "Hold on. If the Teddys are now telling us because they want to solve a problem within their group, does that mean they consider us part of their group?"

"That is accurate," the captain says.

"Oh!" I turn to Doc Elizabeth, smiling. "Now that's kinda cool."

Thirty-One

AFTER SO MUCH HAND-WRINGING and mental stress, we've come to the moment where all we have left to do is wait in anticipation...and worry. We did so much rushing around to get things prepared, we've run out of things to do. Kudos to us for being on the ball, but we should have moved slower because now we're doing the one thing we didn't add to our checklist—worrying.

"Almost there, dude," Grady says, rubbing his eyes as we walk towards our berth. All of us got paired up in rooms, allegedly to get some sleep, but I doubt any of us are relaxed enough to do that. Save for Parrish. He could sleep anywhere. I guess that's why he bunked with the colonel.

"Yeah...can you believe it?" I ask. "Us? About to do something good? Something amazing? If we can pull this off, that is."

"We will, dude," Grady replies, speaking with more confidence than I've heard from him in a while. "With the colonel and the Teddys behind us, we can do anything, including stop a war. And here you thought they only accepted idiots into the military."

I let his statement sink into my psyche. Grady may be right. I had plenty of reason to not like the military. In my mind, they're just an offshoot of the shady Imperial government, and anyone with rank or title is just another self-serving swindler who would do anything to get more than their fair share.

"Yeah, I guess not all of them," I say.

Colonel Nelson's face pops into my head. I guess if there was one shining example of an exception to my blanket hatred of the Imperial service, it would be him. He's been good to all of us, but he's gone out of his way to show me his positive qualities. Sure, he's threatened to drag me off this ship once or twice, but he's also given me the chance to decide for myself. My father never did that.

Now, I don't want to think of my father as some type of all-around poor dad. He wasn't. I enjoyed the moments we spent together...until he walked out on us. Wanting to realize our shared dream brought me here. It's why I stepped on this ship, and it's why I want, almost more than anything else, to make sure we're successful. Grady might believe we've got nothing to lose, but I can't be that upbeat. Plenty can still go wrong. It reassures me that the colonel and his men are with us, so I am glad we're all working together.

In some ways, the colonel has done more for my aspirations than my father ever did. He helped create this opportunity that we find ourselves in now. He's also saved us, more than once, when we were in danger, putting our safety before his own.

I know I've been critical of him, perhaps more than he deserved, and I should reconsider that. Kayley's opinion of him is important to me, too. She's always been an excellent judge of character. So, if she likes him—although hopefully not in *that* way—then that must mean he's a good guy.

We arrive at our little cabin space, and I pause a few steps before the entrance. Grady can stick his finger into that little diamond hole. I don't want to take the risk and get shocked or worse. He doesn't, so I chide myself for being overly careful.

I have been way superstitious lately. I guess I don't want anything to go wrong now that we're so close to success. Just a brief trip to the *Mursilis*, and we'll have taken the next step towards accomplishing my dream. It's a guaranteed success. I can feel it...and then what I've been waiting ten years for will come true.

This hasn't been easy, of course. Kayley and I had a little disagreement, sure, but now that there's no direction to go but forward, I'm sure she understands. Then, once she sees what we can really accomplish, she'll be totally on board. We can't lose!

The colonel pulled us together, but I got everyone here. As everyone is fond of reminding me, I was the first to get on board the Teddy ship—with Grady, of course. So everything is going the way I wanted it to. The only way things could be any better is if I asked Kayley to be my girlfriend and she said yes. In fact, once this part of the mission is over, I'm going to do just that.

"You know what, dude?" I pull my shirt off and throw on the one-piece pajamas that the Teddys made for us. "The colonel has really done so much for us. He's put himself at risk to help us, and he considers us part of his team. I guess he deserves more respect from me. From now on, I'm going to give him the respect he deserves. That's what I should do. Right?"

The only response my speech gets is silence.

"Grady?"

I glance over at my bud. He's fast asleep.

Thirty-Two

"AND SO THAT'S WHAT we'll have to do," Grady says. He's back to functioning in the real world again, though I still see a little of that silly happy face he was wearing before. "Our ship will drop in as close as we can to the *Mursilis*, and we'll just string the insertion team in."

This is the last time we'll get to run through anything before we act out this insanity of a plan we've put together. I'm still one million percent positive about it, but there are quite a few calculations to make. If we don't get them right, we're going to absolutely fail the exam.

"Excellent work, everyone. I think our chances for success are optimistic." The colonel folds his arms and leans against the side of one of the canteen tables.

"As long as the Teddys can do what they say they can do," Grady says.

"Have they ever not been able to?" Parrish asks.

"Not while I've been aboard," Doc Elizabeth replies. She's nibbling on a little piece of black celery, and I'm curious where she got it from. The Teddys shut the canteen down to prepare for the mission.

"So there's no issue with showing up so close to the *Mursilis*?" Kayley asks. "Like, won't we run into them or something like that?"

"Not unless they're moving," Afton responds.

"What about sensors?" Parrish asks.

"Proximity alarms could be a risk, but all other sensors won't focus anywhere near the ship." Colonel Nelson pushes himself off the table and begins pacing around the canteen. Nervous energy—we've all got it.

"If they really wanted to see us, they could just look out the window," I reply. It's an attempt to lighten the mood so everyone doesn't crack in half.

"Visibility is unlikely, Rancid," Original Teddy says as he strolls in with Blue Buddy and a black Teddy. We turn our attention to our hosts. As usual, I can't figure out what their static faces are thinking or feeling. I'm the only one it bothers, apparently. At least, nobody else has brought it up yet.

"Teddy, are we ready to go?" the colonel asks.

"That is accurate," Original Teddy replies.

"Okay then." Colonel Nelson claps his hands together to rally us around him. "It's time. We've done as much planning and preparation as we could. If we succeed, it will be thanks to everyone's efforts. I am extremely impressed by what a bunch of fresh recruits and a few non-combatants could achieve in such a short time. Excellent work, team, I am proud of you and all your hard work. Are our kits packed?"

"Yes, sir," Parrish says. "We put everything we could fit into the suits, and a bit more we had to secure in, uh...other ways."

"Alright, everyone to your stations!" The colonel turns to his two soldiers. "Let's suit up."

Both reply with an "Aye, sir!" before heading out, the colonel right behind them.

"Okay, team." Kayley puts some weight in her words and claps her hands together, appearing to me like a scarlet-haired version of Colonel Nelson. "The colonel is relying on us, so let's get our parts right."

We don't really have any parts at this point, so her words are a bit meaningless. I open my mouth to point this out, but Afton catches me and puts a hand up in front of my mouth before I can say anything. She's right—Kayley's new at this officer thing. Besides, her words do help to pump us up while we wait for something to happen.

"Conclave is welcome," Original Teddy says. "Monitoring is possible."

"Thanks, Teddy. Where should we go for it?" Doc Elizabeth asks.

"Convoy to watch the magic." Original Teddy pushes himself up on his tentacles and pogos down the corridor.

While the colonel and his men position themselves into the airlock—or whatever equates to an airlock on a Teddy ship—we make our way back to the cine theater-in-the-round. The big ball drops as we take our seats. There's anticipation in the air, just like we're about to see the next big blockbuster. The difference here is that the stakes are real.

We can see the bridge and the colonel's team on the screen. There's tons of chatter coming from the bridge, and for the first time I see Teddys suspended from the walls and the ceiling. Meanwhile, the colonel's team is dead silent. That could mean they're not talking, or their suits aren't patched into the ship's communications yet. It might be important to bring this up.

"Hey, Teddy, is the colonel's team communicating with the bridge? I don't hear anything from them."

Original Teddy turns to his Blue Buddy, clicking and whirring at him. BB chirps back before returning to whatever he was doing.

"Colonel is associated," Original Teddy reports.

"Can we talk to them?" I ask.

"Conclave currently not possible."

I nod. The colonel and his team must just be nervous. Who wouldn't be? They're going up against a force they're well familiar with. They know how much power the Imperial military has. If that were me, I'd be chewing my nails off, through my suit.

"Hey, you okay?" Parrish says, turning to me.

"Yeah, why?"

"You're vibrating the entire row with that shaky leg of yours," Parrish replies as he points to my left leg, which is in full jackhammer mode.

"Oh yeah," I say, putting a hand on it to stop it. "Sorry."

"Everything is going to be cool," Parrish says, with more confidence than I've ever had. "The colonel is just going to hop in, get the file, and hop out again. It's easy-peasy."

"I know," I reply. "It's just..."

"Hey, Rance." Parrish drops a hand on my shoulder. "We're all worried. Transracial cooperative mission going on here. It's a first for the entire Empire."

"Good point." It is. There's no doubt we're going to get this done, but now that it's really happening, I might have lost half a percent of the confidence that I had before.

We're going to do this.

"Not to mention, we're about to use a drive to blink ourselves light-years away from our current position, using an engine that isn't all there," Grady adds. "That's putting some sweat on my hands, for sure."

"Thanks for the visual reference, Grady," Afton says. "I don't think I needed it."

"Is this jump drive really going to work?" I look at my friend and give him an *or are we screwed?* face that we'd often use during our secondary school days. We used it a lot because we tended to find ourselves in situations we shouldn't have been in. Like the day we tried to make all the school drinking fountains dispense fruit juice instead of water. Our instructors were often very unhappy with us.

"Hell if I know, dude." Grady shrugs. "I haven't even seen any of this sparkle drive anywhere."

"You sounded way more confident about this last night, dude," I say.

"Yeah, well, I had a chance to sleep on it."

"Glad one of us did."

"Not to get morbid," Parrish leans past me to ask Grady, "but what is the worst thing that could happen if the drive fails?"

"Do you really want to know, now that we're about to do this?" Grady's sharp stare at Parrish is full of warning.

"Just making conversation to keep things cool," Parrish says and shrugs.

"That's how you keep things cool, dude?" Grady shoots back. He doesn't get mad often, but he's definitely on the verge. He's taking personal insult to Parrish's line of questioning as if he designed the sparkle drive himself.

"Okay, okay," Parrish says, holding up a hand. "Let's talk about something else."

"Like what?" I ask.

"How about *all* the ways we could die attempting this blink?" he says with a grin, and he gets pelted with howls and boos for a good minute.

"Listen," Grady says. "It's actually simple. There is only one way, which is that the drive fails while we're in between locations, and we're all severed in two because we can't be in two places at once."

"What about quantum entanglement?" Afton asks.

"Sure, particles can be in two places at once, but we can't. At least not just half of us." Grady's dead certain about that. No one questions him any further on this topic. I'm sure we're all too busy thinking about the many ways we could be sliced in half like a melon at breakfast.

Melon. My stomach rumbles and I groan. It's chosen a really awkward and inopportune time to be wanting food.

"Sparkle is ready," Original Teddy announces. "Engagement in..." He clicks and beeps. "Five minutes."

"Wow, Teddy, you've learned how to tell the time in Common!" Grady says.

"Easy-peasy," Original Teddy replies.

"Do we need to secure ourselves again?" Kayley asks, glancing around for somewhere to do so.

"Nope," Grady replies. "There's no actual momentum with a...well, what the Teddys call a sparkle drive. It just engages, and then we're there!"

Now Grady's throwing up his hands. That may be a sign that he's enjoying experiencing this for the first time, but I could swear that Grady's voice just warbled a little. He'd never admit it, of course, because that would disturb the group harmony and all that, but if I'm freaked, he's also got to be—at least a little bit.

"Two minutes is remaining," Original Teddy says.

"Are remaining, Teddy," Kayley tries to correct him.

"That is accurate. Teddy is remaining."

Afton face-palms, and I chuckle. Parrish and Grady chuckle, too, then Kayley smiles and, after a second, lets out a little giggle. It sets the rest of us off, and we all break into laughter. It lasts for almost the entire time we have left.

"Man," Grady says, catching his breath in between come-down chuckles. "We're totally stressed."

"Totally," Parrish echoes.

"Sparkle in..." Original Teddy clucks five times. Maybe that means five seconds.

"Ooh, here we go!" Grady says, clapping his hands together. "Everyone watch the bridge screens. We're going to phase our hull before we blink out."

"Blink out?" Kayley asks.

"Appear at the *Mursilis*," Grady explains.

We all stare at the screens, but it's a little difficult to see on a big round globe. I mean, I've been thinking this the entire time I've been on the ship. Globe-shaped screens are just not good for anyone's eyes— not even the Teddys'. Why did they build them that way?

"Can anyone see anything?" I ask.

"No, nothing's changed," Parrish replies.

"Yeah," Kayley adds. "I can't see anything different."

"You're all blind," Afton says. "We've already blinked."

All of us, save for Afton, blink our eyes. Nothing happened. I'm sure of it.

I jump up and run to the screen, hoping I can see whatever Afton's talking about. Kayley and Parrish follow me, and we all stretch our necks the wrong way to stare up at the vid. I'm squinting to see if it helps.

It does.

"Oh...there it is," I say.

"What? Where?" both ask.

"You can't see the ship," I say, pointing at the big black space on the screen, "because that *is* the ship."

"Bingo," says Afton.

Thirty-Three

THE *Mursilis* is an impressive bit of military construction. Though we're only seeing about a quarter of its massive hull. If I had to guess, it's three or four times larger than our Teddy ship. I already get tired walking from my berth to the canteen on this ship. I don't even want to think about traversing the *Mursilis*.

We can see an airlock and the creepy hydrogen intakes, covered in hundreds of little spiky cones, all painted crimson like the colonel had mentioned. Grady could tell you what they're for, but I have no idea. I'd hate to be in front of those things when the *Mursilis* moved, however. I hope we can get the colonel and his men inside before that happens.

"Can they see us? Are they moving?" I ask, turning to glance at everyone.

"Motion is not accurate," Original Teddy answers for me.

"That's good," Parrish says. "We don't want them to be moving."

"Excursion is ready," our fuzzy friend announces, and an uneasy static jolt spreads through the room, cutting off our chatter. Parrish folds his arms and avoids eye contact with anyone, while Afton slides her hands under her legs and bows her head.

Grady and I share a nervous moment, but we try to put each other at ease. He gives me a hopeful curl of his mouth, and I return his reassurance with a smile of my own. I guess I shouldn't be a wreck if

Grady isn't. He's a guy who can be like a bug—hard shell outside, but all jelly inside. You'd never know by looking at him.

We are going to do this. The colonel will get this done, and we will stop this war.

"This is Colonel Nelson. We're ready to step out of the airlock." His voice comes from somewhere in the room. I glance around for a speaker or some other type of sound device, but just like the big ball of a screen, it's a mystery of Teddy design. I'm thankful we can hear him at all.

"Airlock is accessible." Captain Teddy's voice comes through in the same way. "Excursion may inaugurate."

"Copy, here we go."

All of us return to the screen, which now displays a wide shot of the *Mursilis*, but the edges of the image are distorted and warped. Not just because we're watching on a spherical screen, but because of what the Teddys are doing to their ship to make it seem like it's a big ball of gas and not a ship.

"Do you see them yet?" Kayley asks, her voice hushed.

"No," someone replies. I think it's Afton, but I'm not paying attention. I've got my eyes locked on the screen and my ears tuned to Teddy radio.

As we wait for them to appear, I wonder how much time has passed. But counting minutes is a bad idea. It's like neglecting to itch when you really need to scratch, and I don't need to torture myself like that. None of us do.

"Is that them?" Parrish points at a small line of dots that seem like they're moving towards the *Mursilis*.

"No, those are stars," Afton says. I hear an edge of annoyance in her tone. Well, she's usually got an edge of annoyance in her tone, but this time I agree with it.

A frustrated sigh comes from Parrish, and he paces like he was doing before the mission started. I can't blame him for trying to expend some pent-up energy, but he better not block my view.

"It can't be taking this long," Kayley says.

"Excursion is visible," Original Teddy says.

"Where?" we all shout at the same time.

"There." Eagle-eyed Afton points at the screen. "Lower right."

Sure enough, they're there, floating across the screen in a much more obvious way than we were expecting. The three EVA suits are making their way to the *Mursilis* at a fairly fast clip.

"Okay, yes!" Grady claps his hands together. "Go get 'em, Colonel!"

I try to gauge the location on the Empire's heavy star cruiser where they'll touch down and hope that they're heading directly towards the access port, just above the intakes. They should have more than enough air to get there and back, but if there's some complication getting in, that could dig into their supply big-time.

"Ten seconds to hull contact," Colonel Nelson declares. "Once we're there, we'll enter the code to unlock the hatch and begin immediate ingress."

While it took forever for them to appear on our screen, getting to the hatch and unlocking it goes speedily. Two seconds more, and the three of them are through and closing the hatch behind them.

I stare at the hatch for a moment, an eerie feeling needling my brain, refusing to go away. I'm not sure what the problem is. They've crossed, they opened the hatch, and now they're in. That's nothing but good.

The colonel is getting this done. He'll be back soon.

"What's up with your face, Rance?" Afton asks.

"What's wrong with my face?" I turn to her with a glare.

"You want a detailed report?" Her smug retort is typical for Afton, but I'm not playing along. I roll my eyes and turn back to the screen. This is no time for messing around.

"No, for real, though," Afton continues. "You've been staring at that hatch for a while now. What's up?"

"Nothing...Just glad this is all going so easily."

"Easy is good," Grady replies. "We want it to be easy."

"Okay." The colonel's voice comes on, whispering. "We've stowed our suits, and now we're heading into the corridor. We'll have to keep it silent from here on out."

"Teddy, can we get a vid-feed from them?" Kayley asks.

"Visual is not possible," Original Teddy replies. "Interception is probable."

"What about the audio then?" Doc Elizabeth asks. "Won't the *Mursilis* pick that up?"

"Convey is possible with Teddy. Interception is unlikely."

I'm hoping that "unlikely" means "not going to happen" in this situation. One slip and the colonel's team become rodents in a very sophisticated rat trap. I'm hoping that the security detachment on the *Mursilis* isn't all that sharp right now. There's no reason for them to be. They're well behind the front line. The nearest Teddy ship—except for ours, of course—is light-years away.

The screen clears, and a two-dimensional map of the *Mursilis* appears. There are three dots on it that are in motion—that's the colonel and his men. I can't say much for the graphics, but at least now we know where they are.

"I think I played this game," Afton says.

"Games like this haven't been around for twenty years, so you would have to have played it before you were born," I reply.

Afton's intelligent reply is to pull her lower eyelid down and stick her tongue out.

"Looks like they're almost there," Parrish says.

"Go, go, go..." Grady whispers.

The three dots file into a small square of space. We can't tell what that is, but it's either a closet or level access. We'll have to wait and see.

"Why can't we see where the ship's personnel are?" Doc Elizabeth asks. "If we saw where they are, we could warn the colonel and his team."

"A great idea, but what we've got is already impressive for the merging of two different technologies," Grady says. "I'm stunned that we can see and hear this much."

"Fair enough," Doc Elizabeth replies but then folds her arms. It's tough on all of us just waiting here. I have to keep my faith in the colonel up. I can feel our success getting closer.

The map redraws itself, and now we're looking at a different level of the ship. The three dots exit the square and enter something long and rectangular, what must be a hallway.

"Hold up," one of the colonel's men suddenly whispers, "someone is coming."

"Back up the corridor," replies the colonel. "To maintenance access."

Their three dots turn a corner and slide down to the entrance to another small square, pausing there. The door must be locked, and I think we all realize it. I hear an anxious shifting of positions from everyone, and I just got an itch I can't scratch.

Nothing happens for a few seconds, and I use my fingers as chew toys to release my stress. They're getting it done, they're getting it done.

"Oh, feck, I wish we could see!" Doc Elizabeth complains.

"Me too," says Parrish.

"Hush. We don't want to miss anything," Kayley scolds.

The dots make it through the doorway and get into the small square. It's not perfectly square, but I'm too anxious to be specific. It's got to be an actual room, with walls, a ceiling, and a floor.

"You hear anything?" the colonel asks, and I imagine one of his team has an ear to the door trying to do just that.

"Negative," comes the answer.

"Alright, we can't stay in here all day. Let's move out. Make sure you check both directions before you head out."

"On the move."

As promised, the dots glide from the space and move back down the corridor. They pause at the corner, then turn and jet down the first corridor, heading for a junction.

"At the junction," the colonel says, and the dots plant themselves on the corridor's right-side wall. They slide up to the turn, then pause before continuing around the corner.

But once they do, they freeze.

"Whoa!" A strange voice comes over the system. "You guys spooked me."

"Sorry about that," the colonel says, then there's a long pause. The dots hold their position just around the corner.

"Hey, where you guys going?" the voice asks in a friendly way. "Oh! Apologies, sir, I didn't realize...um, I mean, Colonel, that way is the archive. Did you want to go there?"

"Yes, Lieutenant, that's where we're headed," the colonel replies. Everyone must be praying to the Goddesses so loudly in their heads, I think I can hear them. When the dots move, Grady shouts, and we all cry, "Yes!"

"Uh, sir..."

"What is it, Lieutenant?" The three dots pause again, and one reverses direction.

"Just curious, sir. You're wearing terrestrial fatigues. Have you been on the ship long? It's just, I've never seen anyone wear them on board before. If you don't mind me suggesting, sir, you should get your SBUs on. If the admiral sees you like that..."

Another dead silence.

"Uh, yeah," the colonel replies. "Thanks for the suggestion, Lieutenant...Dismissed."

These long moments where nobody says anything are really getting to me. None of the dots move, either, and I say a prayer or a few thousand. Get it done, Colonel. Get it done.

"Hold on!" the lieutenant's voice says. "You're not supposed to be here, are you? How did you get on board?"

Oh, crackers.

Thirty-Four

WE HEAR A STARTLED shout, then the sounds of a scuffle. Someone rubs up against a mic, and there's a tremendous rumble and a hard thump as that same someone bangs into the wall. A grunt follows, and a cry of pain. It's all really confusing. We were already worrying before, but now we're going completely bonkers.

"Stop him!" the colonel shouts, and the three dots take off down the corridor, chasing after the invisible lieutenant. Heavy breathing and the clanging of gear are the only other clues we have about what is happening.

"Forget that guy!" Afton yells, disgust and disappointment in her voice. "This mission is over. They should just get out before they get caught."

"No, wait." I turn to her, holding up a hand. "They can still get it done."

"We're still hidden," Grady adds. "As long as we stay that way, there's a chance."

The sudden silence from the Teddy comm brings our attention back to the screen. The three dots have paused, still a respectable distance from the data storage room. After all that racket, they're going to have an interesting time returning there. I'm somewhere between *Wow, I'm so glad no one's seen them yet* and *How are they going to make it back without getting caught?*

"Quick. In there!" the colonel hisses, and six pairs of human eyes jump to the screen to see where they're going. From what I can tell—which is not much because all I see are some lines—it's another storage or maintenance room. The three dots get access with no trouble this time, and they slip in with ease.

"Okay..." The colonel must be out of breath. He doesn't speak for a few seconds. "He's secured, and I don't think we've tripped any alarms. Copy?"

"Information is collected," Captain Teddy responds.

"Thank you, Captain. Is everything still secure on your end? We'd like somewhere to come back to once we complete this mission."

"Can we talk to them?" Parrish asks.

"Conclave is not possible," Original Teddy says, "at ongoing position."

"Any way to hook that up?" Parrish tries. "If we could just coach them a little..."

"Unknown," replies Original Teddy, and that's about as far as that discussion is going. I let out a frustrated sigh. It would require more brainpower than I'm willing to commit to a lost cause of a conversation. The colonel needs our support, not our distractions.

"Ship remains immune," Captain Teddy responds.

"Good to know, Captain. Okay." Colonel Nelson must be looking at his fellow infiltrators because he then adds, "Okay, we're continuing."

As much as I'm tired of seeing three little candies sliding around a floor plan, I can't turn away, and neither can anyone else. The colonel's team is moving slower than before, but I see they're trying to stick to the wall to keep their visibility low. It's all really intense, and I can't stay seated anymore.

"Rance," Kayley says gently. "Sit down...You too, Parrish."

I reluctantly drop in my spot in between Grady and Afton while Parrish takes a seat in the row below. But it's hard for either of us to stay still.

I realize my eyes are going blurry from staring too much, so I squint to keep my focus on the blue Tangy Bleeps—my favorite sugar rush—as they continue to slide towards the data center. Only silence emanates from the colonel's team, and that only makes my skin itch more.

"Hey, Parrish." I lean down to him and whisper in his ear. "You'd come with me if we had to go over there and support the colonel, right?"

"Totally, but..." Parrish considers for a moment. "We're nowhere near as prepared as they are to take on our own military. We don't have any weapons or training...or much of anything, really."

"Well, we would figure something out, right?" I'm really hoping for his support. He's the heavy hitter of our team, and without his firepower I'll be going nowhere fast. He gives me hope when he nods—awesome. We've got to support the colonel however we can so he can complete the mission.

The sound of escaping air comes from Teddy radio. I'm getting whiplash snapping my neck up at the screen every time there's a noise. But the candy dots are almost back at the data center, which makes a little muscle soreness worth it.

"Thank you for the tranquilizer gun," the colonel says. "It works extremely well."

They continue, and they're almost back at the data center. I knew it! They're going to pull this off! A surge of excitement grows in me. The colonel and his men are the ones risking their necks, but I think this happened because we all pitched in. It took an enormous effort from all of us.

If my dad knew what we've done, he would be proud. At least that's what I'm going to keep telling myself—I have to. It's what makes all this worthwhile. That, and ending the war, of course. The Teddys really want that, and once we tell enough of the right people, the Empire's citizens will want it, too. We've really done something significant here. I'm about ready to celebrate!

"Did you hear that?" Kayley asks.

"Hear what?" I ask back.

"I think I heard a shout."

"I didn't hear anything," Grady says, leaning forward and turning his head sideways.

"Back the way we came!" the colonel's voice blasts suddenly over the comm. "Secondary floor access...take it!"

Stomping boots and clanking metal resonate through the comm, sending shivers down my back. All of my former excitement bursts into a flame of terror as I realize they're running away, and fast! Forget the sour balls on the screen. The image in my mind is far more telling: I see them chased by a heavily armed squad of security personnel, all wearing bloodthirsty sneers.

"Captain!" the colonel shouts. "Get the ship ready to blink out. We may need to get out of here in short order!"

"Ship is available," the captain responds in a steady voice. "Recommend evacuation with efficiency."

"No kidding! We're headed back to the hatch now!"

"Well," Afton says, defeated. "Sorry for being the one who called it early."

Kayley puts a hand on Afton's arm and rubs it with a reassuring smile. Afton returns it with a sigh and a shrug. At least they're trying to be calm, even if they're not. I can't say the same for us three guys or Doc Elizabeth. She's been standing the whole time, but now she's dropped into a seat and is clutching her hands together as if saying a prayer.

"Dammit, there's another squad on this floor!" Colonel Nelson grumbles. "Get ready to go on my command. They won't fire in the ship and risk a depressurization. They'll have to capture us by hand. That gives us a chance."

"Colonel, the first squad is just behind us!" one of his men hisses. "They've got the second corridor blocked. We're trapped!"

"We've got to get over there and save them!" I shoot up off my seat and turn to the others.

"Easy, Rance," Kayley replies. "There's nothing we can do, and we'd risk the entire ship if we tried."

I have no idea where she's getting that stony stillness. Her eyes are locked on the screen, even though there's not much reason to look at it. We know where they are and where they can't get to unless there's some major miracle.

"Parrish, let's go." I turn to Parrish, pleading. "The colonel needs our help. You want to help, right?"

"You know I do." He makes a face of exasperation.

"Rance, don't," Afton advises. "We don't need any more problems right now."

"I'm trying to solve the problem, not create one! We've got to go!"

Kayley and Afton glare at me as if they're going to tackle me if I make any sudden moves. I don't want this to become about Kayley versus me again, but the colonel is in trouble. If we can save him, he'll at least have another chance to try again later. He might even have a backup plan in place ready to go. We'll never know if we don't get him back here.

"Parrish, there are two spare EVA suits, right? We can use them! We might not have weapons or training, but you're good at tactics. Maybe we can create a diversion or something, and that could be enough. If we do nothing, they could be executed!"

Parrish chews on his cheek as he looks at me. I know he wants to believe we can do it. He is superb at calling a play. They didn't make him team captain three years straight for no reason. We'd have to make our way to the *Mursilis*, and quickly, but it could work. I've never been outside of a spaceship, but if that's our only challenge, it's worth trying, and it's better than listening to them die.

"We've no choice," Colonel Nelson says. He doesn't sound like he's enjoying that conclusion very much, but he also isn't ready to give up. "Let's move on three before they zero in on our position. Okay?"

"Aye, sir!" his men reply together.

"Alright then. Here we go...Three...two...one...move!"

There's the sound of rustling fabric and clinking buckles, followed by fast breathing and distant shouts. They're running as fast as they can, and the screen becomes useful again. As they pound the decking, there's the rapid squawk of weapons fire in the background.

"They're firing at us, sir!" one of his men shouts.

"They're only stun guns!" comes the colonel's breathless reply. "Keep going!"

The three dots hit the airlock, and a moment later, they slide in.

"Suits on! Forget the safeties. There's no time!" Colonel Nelson bellows.

"This is too much!" I shout, stomping around the room. "Parrish, if you don't want to go, it's cool. I'll go by myself. Just help me put the EVA suit on."

Parrish stares at me, his head shaking slowly. He doesn't want to tell me no, but he's doing it, and it's about to make me freak out.

"No, Rance." Kayley's voice is low and full of warning. "Stay put. You too, Parry. They're coming back now."

"No, KayKay! We've got to do this. We need to get him back!"

"Well, the colonel put me in charge of you, so if I say stay, you're staying here." Kayley puts her hand on her hip and steps towards me. Afton stands, too, her eyes sharp. Kayley might not be able to stop me walking out of here, but Afton sure could.

"Parrish, come on, dude, back me up here." I glance at Grady, who shrinks in his seat when my eyes fall on him. "You too, Grady. I really need your tech smarts to pull this off!"

Grady looks down, his answer clear. I don't blame him—Grady was never one for hostility, not even in games—but it's a spear in my side to know he doesn't have my back here.

I turn back to Parrish. He's gone silent, but I still see the conflict in his eyes. Of course he wants to help, but the fact that he's choosing not to is killing me.

"Fine, don't help," I grumble. "You were never there when it counted, anyway."

It's a cheap shot, but it hits its mark. Parrish's mouth drops open, and I instantly regret saying it. Sure, he wasn't there when my father left, but that's not a fair assessment of how good a friend he is. I'll have to apologize, eventually, but right now I've got someone to save.

"Rance, don't be an idiot!" Afton steps in my way, reaching for my shoulder. I knock her arm away, but she keeps pressing. Soon she's got her claws on me, and we struggle. I shove her hard, but she doesn't let go. My shoulder rams into her abdomen to knock her out of the way. Afton doesn't move. As I lean down, she grabs the back of my shirt and goes to put me in a headlock.

"Rance, please, calm down!" Kayley cries, her voice teetering on the edge of tears. Afton pauses and looks at her. It's just enough time to get my arm free. I twist in her grip, my arm thrusting out to lever myself away from her.

But as I come around, my fist swings around and strikes Parrish right in the jaw. He steps back, blinking. I'm in shock, too. I would never hit any of my friends. Not like that. Never on purpose.

"Parrish...dude...I didn't mean that." My words fall flat as an apology.

Parrish puts a hand up to his jaw and narrows his eyes at me. That's the second attack on him I've made in less than a minute.

"They're about to get in!" one of the colonel's men cries.

We break from our own tension and turn back to the screen. Afton loosens her grip on me, but doesn't let me go. It no longer matters if she stops me. Either the colonel and his men will escape, or they won't. I just punched my friend for no reason.

"Blow the outer hatch, then! We can't get captured!" the colonel shouts back.

"But sir, you're not—"

"I'll be ready! Blow it!"

The entire room shakes with the rumble of the hatch doing an emergency blow. They didn't have time to equalize the airlock to pure vacuum, which means the three of them just got ejected from the *Mursilis* as if it just spit three seeds from its mouth. Now they're burning at high speed on some unknown trajectory. If they don't gain control, they'll simply keep heading in that direction...forever.

"What's happening?" Doc Elizabeth asks. "Did they make it?"

"We're headed back," one of the colonel's men says, his voice low and strangely calm. "We've lost one...and the colonel...he's in trouble. Requesting immediate medical."

"Information received," Captain Teddy's unemotional voice replies. "Doctor is available."

"Teddy," Kayley says, her voice shaking. "Can the captain ask what's wrong with the colonel?"

"It's not him," the colonel's aide replies after a bit of communication tag-teaming. "It's his suit. There's a big hole in it."

Thirty-Five

SILENCE, AS DEEP AS the vacuum of space, pervades the cramped corridor as we crowd in to wait for the airlock to cycle. No one breathes, and absolutely no words come out of anyone's mouth. So when it opens, all we hear is the scrape of feet as the colonel's man pulls his unmoving body through the hatch. I catch sight of the huge rupture in the back of his suit, and I lose all hope for his survival. No one can endure the harshness of vacuum and live. Not for that long.

Parrish shoulders me out of the way and steps in to help the colonel's aide carry his body up to Doc Elizabeth's room. We follow, our heads hung low. I can pray for some miracle, but this time I know even the Goddesses can't change what's happened.

A funny thought pops into my head as we shuffle along. Here we are, sitting next to the *Mursilis*, and they still have no clue. It's going to take some time to figure out what just happened on their ship, and I'll bet they're doing all sorts of crazy scans for ships in their area to figure out where the colonel's team came from. But unless they bump into us, we're just a big cloud of hydrogen gas.

Which leaves us free to be depressed for as long as we want.

They lay the colonel's body down on the exam chair, and his aide removes his helmet as gently as he can, which is to say not very. The metal ring that locks it in place is weighed down by the colonel's body. It's an awkward few seconds as the aide, trying to be respectful of his commanding officer, wrestles with the helmet until he has no choice but to rip it away from the suit.

"Oh Goddesses," Kayley says and turns away, burying her face in Afton's shoulder. Parrish mutters a curse and glances down, but I can't stop looking. It's as if I can't accept what happened unless I see him with my own eyes. Like I could blink and he would be alive again, even though I know that can't happen. One glance at the face of Lt. Colonel Gabriel Nelson, and I know he's gone. Doc Elizabeth does her routine anyway, checking for vitals where we know there are none.

"I'm sorry, everyone. There are no signs of life. If it's any consolation, and I know it's not, whatever happened to him out there went quickly. This contusion on the side of his head means he likely was knocked unconscious. He wouldn't have been aware of what happened."

Kayley lets out a sob and tightens her arms around Afton. Afton squeezes her back, rocking her gently back and forth. I'm trying to be strong, but as I hang my head, I notice my body shaking. My chest gets tight, and moisture surrounds my eyes. If only I had decided a few minutes earlier, I could have gone and helped. Then he'd still be alive, and we could find another way to get the recording. Now...

"Thank you, Doctor," his aide replies. "I'd like to give him full burial rites, in space, if we could. But it can wait. I understand this isn't the best place to do that."

Doc Elizabeth nods and slides off her exam gloves, tossing them on the counter with a sharp sigh. She just kinda stares off into space after that. I can't be so accepting of this, though. Before I realize it, I punch the wall and growl out a few angry words.

"Easy, dude." Grady goes to put a hand on me, but I shrug him off.

"We could have saved him!" I shake my head. "Why didn't you guys back me up?"

"There was no way," Parrish says. "Just not enough time...The EVA suit would have taken you ten minutes to put on."

"That's not the point!" I shoot fire from my eyes, burning Parrish in the blaze. "We could have helped if we didn't hesitate!"

"None of you should blame yourselves for this," the colonel's aide adds. His name is Cortell, and he's a sergeant, and I would have known that sooner if I had just bothered to look at the badge on his uniform. I also could have just asked, and now I feel stupid for not doing it. He could have died just like the colonel, and I would never have known his name. I didn't know the name of the other man, either. It's too late to ask him.

"Rance, you were out of control, and you would have gotten yourself hurt...or killed!" Parrish takes a step towards me. "You should be thankful that we stopped you."

"And what about you? You're the one who was joining the military! You'd be risking your life like that every day, but you wimped out! So much for your big dream."

"Rance, enough!" Kayley lifts her head from Afton's shoulder, and I lose my breath. Her eyes are soaked, and the ivory skin of her face is flushed red with sorrow. "Two people just died! Stop blaming him for that. It's not his fault, and it's not yours, either!"

Parrish stares at me. I know he wants to fire back at me, but he clenches his jaw and turns away. He hangs his head for a moment, then curses and stomps out.

"You're a jerk, Rance, you know that?" Afton growls. I glance at her, but I've got no comeback. I shouldn't—she's right.

"Yeah, I guess I am." I drop my gaze, understanding just how much of a selfish idiot I've been. I wanted the mission to be successful so badly that I didn't care about anything other than that. I abused my friendships and even hit Parrish, if only by mistake. "I should go apologize to him."

"Later," Kayley says. "He's going to need some time before he'll be open to listening to you. I know this has been hard on you, Rance, but what you said was really mean."

My eyes turn back to the colonel's body, wondering what happened. How did it go wrong in such a short time? They were there, right in front of the archive. It would have only been a few minutes more before they achieved their mission. Then everything I've been waiting for could happen.

"Guys." I turn to the three of them. "I'm sorry. Really, really sorry. We all wanted the mission to be a success, but I was in a bad place. I couldn't think of anything but the mission. And now...well...if you're mad at me, I get it. I let everyone down...the colonel included."

Kayley releases one arm from Afton and opens it wide, inviting me into an embrace. Afton does the same, and not thinking much about it,

I wrap my arms around both of them, emotions overtaking me. I try to catch my breath, but I can't without tears. I realize then what high hopes I had for my connection to Colonel Nelson. I wanted him to teach me all the cool things he knew, about ships, about the Empire...about life.

"Bring it in, Mutsumaji," Afton orders, and we open up to let him in. His eyes are already getting moist as he rushes to join us.

The four of us are just silent for a good long time, and my mind wanders. There's only so many depressing thoughts one can have when wrapped tight with friends like this. Eventually, your mind lets go of the grief.

I think of Parrish and wonder how he's feeling right now. If he's anything like the four of us—and he totally is—he's in a world of hurt. I'm sure he needs someone to talk to. If he's up for it, I want to be there for him.

"You guys alright?" Doc Elizabeth asks with a moderate amount of concern. She comes over as we break up and reaches out to rub my back.

"Yeah, we're good," I say, and turn to her with a grateful smile.

"Good, because I have to ask you to leave," she says, a bit of business in her tone. "We've got to, uh, take care of the colonel's body, and you don't want to be around for that."

"I should go talk to Parrish." I glance at Kayley for approval.

"Do that," Kayley says, clearing up the wet spots on her cheeks. "Then the two of you meet us in the canteen. We've got some stuff to talk about."

With some hand gestures and some random sign language with the Teddys, I ask where Parrish is, and a green Teddy guides me up to the ship's solarium garden. Parrish is there, back propped against a tree and staring out into...well, what would be the stars, but the Teddys' hydrogen camouflage is blurring the view a good bit.

"Hey," I try, testing the waters.

"Hey," Parrish says back. He doesn't sound mad, so I press a bit more.

"Not much to see right now." I find a spot on the side of his tree that isn't overgrown with jungle and slide down to the floor.

"Yeah, but would you really want to if you could?" Parrish shoots back. "I mean, there's nothing to see out there but a big Imperial ship full of jerks."

"Yeah, true." I wrap my arms around my knees and gaze upwards. "If you want to see a jerk, all you have to do is look at me."

Parrish snorts—that's a good sign. I can dial down my anxious edge a little, and maybe we can have a genuine conversation without anyone's emotions getting in the way. Not just his—mine too.

"Sorry, dude," I say. "I lashed out at you, and that's not cool. I really wanted us to be a part of this mission. You understand what success would have meant to me, right?"

"Yeah, I understand." Parrish turns his head towards me, pressing his lips together. He's still angry, and I can't blame him, but he's trying to be the awesome guy that he is. "This is hard on all of us because it's all new. I get what you're feeling."

"Thanks, Parrish." I rub a sleeve across my eyes. "Thanks for giving a pebblehead like me another chance. I should have never said that stuff about you joining the military. I mean, I get now why you looked up to the colonel."

"Really?"

"Yeah. He was growing on me, too."

We spend a few minutes gazing up at the blurry glow, our brains drained of all energy for thought. It wasn't what I had intended when I went to find him, but this still feels like quality time well spent with my bud.

"I'm gonna miss him," Parrish says, breaking the silence. "You know how excited I was to join up, as in actually *wanting* to join the military. I was the only one, really. Afton was doing it because she wants to find her dad, and Grady was doing it because his parents probably ordered him to. When I met the colonel, it was like the first big step in achieving a dream."

He's not correct about being the only one, Afton was totally going to officer school. I'll let it slide because I don't want to ruin our conversation.

"Yeah, but why the military, Parrish? Your grades are killer, and once you graduate, you could do anything. I mean it. Anything."

"Really? I don't know." I feel his shrug from around the side of the tree. "Action? Adventure? Honor and duty, and all of that? I just really liked the idea—me as a top officer leading the troops. I could envision it all in my head. It was something worth doing, and I felt that."

"Was?"

"I've got no idea anymore, Rance." Parrish sighs and pulls his legs in, mirroring my position. "I still want to do stuff like that, but...after hearing about this scandal inside the forces...a captain just going rogue like that? Then the upper brass trying to cover it up? I don't know if it's the right place for me anymore."

"The military isn't the only place to find action and adventure. You could go explore new worlds, for instance."

"Maybe. Maybe you're right, Rance. I'll have to think about it."

He glances back up at the ceiling and goes quiet. I know how hard it is on him right now. Once Parrish had made his choice to join up, he really dove in body and soul. I respect him for believing in it as long as he did. Finding a replacement for your dream is not easy, and it's not quick—I should know.

"So...we good?" I ask after a minute. I offer my hand to him, which he takes and gives a good squeeze and shake.

"Yeah, we're good."

"Thanks again, dude. You've always been cool with me, maybe more than I deserved." I chuckle suddenly. "You really are tough competition, you know that?"

"What do you mean?"

"Uh, never mind." Whoa. I can't tell him about my feelings for Kayley —not yet. I just got finished making up with Parrish. I don't want him to get angry again. This would be a good time to move on to another topic, so I get up and dust myself off. "Kayley wants us to meet everyone in the canteen. She said she's got something to discuss."

"Oh, so that's it."

"What's it?" I eye him warily.

"You're totally in love with her, aren't you?" Parrish grins a little, a knowing look in his eye. His grin only gets bigger when he catches the panic I know is all over my face. Is this going to reignite the conflict between us?

My shoulders slump. I was going to have to confess to him at some point.

"Yeah," I admit, cringing. "How d'you know?"

"Anytime you're around her, Rance, you act exactly like I used to."

"So," I say hesitantly, "is it cool?"

Parrish smiles and nods. "You don't need my permission, dude. Go get her."

Thirty-Six

"ALRIGHT, SO," KAYLEY SAYS as she paces back and forth, reminding me of a paler, redheaded version of the colonel. A much more beautiful version, too, I would add. Not that Colonel Nelson was ugly. I just prefer my KayKay.

"I know everyone is feeling bad right now, but this is really important. The Teddys just intercepted a communication between the *Mursilis* and a ship near Angelcanis. The transmission was text only, but it's from a top minister..." Kayley makes sure to catch our eyes before continuing. "A Minister Crowley."

"That guy?" Grady jumps up, his eyes wide. "I never liked him!"

"Easy, dude, we don't even know what the message says yet." Parrish grabs Grady's arm and pulls him back down.

"Well, you won't like it," Kayley says, her jaw getting tight. "He's ordered the captain of the *Mursilis* to destroy any records relating to the original incident and hunt down and capture anyone involved. And it gets worse. He says the war must continue, and I quote, *for the good of the Empire*—that the Teddys are a supreme nuisance and we must remove them. Also, he recommended bombing the other colony planets to maintain support for the Imperial war effort."

My skin goes cold. This is far worse than we knew, but how could we know? Who would ever expect the Empire to murder its own people? And for what? So we'd support the killing of an alien race?

"No!" Grady cries out. Afton gasps and throws a clenched fist to her mouth. I know what she's thinking. Did they kill her dad, too?

"So those weren't Teddy ships that attacked Angelcanis?" Parrish asks.

"That is accurate," Original Teddy replies. "Teddy does not implement aggression."

"Are they sure about the source of the transmission?" Sergeant Cortell asks. "Can they verify it?"

"Transmission source is verified," Original Teddy says. "Originator also en route."

"Yes," Kayley adds, "the minister is on his way here to ensure they follow his orders."

"Then that's it! We've got him!" Parrish cries. "Show the transmission to the right people and that guy is done for!"

"Nope." Afton shakes her head. "Unless we get the real transmission, nobody is going to believe that it's real. The minister could just say the Teddys faked it."

I shake my head. This is too much. Here we thought we were exposing a single captain and a single ship, but this scandal goes all the way up to the Imperial Parliament. I'd be resting back on my cynical laurels right now if I weren't so devastated. This bastard ordered the deaths of thousands of people! I don't even know where to begin with my outrage over that.

"On top of all that, we now need to find our own way home," Kayley says. Her shoulders drop, and her eyes find a spot on the floor to get lost in. "If we can, that is."

"I'm willing to help," Sergeant Cortell says. "Whatever I can make happen from the military's standpoint, I'll do. I know it's probably not much, but you gave us your best. You deserve mine."

"Thanks," Grady replies. "It's got to be hard on you, too, right now."

Sergeant Cortell nods in response. There's not much more for him to say at this point. He's willing to help, which is great, but if the colonel couldn't get us back to Angelcanis, none of us have much expectation that a sergeant will be able to do much better.

"So ideas?" Kayley says, her eyes scanning the six of us and stopping at me. But I can't give her an answer. Not now. My head is so hot with rage, all I want to do is find that minister and make him feel pain for all of the innocent lives he's ended.

"Not all ministers are like Crowley," Parrish says. "Could we contact one of them and tell them what we know?"

"And what makes you think anyone's going to believe us?" Afton counters, her words sharp. "Haven't we been through that already? Come up with something original."

"We..." Parrish doesn't have a comeback. "Well, what's your idea then?"

"I'm working on it."

"Then don't criticize other ideas until you've got your own," Grady fires out, and in a millisecond, Afton goes from mildly annoyed to baring her teeth at him.

"I've got my own, but I can't say them because I have to keep shooting down other people's stupid ideas first!" Afton crosses her arms and huffs.

"Hey! Enough!" Kayley pleads. "We need to work together and solve this. That won't get done if we're all bickering."

"Hey, Rance." Parrish turns to me. "You got a few calls through before, right?"

"Yeah," I reply with a nod.

"I know there's a communications block over the planet, but we could still try."

"Not from here, we can't," Afton says. "We send a carrier wave from here, and the *Mursilis* will be pointing all of its port-side weapons at us before we can even say hello."

"So we move away from the *Mursilis*," Parrish suggests.

"Easier said than done, dude," Grady says. "Remember, with the engine busted, we've only got two speeds on this ship—imperceptible and out of control."

"So we blink out of here," Parrish says. "I mean, that's what got us here, right? Let's just blink out to somewhere closer to home and then make the call."

"Somewhere closer to home is even worse than where we are right now," I say. "The closer we get to Angelcanis, the more ships are going to be around. We broadcast from there, and we'll have twenty Imperial cruisers surrounding us in no time."

"Yeah, I guess," Parrish replies. He drops a heavy fist on a table with a deep thud.

That silences everyone for a good minute, with no one looking at anyone else. We're all off in our own dark little worlds, thinking dismal thoughts about how we'll never get home. Ideas like those don't need conversation to fester. They'll just grow like fungus in a gloomy cave until they rot our brains. Then we'll all become overgrown like moss on a wet rock, covered in our own bitter thoughts.

"I'm not hearing any solid ideas yet," Kayley says, trying to keep us focused. "Come on, we've just got to lighten up and think clearly. Then we'll come up with something."

"You lighten up," Grady mumbles.

"What?" Even KayKay is teetering on the edge of a full atomic chain reaction. She stomps up to him, hands on her hips. "Say that again."

"You heard me."

"You be nice to her, bird-legs," Afton shoots at him.

"Hey," I say. "Let's keep it chill. No need for this."

"You're one to talk." Afton glares at me. "If it wasn't for you, we wouldn't even be here right now."

After that, our discussion collapses. Everyone is trying to shout on top of each other, and Kayley makes every attempt to stop it while hurling a few sharp insults of her own around.

It goes on like this until we are all exhausted, some of us with tears in our eyes. Again, we all find our little piece of floor, wall, or ceiling to stare at, as catching a burning glance will only start the firefight all over again.

As we all pine for our home far away, my thoughts go to the colonel again. I wonder if he had any family back on Angelcanis. He seemed like the type. They have no idea what happened to him, and I don't know if they ever will. Not unless one of us tells them, and one of us should. I hate the thought of his son or daughter wondering if they're ever going to see their father again.

Maybe I should be the one to do it. That edge of guilt continues to dig into me. It's true what Afton said—*I* was the one who went with Original Teddy. *I* was the one who called them and made them come here. It was wrong of me. I wish there was something I could do to make up for it.

Wait, maybe...there is?

"Why don't we finish the mission?" I ask, and everyone snaps their heads in my direction as if I just told them I was going to throw myself out of the airlock.

"You can't be serious," Afton replies, but with less than half of her usual snark. She's still focused on dabbing her fingers around her eyes.

"Rance, no." Kayley shakes her head. "Not a good idea at all."

"I'd be for it," Parrish ventures in a reversal from earlier. I'm not sure why he changed his mind, but I'm happy he did.

"Yeah, me too." Grady nods a few times. He's already thinking it through.

Kayley stares at both of them. Her eyes get wider by the second as she realizes that we're seriously considering of this.

"Well, I wouldn't want any of you to put yourselves at risk, but honestly, I'm alone here. I really would be glad to have help," Sergeant Cortell says, breaking his silence. He kept so quiet while we were all name-calling, I'd forgotten he was in the canteen. "My mission isn't complete until I finish what the colonel started."

"You were planning to complete the mission by yourself?" Parrish has a serious level of shock on his face.

"I wouldn't have to if you joined me," Sergeant Cortell replies. "You were signing up anyway, right?"

Parrish nods.

"Yeah, but he was going to have five months of training before he got put in a dangerous situation!" Kayley says.

"The stuff you learn in basic, I could teach you in half a day." Sergeant Cortell says. "Hell, you probably know half of it already."

"Doc." Kayley turns to her. "Help me here. This is crazy, right?"

"You're asking the wrong person," Doc Elizabeth responds, raising her hand. "Remember, I'm the one human living on an alien spaceship."

"I think we owe it to the colonel to try," I say, looking at everyone. "We owe it to the people who died to try. We have to get the word out."

"Good point." Afton tilts her head at me. "Okay, I'll help," she says with a nod.

"Surela!" Kayley's mouth drops open. She didn't see that one coming.

"What?" Afton shrugs and digs a thumb at me. "He made a good point. Besides, I'm out here to find my dad. If that archive has any data about what happened to him, I want it."

Kayley takes a deep breath, forcing herself to stay calm. I don't think she expected she would be the outsider here. She rarely, if ever, finds herself in such a position. Kayley's a natural-born leader—she's *our* natural-born leader—and on any normal day, we'd follow her anywhere. But today's not all that normal.

She turns to me, her oldest friend and potential last place of refuge in which to find an ally. Kayley might be forgetting that I was the one who suggested this insane idea in the first place.

"Rance." Kayley's big eyes beg me. "Tell me you're not going to do this. We're the ones that were staying behind. Don't you remember?"

I avoid her eyes and stay silent. I know it's going to break her heart when I answer, and that will crush me. I hate to see her upset, and knowing that it'll be my fault only makes it a million times worse. As I'm about to do it, my resolve falters. My open mouth goes shut again, and I look away once more.

"Rance," she tries again. This time her voice comes up with a growl. "Tell me this instant that you won't be doing this, or there's going to be a problem."

I get the courage to connect with her steely blue gaze, and I'm destroyed by it. My legs tremble, and my knees feel weak. Saying no to her is going to be impossible for me. If I go against her wishes, I might as well throw any chance of dating her out the airlock. But then I think about Colonel Nelson. How could I possibly explain to his family that he died for nothing?

"I'm sorry." My apology barely makes it out of my mouth. "I have to... for the colonel, and the people of Angelcanis."

Disappointment hits her eyes first. I know she was desperate to get me to see it her way, but there's also reluctant agreement in her. Kayley knows what I've been through. She was there when it happened, and she gets why I want to do this for the colonel. Some part of her must even want to help. She's struggling, like I struggled, to make sense of this awful place we're in.

I watch with a growing lump in my throat as Kayley's jaw gets tight. Anger and frustration build inside her like a kettle heating up until it boils over. Kayley cries out and slams her fist into my chest. I take a step back, stunned. But it's nothing compared to the hurt and despair that covers her face. She presses a palm against her chest, then turns and bolts.

I take a few seconds to recover, and then I start to go after her.

"Uh-uh," Doc Elizabeth says, blocking me with her arm. "You've got a mission to plan, and healing pain is my job. You stay here."

Thirty-Seven

"DAMN, KID. YOU SURE know how to make a girl cry," Afton says with a grin as she pats me on the back. "All the better for me."

Afton might be right—did I just kill any chance of dating Kayley? I'm jelly right now, so I don't have any witty retorts. That wasn't how I hoped this would go down, but here we are. She's going to be upset for a while, and my guilt will last just as long.

"Dude, you made the right call," Parrish says. "This is for the colonel."

"And the Teddys," Grady adds.

"Yeah, well," I say and sigh. "Why don't I feel so good about it then?"

"Because she just punched you in the chest?" Afton says, still grinning like she just won some marathon. Parrish comes over and gently removes her from gloating over me. I know Afton's trying to lighten the mood in her own way, but her approach is a serious fail. Minus five points, Surela...or, actually, just forget it. I don't feel like keeping score right now.

"Let's get to planning," Parrish says. "We need to get over there before they destroy the data."

"We'll need to choose assignments for everyone," Grady says. "Like, who goes, who stays, who gets to not get space sickness and vomit in their EVA suit..."

"Grady?" I turn to him, surprised. "Do you really get space sick?"

He just curls the side of his mouth and rolls his eyes upwards at my query. Grady isn't the one with the strongest constitution among us, but of all the things for him to be sensitive to, I would never have guessed that a spacewalk would be it.

"Okay, that's one for staying here," Afton says. "I, for one, am going."

"Who said you get to decide that? What if I want to go?" Parrish says. Afton just puts her hands on her hips and smirks back at him, to which he frowns. I duck my head, not wanting to be involved in another round of skewer-your-buddy.

"Hey," Sergeant Cortell says. "Do you kids mind if I run this meeting? I think I can figure out what we all need to do."

"You're the only one here with the military experience, so go for it," Parrish says with a flourish of his hand.

"Thanks." Sergeant Cortell nods. "So I think having four of us go this time will be beneficial. There were a few tight spots, and an extra person could have made a big difference in how the mission went...if only to act as a lookout or a distraction from time to time. We certainly could have used the extra pair of eyes."

"Do we have enough EVA suits for that?" I ask, remembering that we've lost two.

"Well, I've got mine, and the three of us each had backups, so actually, yes."

"Are the backups the same as the regular ones?" Afton asks, suspicious. I don't blame her for that. I was wondering about it myself. If any of us got a half-baked EVA suit, we might think twice about wanting to go.

"Yes, exactly the same in every way," Sergeant Cortell says, raising his hands. "Don't have any concerns about it. I wouldn't put you in any more danger than we'll already be in."

"So then," Parrish says, "are we agreed? Me, Rance, Afton, and the sergeant?"

There are solemn nods all around. It feels like deep down, there's a world of fear and apprehension in each of us, just waiting for when we have a quiet moment to ourselves. That's when we'll all start freaking out.

"Now," Sergeant Cortell says, "before we just jump into our suits and fly over there, we've got a few problems to solve if we can. Number one is security. They're bound to be on top of things now that we stirred them up. Any thoughts on how we diminish that problem are welcome. If there was a way to spoof the security cameras or see who we might be in danger of running into before we actually do, that would be a huge plus. I know we decided it was too risky to hack into the ship's systems last time, but I don't think we have a choice."

"Teddy, can you lend a hand?" Grady asks. Original Teddy bends his tentacles in what could be interpreted as a thumbs-up.

"Good idea," Sergeant Cortell replies. "Next, we need to get some proper uniforms. Mine didn't fool them for very long, as I'm sure you heard."

"Stealing them sounds like a plan," Afton says, with a sly grin.

"Right, well, we'll need to find where we can do that. The ship's laundry might be an idea. That might also tie into our problem number three."

"Where to get in," Parrish says. "That hatch has to be gone after you blew it, and even if it's not, I'll bet they've got serious eyes on it now."

"Perhaps not," Sergeant Cortell corrects. "They may realize it's a gap in their security, but they won't be expecting any other intrusions from there. The minister's arrival might have them really on point, but they could just as easily be trying to hide as many issues as they can."

"What are the chances of that?" I ask.

"Not sure." He shrugs. "I don't have the security clearances that the colonel did, so I don't have any frame of reference."

"We shouldn't take any chances," Parrish says. "Laundry chute it is."

"Yeah, first we have to find where that is," I say. I press my lips together, not expecting much of an answer.

"Most likely on the ass-end of the *Mursilis*, far away from where we need to be," Afton says and moans.

"Rance, this sounds like a job for you," Grady jokes, but Sergeant Cortell misses his sarcasm and nods with an approving glance.

"Yeah, Rance, please find that out."

I guess I'll have to. I give Sergeant Cortell a thumbs-up, and he nods. So great, I'm on the hook for one of the most critical parts of our entire mission. No pressure at all.

"Nicely done," Sergeant Cortell says. "Let's finalize this by choosing our areas of responsibility once we're inside."

"The sergeant and I will be the combat team," Parrish says. "Though I really hope it never comes to that."

"Agreed," the sergeant says. "They're human, and they're on our side, so I'd prefer not to hurt anybody. We, uh, kind of managed that last time."

"Afton can be the distraction," I suggest, and she flashes a narrow-eyed glance at me. Somehow I knew she wouldn't like that idea, but I had no bad intention behind it. I was just thinking—

"Why? Because I'm the girl? Is that it?" Afton crosses her arms. "Maybe they might like your pretty face instead, huh? Didn't think of that, did you, *jaunatabadi*?"

"What did you just call me?" Whatever it was, it wasn't Common.

"Sexist," Grady answers with a smirk.

"Wait a second." I get defensive. "You think I suggested Afton because she's got..." I wave a hand towards her. I'd better be careful about the next words I choose. "A pleasant smile? No way, I just thought she'd be better at deceiving people, you know, in case we run into someone."

"Why don't *you* be the distraction?" Afton sticks her chin out at me. "You can just be the idiot that you are and pretend to be lost."

"Hey, that's not a bad idea," Parrish says. "The being lost part, that is."

"Great, thanks, Rance, for taking that on." Sergeant Cortell is either completely oblivious to that whole interaction, or he's just great at pretending it didn't happen.

"Sure thing," I mumble. Wonderful. Me, a distraction. I guess we'll get as far as the first laundry basket before they're onto us. I've got no idea how to be a distraction. Should I shout and jump around so the others can get away? Not happening—that will only end up with me getting a big hole in my head. Afton must be spot-on with her assessment of me.

"So that just leaves me then." Afton points to herself and smiles. "And like I said, I want to be the one that downloads the recording."

"That's just one part," I shoot back. "What else will you do?"

"Why do I have to do anything else?" Afton says, throwing her hands up. "In fact, why do any of us? We can just bring a few Teddys over, and they can popsicle anyone we run into. Then we just slide into the data room and watch some riveting documentaries."

"That's not going to work," Sergeant Cortell replies. "Any foreign life form detected on board will immediately put the ship into lockdown. We wouldn't even be able to set foot out of the laundry."

"What if Afton is in charge of getting doors open for us?" Parrish suggests. "I remember you guys had some challenges with that the last time."

"Not for lack of trying," the sergeant replies. "Though to have one person in charge of it would be a good idea."

"That means you, Surela," I add with a grin. She wrinkles her nose back at me, but it's in a good-natured way. She'd be really good at breaking into things.

"Awesome," Grady says. "Anything else we need to go over?"

"Don't think so," Sergeant Cortell replies. "This has been fairly comprehensive. Of course, we're building on all the planning and information we had from before, so we skipped a bunch of steps, but I am impressed with what you've come up with. Not even sure if the colonel and I could have done it better."

"Now we gotta get everything prepped," Parrish says. "I did that last time, so I can help the sergeant again."

I take in a breath and glance around the canteen at my partners in crime. That's exactly what we'll be if we get caught—criminals. I get a chill considering that. Not because I'm afraid to die, but because I might not get a chance to talk to Kayley again before we go, and that would be my biggest regret. Well, that, and not seeing my mom again. I wonder if any thoughts like that are crossing my buds' minds.

"You guys realize that we might not be coming back from this, right?" I ask, glancing at all of them.

"It would solve your problem with Kayley, though," Afton replies.

I just give her the side-eye of death.

Thirty-Eight

I STARE OUT OF the translucent wall in front of me, stuffed into my EVA suit like a tube of cheese spread, gazing at the stars. Like cheese, my suit is orange—designed to be visible against the vast darkness that I'm about to step out into. Once we do, there'll be no stopping until we reach the *Mursilis'* aft supply hatch. That's the spot I found to get us in—we're hoping nobody will be there since the ship isn't in dock, and also, it's just a quick turn to get to the laundry.

And then a very long way to the archive.

I didn't get a chance to talk to Kayley before we suited up. None of us did. Doc Elizabeth told us she didn't want to see us. That bothered me a lot—it bothered all of us, and that only makes it worse. It's one thing for KayKay to be angry with me, but for her to be upset with everyone else, that's a major downer. I can only imagine she's got to be feeling really alone, and that really gets me. I can't even find out how she's doing, and that just adds to my regret. I would rather be scraping my insides out than feeling like this.

"You guys ready to go?" Grady's voice comes over our newly installed Teddy comm. He's excited—he might be the only one—to try out his new system. More accurately, *we'll* be trying out the system that the Teddys built for him. Grady didn't have to do much other than tell the Teddys what he wanted, and they pulled some tech off the shelf and jammed it together. I know it's very ad hoc, but they could have at least made the adapter they stuck on the top of my head itch less.

Still, I'm impressed at the tiny little circuit hidden in my hair that allows Grady to see us and talk to us. For an alien race that can create stuff like that, it's kind of curious why they don't have some way to defend themselves. It could be that the Teddys are keeping more secrets, but I thought we were in with them at this point. I put that thought aside for now and focus on diving into the deep end of the outer-space pool.

"Good to go," Sergeant Cortell says. "Ready whenever you are."

"Got it," Grady replies from the bridge. "Starting the countdown at minus ten seconds...nine..."

"Wait! Wait!" Doc Elizabeth shouts from behind us. "Hold up a minute!"

"Hey, Grady, pause the count. I think Doc wants to talk to us." Parrish turns around, and the rest of us follow. It's nice that Doc Elizabeth wants to see us off, but her timing is a bit late. Ten seconds later and we'd be free-floating in a vacuum.

"Not me," Doc Elizabeth corrects. "Well, yes, me, but not just me. Someone else wants to say a few words to all of you."

Kayley steps out from behind the doc, her eyes sharp like a pair of Elizabeth's needles, ready to inoculate us from harm or cause it instead. She's not over whatever anguish she was feeling before, and I'm wondering if she just wants to smite us with some wretched curse.

"Hey." Afton takes off her helmet and steps towards her with an elated smile. "You came."

But when she reaches out to embrace Kayley, she gets rebuffed. Kayley steps back and gives her a *don't you dare* glance. It stops Afton dead in her tracks. She drops her arms, her shoulders, and from the looks of it, her spirits. I feel bad for Afton, but somewhere inside me there is a small part rejoicing over it—I think that makes me a terrible friend. Yeah, well, she started it.

"I came because I didn't want before to be the last time I saw any of you." Kayley's voice is even and measured as if she had planned out what she was going to say before she showed up here. "I won't wish you luck because I'm still angry with all of you. You shouldn't be doing this. It's stupid and reckless. If you die because of this, I...I won't forgive you for leaving me."

Whoa, that's strong and maybe not as well rehearsed as I thought it was going to be. I mean, I get where she's coming from, but to lay that on us right before we leave, what is she thinking? My blood bubbles a little, but I don't want to fight with her. Not now. We need to focus on the mission. I keep myself hidden from her view and stay in the back. It doesn't help my stomach to do that, but the twisting would be a lot worse if our eyes connected.

"Kayley," Afton tries, "I'm sorry. I didn't—"

"Save it." Kayley cuts her off. She drops her head for a minute, fighting with herself to stay collected, but when she raises it again, her eyes are wet. "I...I have to go." As Kayley turns, she raises a hand to cover her face.

"I think what she also wanted to add was be safe, look out for one another, and come back unharmed," Doc Elizabeth says. "And from me: don't be stupid. I don't want to have to patch anyone up. Or worse. Now go, and get this thing so we can bring down the guilty."

"Thanks, Doc," Parrish says with a wistful smile. Then he also switches gears and gets on his comm. "Grady, are you reading? Start the count again. We're back on."

"You might want to put your helmet back on, Afton," I say with a grin. "You don't want to make it too easy for me to be the first one to make up with her."

"Not a chance, boy-o," Afton replies, locking her helmet in place. "Even when we both come back—and we will—you've still got way more stairs to climb than I do."

"Okay, here we go," Grady calls. "We're sealing the inside portal and counting down. Ten...nine...eight...seven...six...five...four...outside portal is opening...three...two...one...launch!"

Despite Grady's thrilling countdown, the trip over is uneventful, even boring. It's still my first spacewalk, and I want to be excited about it, but it's hard. Kayley just gave us the worst pep talk ever, and any amazement about it has been squashed down under the ache in my chest. I wish I could talk with the others about it, but for the sake of security, it's radio silence until we're at the supply hatch. All I can do is be alone with my thoughts and the utter emptiness of space. It's fitting, in a way, to be so alone. Experiencing this is like understanding how Kayley must feel about us leaving her.

That mood doesn't change until we get the supply hatch open and slip inside. Even then, the gloom doesn't fully disappear until we have to shift our brains into mission mode, pushing aside all other thoughts and focusing solely on the task at hand.

"Everybody good?" Sergeant Cortell asks, checking on the three of us. We give him the appropriate nod or thumbs-up, or in Afton's case, a yawn. "Okay, laundry's just down the corridor. Grady, you got eyes on?"

"Yeah, you guys really dropped into the ass-end of the ship." After a brief pause he says, "Looking good otherwise, no movement in your local vicinity, and security hasn't been alerted. I'd say you're good to go."

He's not really seeing what we can see, but with a bit of carrier wave trickery, the Teddy ship is bouncing directed waves off the *Mursilis* to make an extremely crude sensor. Grady says the *Mursilis* won't pick it up because it won't look like anything other than a gravity distortion to them, and that's not something they'll care much about.

We slip into the laundry in no time and instantly regret our plan. It smells—bad. Take the Teddy burp and add some grease and body odor into that, and you're getting close. I try to close my sense of smell off, but it's pointless.

"Ugh," I mutter, "don't be too choosy with your uniform picks."

"There are some clean ones over here," Parrish says, stepping over to a bunch of SBUs hanging off a line.

"Rance, keep an eye out," Sergeant Cortell says. "I'll get you a uniform. You're probably a thirty-six, right?"

"Thirty-six? Are you kidding?"

"He's more like a thirty-two." Afton chuckles. "No muscle mass at all."

"Maybe we should arm-wrestle," I say to Afton. "Then I'd show you just how wrong you are."

"How about now?" Afton shoots back, dropping her elbow onto a table and giving me an *I dare you* face.

"Knock it off," Parrish chides. "This is serious."

The three of them whip through the ready-to-wear stuff hanging off the line, and both Parrish and the sergeant find something in record time. Afton is pickier. I'm not really sure about what, as I'm only glancing their way occasionally. Otherwise, I've got both eyes welded to the corridor in case Grady's brand-new invention, backed by Teddy tech, decides not to work.

"Rance, sorry, I can't find anything for you," Sergeant Cortell says. "Why don't we switch, and you have a look."

"This is taking too long," Grady complains. "You need to be on your way in five minutes according to the schedule."

"What schedule?" Afton frowns, then tries to remember.

"The one I made up."

"The one you made up...and didn't tell us about?" Parrish responds in annoyance.

"Just trying to help..." Grady says in a pouty voice.

I start searching through the uniforms while Parrish and Sergeant Cortell throw their ship uniforms on. They're really nothing much more than fancy jumpsuits, but I guess I could see how they're more useful on the ship. That still doesn't help me find one, and I'm already running low on options.

That is, until I spot an officer's uniform.

I pull it down from the rack and eye it with some interest, but once I do so, Afton catches sight of it and runs right over. She rips it out of my hands and looks it over with eyes sparkling.

"This is a woman's uniform, Rance," Afton says.

"No, it's not."

"No, it totally is," she replies and holds up the waist. "See? It's cut for a woman."

"You just want an officer's uniform," I say, snatching it back. "I found it first."

"No, you didn't."

"Did too!"

"Someone wear it!" Parrish hisses. He's glaring at both of us. So that means I'm just as much to blame for Afton trying to steal my find from my hands as she is. It's not fair, but I'm out of options.

"Okay, fine, be an officer," I say and throw it at her.

"Excellent decision," Afton replies with a smirk. "Now I won't have to stuff you into the dirty pile." She raises her hand and makes a circling motion for me to turn around.

"Forget it. I still have to look. You go find someplace to change." I'm not budging on that. Afton already stole the one uniform I thought might fit me. So maybe it's for a girl, but maybe it's not. I don't really care as long as I find something. I'd be happy with a petty officer's uniform, but at this point, I'll take what I can get.

Except I find no other uniforms, and it's really aggravating. Everything is too big or too small. I could put myself into a larger one, but someone might question why my uniform looks like it belongs to the world's strongest man and I'm not him.

"Don't worry," Sergeant Cortell says. "I've got an idea."

"What's that?"

"We'll say you're one of the infiltrators, and we and the captain there"—he gestures to Afton—"are taking you to interrogation. Only if we run into someone. Otherwise, no need to worry...you look fine."

"So I'm your prisoner, then," I state, not enjoying that idea very much.

"That's right," Afton says, stepping out of her dressing area, her annoying smirk returning to her face. "You're *my* prisoner."

Thirty-Nine

I DON'T KNOW IF everyone is on lunch break or what, but there's no one around. It's creepy, but we're careful, keeping to the edges of the corridor as we work our way up towards the archive. Sneaking around is a waste of our time, though. Nobody's here to challenge us, and the entire scheme we cooked up with me being a prisoner is worthless. So much for that part of our brilliant plan.

While I'm proud to say this is not my first time on a starship, it is my first time on a *human* starship, and I can't help but notice how much brighter and taller it is. The floor, walls, and ceiling are a comfortable light beige, and there are even a few decorative stripes of oceanic blue. It reminds me of the beach, and I even get a little homesick looking at it. We have so much fun at the beach, although we haven't been there in a while. I really hope we make it back so we can go again—all of us.

"Anyone else finding this a little strange?" Parrish whispers. "We've covered, like, half the ship, and we haven't seen anyone."

"You've gone about one-tenth," Grady corrects. "Half the ship is like the other side of town, where the amphitheater used to be...but you're right. There's probably two thousand crew on that ship, not including the fighter wings."

"Keep your guard up all the same," Sergeant Cortell commands. "If they know we're here, they may just be waiting to corner us somewhere."

We continue like this for another few minutes until we reach level access, hop on the ladder, and climb casually. We expected to be avoiding *Mursilis* crew at every turn, but it's been eerily quiet instead. It's bad because I know we're starting to let our guard down. I definitely am, and when I glance at Afton, I notice she's doing anything but watching her back.

"Hey, eyes up," Grady says as we exit the access shaft. "You're getting a visitor in ten seconds."

"Quick! Rance, in between Parrish and me," Sergeant Cortell directs. "Pretend your hands are secured together behind you. Afton, get behind us."

Afton checks her hair—which I think is strange until I realize she's put it up in a bun, military style—and darts in back. I do my best impression of being in restraints, and Parrish grabs my arm. I quickly glance up at him, and he winks. I think his hand on my arm is more for his security than mine.

As we turn the corner towards our destination, a young female ensign with sunflower-blond hair steps into our path. The moment she sees us, her mouth and eyes pop open, and she pauses in place.

"What's this?" she asks, more curious than suspicious, or at least that's the vibe I'm getting from her.

"Escorting this infiltrator to the brig, ma'am," Sergeant Cortell replies. "Apologies for startling you."

"Oh?" She eyes me with interest—maybe a little too much interest. "Is he one of the ones that broke in through hull access fifty-one?"

"Affirmative, ma'am."

Afton coughs from behind, and the ensign's head pops up to search behind me. She checks herself before her face goes all surprise-y again and comes to attention and salutes.

"Ma'am, apologies...I was..." The ensign narrows her eyes a bit, and I cringe, recalling the moment when it went wrong for the colonel and his team. If we mess this up, it's all over. Parrish squeezes my arm but keeps his eyes forward. I know he's feeling the same as me. Let's hope we can clear this one with no problems.

"It's fine." Afton does a good job of sounding the mildly annoyed officer. "May we proceed, please?"

"Of course, ma'am!" The ensign—who at second glance is probably a few years older than Afton, Parrish, and me—salutes again and then steps aside to let us pass. We move forward, and out of the corner of my eye I catch the ensign watching me. I turn my head to glance at her, and she smiles. Now, I know I'm supposed to be the bad-guy criminal or something like that, but when someone smiles at you, it's just good manners to smile back. So I do.

"Eyes front!" Sergeant Cortell grabs my head and spins it forward again. I wasn't expecting it, so my neck cracks like a celery stalk getting twisted too far.

"Sorry about that," the sergeant says once we're clear of the ensign.

"You shouldn't be," Afton says before I can respond. "He deserves any pain he got. Really, Rance? Smiling at an older woman like that? I'm telling as soon as we get back."

"We need to get back first," I reply. "Otherwise, that's going to be difficult."

"Hey, we've got other things to worry about," Parrish snaps, and that ends the argument.

A few more turns, and we're at the entrance to the archive. Sergeant Cortell's face turns pale once we come to a stop a few paces from the entrance. He's got to be playing back the last time he was here, and I'm sure it's not a pleasant memory.

"And here we are," Afton says, coming around to approach the door. "Okay, Grady, now what?"

"Is it locked?" Grady asks.

"What do you think?"

"Okay, so there's usually a master code that will work on all doors on a ship. It depends upon when the ship was built, but I have a few that we can try."

"How the heck do you know that?" Sergeant Cortell asks.

"Two extremely busy ship designers are bound to forget to lock out their home computer systems from time to time," he replies. I guess I just don't give my brainiac friend the credit he deserves. Extra point for effort, Grady.

"Okay, Afton, so here's the first code—hold down the one and the three, then press zero, six, seven, eight, nine, seven, and then five three times."

"Got it, here goes nothing." Afton's usual overconfidence has dwindled down to a hopeful enthusiasm. She does the sequence, and... the door beeps at her and blinks red three times.

"So that didn't work."

"Okay, try this," Grady says. He gives her another sequence, but the same thing happens. Afton sighs out of frustration, and Parrish glances down the corridor with some unease. I do the same, hoping that he didn't just see someone. Luckily for all of us, no one is there.

"Are you sure you entered it correctly?" Grady asks, puzzled. I'm having doubts about his ability to remember strings of numbers. It should be easy for him, but what if he's not as on point with the numbers as we need him to be?

"Of course I did!" Afton reacts more strongly than I expected she would. Even Parrish throws her a surprised glance. "Do you think I can't press a few numbers into a keypad? Maybe you don't remember them correctly."

"Let's keep calm," Sergeant Cortell warns. "We need cool heads to get this done right."

"I'm fine," Afton says. She's not, and we all know it because we're not, either.

"Okay. Okay. Let's try this last one," Grady says, trying to stay focused. "I'll say it slow, and you can just repeat it back to me before you try it. Okay?"

"Just give me the sequence," Afton replies with no amusement in her voice.

As I hear the numbers and instructions that Grady gives her, I get the sense that it's familiar. At least the first grouping of them is the same.

"That's the one you just gave me, idiot," Afton grumbles.

"Oh." There's silence from Grady's end. "Oh yeah, you're right. Sorry about that."

Oh man. Parrish throws his hands up while the sergeant drops his head into his hand, and Afton bangs her head on the door a few times. I'm going to hold back that extra credit I gave Grady before. He might just be stressed out, or maybe he really is as mindless as the rest of us. If this turns out well, I'll consider it a miracle that only the Three Goddesses could have granted. I put it into the back of my mind to do a serious offering when I'm back home—a really big one. That's on top of my other one, of course. I'll be spending a lot of time in temples when this is all over.

"Alright, I've got it," Grady says. "Afton, you ready?"

"Whatever."

"So it's a bit like the first, but it's an older code. Honestly, I don't think it's going to work—"

"Not helping, Grady," Afton growls.

"Sorry, okay, here it is. Hold down the seven and the eight, then key in four, six, six again, then two, zero, two, one. Make sure to hold down the keys for the whole time you're typing in the sequence, then release them only after you finish the sequence. That's really important— seven and eight first, type in the sequence, then release them."

"This is never going to work." Afton sighs, then does exactly what Grady instructed, making a show of releasing the two pads a long time after she typed in the sequence.

Now we weren't expecting miracles—okay, maybe I was—but we get absolutely no response from the keypad this time. No beep, no blinking light. Nothing. I shake my head, teetering on the edge of complete vexation. This was the weakest link in our plan, and now it's the preeminent failure.

"Nothing happened," Afton says. She's not in the least bit surprised.

"Nothing?" Grady's amazed echo comes back. "No beep?"

"Nope."

"Did you hit the enter key?"

I catch my breath. No way. It couldn't be that easy.

"I *will* kill you, Grady." Afton flicks out her pointer finger and drives it into the enter button. Not even a millisecond later, there's a single beep and a solid green light.

And just like that, the door slides open.

"It worked!" I say a little bit too loudly.

"Everyone in, now, before it closes!" Sergeant Cortell pushes me towards the entrance, and Parrish gets dragged along when I reach out and grab his arm. We shove ourselves in as if we're all trying to get into the special cine preview.

The door slides shut behind us, and for some reason, we pile up just inside the entrance instead of moving into the room. It could be that the sheer number of interface terminals in here is intimidating us, or perhaps it's the large bank of biomemory storage tanks lining the walls.

"Uh, guys?" Grady asks timidly. "Did you make it?"

"Yeah," I confirm. "Yeah, Grady, we're in."

"Great! Don't forget to lock the door behind you."

There's a sudden jumble of hands trying to find the switch before one of us engages the lock. That better do it. Now on to more important things.

Forty

"OKAY, AFTON, YOU'RE UP," Sergeant Cortell says. "We'll do a quick sweep of the room while you're working. We don't want someone to pop out and surprise us at an inopportune time."

Afton salutes with way too much embellishment and spins off to choose a terminal. It doesn't take her long—Miss I Know Better Than You knows what she wants. She usually gets it, too, which is why I'm jealous of her. Sometimes.

"If you actually want to be in the military, Surela, you'd better learn how to do that right," I say. "Salutes don't include dance moves."

Her response is to twist around and stick her tongue out at me before dropping down in front of a terminal. I roll my eyes and shake my head. Only she could get away with that as an answer.

"Rance, you've still got a long way to go when it comes to girls, don't you?" Sergeant Cortell asks with a grin. "Come on, let's check the room out. Start out on that side, and I'll start on the other. We'll cover everything twice that way. Make sure to touch everything and look for hidden openings. Parrish, if you would, please stay by the door."

"Sure."

"Grady, we get any visitors, let us know," I say, and he responds in the affirmative.

The biomemory tanks are warm as I slide my hands over them, but not burning hot. Boiling temperatures would kill all the organic material inside, which would be contrary to the tank's purpose. It's disturbing enough that we use living tissue to store data. The pungent smell of the tanks doesn't help the creep factor, either. I once had a fish tank that gave off a better scent.

I make my way down the left side of the room, as the sergeant directed. The room isn't that big, but the dim lighting makes it difficult to tell just how big it really is. Someone could be hiding in here and we could miss them. I guess that means it's a good thing we're going over the area twice. More if Afton takes too long.

"How you coming, Rance?" Sergeant Cortell asks, just a little ahead of me on the opposite side. He's sliding his hands around the tanks and shining a light in between them.

"Fine, though I don't have a light like you do." That comes out sounding more envious than I meant it to be.

"Don't worry, I'll handle that," he replies.

I return to peering into the data tanks, feeling around their edges for anything out of the ordinary—not that I'd know what that would be. As I check, I consider how amazing it is that somewhere within one of these nutrient-rich tanks filled with trillions of neurons, the vid recording exists. At least, I hope it does. We have no idea if someone already beat us in here and erased the data. Grady claims that's not easy to do, but I'm still worried.

"Shoot! He's not in here!" Afton pounds the terminal as if it's a defective vending machine.

"He?" Parrish queries.

"My father. No record of him being rescued!" Her voice is defeated and sullen. I can't help but feel bad for her. She's been carrying the hope that he's still alive this whole time. Other than the first time when she told me and Grady, she's never really mentioned how worried she was about him. Maybe she told Kayley, but I doubt even that. All of the negative thoughts I've ever had about her go floating off into space, and I'm left with just wanting to give her a hug. She wouldn't accept it, of course.

"Afton, you're supposed to be looking for the recording of the attack!" Parrish says. "We don't have time for anything else!"

"Easy, Parrish," I advise. Not that he's going to listen to me.

"I already looked," Afton replies, nonchalant about the whole thing. "It's not here, either."

"Now's not the time to make jokes!" I hiss. "We need to get that vid!"

"I already told you, I can't find it. They must have erased it."

A stream of curses and growls comes from my mouth. This is beyond pathetic. We were too slow, and now we're paying the price. If we don't get any data to help us, we lose the chance to stop the war. Then where will we be? Where will the Teddys be?

I can't give up hope yet.

"Maybe we've got no vid, but there's got to be something we can use," I say, jumping over to Afton's terminal. Parrish is right there with me, and we crowd around her screen.

"Not both of you at once!" Sergeant Cortell sounds like an elementary school teacher trying to corral rambunctious students. "Parrish, you help Afton. Rance and I will continue to search."

It's hard to pay attention to what I'm doing when our entire reason for being here just vanished. Without that vid, we're nowhere, and all the risks we took were for nothing. Kayley might have been right, after all. We shouldn't have come.

"Grady, I thought you said stuff is difficult to erase from these kinds of data storage units." I'm reaching, but if he's got a better insight about these tanks, then I'm all for it.

"Difficult, but not impossible," Grady replies. "Especially for someone really determined...and I'd say the captain on that ship really wanted to get rid of that vid."

I can deny it all I want, but that's not going to magically make the vid reappear. I can only hope that we can find another way to take Minister Sinister down. He's got to face justice. I don't want to see anyone else die.

"Alright." Afton sighs. "It's not much, but I found a few messages between Crowley and the captain of the *Mursilis*. If nothing else, it proves they were in contact before the first attack."

"That's good. Did you copy it?" I ask.

"Who do you think I am, buddy?"

"Alright, listen, our main objective wasn't successful, but we're not leaving empty-handed," Sergeant Cortell says. "Let's get out of here. We don't need to take any more risks at this point."

"Yeah, that's a really good idea, guys," Grady pipes up over the Teddy comm. "About a hundred targets are coming your way."

"What?"

"It's a trap!" Parrish cries. "They knew we'd try again, and they waited for us to lock ourselves in here!"

"Don't panic." Sergeant Cortell takes a moment to think. "Okay, this is what we're going to do: Rance, you go out first. The rest of us follow like we're chasing you down."

"Got it!" Afton logs out of the terminal and hops up, her eyes locked on me. "You'd better run like you never have before, buddy. You're going to have two athletes and a soldier chasing you. It wouldn't look good if we caught up with you too soon."

"Grady, how soon until they get here?" I ask, positioning myself by the door.

"About twenty seconds, give or take. Better hurry..."

Parrish nods at me, and I nod back. There's no reason to say anything more. It would only come out sounding like some action scene from a cine.

He mouths out the numbers *three, two, one* and punches the door open. Once there's enough space to slip through, I blast out, sliding around the left turn and heading down the corridor. I dive into the access shaft, getting there in what I think is record time. For me, maybe it was, but I'm only about halfway down the ladder when the others show up.

"Rance, get moving!" Afton hisses.

I chance it, putting my feet on the sides of the ladder, and slide the rest of the way down. Afton is a half second behind, doing the same maneuver, but her attempt is far more graceful than mine.

"More like it!" she says, putting her hand on my shoulder and giving me a shove out the door. "Don't forget, right turn at the fork!"

I fly down the corridor like I have wings to soar down this beach-tinted hallway. It's almost enjoyable, and I nearly forget where I am, but as I pass a sea of blue down a connecting passageway, I get a frightening reminder.

"There!" one of the crew shouts.

I swallow hard and hope the others don't get caught up in that mass of bodies. They're already after me—a rumble of boots accelerating to attack speed. My legs are burning. I swallow as much air as possible and redouble my efforts.

This corridor seems way longer than I remember, but I push thoughts like that out of my head. Speed is the only thing that I need to focus on, but it's hard not to wonder where the others are. I can't look back right now to find them. I'll slow down, and that's bad.

The pounding of a hundred pairs of feet picks up behind me, and I brace for weapons fire. It can't be easy to fire and run, and I hope they don't. I won't be able to outrun plasma bolts.

"Stop, or we fire!" one of my pursuers shouts, killing any hopes that they weren't going to do that.

I cut around another turn—too fast—and I go sliding into the wall, smashing my shoulder hard. It hurts, but I have to push that out of my mind. My breathing is heavy, and my chest is burning just as much as my legs are. I'm not sure that I can keep this up for much longer, but I have to.

"Hey!" Afton is beckoning me from the fork in the corridor. It's not far now. I have no idea how she got ahead of me, but I can ask later. We're almost home free. Then that army behind me—

Oh shoot! I'm leading the guards to the three of them. No—they've got to get whatever data Afton got off the ship. This is our last chance at this!

I wave her on, but she doesn't move. I do it again, and she spreads her hands out and shakes her head. That is, until she sees the horde of soldiers behind me. Her eyes go wide, and she darts right, heading towards the way back.

So I go left.

I use all the energy I have left to move my body as fast as I can. Those military idiots better follow me. I'm doing this for everyone, so it has to work. Afton and the others have to escape.

The rumble of feet dies off behind me, and I panic. Was I too fast for them? Or are they not used to sprinting down the corridors of the *Mursilis*? I can't believe I've lost them. There were so many. I think their commanding officer is about to face a serious demotion.

Then I see a group of ten soldiers step out of a room ahead of me, led by that blond ensign we saw before. They raise their weapons, and I dig my feet into the floor, trying to slow down and turn back around.

It's only then that I see the mass of pursuers there, wicked grins all around. They'd stopped running not because they weren't up for it, but because they knew I was caught.

So this is what it feels like to sacrifice yourself for others.

Forty-One

AS I DROP TO the floor on their command, I wonder if the others made it out. Of course, they were wearing ship uniforms, so nobody would have taken too much notice of them in the frenzy to catch me. That could mean that Grady's little trick with the subcarrier wave worked. If they think it was only me who infiltrated the ship, they won't be looking for the others. That's what I want to believe, anyway.

I count about twenty guns aimed at me. A little overkill, given the sheer number of bodies surrounding me in this tight space. The corridors get smaller towards the ends of the ship, and a hundred people must take up a lot of space.

The blond ensign steps up to me, hands on hips and a flirty little smile on her face. I look up and return the smile, though not to flirt. My flirting days are over. The only thing I need to do is get back to the girl I love. I'd want to look for my buddies, too, if I didn't think they were already floating back to safety.

"Well, if it isn't that cute boy from before," she says, taking another step forward to stand over me. "Too bad you're in trouble. I might have liked to get to know you."

"Well, sorry to disappoint," I reply. "Besides, my heart belongs to another."

"What a lucky girl she must be." Blondie is still trying to flirt.

"Yes, how lucky," comes a deep voice from behind, "but she will only have your heart. Your brain belongs to me."

A heavy hand falls onto my head, gripping hard, and begins to turn it around. I have to start turning my whole body before whoever it is overextends my neck to the point where it breaks. As I catch that snide face, instant recognition hits me like a sharp smack from Afton.

"Minister, I can say confidently you'd never win my heart."

Minister Crowley sneers back at me and rises to his full height. From my position on the floor he looks like a giant. I have to crane my neck back just to see his ugly face.

"Take him to my shuttle," Minister Crowley says. "And don't be gentle about it."

Three blue-suited tough guys follow these orders strictly, throwing me into a seat in the aforementioned shuttle and strapping me in. They use more than just the safety harness to do so, taking a good amount of binding tape to ensure I'm not thinking about an unscheduled spacewalk without a suit. They must not realize I'm not that daring.

When I see the massive space station in orbit around a green planet, it becomes obvious where we're going to end up. This is the rear staging base at Herdewyke. I've seen so many images of it that it's strange to see it with my own eyes. I've always wanted to visit to see the city-long space docks where they build and repair star cruisers, but not like this.

The rough boy trio continue to follow orders and bang me about as we make our way to an unknown station level. I should be excitedly taking in the sights of military might in motion, but my head is now so banged up, it hurts to look straight.

I guess that's for the best, since the room they drop me in isn't really worth looking at. There's only a metal table, cold chairs, and no windows, except for the one on the door and the unmistakable two-way mirror on the wall in front of me. The light in here is so glaring that I'm strangely glad one of my eyes is nearly shut from the not-so-accidental fist that slammed into it when they were getting me out of the shuttle.

Moments after they secure my arms behind my back, Minister Sinister comes in holding a tablet. He gives me a quick examination and smiles approvingly at the black ring forming around my right eye.

"Since you referred to me as minister earlier, I'll assume you know who I am. What you may also know is I oversee the Empire's entire frontier defense." He pulls out the metal chair across from me and the legs make a creepy shriek. "Infiltration of our star cruisers, by a human or otherwise, is also part of my jurisdiction."

As if he had rehearsed this entire moment, Minister Sinister smirks at me, then drops the tablet on the table. It makes a tremendous clang that reverberates around the room, but I'm not impressed. If he wanted the noise to frighten or intimidate me, then maybe he shouldn't have let his thugs knock me around to the point where I'm numb.

"Now." He sits down. "You and I are going to have a talk, and you will answer all of my questions, and if you do, then and only then will I consider locking you up for your entire life instead of executing you on the spot."

There's a knock at the door, and a man in pale-green medical scrubs comes in pushing a small cart. On top of it is a small device with a screen and a large needle attached to a tube. They really have the timing of this intimidation thing down. I would roll both my eyes if I could, but I'll settle on one.

"So let's start with you telling me what your name is, boy," the minister says. I'm picturing him pulling off long gloves in dramatic fashion, and I enjoy that vision so much I forget to answer him.

"Deciding not to cooperate is a poor choice." He waves the medical guy over, who rolls his cart up behind me and switches on his device. A sharp pain hits my arm, and I cry out. Minister Sinister grins and leans back in his seat.

"No record match," Med-Man says. "Though the DNA says he's human. He could be from a colony or one of the separatist planets."

"Or maybe just an excellent deception by an alien race," the minister adds. "What say you, boy? Where are you from?"

"Angelcanis," I reply through clenched teeth. That needle jab stung more than any pummeling that a stone-fisted bully could give me.

"Angelcanis, you say?" Minister Sinister crosses one leg over the other and folds his arms. "How...convenient. So you must have been there when those savages attacked, yes?"

"No," I manage to squeeze out before I cough.

"No? You weren't there?"

"No, the Teddys didn't attack us." No need for me to hold back at this point. If I show him I know the truth, I might just knock him down a few notches—enough to make him negotiate with me.

Or, on second thought, it might have the complete opposite reaction. Better not.

"And who are the Teddys?"

"Sounds like some singing quartet," Med-Man jokes, though he's the only one to laugh. He stifles it when the minister gives him his sinister eye.

"They're not savages," I wheeze.

"How would you know that?" Minister Sinister's tone turns suspicious. He uncrosses his legs and leans forward, his fingers pressing together like he's about to pray.

"None of your business," I reply, despite knowing the answer will result in more physical assaults on my person.

"Now, Mr...." He frowns. "What did you say your name was?"

"I didn't."

"Yes, that's right, you didn't." He motions to Med-Man, and suddenly every muscle in my body convulses as if someone else controls them. My arms and legs cramp, and then the sensation disappears. Minister Sinister smiles pleasantly and puts his hands back on the table.

"Felt that, didn't you?" He doesn't wait for my reply. "Every time you fail to answer one of my questions, I'll have Max back there give you another jolt. Understood?"

I'm still trying to recover, so I don't answer.

"You're not answering!" he sings.

"Got it," I mumble.

"So then, your name, please."

"Rance."

"Rance? As in Ransome? And the rest?"

"Rance Quigley He'."

"Oh, maybe a descendant from the Han Expedition then?" He doesn't wait for my answer, as if he wasn't asking me at all. "A pleasure to meet you, Ransome Quigley He' from Angelcanis." His eyes dart past me, up to Med-Man Max.

"Look into that, would you, Max? But before you do, let's give our guest here the shot."

"A shot at what?" I wonder aloud. My question is instantly answered by a pinch on my neck. It's not painful—not compared to what I just went through—but I jump at the surprise. "What was that?"

"Well, let's just call it a little positive reinforcement," Minister Sinister says with that pleasant smile that's starting to make me sick. "If you choose to cooperate, then it will help you remember everything you'd like to say. Of course, if you don't cooperate, we also have negative reinforcement at our disposal. I already know which one you're going to like better."

"Me too."

"So, Ransome, you said something curious to me before. About there not being an attack on Angelcanis. Did you not witness it? The Prime Minister and I both gave a grand speech about it, about how we must... now, what did I say? Ah, how your decision may mean the difference between your survival or the horrible destruction of this planet that has given you so very much...Yes, that was excellent. Did you not see that?"

"I was there," I say, the words coming out of my mouth before I can think them. "I almost got killed by one of those bombs and had to spend half the day in a shelter."

"See how well positive reinforcement works? That's more words in one sentence than you've said to me this entire conversation." He sits back again. "So then, why would you say there was no attack?"

"I never said there was no attack." My eyes go wide as I speak before I can stop myself. "Only that the Teddys didn't do it."

"And who are the Teddys? A separatist movement?"

I tighten my jaw and clench my fists, but my mouth still wants to open and tell this jerk off.

Minister Sinister waves Med-Man Max off from what was going to be more negative reinforcement. Despite not being scared, I'm not looking forward to having that happen again. My brain still feels like it's been scrambled and cooked like one of my mom's stir-fry meals.

"They're what you call 'savages,' though they're more civilized than you'll ever be." I manage to let out only what I wanted, and I'm proud of the little dig I got in.

"So...the Teddys are what you call our enemy, is that it?" Minister Sinister puts his fingers back together.

"It's what they call themselves."

"A rather common name for such an exotic animal, wouldn't you say?"

"It's for our benefit." My eyes close for a moment, as if I'm getting sleepy. Maybe I am, or maybe the minister's little helper is making me drowsy. I might not be able to keep myself awake for much longer.

"I see. So you think these Teddys didn't attack you then?" the minister asks.

"I know they didn't." Shoot, I didn't want to give that up. Not yet. But as my eyes drift down to the table's surface, I think about laying my head down. That would be great. The surface of the steel table is nice and cool. It would feel good on my beaten and slowly warming face.

"Stay with us, Ransome." Minister Crowley snaps his fingers in front of me. I blink and jerk my head back up. "That's better. Now what proof do you have that they didn't attack your planet and kill all of your innocent people? It seems far-fetched if you ask me."

"I was on their ship." No! Stop staying things! My mouth is giving my brain a real struggle. "They're not fighters...They don't have weapons..."

As the battle rages on in my head, I feel my will slip away. We might not get him locked up, but that won't stop me from calling him out for what he's done.

"You," I say, and the minister leans in, curious to know where I'm going with this. "You did it...You bombed us...You killed us! Why?"

The minister drops back in his seat, looking chagrined.

"Max, would you give us a moment? Well," he says as Max leaves the room, "how unfortunate for you. You guessed our little secret. I don't mind admitting it to you since you're here with me, and you won't be leaving anytime soon to go tell anyone else. I'm going to suggest to the Bar that they sentence you to life imprisonment for treason."

"You can't do that." After a moment of being awake, my head is getting heavy again. "I've got rights."

"Actually, no, you don't." He waggles a finger at me. "Parliament has not formally recognized Angelcanis as a member of the

Commonwealth, so you are not a citizen of the Empire, and therefore, I can do whatever I want with you.

"You see, Ransome Quigley He', the Empire is on *my* side, not yours. We must ensure the survival of our grand establishment and of the human race, as the Most Holy intended. If a few inferior creatures of the universe get pushed aside to make way for our expansion, then so be it. Oh, now, don't give me that look, boy. We won't kill any more than we need to. Only enough to get them out of our way. The Goddesses will forgive us. It is our most sacred errand, after all."

"You... you..." I clamp down and tighten my jaw with whatever amount of focus I have left. He's using the Three Goddesses as the reason for killing innocent people? Aliens and humans alike? Oh no...he can't get away with this. I have to stop him...if I can only stay awake...

"Going to call me an unsavory name, are you?" He is amused. "Insult me in some way? Go on, go on, Ransome, let's hear a good one."

My head drops on the table, and I blank out.

Forty-Two

I WAKE UP IN my brand-new home, head hurting worse than all the times I banged my skull on stuff hanging from the Teddy ship's ceilings. Of course, I'm not the tallest, and Parrish and the colonel did it way more times than I did, even though they hadn't been on the ship as long. I felt bad for both of them, but I feel a lot worse now, and not just because of the beatings I got.

They must have brought me in here after I conked out on the interrogation room table. How nice of them! Someone even took my boots off and covered me with a synthetic blanket. If I have to spend the rest of my life in here with someone tucking me in every night, well, that would be creepy at first, but I might grow to enjoy it.

That would be the only thing I would enjoy, however. This closet of a space makes the room where we hacked into the military's network look like a luxurious cavern. The ceiling is taller here, but not by much, and I could easily touch both side walls without even stretching my arms all the way out. I don't know if this is a real stockade, but it's doing the job pretty well.

I slide my legs off the bed, which is more like a shelf, and drop my feet to the floor. It's cold, just like this whole station, or at least the parts I've been to—I'll bet the officers' quarters are nice and toasty. I must be on the farthest ring from the center, and the outer edge, at that.

If I poked a hole through the back wall, I'm sure I'd see the spiral arm of our galaxy.

The front of this cell, at least from what I can tell, is solid but transparent. With the blanket wrapped around me, I shuffle up to the front and peer out. There's not much to see, just a clear, bright corridor that stretches on for a bit then turns left. There might be some stairs there, too, as I glimpse the hint of a handrail.

This is an official brig, after all. I might be the only one down here; the other cells are dark. They even put me in the next-to-last compartment, just for spite. Minister Sinister really wanted to drive home that I'm here permanently. Though, if my sentence is life in prison, I'll be here a lot longer than he will, and he'll be getting to the big judgment in the sky before I do. My guess is he'll be headed down, not up, after his little chat with the Goddesses. Who gets the last laugh then, Minister?

"Teatime, ladies!" someone announces over the intercom. I peek out again to see four guards coming down the corridor, one of them pushing a box with wheels. They stop a few cells down, and the guard takes a carton from the box and brings it to the front of the cell. I can't see what happens after that, but my guess is the occupant of that cell takes it from them. I'm not so alone then.

One guard gets to my cell and glowers at me for a moment. He's slapping a thick rod in his hand. He definitely wants to use that on me if he gets the chance. I'll have to make sure I don't give it to him—I'm done collecting bruises.

"Step back, criminal," he says. I do because I'm not going to give him the satisfaction. Also, I really don't want to find out if that rod is electrified or not.

A section of the translucent door slides open, and the gift-giving guard slides a box halfway through.

"Take it," he orders.

"What is it?" I ask.

"A slow way to get yourself into the infirmary," he replies with a sneer. "Now take it, or you lose out for the next eighteen hours."

I reach out and snatch it from him before he can change his mind. I'm not hungry, but I might be later. Though, with the guard's sparkling review of the food, I might just abstain altogether.

The guards leave me, and the door slides shut again. I sigh and drop myself back down onto my sleeping shelf. That was about the most exciting thing that's happened so far.

Out of sheer boredom or morbid curiosity, I open the carton. There are only four flaps that make up the lid, but it still takes me a minute to figure out how they work. My brain must still be fuzzy with whatever poison they injected me with, because when I do figure it out, I laugh at myself for not getting it sooner. If Kayley were here, she'd be giggling her head off at me.

I sigh again. If I wasn't hungry before, thinking about Kayley just killed any interest I had in food. Not that I really wanted to eat whatever that gray slop is inside the carton. I can tell it's got animal flesh in it. Ugh. My stomach does a triple loop combined with a few twists, and I gag.

Maybe they've got a vegetarian option. I'll have to ask because I'm definitely not eating that.

The hours go by, and I find out quickly enough that there are two options for food—eat it or don't. I can't, so I refuse whatever meals they try to shove at me. Now, after two days, I'm paying the price for my decision. My body is getting too weak to move. If I hadn't at least stayed hydrated, I might have found myself in the infirmary already, but I suspect it won't be long until I am. This must be the fast way to get there.

Ah well. If I have to stay here for the rest of my life, I might as well make it a short one. I won't achieve any of my dreams at this point, anyway.

Static crackles in my head, and I jump as far as my malnourished body can move. Was that over the intercom? I glance around my cell, then push myself up and try to see if someone's coming.

"Rance?"

That sounds like Grady! His voice is distorted and garbled. But unless I'm hallucinating—and I might be—he's communicating to me, from...where?

Oh...Teddy comm! I'm amazed it still works. Or that I even still have it. They took everything else I had on me, but they must not have dug too deeply in my hair. Not that they would have thought it was anything more than a flea if they'd found it.

"Grady? Are you there?"

"Oh, thank the Goddesses! Dude—" His voice cuts out for a few seconds then returns. "So that's why you haven't heard from us, but don't worry—"

"Grady?" I sigh as the Teddy comm goes silent once again. I didn't get a chance to find out about the others, and now that he knows I'm still alive, they're going to come and save me. Shoot. I don't want them risking themselves for me. I should have just stayed quiet. What's to go back to, anyway? Kayley's angry with me, which means I'll probably never get to date her. They erased the vid. Now we don't have a recording...

Wait—recording? Didn't Grady say something about the Teddy comm adapter having a buffer? Yes! It stores a recording of the voice before sending the signal out, which means it captured everything Minister Crowley has said to me...including an admission of guilt! I've got the proof we need!

"Get up, criminal." The mean guard with the rod taps it on the door, shaking me out of my delirium. "There's someone here to see you."

I don't know if the Three Goddesses are that pissed at him or if they're looking out for me, but when Minister Crowley shows up, staring at me with an unemotional gaze, I can't help but get a tiny burst of excitement. Here's my chance to capture some more of his confession!

"You're not looking so good there, Ransome," he says with mock concern. As someone brings a chair for him, my cell door opens. He steps inside and pulls the chair in behind him. "The guards tell me you're not eating. Why not?"

"Have you seen the rotten flesh they want me to eat?" I reply with as much snark as I can muster. "You wouldn't want it, either."

"Nonsense," Minister Crowley says, crossing his legs at the knee, one foot sticking out. "It has been specifically designed with all the nutrients and amino acids that your body needs to keep healthy. I'll bet it even tastes good, too."

"I don't eat dead animal," I say, glaring at his outstretched foot. I don't know why, but his choice of sitting position is getting on my nerves. It's the most wasteful use of space someone can make while sitting and is outright rude to anyone who has to stand in front of you.

"Well, like it or not, Ransome, you will eat it, or I'll have the med team stuff a feeding tube down your throat. You'll be alive to stand trial when we're ready to have one...that much I can guarantee you."

My eyes rise to his face, and I narrow them like I'm a real felon. I must really look the part, too—messy hair, eyes deep in their sockets. Oh yeah. I wish I had a camera to take a picture. Now how to get him to say some stuff that'll incriminate him?

"So will you cooperate?" Minister Sinister asks. "I don't care if you starve yourself, honestly, but you don't get to do that until after the trial."

I roll my eyes, but he ignores it and digs into the pocket of his long ministerial robe.

"Yes, so that is not the main reason I came down to see you." He pulls out something from the pocket, and I recognize it instantly. It's the heirloom my NaiNai gave me that Grady got all excited about. I had shoved it into one of the side pockets of my pants and forgotten about it. Great, another thing I forgot. It's got to be the lack of nutrients in my system causing my brain to go dopey.

"So you recognize it," he comments, catching my reaction. "Tell me... What is it, and where did you get it?"

"My grandmother gave it to me."

Holding it by the circular part at the bottom, he turns it around in his hand and examines the plastic feather-like things sprouting from the top of it. "Hmm, so, you say the origin of this item is human and not alien? Why should I believe that?"

I'd burst out laughing if I didn't think it would get me a beating.

"Listen," I say. "It's probably worthless. Why don't you just leave it here and let me have something to amuse myself with?"

"Ransome Quigley He'." He gives me a disapproving stare, the kind a mother would give her child when they say a bad word for the first time. "Do you realize how many things are wrong with what you just said?"

"No." We're getting off-topic here. I've got to get him back on track if I want more confession. "You want to talk about saying something wrong? How about killing a bunch of humans and blaming an alien race for it? Oh, and another thing...I know you gave the order to fire that started the war!"

He smirks, then glances behind him before leaning in and getting really close to me. I don't flinch or move...mostly because I'm too anemic to do so, but also because being this close will ensure I get his voice nice and clear on my adapter.

"Now listen here, you half-breed hick. Your planet, and all the people on it, are expendable in the eyes of the Empire. Just like those Teddys you seem to be so fond of. Nothing will stop our expansion or control of whatever planet or resource on it we so choose—as divine will commands. It is our Emperor's destiny to become the greatest ruler in history. If that means executing every one of you to achieve it, I will not hesitate in the slightest to give that command again and again!"

"So you admit you gave the order that started the war?"

"I admit it freely." Minister Sinister leans back again, a satisfied smile on his face. "Because, as I said before, Ransome Quigley He', you are in here until you die. No one will ever find out anything. My tracks have been covered all too well."

Oh, we'll see about that.

Forty-Three

MINISTER SINISTER RETURNS EARLY the next morning. I can tell it's early in the morning because the lights in the corridor haven't come back on yet. The mean guard, who's hefting a seriously heavy lamp, and two burly men in medical scrubs accompany him. Neither one of them is Max, and for that small favor I am thankful. I don't think I could handle any more shocks. I'm hurting as it is.

"Get up, Ransome," the minister says, rapping his knuckles on the cell door while Mr. Mean shines his light in my face. They continue this annoyance as I struggle to sit up in my weakened condition and only stop when I squint and throw my arm in front of my face.

Minister Sinister steps inside after the door slides open, this time with no chair.

"Now, Ransome, you have a decision to make. Will you choose to eat the food we give you, or will you choose to make these two gentlemen here shove a tube down your throat?"

"I have a question first," I say, my hoarse voice barely above a whisper.

"Yes, what is it?"

"You've got me...Why bother to hold a trial? I mean, you said yourself that you've already covered all your tracks well."

"I did, didn't I?" He sits down on the edge of my plank of a bed and puts his hands in his lap, as if he's about to lecture me. "Well, that would be an accurate description, certainly. Are you familiar with the term *scapegoat*? It hardly gets used much these days, but—"

He pauses as an alarm goes off somewhere in the distance. Minister Sinister frowns and listens for a moment. It's an odd kind of klaxon, rising and falling with a strange vibrato. I've never heard it before, and apparently neither has he. Rather than investigate, he turns his attention back to me. But before he can open his mouth again, someone calls his name from beyond my field of vision. Minister Sinister gets annoyed and drops both his feet to the ground, twisting around.

"For heaven's sake, what is it? Can't you see I'm in the middle of something?"

"Apologies, Minister, but the system has just detected an alien life form."

Alien life form? I know what that means.

Teddys!

"What?" Minister Sinister shoots up. "How is that possible?"

"It goes off if the sensors detect an alien life form," the officer says, coming into view.

"Well, I got that much, but what does it actually mean, man?"

"Minister"—the officer stares at him with a blank face—"there could be an alien on the station. The situation could become dangerous. We must evacuate you immediately."

Minister Sinister stares at the man as if he just spoke some strange language. The officer blinks and waits for a reply.

"Do you mean to tell me that our base...our *military* base has been infiltrated by the enemy?" The minister is well past annoyed. It's obvious he's looking to take his irritation out on someone, so no one offers an explanation. "Well? I'm waiting!"

Before anyone around the minister gets brave enough, another assistant comes up holding a tablet.

"Minister, I need a moment," the assistant says, his voice tight and assertive. This is getting more enjoyable than the daytime drama I watch with my mom. That reminds me, I'll have to ask her about what's happened on *My Doctor, My Chef*. I've missed so many episodes.

"Not now. Can't you see I'm busy?" The minister flicks a hand at the man.

"Minister, you need to see this." As he holds out the tablet to him, I catch a glimpse of the screen. There's a news report playing on it, but I can't read the headline. The minister glares and snatches the tablet from the man's hands.

As Minister Sinister watches, his face goes pale, and his jaw slackens. All he can do is stare at the screen until the newscast is over. Even then, his eyes stay locked on it, knuckles turning white. I'm getting anxious myself, watching his panic attack. But I can't say I'm not enjoying it.

His head lifts, and I see his face. There's murder in his eyes, and now I really need to know what has gotten him so scared. Whatever it is, it's really making my day and freaking me out at the same time.

"You," the minister growls, and he holds the tablet out to me. "Did you know about this? Was this why we caught you on the *Mursilis*?"

I glance at the tablet and catch the headline: *Minister Crowley Under Investigation for War Scandal*. Oh! So that's what's freaking him out. He thinks we got the vid that we didn't actually get. Does that mean the messages Afton found are enough to incriminate him? I don't know, and I'm not sure I care...We got him! A hundred points for everyone involved.

It's so amazing. I have to feign a cough to stop the elation from reaching my face, but he notices my play, and I can see a rage building inside him.

"You *did* know!" Minister Sinister roars and raises the tablet over his head as if he's about to smash it over mine. Then he turns around to the guard. "Give me your weapon! I'm going to provide the expediency of trial right now by being the judge, jury, and executioner!"

Oh, that's not good. I'm starting to not like his extreme mood swings. They're affecting my own mental health, and that can't be good for my heart. I watch him as he holds a hand out to the guard, and my pulse beats faster than it ever has before.

Is he really going to kill me?

The guard is reluctant, so the minister rips the weapon out of the man's holster and shoves him back. He has to fumble with the gun to get it fit correctly in his hand before he can step back into the cell and take aim. I remember to take a breath, and I hold it, as it's going to be my last.

"By the authority granted to me by His Imperial Majesty and the Accord by which our Emperor rules, I hereby declare you, Ransome Quigley He', guilty of the crime of treason. For this, you shall receive the punishment of execution, to be enacted immediately!"

I cringe as he squeezes the trigger, but nothing happens. I was hoping that he didn't know how to use it correctly, and I am thanking the Heavenly Goddesses that I was right. Someone must have done a few extra merits and passed them on to me.

It's only temporary, however. The minister curses and spins around to the guard, waving the weapon at him, and the guard takes a step back.

"What is wrong with this thing? I pressed the trigger! Why didn't it go off?"

"Minister..." His assistant cuts in before the guard can answer. "We must go."

"Enough with that, man! Can't you see I'm trying to perform my royally decreed duty?"

"It's a secure weapon, Minister," the guard explains, "so the inmates can't steal it and use it against us."

"So fix it!" The minister shoves the weapon in the man's chest. The guard just stares at him, and I'm guessing that there's no fix for that. The breath that I've been holding in for the last minute comes out. I owe some serious karma to someone and will happily pay it.

"Minister, please!" The assistant is really getting scared. "We have —"

The assistant turns around, then takes a step back and raises his hands. The guard notices, turns his head in that direction. His jaw drops as far as it can go. He moves back, too. This is too much. I need to know what's going on.

"What...is that?" The guard steps back again.

It's enough to make Minister Sinister look towards the excitement that's out of my view. "It's them!" Minister Sinister raises his arm and points. "Shoot—"

All of them freeze in place, as if time just stopped. They're completely immobile, and my level of anticipation clicks up a few notches. I hold my breath and hope for the best.

Parrish's smiling face pops around the corner, but he frowns when he sees me.

"Rance, you don't look so good," he says with concern.

"I'm—" I cough, betraying any lie I was just about to tell. "No...I'm not."

Though I am really glad to see him!

"Let's get you out of there and somewhere safe, yeah? Let Elizabeth take a good look at you."

He uses the minister's outstretched arm as a handle and pivots him out of the way. Only he tilts him too far, and Minister Sinister tips over and smashes into the guard. They fall to the floor like a pair of dominoes. Parrish winces apologetically, but then gets back to me, putting an arm around me for support.

"Wait! I need that!" I point to my heirloom that tumbled out of the minister's robe when he fell. Parrish leans down, grabs it, and shoves it in my back pocket. Then we get on our way.

"Teddy!" I croak as I see...wow...maybe ten of them standing there with their biscuit-dish-sized eyes.

"Well done, Rancid." Original Teddy steps forward from the group. Good thing, too. I don't think I could have picked him out from the rest.

"Good to see you, too," I reply. "But we're going to have to work on that phrase. It doesn't mean what you think it does."

"Conclave later," Original Teddy says. "Disembarkation is paramount."

"I'm totally with you on that."

As the sharp bark of plasma fire bites our ears, Afton hops down the stairs, a large rifle in her hands. She looks every bit the mercenary she's trying to be. It's totally impressive, and I wish for that camera again.

"Do you know how to use that?" I ask, out of curiosity.

"Nope, but he does," Afton replies and tosses the rifle to Parrish. "I'll help Rance. You're on point."

"So, besides escape"—I take a quick glance at the minister and the two others as Afton wraps a helpful arm around me—"what's the plan?"

"Sergeant Cortell is holding an exit for us, not far from here," Parrish says. "He's got enough Teddys with him to freeze a small army, but they won't be able to do that forever."

"All from our ship?"

"Not exactly." Parrish grins.

"How many Teddy ships are there?"

"I think all of them?"

"*All* of them? How did...I mean..." My tongue breaks down because I'm trying to fathom just how many Teddy ships that might be. I know they can blink in and camouflage their ships, but I never imagined it working on such a scale.

"This is really important to them, Rance," Parrish says. "They're here to save their hero."

I blink because I don't think I heard him right. A hero? Me? I'm the one who got caught. How does that make me a hero? I mean, Teddy logic isn't exactly a straight parallel to human reason, but I can't see how I'm deserving of that title. I'm the one who's getting rescued.

"Parrish, he doesn't know," Afton says. I glance at her, then over to Parrish, who grins big.

"Grady was able to download all of your conversations with Minister Crowley." Parrish squeezes me in a rough hug. "We sent all the messages we downloaded to every major media outlet we could think of...and Colonel Nelson's boss, too. Nice work, buddy!"

"Let's go, hero." Afton teases.

Forty-Four

WE DON'T GET FAR before station security finds us. It's not too difficult, after all. Three humans—one wrapped in a shiny blanket—plus a dozen multicolored aliens wouldn't be hard for a blind squirrel to find. The Teddys popsicle a bunch of them, but they keep coming, and popsicle range is a lot shorter than the beam of a soldier's rifle. At least we have one of those as well, but Parrish isn't a practiced shot. He may know how to fire the gun, but that doesn't mean he's sniping anyone.

Their fire comes heavy, and we get pinned in place behind a few cargo crates. Their beams screech by and burn into the wall behind us, hissing as they impact. Smoke is beginning to fill up the area around us, and pretty soon we're not going to be able to breathe.

I keep glancing down the passage behind us to make sure no one's coming. The corridor splits off in two ways, so there's a double chance that angry security guys could surround us, and then it really will be game over—no more arrests. We're the enemy now.

"Let me pull these guys off you," Parrish yells, ducking after a shot nearly shaves his hair off. "Take Original Teddy with you and meet us back at the airlock! Afton knows where to go."

"No, Parrish!" I protest, but he just shakes his head. I've got no strength to argue, so I've got no choice but to go along. "Lead on," I say to Afton. "You're driving."

"Always," she replies with a smirk. "Don't worry. I'll get us there."

With a grunt, Afton hauls me up, and we sprint down the corridor. It's not much of a sprint since I'm way low on energy, but this isn't the first time I've been dead weight for her.

We get to the junction, and Afton pauses, glancing both ways. She starts in one direction, only to stop and reverse, then do the entire thing again.

"I thought you said you knew the way!"

"Parrish said that. I didn't!"

A plasma blast ricochets past us and strikes a power box along the wall. It explodes in a spectacular shower of sparks. We spin away and hit the ground, hiding our faces from the burning metal.

"Okay, maybe not that way!" Afton shouts, helping me up. Original Teddy heads in the opposite direction, so we follow. Another blast impacts the wall behind us, and I really hope Parrish is okay. I want to go back and help him, but Afton would never let me go. She's stronger than me, even on my good days.

As we barrel away from the fight, the cacophony of battle dies down. It becomes quieter and quieter until we turn down a softly lit corridor where you'd never know that a firefight was going on not far away.

"Recognizing any of this?" I ask Afton.

"Not at all," she replies, glancing around.

"Teddy, can you help? Like, do you have a map uploaded or something?"

"That is not accurate, Rancid. Cartography does not exist."

With a bit more questioning, I find out that another Teddy couldn't upload the information to Teddynet before getting hit. I grimace at the idea that someone just sacrificed their life to save me. Someone that's not even human.

We move forward cautiously, listening for signs of approaching soldiers, but all is calm. It's eerie. There's a bright light bleeding out into the corridor ahead from a room with tall windows surrounding the entrance. As we get closer it becomes clear it's a medical bay, which is good because that means no guards, and patients are unlikely to attack us.

"Just keep going and pretend we're supposed to be doing whatever we're doing. Don't look in." Afton speaks in a low voice. "Teddy, try to look inconspicuous."

"Teddy will camouflage."

"Surela?" A man's hoarse voice calls out from the room as we pass, stopping Afton cold.

"Insulting me while I'm saving your neck a second time? Thanks a lot, buddy." But Afton's not glaring at me. She's staring straight ahead.

"But I didn't say that," I reply, turning to her in confusion.

Afton swallows hard. I feel her muscles tighten as she turns her head to scan the room. She does a full sweep, then turns back as if she had just imagined the voice. Except we both heard it.

Then she looks again and her eyes lock on someone inside, and I hear her whimper, her whole body shaking with the sound.

"Dad?"

A well-bandaged patient in the second bed to the right raises a hand and attempts to sit up.

"You're—" Afton's arm slides off of me, and she's pulled into the room like a rogue satellite caught in a gravity well. "Alive...Dad...you're alive!"

The pull becomes stronger, and she rushes in, opening her arms wide to trap him in a hug. He's caught off guard at first but then smiles and returns her embrace, though a bit more gently. For a moment, I see her as a little girl, welcoming her daddy home after a long tour in space. She's no longer the cool, confident scholar-athlete but just a vulnerable young woman who missed her father. She buries her head into his shoulder and sobs.

"Dad, I thought you were dead!" Afton's voice breaks when she says the word. "We received the notice from command HQ...you know...*that* one..."

"Wounded, yes, but not dead by a long shot." Commander Jee frowns as he sees me shuffle in, then turns back to his daughter. "What are the two of you doing here?"

"Uh." Afton turns to me, looking for help, but I don't have an answer. So instead, she changes the subject. "Dad...what happened to your ship?"

"The damnedest thing, actually," Commander Jee replies. "We were about to run a test on our new weapon, and we came across debris from a ship...an alien ship. Our hull must have bumped into something reactive—like antimatter or something like that. It tore the whole side off the ship. I was lucky enough to be near an escape pod, but that got hit by debris when our ship's engine exploded. We got picked up by a merchant freighter, and well, here we are."

"So the Teddys—I mean, you weren't attacked?" Afton asks. Commander Jee raises an eyebrow when she corrects herself.

"No." Commander Jee smiles. "Just an accident."

"Uh, Afton," I say, trying not to sound impatient. "We have to catch our shuttle, or it's going to leave without us."

"Yeah...right." Afton doesn't want to leave, but we can't be caught here, and I know she doesn't want to put her father in harm's way.

"You'd better go, then, but thank you both for coming." Commander Jee rubs her arm. "Don't worry, I'll be home in a few weeks, and we can always talk on carrier wave."

She nods and hugs him once more, holding on just a little longer than she did before.

"Come home soon, Dad." Afton turns and takes me by the arm, pretending to help me walk, but I'm wondering who's supporting whom right now. She glances back more than once before we exit. I can tell Afton is fighting herself not to break down in the middle of our escape. I give her a gentle squeeze on her arm, as if that will save her from bursting into tears.

"You'll see him again soon," I say, hoping that it helps. Maybe it does.

"Where's Teddy?" she whispers, changing the subject. This isn't really the time or place to have a heart-to-heart chat, anyway. We need to focus on getting out of here.

Original Teddy comes sliding down the wall, using his tentacles and claws to slow his descent. Afton and I watch as he hops down half his height from the floor and turns to approach us.

"Teddy is now available."

"Great, let's fly." Afton takes a deep breath, grabs my wrist, and takes off at a speed that I'm not sure I could keep up with even if I was okay. My malnourished brain tries to focus on the task at hand, and if I think about what my feet are doing I'm going to take a hard crash into the deck. Original Teddy must be struggling to keep up, too.

"Afton!" I cry out. "Cut the turbo! Teddy—"

As we skid around a corner, we smash into two security guards. They spin and crash into separate walls while Afton and I take a dive onto the deck. I hit my head hard, and I lose a sense of which direction is up, but Afton recovers faster and is on her feet before the guards can even understand what just happened. Then we're off again, flying down the corridor and around the next corner. Before we turn, I catch one of them grab his radio from his belt.

"We got two of them! Section B, fourth level...headed your way!"

I wonder if that means they won't give chase.

After another minute of running, we come to a corridor that Afton remembers. There are scars up and down it from weapons fire, and the acrid smell of melted metal is ripe in the air. I don't hear any guns, so that could mean the battle is over...but who won? And how many died?

I drop to the floor, my knees weak. Afton tries pulling me up, and I try to help, but I'm spent. I really need a minute...maybe ten. Just to catch my breath. That's all I need. Then we can go.

"Come on, Rance!" Afton gasps, out of breath, too. Still, she tries to keep us moving. "Do I have to carry you again?"

The sudden *tap-tap-tap* of heavy boots on metal decking interrupts my answer. It's coming from down the passage. We glance up, and a second later three men pound into sight. I sigh the moment I see who it is.

"An excellent trick, but it didn't really work, did it, Ransome?" It's Minister Sinister, unthawed from his frozen nap. He's got his assistant and the mean guard with him, and what's worse, he's got his gun drawn. "Fortunately for us, we've found you here, lying on the floor and not taking advantage of your temporary freedom."

"Teddy! Popsicle!" I shout, but I get nothing. I glance behind me only to see an empty corridor. Damn.

"Your fuzzy little ally has gone missing, has he?" Minister Sinister smirks, but then gives Afton a once-over. "Who are you then? You going to step aside, young lady, or do we have to arrest you for assisting a known criminal?"

"Him?" Afton glances down at me with a chuckle and gives me a wink. "A criminal? Well, that's a seriously wrong assessment of my friend. Try again."

The wink means she wants to try something. I can't think what that might be because there's a sharp pain digging into my backside—my grandmother's heirloom. I shift myself around so I can pull it out of my pocket. As I grab on to it, I feel the weight of its coin-like bottom in my hand. It's heavy—really heavy.

I wonder...

"Not so, miss." The minister wags a finger at her. "I've already tried and convicted him of treason. All that's left is for his execution to be carried out. Now I suggest you step away, or we may need to convict you on the spot as well."

"I don't think so," Afton replies. "The only one going to jail is you. We know what you've done. The entire Empire knows, thanks to us. Try escaping that, murderer!"

"Yes." The minister nods respectfully to her. "That is unfortunate for me, but it is worse for you. Neither of you will be around to enjoy the fruits of your labors. Execute them both!"

The guard just stares at him.

"Are you deaf, man? They're criminal non-citizens! Do it now, or your entire family will be joining them!"

As the guard glances down at the weapon in his hand and considers, I get a bad feeling. I don't think I'm going to escape death twice. Way too many karma points have already been expended on my behalf. Though it's worse for Afton. She just got her dad back.

"Sorry," the guard says, and raises his weapon. This is it...I'm dead now.

A pink and a blue fuzzy thing drop down from the ceiling—Original Teddy and Blue Buddy! The minister and his men jump back, and their attention is pulled away from us.

Now's our chance!

"Surela!" I yell and throw the heirloom up in the air. She sees it, but instead of grabbing it and throwing it at them, Afton flies up, arms spread like some avenging angel. She drop-kicks it straight towards the minister. Like a projectile from a cannon, it blasts out, flying straighter than I could have expected, and whacks him right in the face. Minister Sinister goes flying back, throwing his arms wide, and knocks the other two men down like a pair of ninepins. All three of them land with a deep, resonant thud.

"Teddy," I say with a grin. "Popsicle, please."

Forty-Five

"WHAT DO YOU THINK will happen to them?" I ask Doc Elizabeth as I lie on the exam chair in her room. I'm still drained, and she's got a line in my arm, feeding me some nutrient mix direct to my bloodstream. She said it would help me recover faster than just eating. I still made sure there were no animals in it.

We're headed back to Angelcanis at a leisurely pace. No emergency FTL required. It'll take us a month or two to get there, and our families will be anxious, but we'll get there. Eventually. After all the trouble we've been through, it's better to be safe.

"Who? That minister?" she asks. "Well, I suspect if he gets convicted of treason..."

"Yeah, I know how that ends." I roll my eyes, and maybe that's not appropriate, but it's pretty much sums up my feelings. "I doubt he'll get tried for treason, though. Too many in the government on his side who will protect him from any real harm."

"Well." The doc leans over me to check on my tube or some other medical thing. "Unfortunately, I think you're right. No treason, but he won't be appointed to any high-profile position again."

"At least the war is over, not that I'd call it a war. The Teddys weren't even fighting!"

That last part comes out more like a croak than a raised voice. Doc Elizabeth puts her hands on her hips, gives me a disapproving look, shakes her head at me, and clucks her tongue.

"Rancid," she says, borrowing Original Teddy's misconstrued name for me. "Whatever made you decide to starve yourself?"

"You should have seen the stuff they wanted me to eat! Mutilated animal flesh! As if I ever could."

"Fair enough." Doc Elizabeth chuckles. "I understand, even if I don't approve. Not eating can do long-term damage to your body, and after a month, you would have died. At some point, though, they probably would have sent you to medical."

I just shrug and look down.

"What's wrong?" The doc folds her arms and frowns.

"Everyone's come to see me while I've been in here. Everyone except for Kayley."

"You need to give her time, Rance." Doc Elizabeth gives me a light pat on the shoulder as she speaks. "The four of you going against her really knocked her down hard...and then when the others came back without you, it took a long time before she would talk to anyone."

"I thought doctors made patients feel better, not worse," I complain.

"Ah, but sometimes we must do things that hurt temporarily to heal the body for the long term." She pokes a finger on my forehead. "And that's what we're doing here, Rance, healing you for the long term. You and Kayley both."

"Now on to brighter and happier things. I'm curious about something." Doc Elizabeth sits down on the edge of the chair. "Tell me again how you took that miserable bastard of a minister down. Before the Teddys popsicled them, you and Afton distracted them, yes? Something like that?"

"Yeah," I say with a smile, and I explain how I came up with the idea to use the heirloom to distract the minister, but Afton wound up bowling them over when she kicked it at them instead.

"Amazing!" Doc Elizabeth claps her hands. "And where is this heirloom now? I'm stunned you would you use such a valuable antique like that."

"I didn't expect to, actually, but it's there, on the counter." I tilt my head towards the top of the medicine chest where Afton left it.

"That thing?" She goes over and holds it up to the light. Her eyebrows knot as she examines it. After a minute, her face brightens.

"Jianzi!" she shouts, and I nearly fall out of the chair, not at all ready for her outburst.

"What did you just call me?"

"Don't be ridiculous." The doc smiles and shakes her head. "That's the name of it—it's a game. You play with your feet and try not to let it hit the ground."

"Guess Afton got it right," I murmur, remembering her flying field goal of a kick.

"You know what else?" Doc Elizabeth appears to digs deep into her memory. "It's...it's from Earth!"

"Erf?"

"Earth! It's a planet...and..." Her eyes dart up, and her mouth opens. "I think I'm from there."

"Wow...really? All that from a...what did you call it?"

We spend the next few days trying to help her recall things about this Earth planet. It's not much, and what she does remember is strange. Just like its name, I suppose. I'm surprised that anyone would choose to name a planet after dirt. Whoever did must not have liked it all that much.

When we try to figure out where it's located in the Empire, we can't. Doc Elizabeth thinks it's on the spiral arm somewhere, but where exactly is a mystery. Also unknown is just how long she's been with the Teddys. I can't get her to tell me how she got on board in the first place, but I suspect it's been a really, really long time.

I enjoy my time hanging out with Doc Elizabeth, despite my reason for being there. I get to know her better, and it makes me realize how much she fits in with our gang. She's kind, intelligent, friendly...and neurotic, just like the rest of us. It'll be difficult to say goodbye to her.

The time finally comes for me to be released from Doc's care. I've rested and felt better every day that I was there, but today my stomach is twisting into knots. My heart's beating a bit fast, and I have to keep taking slow, deep breaths so I don't feel like I'm suffocating. Doc says it's nerves, and since she's the expert, I suppose she's right. Nerves because of what, though?

As I make my way to the canteen, it hits me—Kayley. It'll be the first time I've seen her after that horrible moment I don't want to think about ever again. What's got me freaked is that I have no idea how that's going to go. If she hates me now, I might just return to Doc's care for a little while longer...or maybe a whole lot longer. I couldn't handle Kayley despising me.

I pause a few steps before the entrance to the canteen. It's packed right now—Teddy dining time—and I can also hear the sound of human speech, and laughter too. I can't pick out any one voice over the clamor of Teddys, but I'd expect that everyone is here. Everyone, including the girl I love.

My feet don't want to move forward, and at the same time, I've no idea what I am afraid of. I mean, I do, but how likely is that? How realistic is it to say that she would choose to cut any tie that she ever had with me after knowing each other our entire lives? That's crazy, isn't it?

Yet, here I am, not moving.

I have to get this over with. We can't avoid each other for two entire months. Well, actually, it's a big ship, so maybe we could, but I need to do this. Just like I chose to step on this ship, I need to step forward and do this.

With a shaky leg, I take one step forward and then another. And another, and soon enough I'm standing inside the canteen. I glance around. Everyone, Kayley included, is at our usual table with our favorite Teddys.

A hush comes over the room, as if everyone has noticed me step in. Our human table takes a moment longer, but then it quiets down as well. Their heads turn in my direction, and the reaction seems mixed. Parrish and Grady smile, but their eyes dart over to Afton and Kayley, and their smiles fade away. I think Afton is happy to see me up and out, but she's keeping her volume down to see what Kayley does. They all are. Even the Teddys. If I wasn't shaking like a tree in the wind, I'd have to wonder: What do they know, exactly?

Kayley slides off her stool backward and takes an eternity of tension to come over to me. She stops a few paces away, her eyes piercing me straight through. The rest of her face is stony and unemotional, and I get no clue as to what she's feeling.

"Hey, KayKay," I say lightly, trying to break through the emotional glacier between us. It's another eon before she responds.

"I told you," Kayley starts, her voice low, but she steps closer to me, and I begin to wonder if I should be afraid.

"I told you," she says again, louder this time and taking another step forward. "To never do that to me again."

"Yeah, I'm sorry, Kayley...I—"

While I'm thinking about how to word this, her hand flies out and catches my cheek. Sparks fly across my eyes, and my mind gets hazy. Did she just slap me? The answer comes soon enough as I begin to feel the sting. I lift my hand up to touch my cheek but then forget all about it when I see Kayley's wet eyes.

My mouth drops open, and I've got no words. I don't know whether I should be happy or sad, angry, or...what? I'm not even sure how my body is reacting because I can't feel it at all. The only thing that exists for me in this moment is her...and what she'll do next.

"Don't you know?" Kayley asks, the tears beginning to fall down her cheeks. Her voice is barely above a whisper, and my heart is coming up into my throat. I get this is hard on her, but it's killing me, too. I really wish she would just say what she means.

"Know what, Kayley?" I'm begging her to tell me because I need to know.

"Do you not get it?" she asks again. "Do you even have the slightest idea how much I care about you?"

This is dangerous territory. I'm overjoyed that she's trying to tell me that, which means she doesn't hate me, but I might get ejected from the ship if I answer this wrong—no, wait. That doesn't matter. Telling the truth is the only way here, and if I have to tell her how I feel and face rejection, or completely confuse her, then that's a risk. I have to try. I need to tell her too.

"I do, Kayley. Of course I so," I say, closing the distance between us. "I know you care about me because I care the entire universe about you. You're all I think about, and it's been driving me crazy to even consider there was a chance I would never speak to you again."

This doesn't completely confuse her, and I think I even see her eyes brighten up a little. There was something in what I said that she likes.

"What are you trying to say, Rance?" There's hope in her voice, and that spurs me on. This is my chance, my chance to let my true feelings come out.

"Well," I begin, but almost choke on the first word. What a brilliant start, you idiot. My hands are getting sweaty, and I can't believe I'm really about to confess to her.

"What I'm trying to say...Kayley...um...is...Kayley...I...I..."

Kayley shoots forward and wraps her hand around the back of my head. Not a millisecond later, her lips touch mine, and, and...she kisses me! It's tender and sweet and full of everything that I know my—dare I say it—girlfriend-to-be. That thought alone fills me with such elation that my feet practically rise off the ground.

Better sense comes over me, eventually, and I wrap my arms around her, kissing her back. Somewhere in the back of my mind, I think I hear all the Teddys warbling in joy. I would know for sure if I wasn't completely lost in this moment.

Oh, this is way better than when Afton did it.

Forty-Six

IT FEELS GREAT TO be back on Angelcanis! First of all...there's sun! Its golden rays shine down on us as we gather outside the town hall for our—get this—honor ceremony. That's right, the Prime Minister is giving us all commendations for saving the planet. Sergeant Cortell and Doc Elizabeth included. Colonel Nelson and his other aide will have their own separate one, along with a full-service funeral. I think we should recognize them here, too, though.

I feel funny wearing a formal robe. It's like someone just threw a blanket, a velvet blanket, over my shoulders. It's itchy and hot, and I'm about to boil over, even here in the shade. I'd prefer to be right out in the direct sun, but I don't want to melt before I get my award. I heard there might be some money that goes with it. I think I'll splurge and go grab some water for all of us from an auto-server in the town hall.

"Hey there, lover boy," Afton calls after me as I head down the corridor, looking for the vending machine. I turn and wait for her to catch up. She's also drowning in a robe made from leftover curtains. At least they're light in color, or we would faint from heat exhaustion.

"Hey," I call back, smiling.

"Not trying to run out on the ceremony, are you?" she asks, leaning a shoulder against the wall.

"Not at all. Just trying to get us all rehydrated before we sweat to death," I reply. "Want to help?"

"Sure."

We make an adventure out of it, exploring the town hall in search of liquid refreshment. At first we continue down the same hall, but we get lost and have to ask for help. A janitor gives us some vague directions, and we try to make sense of them, but we wind up getting lost again.

"So..." Afton's sing-song conversation starter gets me suspicious right away. "Haven't seen much of you the last two weeks."

"How is that possible?" I counter. "We've been on the same ship for two months with like...three places all of us normally go."

"Except for your room..." She smirks. "Or Kayley's."

"We didn't spend a lot of time in either of our rooms." My defense is accurate and solid, but there's still heat coming to my face, and it's not because of the sun. "We were up in the solarium a lot."

"Doing what?" Her question is meant to provoke me, and it's working.

"Talking! What are you, a middle school student?"

"You're the one who's getting flustered," Afton replies coolly.

I stop and spin towards her, ready to take her down. She could be poking me because she's jealous and a bad loser, and I'm not going to let her. She dared me and I won, fair and square. Though, now that I think about it, maybe that was her plan all along? Let's test the waters.

"I'm not flustered at all. You just can't admit you lost, Surela."

That pushes the right button, though I'm not sure which button it is. Afton invades my space, forcing me back against the wall. She plants an arm on it, right next to my head, and leans in like she's about to kiss me again. I grit my teeth, ready to push back on whatever she tries to throw at me.

"Oh, buddy...are you that stupid?" Afton's face is just centimeters from mine. "Didn't you realize what I was doing this whole time?"

"What are you talking about?" I turn my head. Now that I've kissed Kayley, I can't kiss Afton again. It wouldn't be right on so many levels. That's not what she's trying to do, right?

"Rance, I've been trying to get you and Kayley together for the past year. You've just been too dumb to notice."

"I knew it!" I push my finger into her face. "I knew that's what you were up to!"

"You did not, liar."

I start to shoot something back at her but just wind up laughing. Afton laughs with me, and we wind up in a hug. She gives me a tight squeeze—which is just a little painful—before letting me go and smiling at me.

"She's crazy about you, you know, but she's been so afraid you wouldn't feel the same way that she couldn't tell you. And since I also knew how you felt, how could I not try to get my two best friends together?"

"Just so I'm clear on this"—I have to think about this for a moment —"you weren't actually trying to date her...right?"

"Yep." Afton nods, then glares. "Unlike some people I know, I don't date my best friends."

"But you did," I correct her. "*We* did."

"That was six years ago, and we went out once." Afton wrinkles her face at me. "Get over it."

"So." I think about it. "You're not jealous? Not at all?"

"Nope!" Afton plants a kiss on my cheek and goes to walk down the hallway, but then turns back. "But if you break her heart, I will break every bone in your body. Got it?"

"Yeah, your threats are always clear." I grin. "Surela."

"Remember, maggot, only my father gets to call me that."

"And me!"

"Do you really want to die so young?"

The ceremony is stuffy and dull, but to see so many people attend, just to support us, is amazing. They have to put monitors and speakers outside to accommodate everyone, and they broadcast it live on Angel-1. We get a little bit of money, too, but I'm just going to give my mom my share. Not that she needs it—the government already paid for the repairs to our home, and then some—but I don't really know what else to do with it.

The parade that follows is more exciting. Throngs of people cheer for us as we ride down the main street of the capital. We're celebrities just like all the big stars of cine. The big difference is we actually did what they only pretend to do.

Kayley sits next to me on the back of the presentation vehicle. We hold hands, our fingers interlaced together, our other hands waving at the crowd. It's so natural, so comfortable, I can't think of a reason why it wasn't ever this way before and why it won't be this way forever. I only live to see her smile, and she bestows it on me every day. Ever since our confrontation, Kayley has done nothing but smile every time she sees me.

The time comes for the Prime Minister and his cabinet to meet the Teddys, and everyone is apprehensive. No one knows what to expect. Until we returned, everyone thought the Teddys had bombed us. Some still do, and that's what's making things uncomfortable.

The smooth dark shape of the Teddy ship has been looming over a clear field near the capital since yesterday, ominous to all gazing upon it. If I didn't know better, I would be afraid, too.

"Rance," Kayley says, her low voice tickling my ear. "Let's make sure we put them in the best light. I want everyone to accept them."

"Of course," I agree, then glance at Parrish and Grady. I'm hoping for some support, but they're too busy focusing on the people surrounding us. One of them is nervous, the other basking in all the attention, and it's not who you'd think it would be. Grady must get the exhibitionist gene from his parents. Parrish, on the other hand...

A shuttle brings Captain Teddy, Original Teddy, Blue Buddy, and a few others down to the landing platform where we're standing. The sun is pounding down on us once again, and I'm growing concerned that our guests will fry from the inside with all that fuzz covering their bodies.

"Let's get them inside as soon as possible," I suggest. The Prime Minister nods agreement, and I instantly feel better about the potential for a real interspecies scandal.

As the shuttle doors open, a hush settles over the crowd. Kayley squeezes my hand and gives me a comforting smile. I want to believe everything will be alright, but we won't know until they come out.

The Teddys don't waste any time and jump down the ramp, one right after another. There are a few gasps from the crowd, and I say a small prayer to the Goddesses that it won't turn into a full-on riot. The Goddesses have had my back so far, so I'm hoping they don't mind doing a little more for cross-species harmony.

Captain Teddy is wearing some type of strap, which separates him from the other Teddys. Original Teddy and Blue Buddy are right behind. Four others come out, but if I've met them or remember them, my brain isn't registering it.

They turn to the crowd and raise their arms and tentacles. I'm guessing this is some sort of greeting, or at least something they thought would make them seem less dangerous. The crowd remains silent, a thousand pairs of eyes staring back at them. There's tension in the air, and I can see a few angry and fearful faces in the crowd. I don't know if the Teddys notice it, but it doesn't seem to bother them.

It bothers me, though, and Kayley knows it. She tightens her grip on my hand, ensuring that I don't go running out into the mass of people, aiming for those spreading bad vibes. I wouldn't, of course. Even with everything we've accomplished, I still don't consider myself any sort of hero type.

"Murderers!" someone shouts, but there's no way to tell who said it. The Prime Minister is grim but decides to step up to the podium and address the people. I'm hoping that whatever he says, it calms those who are ready to cause trouble.

"Fellow citizens of Angelcanis, I am standing before you today to mark a historical event in the history of our planet and the entire Empire. For three hundred years, we have endeavored to create our own civilized world. We have labored to develop and initiate a lifestyle that no other planet in the entire Empire could achieve...and I can stand before you today and say confidently, we have achieved everything our forebears set out to create!"

There's huge applause and cheers from the crowd, and I relax just a tiny bit.

"Today we also mark another milestone in our relatively short history, one that is not just important for us, but for the entire Empire. Today we will recognize formal relations with another race, another species...and, I am proud to say, once again, we of Angelcanis were the first to achieve it!

"Let us welcome our new friends...the..." He has to turn around to one of his deputies to ask a question, then quickly turns back. "Teddys! Welcome, new friends!"

As Captain Teddy steps up to the podium, the frenzy of excitement dies down. Even after such a rousing speech, the people are still apprehensive, but Captain Teddy does not flinch. Not that I know what that looks like on a Teddy, but I think I'm starting to get it.

His big black eyes scan the crowd, and then after a very uneasy moment, he throws his hands up in the air, followed by his tentacles.

"Have a great day!" he says, in what is a loud voice for a Teddy.

At first there's no response, but then someone shouts "Yeah!" and begins to clap. His neighbors begin to join, and pretty soon the entire crowd gives a round of muted applause. It's not a full welcome, but at least it's a positive response.

Then Original Teddy steps up next to the captain and pulls the microphone down with a tentacle to talk into it. The crowd once again gets quiet as Original Teddy scans the mass of people. I'm hoping that whatever he comes up with, it's better than what his captain said.

"Thank you for saving us! You are all awesome!" This time the response is tenfold. Cheers and yells abound, and just about everyone has a smile on their face.

I turn to Kayley, and she beams back.

"Well, one more problem solved," I say.

EPILOGUE

"THIS IS MORE LIKE it!" Grady says. "No crowds, no politicians, no ceremonies...just the five of us!"

"Teddy is also present," Original Teddy says.

"Six of us," Parrish corrects himself.

"Boys and girls, I will never as much as put a bandage on your finger if you leave me out." Doc Elizabeth folds her arms and narrows her eyes at all of us.

Grady's face turns red, and he smiles apologetically. "Okay, sorry... the seven of us."

Seven is the right number for us. It's also the maximum number of occupants possible in my new living room. Well, not actually mine. My mom owns the house, and the government paid for the repairs to the kitchen and then dropped a room in the back, just for our trouble. Mom prefers to call it a "winter garden," but I don't really know why. There are no plants here, and we don't get winter in our town. She might be hinting that this will be the last time she'll allow us to gather here before she takes it over. It's okay with me—anything for my mom. We've certainly put her through enough.

As I glance about the room, I get a heaviness in my chest. Not only could this be the last time we're in this room, but it could be our last time being together entirely.

We've accomplished some amazing things together, but our planet-saving days are behind us. Now it's back to where we started—off to compulsories and then specialized training. I know I wanted something different, but Kayley and I have been talking. Nothing definite yet, but if I can do my two years' penance, then come back and start doing some small stuff here and there, hopefully she'll come join me once she's done with the publicity tour around Angelcanis that the government has asked her to do.

Parrish might still join the military, though I don't think he's convinced that's the right path for him anymore. I think he'd prefer a job far away from the front lines. Maybe a gig in space exploration where the ship goes out for years to discover new planets suitable for human habitation. If he chose that, I would miss him big-time.

"Seven is the lucky number. We chose right!" Grady takes the initiative to cover up his social misstep. Honestly, I think he should own up to it and let us take him down a notch or two. We'd be nice about it.

Grady is destined for great things, and he could be another one that floats away. With his parents' connections—and their high expectations for him—it won't be long before he's the head designer at some major firm, making a stipend that will put him in an enormous mansion in Bradbury. I'd never get a job like that, so the capital would be completely out of reach for me. Unfortunately, that means so would Grady.

"We weren't planning on any particular number, Grady," Kayley chides. "We're just lucky we could work together so well."

"And that's what makes us awesome," I add with a grin.

"If you two start finishing each other's sentences, I will vomit in your mom's nice new living room," Afton warns. I hope that she'll be around to keep Kayley and me grounded. The two of us are often so sweet-faced with each other, I get dizzy sometimes.

"What are you gonna do after you graduate, Afton?" I ask, and my question catches her off guard. "Still going to join the military?"

She shrugs and turns her head away. Afton doesn't know what she's going to do, and it's grinding on her. I didn't intend to rub a sore spot, but I guess I did. Still, she wouldn't be the ever-resilient Surela Afton Jee if she didn't hit back at me.

"Maybe I'll stick around and annoy you until you either marry Kayley or give up in sheer frustration." Her grin is her best shield from things that trouble her, but I know better. I saw how she was with her father. There's a sweet and loving person under all that toughness.

Now, I could fire back at her, as per my usual habit, but I'm not about kicking a lady when she's down. So I'll let her get away with it this time. Besides, I've got a girlfriend now. There's nothing in this world that can pull me down off my cloud.

"How about you, Elizabeth?" Kayley asks. "I heard from Rance that you've got some of your memory back. Will you try to find home?"

"Absolutely not," Doc Elizabeth states with determination. "There's a good chance that anyone I knew there is long gone by now, and besides"—she glances at Original Teddy—"I already have a place that I can call home."

"Teddy is jubilant," Original Teddy says, and he moves his face in what I am currently interpreting as joy or pleasure. Honestly, after being with them for a few months now, I still have no idea.

"What about you, Rance?" Afton turns the serious question into a dig. "Are you going to specialize, or are you just going to become Kayley's parasite?"

It's a fair question—the specialization part, not the parasite part—and one I've been thinking about ever since our drowning in honors died down. I still really want to make my dream happen, but even after our whirlwind world rescue, I still don't have a clue just how to put it together. I could try law like my dad did, and maybe that would get me to where I'm going, though I might be doing that all alone.

Maybe becoming Kayley's leech wouldn't be a bad idea.

When I think about the incredible thing we accomplished together, it fills me with sheer craving. What we did, we did as a team, and when I think about my dream, that's how I see it happening—together will all of my buds, old and new. I now realize that's the only way it could happen.

"Well, I was thinking about more ways I could do good for regular people. You know, save the Empire from itself again." I mean it as a joke because I'd never expect them to drop their dreams to make mine happen.

"Dude! That's a great idea!" Grady says. I've got to love the guy for being so positive and supportive of me. It could be because I've got his back, too, but he's always given me a bit more encouragement than I've given him.

"Don't be an idiot, Grady," Afton says. "Rance was kidding."

"Were you, Rance?" Kayley turns to me, a thoughtful look in her eye. "Kidding?"

"Yeah, of course I was." I shrug, not wanting to be caught in a lie.

"Ha!" Grady points at me and gets up on his knees. "See? He meant it!"

"What a pebble you are!" Afton sneers. "Cut the fake play, Rance. We know you too well."

Everyone laughs and chuckles. Even KayKay smirks at me a little, but she squeezes my hand at the same time. I'll forgive her for a little tease here and there, but if she pushes it into Afton's realm, I might have to retaliate. Though that retaliation might be similar to a cat fighting with no claws.

"Wait a second," Parrish says, getting serious. "Rance deserves the benefit of the doubt. After all, he's the one who took one for the team. Without which, we may not have made it off the *Mursilis*."

Parrish, ever team captain, decides that I'm the MVP of the day. If all this Rance support keeps up, I'm going to get sappy.

"So, what do you want to do, Parrish?" Doc Elizabeth asks. "Put it up for a vote?"

"We need some debate before we put anything up for a vote," Kayley corrects. "That's always been the way we do things."

It's true, we did always debate before we took a vote, but then we'd follow whatever Kayley decided, anyway. I'm not really considering any of this to be real, but as I consider the possibility, I feel the adrenaline pump into my veins.

"What are we talking about, exactly?" I ask, putting reality back into the conversation. "We can't just call ourselves some league of justice and expect someone to throw up a signal anytime they need help, can we? We barely scraped out of this one alive, guys. We need to level up if we want to have any real effectiveness. We can't just rely on the luck of the Goddesses to pull us through every time."

"Good point." Parrish gives me a nod. "We would need to pick up some new skills and experience before we jumped in again."

"What else?" Kayley asks, channeling the colonel again. My heart twitches when I picture him up front, leading the team.

"For certain, you'd need a base of operations," Doc Elizabeth states. "Your home is lovely, Rance, but rather inappropriate."

"True. My mom would prefer a peaceful existence from here on out."

"Then the only other thing we'd need is someone to hire us." Grady's eyes are getting wide, and I'm getting anxious. "We could start small. You know, like find someone's lost child or something like that, then as we get more experience, take on bigger challenges."

"Good idea, Grady." Kayley gives him a smile. I don't know what's going on here, but I'm waiting for one of them to turn to me and confess this is all a big joke. It wouldn't be the first time they got one over on me like that.

"Are we seriously considering this?" Afton asks, ever the advocate of the opposition. "I mean, didn't Rance just say we barely escaped with our lives? I'd like to keep mine for a little while longer if that's alright with everyone."

"Teddy will collaborate," Original Teddy says.

"Really, Teddy?"

"That is accurate. You are Teddy."

"Wait," Afton says. "You're saying we're now a part of your...race?"

"That is accurate," Original Teddy says, standing up. "You are Teddy. Teddy will engage in participation as Teddy requires."

It's cryptic, as per usual with Teddyspeak, but it makes sense to me. He's saying they have our backs, and if we're going to do good things, then they'll support us. I find it hard to believe, but that's now the strongest argument for actually giving this a go. I don't mind risking my life, not for the right reason. It gives me purpose, just like taking care of Kayley gives me purpose. And I want to take care of her.

"Okay then. Time to put it up to a vote," Kayley says, sensing the buzz in the room. She's reading it better than I am, but any fool could see the excitement on everyone's faces—everyone but Afton, that is. She wants to be a part of whatever we decide to do, but I don't think she agrees with it. It would suck if she voted against it, but that could happen. We'd likely decide not to if that was the case, and I would have to agree. She's as critical to this as any of us. Trying to do it without her would be like attempting a marathon without a left leg.

"I'm in," Parrish says.

"Me too." Grady claps his fist into his hand. "This has got to be more exciting than designing ships."

"I like it," Doc Elizabeth says. "And I'm impressed with your initiative. Count me in as well. Someone's going to have to patch you up when you fall."

"Let's none of us fall too hard," Kayley says, then turns to me. "Rance? It's your idea. What do you think?"

Nearly everyone really wants to do this? How can I say no?

"If you're in, I'm in." I smile at her, and the expected groan from Afton comes with perfect timing. But this time, Kayley's on my side. She turns to Afton, all business.

"Come on, Afton, you've made your comments, time to answer." Her voice is like that of a Goddess come down from heaven to demand us mere mortals choose our destiny.

Afton wrinkles her nose, feeling all the attention on her. We'd never force her into this, but she's got to know she'd be holding the rest of us up if she declines.

"Fine." Afton pouts. "But only because I'm going to enjoy watching you all make fools of yourselves."

"Rance," my mom calls from the kitchen. "Is everyone staying for dinner? They're all welcome, but I'd appreciate some help."

"I'll go," Kayley says and kisses me on the cheek before she gets up.

I survey everyone's expectant looks, and I get warm inside. Nobody's got friends as awesome as mine. I hope we can be together for a really, really long time—especially Kayley and me. I couldn't ask for anything else.

"Yes, Mom, everyone's staying," I reply with a grin. "We've got a lot to talk about."

About the Author

Marc B. DeGeorge has made every attempt in his adult life to maintain a balance between how much science and how much art he dabbles in. Sometimes, he's even successful. When he was young, he wanted to be an astronaut, and then an aeronautical engineer—he even went to Space Camp! But then he learned how to play guitar and his space dreams took a back seat. He spent a decade playing professionally in bands and studying music in college (university only took five years). These days, things have come round full circle, and Marc envisions the future by writing books that imagine what challenges humanity may face, and what we might accomplish together.

When Marc isn't writing, he performs traditional Japanese music on shamisen and writes, shoots, and edits performing arts photos and documentaries under the MuseMarc Studio name.